OPERATION POPPY PRIDE

OPERATION POPPY PRIDE

Richard Joyce

OLIVER & LEWIS

British Library Cataloguing in Publication Data
A catalogue record for this book is available from the British Library

ISBN 978-0-9935750-2-0

Typeset by Amolibros, Milverton, Somerset
www.amolibros.com
This book production has been managed by Amolibros
Printed and bound by Lightning Source worldwide

ACKNOWLEDGEMENTS

Although there are references made to true military operations and people in this book, none of those in this novel happened. However, I have tried to make the book as factually accurate as possible, and to portray the courage and sacrifice.

If I haven't mentioned you on this page, please accept my apologies, and at the same time, my sincere thanks.

First, I would like to thank those who have continued their support by purchasing *Operation Blue Halo*, and *Operation Last Assault*; without whom I would not be able to continue to raise funds for military charities.

I can't thank enough the talented artist Anthony Holder from Maverick Art for the hand-painted book cover design. His artwork and support are an inspiration. www.anthonyholder01.wixsite.com/anthonyholderartist

A huge 'cheers' for your detail, Chris Buswell and Hendrik Stolz.

I would like to give appreciation to all the music agents who helped me achieve the lyric licences, and to the every busy front-line worker, Keenan Gorrie, for the book trailers.

Lastly, 'Lest we forget' those who protected us in the Great Wars, especially the crazy bunch serving in the Elite.

*I dedicate this book to the late Sir Archibald David Stirling,
and all those who have shared his vision.*

ABOUT THE AUTHOR

Following the success of *Operation Blue Halo*, and *Operation Last Assault*, Richard Joyce has also published the third novel in the series featuring Johnny Vince: his next mission: to track and locate the Sumatra tiger poachers' stronghold; relatively easy for an ex-Special Forces, or so his boss said. With a truly strange turn of events, Johnny is emerged into a world that not even the complex himself can prepare to fathom. Even with Johnny's Elite skills, can he take this young, new squad into the hornets' nest with little knowledge and weaponry? You want action, adventure, and emotions—is the edge of your seat ready?

LYRIC PERMISSIONS

PROLOGUE

May 20th, 2015

It had been a long-awaited mission to get started after the first phone call from Ocker, nearly nine months ago, when I had been sitting on the beach with Lena and friends. The good news was that my family and I had suffered no more troubles with Abishua's mob. In fact, I'd never heard anything again about the L16BY formula or any of the groups involved. Occasionally, the fight at the apartment would be brought up in the pub by Trevor and Simon. Craig had returned to Aldershot, but before he'd left, I had managed to get a few more words out of him. He said he had enjoyed the experience and would gladly help again. Oliver never mentioned that I'd shot Ramario and left Abishua to burn in hell, but maybe he didn't want to relive his ordeal, surf and girls were his preferred subjects. With Oliver's brutal ordeal, the guilt still consumed me.

The bad news: I had been pressurising Lena to start a family. Rumours started to surface that she had been involved with another lad. Before I could launch an investigation, I returned home from work and found the house cleared of her possessions. A letter explained the blame I had put her under as she couldn't have children, a secret she had kept. It went on to say that she had moved to a new area, with a new man. It wasn't the fact she couldn't have children that bothered me, it was the bit about having an affair. It damaged my ego. I thought I was clued up on reading body language and had a good perception of attitudes and situations. It wasn't the first time a partner of mine had an affair. Now, it was back to the drawing-board to understand women, emphasised by the fact that my divorce had been finalised.

Being wounded, but a free man, the very same evening I visited a local Australian Bar. I found a seat away from the loving couples, when the manager strolled over with two bottles of beer and a JD.

"Think you'll need these, mate. Plenty more in the sea. You've just got to catch the right surf," he said—so, word had got out then.

As I drowned myself in the endless drinks, I overheard a family on the table next to me telling the old gentleman not to make up stories to the grandchildren. The children were in awe and questioned him excitedly. Every time he had talked about the war he was rudely interrupted by one of the adults. In the end they all left, except the great-grandad who put up a good fight to stay.

When I returned to my seat with another pint, the table had been taken. The elderly man dragged out the chair next to him. His frail hands were shaking. For a while he just stared at me as if waiting for me to say something. The only part of him that looked young was his crystal-blue eyes. The first thing he asked was why was I still in uniform as the war was over. Maybe he was a bit fruit-loop, I thought. However, I spent the rest of the evening listening to Weaves, as he liked to be called, intrigued by his war stories. I was especially captivated by his revelation that he had been in the SAS, and the stories of the missions he had taken part in during World War Two. The most chilling was Operation Bulbasket which had gone drastically wrong after losing his mates evading the Germans. As a former top cricketer he had used his stamina to run, and just kept running.

Since that evening, I've been mulling over something that Weaves had said at the end of the story. Talking about the loss of his friends in Bulbasket, he said it must have felt the same as when I'd lost Planet, Shrek, and Fish on my mission. I was flummoxed and asked him to repeat himself, but as the last kicking-out rights were shouted, he staggered away. I knew I was drunk, but was sure that I had heard him right. I never saw him again. I had even asked my parents if they knew him or had they been telling stories about me, but they denied all knowledge.

CHAPTER ONE

After nearly seven thousand miles of travelling, I was relieved to land at Minangkabau International Airport. The fourteen-hour flight had numbed my brain, and arse. The only real comfort, still being single, were the sexy stewardesses. I set my new watch forward to the local time: 06.36 hrs. On the previous two missions, I had returned without my watch, both had been expensive gifts from my parents. I tried to shake off the memory of my big argument with Dad before I'd left. Yeah, we were a shouty family when me and my bro were teenagers, but this fight had topped anything so far. When I'd handed over the flowers to Mum, she burst into tears, leaving the room in a hurry.

My dad started ranting when I'd bragged about my new watch. I tried to apologise for losing the other two and, feeling the time was right to quash his mood, I presented him with the latest Rolex Sea-Dweller. He wasn't overjoyed and he threw a book at me. Whilst I read the front cover, *How to Stay Safe as an Adventurer*, he continued to rant.

"You just don't get it. You're so bloody selfish."

He told me that I had wasted the education that he and mum had worked so hard to give me.

"Why can't you be more like your brother."

The argument escalated. For the first time ever, I had threatened him verbally and physically. The tears in his eyes said it all. I let him know by the slamming of the front door that I was seriously pissed off.

I still was a little apprehensive as I went through passport control, thinking that Will and Ocker may have set up another airport prank. At least the flooring wasn't as hideously designed as the carpet in Yemen had been; it was highly polished tiles.

The blissful sun was rising as I went through the main doors. Feeling its beauty and warmth, I strolled into the almost empty car park. Sitting on the small brick wall under the main airport sign, it had an extravagant design similar to the red-tiled roof over the main building. I stretched my arms and legs. A cool breeze fluttered the three red and white flags high up on their poles. I sucked in the fresh air and then released it, feeling good. Where was my lift? I was supposed to be picked up by a bloke called Gavin Applegate. I had studied his photo that Ocker had emailed, but his personal profile report was very sparse. Every person that drove in I checked for Gavin.

Time check: 07.15 hrs. I was about to phone Ocker when a motorbike squealed alongside me. I glanced up to see a skinny brown kid, no more than twelve years old, smiling at me. He had insects between his teeth, some in his dirty ears and matted black hair. I looked back at my phone and scrolled down the list of names. He sounded the weak horn.

'You Mr Vince?' the kid asked.

You're fucking joking, I thought, and frowned at him.

'You Mr Vince?'

'Might be. Who's asking?'

'You the only white man. Get on,' he said.

'Did Gavin Applegate send you?'

'You not say his name here,' he whispered.

'I take it no helmet then.'

'My head too small.' He stupidly grinned.

'I meant for me,' I said, fixing him a glare.

'Your head too big.'

I hooked my heavy Bergen over my shoulders. The motorbike creaked as I sat behind him. It appeared to be built from several bikes slapped together. There was nowhere to hang onto except the kid's scrawny waist. I was sure it would be me making sure he wouldn't get blown off by any headwind. I cursed under my breath when he stalled it. We sat in the middle of the road holding up the traffic coming into the airport. I apologised to the impatient drivers, but began to slightly redden.

'Do you want me to drive?' I asked.

As soon as I had said it, the heap of junk restarted, jerking forward through its plume of choking smoke.

Instead of taking the smooth main road, the lad took a sharp right detour down a cobbled lane. He could only just keep hold of the handlebars as we were almost vibrated to death. For once, I was glad I hadn't indulged in too much in-flight entertainment. I tried to take in as much of what was going around me as possible, but he was zigzagging through parked cars and oncoming people. The lad didn't slow when a group of children dressed in red and white dresses with white headscarves crossed in front of us. Their screams were drowned out by the noisy exhaust. The houses we raced by had an oriental architecture about them, but I hardly had time to admire. From time to time, I got the distinct smell of strong fish. It wasn't till we reached the main road again and crossed a bridge over a river, that I felt slightly more at ease, along with my back. From then on, the views of farmlands and countryside were spectacular. However, trying not to get a face full of insects was becoming a pain, and I tried to hunker behind the lad.

After an hour of weaving through the traffic consisting of motorbikes, four-by-fours, coaches, and even a near collision with a man crossing the road with what I guessed were two water buffalo, I tapped him on the shoulder and told him I was desperate for a piss. He quickly diverted down a bumpy, dusty track which ended by some trees. The dust cloud dispersed and I was relieved to get off. Whilst straightening my seized back and letting go my aching bladder, I admired the beautiful scenery: there wasn't a town in sight, just pure greenery and mountain ranges. The breeze had dropped, the humidity had increased. The mist rising off the mountains was stunning.

All finished, I wiped the dead bugs from my face. After a long swig of cool water, I breathed in the tranquillity.

'How much further, lad?'

'Five minutes.'

'What's your name?'

'You get on, now. You make me late,' he said, tapping the split seat behind him.

'Well you should have got to me on time.'

He revved the engine. The rickety machine jumped forward as he clunked it into gear. I dumped my Bergen back on and reluctantly climbed aboard to the now familiar sound of creaking springs. Time check: 08.20 hrs.

The enthralling forestation was becoming denser as we gradually climbed in altitude. Again, I got the smell of burning oil. Every time I had checked the hot engine, the bike went into a wobble. Was the lad doing it on purpose? I checked the time again: twenty minutes since I had reminded him that his five minutes had lapsed.

The engine's drone suddenly stopped and we freewheeled to the side of the road. The lad ordered me off. When I had dragged my sorry self off, he pushed the bike into a bush and tried to cover it. Why would anyone want to steal that? The ringing in my ears was interrupted when he asked me to follow him. This is getting weirder, I thought, but decided to trail his disappearing spindly brown legs up a steep, rooted path. When I had caught up with him, he had his back to me. I was more out of breath than him, the low oxygen and high humidity both playing their part.

Our view was of an idyllic village amongst captivating tall trees, all set back on a plateau. You wouldn't have even guessed it was there. My senses came to life: a faint trace of cooking wafted through the smell of damp woodland. Birds sang hypnotic tunes high in the trees. The longer we stood there, the more joined in the chorus. Houses were dotted around, all having the typical pointed roofs, but had turned green and were covered in foliage. A door creaked open to one property situated at the far end. The man standing there waved at us to come to him. It was only a brief sighting, but I registered he was white, short, with tattoos.

I stepped forward, but the lad held my arm back. As I faced him, he held his hand out.

'You pay me,' he demanded.

'You mean for that exquisite luxury ffff... flipping taxi ride?' I said, minding my ps and qs.

'You tight fucking English man.'

My jaw dropped as I watched him stomp off.

The sound of his junk-heap motorbike played off into the far distance as I walked the slight incline to the house. There was freshness in the air, twigs cracked underfoot. The roof point was an imposing piece of engineered architecture, the shape of a tepee. The front wall had an inlay of patterns between the maroon wooden frames, and the ornate suffix was painted in gold paint. I walked up the grand, solid, white balustrade staircase. Taking the first step onto the porch, the right-hand mahogany door swung open.

'You made it then, Johnny. Welcome to Solok. My name is Gavin.'

I stepped forward and shook his hand. 'Nice taxi service.'

'Safest fucking way, buddy. Especially around this fucking neck of the woods. Come in. We've got a few things to sort before we head off.'

'Gobby shit he was, too. Should I have paid him?'

'Sometimes it's the gobby ones you can trust around here. His name is Setiawan, meaning faithful, and his reliance is solid. I'd already paid him.'

'Can't be that trustworthy if he asked me to pay him,' I said.

'Good fucking lad. I taught him well.'

I caught his smile before he turned and went back inside.

Gavin was five four, skinny but muscular, and had an immaculately smooth bald head. His tattoos flowed across his left upper arm and right shoulder, from where they continued across his chest. He also had a phoenix and a Saint George's cross. On his left bicep he had a yin yang with a Chinese dragon and wind bars. I had seen the symbol somewhere before, but couldn't think where. Amongst the tattoos were many new and old scars. He was English, but had no distinguishable accent. His voice was slightly high-pitched with a gravelly tone, like he had been sucking on helium. Dressed just in shorts, he showed off further tattoos on his legs and back.

I followed him into the cool gloom of the house.

'Take a seat, but don't get too comfortable as we've got to head out,' he said.

'Not even a nice brew first?'

'Bollocks.'

I was about to thank him for his hospitality when a woman walked through one of the slatted doors. Her ivory long dress elegantly flowed as she floated past.

'Johnny, this is my trouble and strife. Well, we're not quite married yet, but soon. Hey, babe?'

The woman didn't reply when he smacked her on the arse. She turned and adjusted her ivory headscarf, then smiled. I beamed back, trying not to let it show I was mesmerised by her soft brown skin, sultry brown eyes, and plush pink lips. What a stunner. The front door creaked open, breaking my stare. A voice shrieked from the lobby. Instantly, Gavin's bride-to-be shuffled into the kitchen.

'Time we fucked off, buddy,' Gavin said.

The door to my left nearly swung off its hinges. Stood there was a woman, or maybe a man, with a bolshie attitude. The person pulled the black veil from their face and started ranting in her native tongue. Jesus, it had gone from beauty, to the beast, I thought.

'Johnny, this is the mother-in-law,' Gavin said.

I grimaced, but then quickly stopped as I didn't want to offend Gavin's girlfriend, and certainly not the mother-in-law, who by now had her arms flailing. It was hard not to smirk as the thought of the evil Zelda from the Terrahawks had entered my mind. Zelda was still carrying on when Gavin, unconcerned, disappeared into the kitchen. Through the slats I saw him give his lady a loving embrace and kiss. Zelda stopped her abuse, her cold beady eyes staring at me.

Fuck it, I thought, and said, 'Nice to meet you, Zelda.'

I was a little unnerved by Zelda, still standing there in the same pose as a waxwork, glowering.

'Ready?' Gavin said.

'Too fucking right.'

Her glare followed me as I squeezed with the Bergen through the small gap she had left; a waft of old broccoli fragranced from her. Gavin grabbed a handful of clothes and marched out the door. As I caught up, he put on a pair of black baggy tracksuit trousers and a tight-fitting white T-shirt.

'Fucking bitch,' Gavin blurted.

He continued to curse under his breath until we reached a battered, grey Pak Suzuki Jeep with a red stripe down the side. The chilling thoughts quickly returned: the same model as the one Ghulam had sold to me in Haleema's village during Operation Blue Halo.

'What the fuck's wrong, bud?' Gavin asked.

'Just admiring your shit piece of scrap. Think I might take my chances by going back and having tea and cake with Zelda.'

'Zelda?' He roared with laughter. 'I haven't heard that name for years. That programme scared the shit out of me when I was a kid. How the fuck am I going to sleep at night with the thought of her wandering in and out of the house?'

'Claymore is your answer.'

Gavin's thought process was in motion as he stared into nothing, and then he grinned.

He yanked hard at the stiff driver's door, got in and then repeatedly slammed it until it properly closed. Even though I had tried to block out the past nightmare events in Afghanistan, it felt eerie as I sat in the passenger's seat. The engine's fumes filled the front. Eventually, after a lot of cursing, he managed to select a gear.

'Where are we heading to?' I asked.

'As the women own the houses here, we need to find a man's shack. We can have quick drink and a chat before I take you to my guvnor.'

'Who's that?' I said. 'Will or Ocker never mentioned him.' Typical, I thought.

He shook his head, the car slightly wobbling along the track. 'Ah, Ocker. That loud-mouth wanker. I'm glad it's you here and not that prick.'

I snatched up the handbrake, the jeep snaked left and right. Gavin fought for control, but stalled it to a stop just short of a canyon.

'Now you can slag off who you want, but none of my mates, especially the ones who I've fought side by side with. You've only scratched the surface with him. So wind your fucking neck in.'

'Are you trying to stamp your authority?' Gavin asked.

'Fuck off, and drive on.'

'What, over the edge?'

'If you've the bottle,' I said, steely glaring.

Gavin wanted to take it further, but instead he took his anger out on the jeep by slamming it into reverse. He then span the wheels forward.

After about five minutes of crazy moody driving, which I'd enjoyed, Gavin slowed down. Our tension was adding to the already thick dust and exhaust-fumed air, the flapping soft-top roofline letting some of it out. It was uncanny that the same vehicle could bring back so many memories, none of them good.

I thought I would break the tension tactfully and said, 'I thought your mother-in-law was the guvnor. I saw how you cowered in the kitchen.'

'Bollocks,' he replied, and scoffed.

'Now we're back on track, no pun intended, where do you fit into this mission if you aren't the boss?'

'I'm just his bodyguard.'

I tried not to laugh, but it came out.

He scowled at me. 'You're so fucking easily blinded,' he snapped.

'And you swear too much.'

His erratic driving manner increased. I held on as we hit a ditch crossing the track. My Bergen in the back had fallen off the side seat and clattered to the floor. He then swung the jeep sideways down a small lane, the branches and bushes scraping the side. Just before the large tree at the dead-end, we skidded to a halt. Gavin slung off his belt and body-slammed open his door.

'You coming for that drink, then?' he asked, waving the dust from his face.

I couldn't get out my side due to the thick bush, but I've good previous for climbing across using the opposite door on this type of vehicle. I made it look easy, then followed his energetic stomp through a gap in the undergrowth.

In a clearing, two corrugated roofed wooden shacks stood opposite each other. Four saddleless horses were tied up to a wooden rail, like one from a wild-west movie. The door to the left building creaked open and out ducked a nearly naked, overweight giant. He wore a loin cloth that was folded at the front, hanging down between his groin. Black stripes were painted on his fat arms and legs. His huge bulk strode over to Gavin. I stayed where I was. The giant looked at me as Gavin stood in front of him. Whilst Gavin softly spoke, the large man kept shaking his head. Goliath, as I'd named him, put his gigantic hand on Gavin's shoulder to stop him going into the other shack; the grip even more colossal against Gavin's body. I was getting a bit twitchy from their body language.

Goliath paced back to where he had come from without taking his curious stare from me; I stared back at him.

'Fancy a proper drink?' Gavin asked.

'Blimey yeah, especially if that was the bar lady.'

'Your round then.'

'If it calms your angry outbursts, sure.' I grinned.

'Makes us even then, buddy.'

'Fair point,' I said.

Gavin held out his hand, and I shook it.

Inside was even stranger: two gambling-style round tables with four chairs each stood at the edges of the dimly-lit area. A crude wooden bar was constructed at the far end. The heat from the sun enhanced the smell of timber, blending with cigar odour. In the lantern's glow stood two blokes, with another sat on a bar-stool. All had their backs to us. I was going to make a quip about having a game of poker in this saloon, but Gavin took a deep breath through his nose, slowly exhaling. My sixth sense rattled me; hairs stood up on my neck. I swung down my Bergen to the wooden floorboards, the thump didn't even make them look. However, as Gavin purposeful stepped forward, the floorboard creaked. One by one they all turned around; all having been in recent fights. The bloke on the wooden rickety stool slipped to his feet. Their eyes narrowed. The largest man dressed just in jeans spat at the ground. This was fucking weird. All they needed were cowboy hats and holstered guns to top it. As soon as I thought of the last weapon, I wished I hadn't, I was unarmed.

The front man put his hand behind him and slid a machete to the front. Now I knew what the thin leather straps were around his naked tattooed chest. Oh great, fucking scalping Indians, I thought. The man on his left pulled out a scary-looking hunting knife from his side sheath. The bloke who had slid off the stool leant to the side of the makeshift bar and then held up a baseball bat. They drove their hate towards Gavin, but then simultaneously they observed me, their intent clear. Instantly, my right foot went back into a short fighting stance and I raised my hands to the front. My mind processed objects that could be used as a weapon, and how each of them carried their arms. I turned my fear into aggression. It was them, or me.

'Johnny, meet my future brothers-in-law, Pepen, Rede, and Wayan.'

'This is for real, right?' I said.

'Yes. They don't like their sister shacking up with me. We've had a few encounters. Isn't that right, boys?'

The bloke with the machete stepped closer. With my heart beating faster, I moved a step in, but weirdly I found myself searching for any family resemblance to Zelda.

'Ocker tells me you're a martial art nut and fucking crazy, but leave this one to me. Take a seat on your rucksack, and enjoy.'

Gavin took off his white T-shirt and handed it to me. He then went into a martial arts stance, different from my karate style.

CHAPTER TWO

Gavin held his hand out with two fingers pointing towards the three of them, his other hand across his chest. His tattoos twitched as his muscles flexed. He then went perfectly still, relaxed. The brother-in-law holding the machete nodded at the baseball bat-wielding family member. Wayan tapped the bat in the palm of his hand as he walked casually closer; dried mud fell off his boots. I shouldn't have taken my eyes off the other two, but I was entranced. With a short sharp grunt, the bat arced towards the left hand side of Gavin's head. In an instant, Gavin exploded with speed and an unerring accuracy with both hands open, blocking the arm with the bat. In the same flowing movement, Gavin fired a powerful snappy back-fist to the assailant's right temple, sending a searing pain through Wayan's temporal artery. He dropped the baseball bat. Moving with as much fluidity as water, Gavin's left hand grabbed Wayan's right wrist. Still gracefully flowing, Gavin seized Wayan by the back of the neck, squeezing his nerves. Gavin's face was contorted with aggression and power. As his attacker squealed, Gavin pushed up Wayan's arm and then pulled his head down towards a vicious knee strike to his face; Wayan's nose shattered. Spewing blood followed the descent of Wayan's unconscious body to the floor. Gavin turned his back to his opponent to face the other two assailants. I was in awe at the speed of it all.

A charge from Rede with a knife in his left hand lunged at Gavin's head. In a lightning reaction, Gavin ducked; I flinched. The blade came back at chest height, but Gavin arched his torso in, missing him by millimetres. As the scary-looking weapon sailed passed, Gavin forced Rede's arm away with a right-handed open-palmed block, pushing the knife in an opposite direction. Rede spun around.

'*Membunuhn ya*,' Pepen yelled.

Face to face again, Gavin had reverted to a martial art stance, his tattoos now reminding me of something to do with Kung Fu. Rede thrust the knife again, but Gavin's wrist blocked the knife hand at the wrist. In the same sinuous movement, Gavin grabbed the wrist and, twisting it, caused the point of the assailant's elbow to point skywards. Immediately, Gavin, with the inner part of his forearm, struck a hammer blow with an almost steel-like bone, forcing the attacker's arm to bend in an unnatural way, the tendons separating. With an unnerving scream, Rede dropped to his knees, choking from the pain. However, Gavin showed no mercy with a spinning outer crescent kick to Rede's jaw. Sprawling across the floor, Rede now lay motionless at the Pepen's feet.

Gavin picked up the Rede's knife that had stood upright in the floor and whipped it to the side of him, the point fixing into the timber wall.

'Gavin,' I shouted.

Gavin twisted as it swished by, the large metal blade missing him by a whisker. Amazingly, he leg-swept Pepen, who crashed to the floor. Both men stared at each other in defiance. Gavin invited him off the floor with a hand gesture. The brother-in-law slowly stood up, smiling, but then turned into a screaming madman. He raced at Gavin, swinging the machete up in an arc. It seemed in slow motion as Gavin's eyes followed the tip of the blade as it travelled up his entire body, simultaneously curving centimetres away from it. As it reached Gavin's face, he fell back on to his hands and struck Pepen in the bollocks with a powerful toe-punt. The smack was chilling enough, let alone the yell of pain. The machete clanged on the floor. Pepen held onto his groin for dear life.

Gavin flipped onto his feet and kicked the machete back to Pepen. I watched with bated breath to see if he would pick it up. Through grunts and groans, Pepen dribbled onto the handle that lay at his knees. My mind was telling him to leave it alone. I glanced back at Gavin who had blood dripping, but I couldn't see where from.

Stupidly, Pepen picked up his weapon and, gritting his teeth, straightened upright. Pepen vented his aggression by swinging at head height with extreme force. Instead of ducking, Gavin stepped in swiftly, seized Pepen's arm and pushed it upwards. The power forced Pepen's bicep into his cheek, blocking his vision of where Gavin was. At the same time, Gavin's right inner forearm arched around and struck the left side of Pepen's neck. The shock unbalanced Pepen, the machete dropped to the floor. Gavin put more pressure on Pepen's neck, causing him to almost lose consciousness. Eventually, Pepen slithered to the floor. Gavin released his strangle-hold and took a step back. Pepen gasped for air, but dazed, Pepen slowly rose to his knees with his back to Gavin. Pepen put one sole of his foot on the ground. Gavin placed a powerful kick in Pepen's spine, crashing him to the floor. This time, face embedded in the wood, the dust around his mouth being snorted away, Pepen didn't get up.

Gavin was in his solid stance again. It took me three shouts to release his stare before he turned to me. When he stood up, he began to slightly tremble; blood dripped off his elbow and ear. I didn't know what to say. The door swung behind me. I turned, expecting more trouble, but Goliath trudged by and threw an already blood-stained white towel at Gavin.

'Cheers, Ahmad,' Gavin said.

Incredibly, Gavin helped Ahmad lift and lay all three beaten blokes onto their horses, and they were sent on their way down the winding track.

'Do you want that drink now?' Gavin asked.

'Fucking need one. Remind me not to get on the wrong side of you. I would have slotted the motherfuckers.'

'So I've heard. Remind me not to get on the wrong side of you. Ahmad, bring me two shots, please.' Gavin picked a chair up and slumped into it. 'Sorry, Johnny, this is Ahmad. Ahmad, this is Johnny.'

The big lump grunted. Grabbing the handful of rupiah notes on the top of the bar, Ahmad went behind it.

'You want me to look at your injuries?' I asked.

'Nah, it's fine. Not the first I've received off that lot, nor the last, I expect. Just pissed off he caught my tattoo.'

'Families, hey. I hope she's worth it.'

Ahmad brought over two shot glasses, looking minuscule in his hands. The liquid he poured was brown, like brandy.

'One for the road,' Gavin said, and downed it.

He screwed his face up, shook his head, and exhaled as if breathing fire. I knocked it back, the burning urged me to cough as I exhaled the heat. Through gritted teeth and sheer determination, I winked at Gavin, shaking the glass at Ahmad for another one.

'Fuck off. No way,' Gavin gruffly said—he didn't have to twist my arm.

Ahmad slammed the bottle down on the table and then picked up all the weapons, before disappearing out the door, shutting it behind him. Ah, lock-in; now this is what I call hospitality, I thought.

I'm sure that as Gavin drove back along the narrow track to the main dirt road, he was reliving the attack in his thoughts; I was. It was the strangest situation I had ever been in. I know I would have dumped them over the canyon instead of helping them on their way, but I suppose it was in his best interests to keep his family-to-be on his side.

On occasions, his driving had come very to the edge, but with the amount of alcohol I'd had, I didn't really care; the paint stripper drink still warmed my chest. Gavin adjusted the white towel on his arm, the jeep swerving closer still to the gorge on his side.

'How long you been out here, Gav?'

'Five years now. Only fucking passing through, when I met this guy who was desperate for help tracking poachers. Fucking scumbag wankers. After two or three bottles of that gut-burning brown shit, I agreed. I wonder if my boss back in the UK has realised I've been away for five years.' He sniggered.

'Don't you mean one or two glasses of the gut-burning brown shit,' I said, and laughed.

'I'm sure it was at least a bottle, you bastard.'

'Oh yeah, same truth as like when you met this ugly bride-to-be, and her family welcomed you in.'

'Whatever.'

I thought of Ocker's annoying wind-up about my karate. 'Then you had to do some jujitsu shit on them, after getting drunk on a whole bottle, that is,' I added.

'It's Kung Fu, you twat.'

I grinned. 'I take it this guy you met is the bloke I'm going to see now.'

'Yep, and take my advice: you love tigers more than humans.'

'What's his name?' I asked.

'Nico Stolz.'

'Is he German?'

'No, Swedish, and very proud of it, so make sure you make a fuss.'

Feeling relaxed from the brown shit, I turned my attention to the stunning backdrop against the pure-blue sky and crisp-white clouds. My passion for animals and their conservation had returned, something I hadn't properly felt since I was a young lad. I couldn't wait to explore this splendour. Even if I didn't get to spot the tiger, there were plenty of animals to see that I had studied before leaving. If this turned out to be a brilliant mission, I didn't really care about the payday. The only downside was that I would have to thank Ocker and then listen to him go on and on about it.

Time check: 10.30 hrs. The humidity and temperature had risen. I was starting to soak in my own sweat. No wonder Gavin only wore light clothes, me still in my walking boots, cargo trousers, and thick cotton shirt. I turned the knob for the air blowers, but it came off in my hand. I lowered the window, but it clonked, dropping of sight.

'Stop fucking fiddling,' Gavin said.

'Typical eighties Suzuki junk.'

'I take it you owned one then.'

'Only for a short while, but it got me out of a hole and across Afghanistan,' I said, and scoffed.

'Special Forces, I've heard,' he probed.

Big mouth Ocker, I thought. Shit. I was supposed to have contacted him.

'My mate was in the SAS. He said he was at the embassy siege,' Gavin continued.

I smirked. 'Yeah? That makes about a thousand I've heard so far.'

'Were you there?' he asked, still prying, knowing I would have been too young.

I took out my phone, but the signal was shit. Leaning back in the rear, from the top of my Bergen I pulled out my latest gadget: a mini-satellite. Rigged up and with it held out the window, I phoned Ocker. It rang for ages, until he answered.

'Strewth. What the fuck time do you call this, mate? Better be bloody urgent.'

'Morning, Ocker. It's ten thirty-five. Just …'

'Jesus fuck,' Ocker interrupted. 'It's five thirty-five, fucking A, fucking M, here.'

'How's the hangover, dude? Anyway, you should be up and ready for me to report in every hour, twenty-four hours a day. That's your new role.'

Gavin laughed and put his thumb up.

'Sorry, mate, didn't catch that over the fucking whining. What do ya want, ya stupid pommy?'

I laughed. 'Just signing in.'

'Well, hash-tag fuck off. I'm gonna now have to use my fat on the shelia next to me, be a shame to waste it.'

'You sure you don't want to join me and Gavin out here?' I asked, knowing the sort of response I was going to get.

'I'd rather fill me shorts with croc shit and do a bungee jump, mate.'

It was a worse reply than I'd thought, and he then ended the call.

'What was his answer?' Gavin asked.

'Said he would like to join us and make amends.'

'Sounds like he has his marbles in the right place.'

'Oh yeah,' I said sarcastically.

Along with the screen, the satellite and my arms were covered in dust and insects. As if reading my mind the wipers went on; well, the driver's did. Gavin took a left turn at speed down a rutted track. The dust billowed in through my window, sticking to my soaked body. The off-road experience worsened. I had to take my cupped hands from around my mouth and nose to hold onto whatever didn't fall off. Eventually, he skidded to a stop. I spat out the grit.

'Welcome to paradise, sir. Hope you enjoyed the taxi ride,' he said.

'It wasn't as nice as Setiawan's. How much do I owe you?'

'It's all for charity, mate,' Gavin replied, impersonating Mr Nicey.

Gavin shoulder-barged his door and got out. I shadowed him around to the rear where he collected a beige holdall from the inside. He checked the sandy track both ways before telling me to quickly follow him. We jogged the ten metres up the slight slope through the trees. Fast-flowing water raged nearby. Coming out from the bushes, I was confronted by a spectacular wide river. The air was fresher. There was no way we could cross that swell and current, I thought. Gavin squat-ran along the edge, the shingle falling into the danger below. Where was he going? More of the bank fell in as I trailed him.

Approximately twenty-five metres later, the river slightly narrowed on a bend. A wire expanding the width had been set up, moisture dripped from it. Gavin rapidly pulled a contraption out of his holdall and held it out to me.

'Being what you are, you've probably done this a million times,' he said, voiced raised above the torrent.

'I've never been in the circus.' I took it off him and unravelled the two bits of rope crudely attached to two steel wheels. 'Did you make this?'

Gavin folded his arms. 'Yeah, why?'

'Have you tested it?'

Gavin pulled at the thick wire. 'Sure, when I was a circus trapeze artist. Now get a fucking move on. You don't want to keep Nico late.'

I placed the two wheels on the wire. 'Is that because he has a Swedish watch?'

'Yep, pure Swedish blood, bud. By the way, he see's swearing as a sign of a real man.' Gavin helped me on with the heavy Bergen.

'Why do you tell me that?' I asked, knowing I shouldn't have.

'Coz, you don't swear much, sign of being a fucking wuss, bud.'

'I fell right into that. Let's hope your Heath Robinson contraption doesn't let me fall any further.'

Placing my hands in the rope loops, I checked the angle of the wire that descended towards the tree on the far bank.

'How the fuck are you going to get across?' I asked.

'I'm not.'

Gavin pushed me over the edge. My Bergen bounced into the water, slightly tilting me off balance, and then it sprang out. I immediately checked the wheels above. Thank fuck they were still on. Gaining speed, I arched my neck back to Gavin, who was grinning big.

'You wanker,' I shouted. 'How the fuck am I going to get back?'

'Oh, now you're swearing like a trooper. And, that's if you get out of the jungle, alive.'

I had to keep my legs up from the fast flow as the opposite bank came nearer. In the last two metres, my Bergen became completely submerged. I came to a stop. Again, I cursed Gavin. He obviously was finding this amusing. I couldn't wait tell him that his calculations for my weight and Bergen compared to his lightweight frame were completely useless.

Dry land was within spitting distance. Hooking both legs over the wire, I tried to shimmy along. With both biceps burning, I decided to unlock my legs and dangle, land below being my salvation. Once I had stood up and taken my wrists from rope, I sharply looked back at the opposite bank to give Gavin abuse, but he had disappeared.

The wet backpack's weight had increased; however, through jungle excursions, I had learnt to keep everything that was crucial in a dry-sack. The area I was in was dotted with trees. The further in, the denser it became. The odd bird noise came from deep inside, but life seemed to have stopped. Was I supposed to wait here for Nico? Maybe I was late and he had gone.

After ten minutes of tuning into my surroundings and watching different insects on the trees and floor, I got a sense of my meagre existence compared to Planet Earth's Mother Nature. I wondered how many other people at this moment were sitting in such isolation from other humans.

A faint sound alerted me, different to what I was tuned into. I had a feeling of being watched. There it was again: a slight wood-on-wood tapping. Peering into the forestation, I noticed a tiny movement. I blinked the sweat away, focusing hard. Inconspicuously, I undid the Bergen's side pocket, drawing my knife. I knew leopards lurked around this part of the world, but knowing their precarious existence, I would only use my knife as a last resort. Making out I hadn't been forewarned, I slid the knife up my sleeve and hauled up the Bergen over one shoulder. I purposely headed off left of the target, still acting casual, though my mind raced with different scenarios.

Pushing my way through the thick bushes, I found a small clearing that appeared to be man-made. Immediately, I checked the ground for traps, like a hole covered in leaves, at the bottom of which could be spikes. Between the loose branches, twigs, and moss, I also searched for snares. Down on one knee, I slid the weight off my back and listened— silence. Keeping in a slight curve, I began heading back towards where I had seen the movement. My heartbeat increased, pushing adrenalin through my veins. Within about three metres of where I had predicted whatever it was to be, I slid the knife into my hand. I deciphered each leaf, twig, and bush to the point I knew I was positive what I viewing. Maybe it was Nico, but why was he hiding? I regripped the knife.

'Psst... Nico,' I whispered—nothing.

Bollocks to this, I thought, and charged through. With a metre to go, I suddenly halted, waiting for a reaction. I probed deeper: a small clearing had been hacked away. In the middle was a rock, like those I'd seen at the river's edge. First, I looked around it. With the tip of my blade, I cautiously poked under it, then slowly lifted it. Underneath was a piece of folded paper, no bigger than a fifty pence piece. Feeling exposed, I scanned the area again. Was I a sitting target? I squashed the negative. Only two people knew I was here, and I'd not upset anyone; well, except for the kid on the motorbike that I had not paid. I doubted Zelda would have left her village, in the fear she may be identified as Bigfoot. There was no way Gavin's brothers-in-law would have recovered by now. Opening the note, it read: Rendezvous: 0°41'42.8"S 100°35'46.3"E

CHAPTER THREE

Trying to find a direct route through the jungle, the same as the crow would fly above, wasn't easy. However, at least I didn't have to go at the deathly slow pace I'd had on other SF missions. With one hand on my GPS, I kept as close as I could to the destination coordinates. The call of monkeys and birds kept me cheerful. I had given up trying to find the tell-tale signs of whoever had left the note. Maybe Nico was tracking me? I did think at one point of doing a dog-leg ambush, but had decided it was too hot for games. I pondered why there was so much secrecy in Gavin and the elusive Nico since I had landed. Even Will had not informed me of the whole picture, but then, he never did, thinking back on Operation Last Assault.

The rendezvous was only one kilometre from where I had found the note. Even though I was sweating buckets, at least I had shade from the tree canopies, unlike the crow. Apart from my drinking bonanza on the couple of days leading up to this mission, I had put in extra physical training and gorged on high protein and fresh foods. I was in damn good shape. This wasn't a survival mission; I wouldn't be snaring animals and living off the land. I had plenty of rations, water, malaria tablets, and medical aids.

Ahead was a large clearing, and in the background was a huge blue lake. It was idyllic, tempting me to strip off and wade in. Checking again that this was the rendezvous, I then slung off my Bergen, put away the GPS, and took a well-earned drink. Again, my sixth sense told me I was being watched; yet, this time I couldn't be arsed to play the game. Instead, I sat and marvelled at the wonderful lake Danau Singkarak and its stunning scenery. Groups of mosquitoes buzzed above the calm surface. It wouldn't be long before they tested if I had the correct repellent. The white clouds rolled over the top of the mountains and then faded out, descending on the trees that covered the slopes. The pure-blue sky mirror-imaged its colour on the lake, itself tranquil, with only the occasional ripple from a jumping fish.

Dotted between the trees in the far distance was an infrequent house with the typical pointed roof. I almost had to pinch myself that this was a mission and not a holiday. Was this really going to be a "cracker job" as Ocker had put it? No terrorists, Russian thugs, drug cartels, deserts, Somali pirates, attack boats, bent Yanks, or weird desperate old men that tie up young girls. For a change, perhaps trouble wouldn't find me and I wouldn't look for it. So far, well, except the Gavin incident, it had been trouble-free. I didn't even need an operations name.

Time check: 12.43 hrs. I had been sitting on my rucksack for nearly an hour. My impatient mood was growing, which was a shame due to the amazing ambience. What the fuck was Nico up to? I finished off the second energy bar, then decided to turn my attention to the small log-cabin set on the edge of the wood. The surface had turned a damp green, even with the sun out. I wiped the green-tinged window and peered in—disused. Surprisingly, the door wasn't locked, so I walked into the shadows; must filled my nostrils. Not only did the room look abandoned, everything that should have been in the cupboards had been strewn. The candlewax in the wall lanterns had dripped, leaving only the wick. A rickety ladder led up to the next level. I decided to climb halfway and poke my head over, but all that was up there was an empty bedframe. I questioned if I had punched in the right GPS co-ordinates.

Back outside, I checked the near vicinity. Apart from a few empty fuel containers and signs that someone had a fire going a long time ago, it was bare. This was ridiculous. I was getting seriously pissed off. Suddenly, goose bumps layered my arms. I turned, knowing someone was behind me, and I was right: a large-framed and broad-shouldered man stood, most probably six foot five. His entire clothes and hat were green kaki. His hands and face were covered in cam-cream and he had a veil around his neck. Johnny, meet the stalker, I thought.

'Johnny Vince. Welcome,' he said in his thick South African accent.

I realised Gavin's 'Swedish' wind-up. 'Nico, where the fuck have you been? Why the fuck did you not greet me back at the river's edge?'

'I wanted to make sure you were who you were meant to be. And I do not take kind to your foul language. It should be only used when appropriate.'

I scoffed at Gavin's second wind-up. 'I think this is fucking appropriate.'

Nico took his hands off his hips and folded them. 'I am being serious.'

'So the fuck am I.'

Nico shook his head. 'Obnoxious.'

'Maybe I'm a little pissed off with the hospitality. Where I come from, everyone says hello.'

'You really ought to move out of that telephone box, and get a real life.'

That was quite witty, but I didn't want to let him have the pleasure. 'Now, shall we get a brew on and get down to the niceties? Two sugars in mine.'

'No milk in mine, Tom,' he quickly replied.

'Tom?' I snapped. 'It's Johnny.'

'As you wish, Hardy.'

'Tom Hardy? Have you been smoking the natural weed?'

A broad grin to match his shoulders broke up his rugged facial looks. 'Ocker and Will had warned me.'

'Warned you?'

He strutted over and held out his large spade-size hand. I shook it hard. Nico eventually let his vice grip go.

'Anyway, it could have been worse,' I said. 'You could have had Ocker here, or you could have been a Swede with a foul mouth.'

'Ah, Gavin up to his old tricks.' He laughed and, stepping in closer, patted me hard on the back. '*Howitz.*'

He stank like the log-cabin, but I thanked him for his greeting. With his hands on both of my shoulders, he looked me straight in the eyes.

'I am glad you are here,' he said. 'You have a big reputation, and I hope you can deliver it. Now, follow me.'

He slapped me on the arm and then strode off towards the shack.

'I'll get my luggage then,' I moaned.

I rubbed my arm and then followed him, surprised, but relieved, when he walked past hotel shit-hole cabin.

Twenty metres on, Nico turned and held his hand up for me to stop. He scanned the area first. With his big smile grinning at me, he turned his back and foraged in the leaves at his feet. He pulled out a loop of rope and heaved it up, which then pulled up a thick wooden slatted door.

'What are you waiting for? Come into my house,' he said.

I held back a bit, curious as to what he had in surprise for me. 'Your home?'

'Quick, inside.'

I dumped the Bergen in front of the aperture and peered in, my shadow covering the natural light below. Showing what appeared to be the inside of a log-styled cabin, I thought of a joke that he was indeed Swedish, but decided not to speak. He seemed to lack any humour, and he was a straight talker all right. My feet fumbled through the ladder rungs, but eventually I felt the floor. The light from above was shadowed by my rucksack. He barked at me to hurry and take it from him. It was surprisingly cool compared to above and it didn't smell disused.

Once he had reached the bottom after pulling the door shut, in the dark he gave me another manly bear hug. After letting go, clanking came from the far end. A flame from his lighter lit a lantern. In the nearest corner he lifted a lid off a box and fiddled around inside. The lantern jerked, making weird shadows on the walls as he pulled at something. The familiar sound of a generator filled the air. Slowly, the lights on the walls and ceiling flickered on.

The room was about sixteen metres squared, with a bed, chairs, and a basic kitchen area. At one end were two doors, one padlocked. Another ladder was situated at the far end wall with a closed hatch above. I was impressed with the set-up.

'Nice shelter,' I said.

'This is my home,' he snapped.

It was like walking on eggshells. 'Did you build it yourself? It's far better than the guest-room above.'

'What do you know?' he said.

'I know I'm getting a bit pissed off with your bark.'

'I meant about the demise of the Sumatran tiger.'

'Oh... a little,' I said, feeling I'd jumped in with both feet.

'I am going to tell you then.'

'Fuck me. Do you all speak so direct?' I said. 'Sorry, Gavin's foul mouth has rubbed off on me.'

Nico laughed. He turned around and plugged in a kettle—Jesus; this bloke was hard to read and he changed like the wind.

Nico handed me a large mug of black coffee and then sat down on a chair, leaving nowhere else for me to sit.

'Sit down. I need to tell you your mission,' he said.

'I would love to, but the comfort is a bit frugal.'

He had taken offence, but instead of barking, he said, 'You are right. Please, sit here. I will stand.'

Was this his sarcasm? 'No, it's fine,' I said. 'I've sat on a long boring flight and then on an uncomfortable part-built motorbike. I then had to sit in a beat-up piece of shitty junk to the river. And lastly, I had to take an extended seat on my Bergen whilst waiting for the Swedish non-swearing invisible man to show.'

'Lay on the fucking bed then, Hardy.'

I sprayed my tea, coughing after. I went to tell him he swore, but then I thought it was puerile. As I wiped my shirt, I caught him smiling. I sat on the bed and loudly stretched. He went to the kitchen area.

'I can see why you love tigers more than humans.' Or is it tigers love you more than humans do, I thought. 'This is a lovely home. How long have you lived here?'

'If you are hungry, I will cook for you.'

'Sure, Nico, that would be nice. What have you got?'

'You get what you are given,' he snapped.

'Yes, Mum.' I sniggered. 'So, tell me more why you're here.'

Nico lit the gas and started to boil some water. He then proceeded to chop some raw meat. I'm not asking again, I thought, but then he cleared his throat.

'I have lived in Sumatra for fifteen years. This job has turned me into an *ou ballie*, that's Afrikaans for "old man", but it is my destiny to save the tiger. At first the government did not help, but now they are under a lot of pressure.'

'From worldwide animal organisations?' I said.

'Yes, the same pot that pays my wages and this mission. Now let me finish. With funding I have built up a network of people I can trust, and a dedicated ranger patrol to combat the poachers who disgracefully and brutally kill the tigers. They have no morals. To see such a majestic iconic creature barbarically slaughtered for export is...' Nico thumped his fist on the chopping board, sending up splats of blood. 'Fucking subhuman. Sorry, my *bru*, I have digressed. The rangers do a fantastic job dismantling the wire snares that catch the tigers. However, the poachers are on the increase due to the greed of the world. Animal trading across the board is on a massive increase. Do you know, less than five hundred tigers remain in Sumatra due to the deforestation and bastard poachers? In twenty years the epitome of the world's animal kingdom will be gone, unless we stop now.'

Nico poured boiling water into a drum next to him; steam rose to the ceiling. When I turned back to him, he was looking at me.

'Don't worry, any smells are filtered,' he said. 'Once I cover the main hatch with leaves, I come back through this tiny one that leads secretly into a bush. You could have someone straight above us and they wouldn't hear or smell anything. And yes, even your perfumed body, something you will have to change when you go into the jungle.'

'I know a lot abo …'

'Why do I live like this?' he interrupted. 'I will tell you.'

Really, I sarcastically thought.

'The bastard poachers are bribing officials in high places to turn a blind-eye. Even the paperwork at the docking yard is falsified. The five-year imprisonment passed in 1990 for such a crime is laughable, but it is sickening when the poachers get out after a year, just to do it all again, the next time wiser not to be caught. Bastards. My first home in town they had turned upside down many times, and they steal my stock. I moved out the area and lived in the jungle. It is what I know best. After the log cabin was trashed, I set up another further inland, as a ruse. My nickname is *Boastman*; Afrikaans name for 'bushman'. After seeking new funds, I returned and built this new home with all-round protection. You did well to miss the abundance of traps.'

'Like I said, I'm trained.' I was lying through my teeth as I'd not seen any; maybe my luck was in.

'Here, eat this.' He handed me a plate of food. '*Mielie* and *sosatie*. Tuck in, my *bru*.'

I recognised the first as corn-on-the-cob with lashings of oil and salt. The second was a meat kebab, but it didn't look like chicken, and was too dark for beef. Tasting it, it was deliciously rich in flavour. Nico called me Hardy, and when I looked up, he chucked me a can of something. I caught it, nearly dropping my plate. It was a can of Castle Beer.

He continued his story of how he had survived out here. It was no revelation to find out he had learnt his survival skills from his dad, who had been in the Rhodesian Special Forces. He told me how he had met Gavin, the bond of trust between them, and his loathing of Gavin's cursing. He continued down the trust road, saying only three people knew what I was really doing here: himself, Gavin, and Setiawan. Not even the team of rangers had been told. I dared not tell him that I had met Gavin's new family.

After we had tucked into more food and beer, Nico was more relaxed, as was I. He went over to the locked door. After going through three combination locks and, opening it, he switched on a light. I moved my head around to get a better view of what was in there, but he quickly closed the door behind him. Without as much as a decent peek, he slid out, locked up, and sat next to me on the bed. Nico proceeded to hand me a large old rucksack, but kept a faded-pink folder in his hand.

'Take this,' Nico said.

'I've got everything I need, thanks.'

His look said not to piss him off, but to look inside. Opening it up, there were bits of old wire, a large machete, a compass, and a map.

'Cheers,' I said, hopefully not sounding as sarcastic as it was.

Nico then opened the file's flap and said, 'I want you to listen, and listen hard.' He pulled out a pile of A4 photos. 'This is the ranger field manager, Dian, and this is his team.'

He passed me the photos. I studied the dusky-blue uniform and cap. None of them were carrying rifles, only rucksacks and machetes. The next photo was of a haul of dried skins and body parts. As I studied to work out what they were, it reminded me of the bodies dumped at the bottom of the factory stairs in Operation Last Assault, turning my stomach. Nico never said a word whilst passing me the photos. His eyes were filled with sadness. The images continued to portray more atrocities: tigers that had chewed through their legs after being caught in a snare, decomposed carcasses, and more skins and bones. The last two photos were of some of the poachers: one of a pair who had been caught, the other of a group of five heading through the jungle. I noted the dated rifles slung over their shoulders. Some of the weapons had blue and orange painted action frames.

'Where's my Heckler & Koch?' I asked.

'You will not be taking any guns into the jungle.'

'What?'

'There is a very good reason not even our rangers carry guns. Can you imagine what the poachers would do if they manage to get hold of just one. I know the...'

'But I won't let them get hold of any weapon I have,' I butted in.

'No weapons. OK?' he said sternly. 'I am going to finish what I was saying. I know the poachers are armed, but they have a limited amount of ammunition. The guns are very old. However, I have lost three rangers in the last sixteen months.'

I let the pause of silence go on for a bit. 'Is it OK to speak?'

'*Eish.*'

I smirked. 'What are the mission details?' I pulled out the wire from the rucksack. 'And why do I need this?'

'Those, my *bru*, are what you need to look out for.' He stood up and untangled the mess. 'The loop snare end of the wire is placed in a small hole in the ground, three in total. Then logs are placed each side of the hole and the middle is covered with leaves. The tiger will tread over the logs and into the trap. Once the tiger pulls at the snare, it will fling up at the end tied to a pressurised bent branch. The other two wires will be secured to the ground.'

Nico put his thick forearm through one of the loops and thrashed it around. New marks appeared over old scars. He had broken the skin where he vigorously demonstrated. I wondered how many times he had done this show.

'You see, the more I struggle, the more it tightens and cuts in. The tiger sometimes gnaws through its own leg to escape. It is macabre. The pain and anguish they go through. Just for fucking fur and meat, and bone and skull trophies. They are supposed to be in protected fucking areas.' He stopped to compose himself, breathing hard as he did.

Energised by his passion, I said, 'I won't let you down. What are my mission details?'

'There is believed to be a one hundred and fifty tiger stronghold in the north in Kerinci Seblat National Park. Now that might sound a lot, but bear in mind that its nearly fourteen thousand square kilometres. The Sumatran tiger is generally a solitary animal, but reports say that streaks of them have been seen heading towards the outer edges, to the mountains. It is said that the poachers have set up a camp there, and many traps have been laid. The rangers will not travel this far. You are to track the poachers to their camp, plot it, and destroy any snares along the way. Each time you find a trap, you must note its location. Can you manage that?'

'Easy,' I said.

Nico threw the wire to the side in disgust, blood dripped from his forearm. 'I want to ask you one question: why are you here?'

I pondered, then said, 'I need to ask you a few questions, my *bru*,'— which I think meant male friend—'and I want you to answer directly.' I smirked. 'Why won't the rangers travel to this region and the mountains?'

'*Tokoloshe*,' he said.

'Not as directly as I can't understand you,' I snapped.

'Afrikaans for evil spirit.'

I kept silent, waiting for more...

'It is believed that these natives who live in hiding have sided with the evil spirits. If you are captured, you live in hell for the rest of your days.'

'Big fucking pile of shit. And that's worth swearing about.' I took a swig of beer. 'Has anyone ever seen this tribe?'

'It is said that if anyone looks into their eyes, they will take your mind. You will not know what is real, and what isn't.'

'Really?' I shook my head at how silly it was. 'What a load of bollocks. If your rangers haven't seen the camp and traps, then how do you know they are there?'

Nico sat back down and rubbed his smoothly-shaven jaw, smearing his cam-cream. 'I have lost two men who have travelled into this area to search. One of ...'

'Lost?' I said, cutting him short. 'What, just disappeared without a trace? They couldn't have been from an Elite background.'

He looked at me sharply, his eyes narrowing. 'One of them was my brother, Georges Demblon.'

'Demblon? How can this be your brother?'

'Brother in arms, *jou poephol.*'

'Georges? Bit of a girl's name,' I said, and laughed to cover up my previous mistake.

'You really should not upset me by slating my friends and family.'

'Blimey. You're a bit touchy on that front. So, your *brother* is shacked up high with the Korowai tribe?' I grinned.

He sighed, slightly shaking his head. 'Georges sent a sitrep saying he had found the camp and had dismantled many traps. I've never heard from him since. He has been missing for three months.' He closed his fingers together and squeezed.

'Why haven't you gone to look for him? I would if it was my best mate,' I said, but wished I hadn't.

'You are not fucking here to judge me,' he yelled. 'I need to know why you are fucking here.'

'Because I like tigers... more than I like you.'

'*Eish.* I am so tired of listening to your shit. Meet me up top when you are ready.' Nico threw his beer can aside and headed back up the ladder.

CHAPTER FOUR

After changing into my green camouflage jungle clothing, I slapped on more non-smelling insect repellent. Deciding what I wanted in my Bergen, I left the rest, including what Nico had given me. I had planned a maximum of two weeks, but as most plans could go rat shit, I took enough for three weeks. I double-checked the mental list as it went in: escape and evade Pelican case, fire-starting equipment, torches, GPS, compass, satcom, dehydration and purification tablets, a second mobile phone with plug-in mini satellite, dry clothing for the sleeping-bag, waterproof smock and poncho, knife, first-aid kit, latex and leather gloves, climbing equipment, water and spare containers, sealable bags, Hexi-stove, ration packs, trusty mug, binoculars, mosquito repellent, cam-cream, and spare batteries for everything that needed them. Being in the jungle, I'd brought some Broad Spectrum Antibiotic pills. One piece of kit I didn't leave behind was a pair of night vision goggles.

Back up on level ground, there was some rustling from the bushes, but I couldn't see Nico. He could obviously see me as he had ordered me to come and help. Moving the thick overgrowth aside, Nico was clearing a pile of already cut forestation that concealed a green tarpaulin. Underneath revealed a naval khaki-patterned long one-man kayak. I had not seen one like this before and it looked decent. Nico grinned like a Cheshire cat.

'You're not coming with me then?' I asked.

'The water-jet propelled engine has been sound-proofed.' He moved his finger down the length. 'You will find fuel and water in where you sit. Notice the steering modification fitted to the side, that is the bracket where you put your GPS. I know, obvious, before you butt in. Impressed?'

He had this knack of only answering what was important to him, I thought. 'Your typical Elite stuff,' I said.

He grinned. 'Oh really? Please tell me the facts, as I forget.' He knew I was talking shit. '*Eish*. Johnny Vince is speechless.'

'Johnny who? Thought I was Tom Hardy.'

'I will tell you the facts you do not know: the three-gallon tank will give you a hundred and thirty to a hundred sixty kilometres, depending on your weight and speed. It has a top speed of twenty-five kilometres per hour. I hope you like the specially designed paintwork.'

'I do. Whose idea was it? Who paid for it?'

'A gutter-mouthed Australian ordered it. The charity stumped up the cash.'

I'm surprised Ocker hadn't added a Gatling gun, I thought. 'Who's the charity?'

'Right, help me out with it,' he said.

'Oh that's right, body-swerve what you don't want to answer.'

Once I had loaded up and was sat in it, Nico waded into the water and handed me the GPS co-ordinates, and then the map I had left behind. I tucked the map into my shirt, then set the GPS.

'Take this, Hardy,' Nico said.

'Why do you keep calling me this?'

He grinned.

I took something off him which was wrapped up in tinfoil. 'Sig-Sauer P228?' I joked.

'*Padkos*. Food for the journey, my English friend.'

'Friend? You're going soft.' I took a sniff. 'What the fu... flip is that?'

'*Eish*. You held your tongue. *You* must be going soft. It is biltong. Dried and seasoned meat, similar to jerky.'

I went to reply facetiously about it being tiger meat, but decided not to. Even Ocker wouldn't have stooped that low. 'Mmm... thanks.'

'I want you to use some of my rat-packs. Seems a shame to waste them.'

'Rat-packs?'

Nico handed me a tatty square box. Inside were discoloured tins, biscuits, and energy bars. 'Ration packs from my army days.'

'Jesus,' I said. 'How old are these?'

'Hey. They last for ever. And don't be so rude.'

Time check: 14.37 hrs. The insect life had already started to congregate around me. I pulled back on the starter handle between my legs, like that of a chainsaw. Nico was right, the engine was very quiet.

'I thought you said it was quiet, my *bru*,' I said in my best deep South African accent.

'Was that your best?'

'See ya around,' I said, and gave him a wave.

'If you bother to check the old map, Lake Singkarak is roughly twenty-one kilometres long and seven wide.'

'Only roughly?' I said flippantly.

Nico waded back towards dry land. 'Don't get lost.'

'Cantankerous.' I threw the biltong over my shoulder.

Sailing the stunning vast open, calm water, I thought back on what Nico had said, "Don't get lost." Did he mean on the lake, or in the jungle like my two predecessors? I soon dismissed it, enjoying the magnificent views, wondering if I was the only one in this lost world. It certainly easily beat the sweaty and sandy bollocks of the desert. Impressed by this Mokai kayak whilst I plodded along, I thought of a business venture to use them back home in Newquay. I kept the craft as close to the middle of the lake as possible, speculating how deep it was and what sort of creatures lurked below. This was a first for me: to go on a mission and not think of the battle ahead, my squad, and weapons. I had never been so relaxed and I'd not even longed for action, being careful what I wished for. I was confident I would find the camp, if there really was one. I hoped I would get to see the awe-inspiring Sumatran tiger, but not up close. The many hours of animal research, especially the dangerous ones, now played through my mind. I couldn't wait to take some photos. A small part of me felt guilty that I was accepting money from a charity; maybe I should give some back.

With less than an hour of delights, the soothing, peaceful journey was over. Flicking the red kill-switch on the side, I drifted the last few metres. Sitting there for a minute, I tuned into the almost silent environment, before climbing out, the water cooling me. I hauled the kayak up the bank. Unfastening the Bergen, leaving the rat-packs behind, I hid the boat the best I could. I'm not sure why I made such a good job of it; I doubted there would be any passers-by. On the GPS I marked the position on the map with the co-ordinates, then set up the phone satellite. Breaking the lonely harmony I phoned Ocker. It rang for ages, so I ended the call. Time check: 15.40 hrs. Now what the fuck was he up to? I phoned again, but this time I didn't end the call; at least two minutes agonisingly went by.

'G'day, Vinnie,' Ocker said, upbeat.

'About bloody time. Don't tell me, you had another shelia on the go?'

'Nah, I'm at work now. Honestly, she did my head in with her bloody moaning about life, mate. She told me she was stuck in a rut, reckon a creek more like. She was fatter than I remembered last night.'

I tried not to laugh at the images in my head. 'Cut the shit, Ocker. Take down these co-ordinates...'

'Hold on, need something to write with.'

'You can write?'

No reply came. I waited.

'Strewth, found one at last. OK, ready.'

'0°33'23.4S. 100°29'01.2"E. What time is it there?'

'It's ten forty-seven, mate.'

'Remind me to not take another mission off you.'

'Why? Tell me what's happened. Are ya in trouble?'

'Yeah, big time,' I said seriously. 'I have had to travel across a lake in a boat designed by a fucking moron.' I quickly ended the call.

The map, as always, was cumbersome to put away. As well as the GPS, I had made a bearing with the compass. After filling up the spare container from the lake, also adding purification tablets, I heaved on the Bergen and then set off. Different bushes and trees tried to either block my path or snag me. Half an hour later, I was stunned to find a narrow vehicle track, seeming to follow the curve of the lake through the trees. The tracks were of a vehicle with chunky tyres, but the sun had baked the sand, so not that fresh. Down on one knee I checked the map, but this trail didn't show on it. Surely Nico would have made me travel by vehicle. Maybe he didn't know it. I quashed that thought as he knew the area well. It was probably unsafe to travel this way due to the poachers. With another measured sip of water, I headed across into the forestation. Looking back I could see my footprints. A little further in, I cut off a small pine-needle branch. Returning to the prints, I brushed them away so they didn't look obvious.

The jungle had become denser, making it awkward. The slicing of my machete sounded alien in this wonderful paradise. Whilst waiting for the cries of birds to subside, I contemplated how many rangers might be in the vicinity. An hour in, trying to go as the crow would fly, it was becoming impossible and I needed some rest. On the map it showed a higher contoured ridge. Below this was a river. It meant I would have to take a serious detour from the intended straight route, but weighing up continuing forwards, or turning back and seeing where the track went, I decided to go for the detour.

Two hours of hacking forwards, and trudging back to change direction, I found the slope to the ridge. I was hot and soaked in sweat. The sun was in the last stages of going down. My eyes were straining as it was. I raced through the small shrubs and stones to the ridge. On top and slightly out of breath, I wasn't expecting to see a narrow path; well, more of a trail. The earth was soft but compact. Through the dim light, I felt the animal tracks. I fumbled through my rucksack until I found the torch. On closer inspection the prints headed the way I was heading, but I had no idea if they belonged to a tiger.

Unexpectedly, the sound of an engine filtered in. I quickly switched off the torch. Clipping it to my Bergen, I foraged for the NVGs, but couldn't find them. I stopped and listened to the sound. It was far away, unsure if it was a boat or a car. Then a strange glow bounced out of the tops of the trees into the clouds. It was a car. As the noise came closer, the sound of the river below me became insignificant. It was dark enough for me not to be seen by eye and there was no way the vehicle could venture off the track.

Feeling more relaxed, I took out the equipment until I found the NVGs. It took me a while to get used to the weird green world. I thought back to when Kyle had only seconds to adjust his when on a collision course with death. I still had nightmares since returning from the last mission and they had increased as this one loomed. Now wasn't the time to get negative, I told myself. For reassurance, I put in one earpiece, playing Coldplay at low volume from my phone. Even though I had almost stopped seeing the psychologist, she had told me to play my favourite music, that's if it didn't remind me of any negative events.

Following the ridge wasn't easy, even with the goggles. In places the bank and path had eroded, leaving a perilous jump across. Most of the way the branches and bushes had stuck out at waist height, and I had to cut them away. It proved this path wasn't man-made. I thought back to what Nico had said: "Most tiger trails are close to water. This is where most traps will be laid." I concentrated on the ground even more.

Guessing that an hour had gone by, I stopped, lifted my goggles, and pulled the earphone out. Tuning in, I rubbed my weary eyes, taking a while to adjust to the blackness. The light from the GPS appeared ever so bright. Apart from the cascading river a large drop below, and the night insects' vocalisation, it was shrilly quiet. The vehicle's lights and engine had disappeared ages ago. Time check: 20.15 hrs. I cursed myself for leaving Nico's late, now not having found a lie up position. I knew I should have waited till dawn. I hit the side of my head, my own worst critic.

I was within ten kilometres of the main area where the suspected poachers' camp was, but now was the time to set up a camp and take some much-needed food and water. Physically, I felt fine, but I was sweating like a pig at a hog-roast. My GPS told me it was thirty degrees and eighty per cent humidity. A comfort was the cooling breeze that sometimes whipped off the river below. The question was: where do I set up a LUP? I was sure dangerous animals would use the path at night and would easily find my scent if I set up below in the woods. I knew tigers, like most dangerous cats, could climb trees.

Flipping my goggles down, I waited for the adjustment, then scaled down the steep riverbank. It was precarious and, a few times, I slipped down further with the stones and shingle, my heart giving a fluttered burst. Ten metres down it had become a near vertical drop, so I wedged my foot at the base of a small overhanging tree, but it didn't feel secure. Looking back at the route I'd taken, there was no way I could safely climb back. Why the fuck didn't you secure the rope? I'd reasoned that I would have to go back and untie it. It was the only excuse I could think of—pathetic. A simple loop knot and I could have pulled the rope back. I hit the side of my head, again.

Below to the right was a jagged slab of rock. Far below, the water cascaded over a mass of large boulders. From this angle I couldn't see how far the slab went back and how secure it was. The problem was: getting near it. However, I couldn't stay at the base of the tree much longer, it was about to join the fallen rocks below.

'Fuck. Not the best fucking decision you've made.'

I carefully turned so my Bergen faced the tree, the earth under the roots crumbled away. The ledge was only a stone's throw away. I went for it, digging my feet and hands in as I crab-traversed across. However, as soon as my last foot left the base of the roots, the tree fell. Trying not to get caught with it, my crabbing movement increased in speed, but I started to slide down. I gripped with my fingers; sharp little stones shot under my nails. It was no use; I was going down too fast. In a final attempt I pushed off to my left. Fortunately, my foot landed on the ledge, the momentum slapping my body on to it. Unfortunately, the largest tree branch crashed across my rucksack and legs. A loud cracking followed.

Eventually, silence fell and I slowed my breathing. The weight wasn't horrendous, but the pain was. I also wondered as I lay still, would the ledge take the weight? Lifting my scrunched-up face off the NVGs, only one of the lenses was green.

'Bollocks,' I grunted.

Whipping them off my head, I moved them aside. My face was swollen from the impact. Holding my hand in front, there was no blood. On my elbows I inched forward. Once the branches were off my legs, it was relatively easy to crawl out. I unclipped the torch. The beam ahead lit up my morale when I saw a small cave entrance. Energised, I twisted over and sat up. I had no obvious blood from my legs. Moving them, they weren't broken, but bruised, along with my pride. I shone the torch at the mess I had crawled out from; insects danced in the beam. Luckily, the main thick branch had struck me on its concave arch. Further along, it had hit the slab, a piece had cracked off the edge. I was damn fortunate it landed as it had.

I sat for a while reliving the event, shaking my head. The crashing of the torrent below reminded me how close I had come. I ventured into the small cave entrance and shone the torch around. At some point a large tree must have been here as twisted roots remained, it also having fallen to its death. I reckoned it had taken down a giant boulder, leaving enough room inside for me and my kit. Then a thought hit me: in retribution, I would use the branches that had tried to claim me, as firewood; I smiled. First, though, I needed to set up a call to Ocker. Again, the phone rang forever. I was about to end it in frustration, when he answered.

'G'day,' he said. 'Are ya having a ball?'

'Oh yeah, just had a fight with a tree, but I won.'

'Was that with your jujitsu shit?'

I didn't take the bait. 'Listen, take down these co-ordinates: 0°32'39.1"S 100°23'58.9"E. It's my first LUP.'

'Good call. You meeting Nico must be like meeting yourself. Have you killed him yet?' Ocker was trying to keep his childish giggle in.

'What do you mean? I'm nothing like him.'

'Like two dingo balls in the same sack, mate. Obnoxious, courteous, moody, blunt, funny, all in one breath. Quite complex, hey? I wonder if he's made a nickname for you. You know, like you do for others.'

'I think you mean two peas in a pod, you Australian pikey. Now don't go using those big lawyer words. You haven't a fucking clue what they mean.'

'You body-swerved my question,' he said.

'Was that your idea to name me Tom Hardy?'

'Who the fuck is Tom Hardy? So, ya miss me then?'

'No.'

'Bull dust. I reckon ya must be getting lonely. Why don't ya set your satnav to minge, mate? It's been a while since that Russian he-she ran off with someone better.' He ended the call.

I roared with laughter, the sound bouncing off the walls. I did miss him, sometimes.

Carefully, so as not to lose the tree over the edge, I cut off all the smaller branches with my Gigli saw. At the foot of the entrance, from a tampon and small twigs, I started a fire. Slowly, I added the dead wood until it was ablaze. Once this had died down to embers, I added larger logs in a flat triangle formation. After heating water in my billycan, I poured some into my mug to make a brew. The rest, I added an MRE.

After devouring it, I sat back and finished off some oat biscuits. I had enough logs to see me through the night, not to keep warm, but as some protection from any wild animals that might decide to check me out, that's if they managed to get down the sheer, gravelly slope. I hoped any insects and mosquitos would be fried before they reached me, but even so, I sprayed all my bedding and clothes.

I congratulated myself on finding the cave after the epic jump. Three more large logs on the fire boosted my positivity. I got comfortable on top of my sleeping bag, watching the spellbinding glow. This was my territory and no one was having a piece of it. My mind wandered off listening to the jungle life, louder than through the day. I was in a good place. This was the life. All I needed now was to listen to more Coldplay or Swing. I wondered again why Ocker had said I was like Nico, but shrugged it off. As I drifted into a world of happiness, I tried not to think about Lena, and my ex-wife, Ella. Instead, I tried to imagine Rabbit meeting with Ocker—fisticuffs. I quickly changed my mindset to my old SBS mates, fallen, but never forgotten.

CHAPTER FIVE

It hadn't taken long for me to fall asleep, and I'd managed to sleep all the way through without any unwanted dreams. Perhaps this type of world was what I needed: no unnecessary loud bangs and crashes from drunks walking home, or sirens, and low helicopter fly-overs to provoke flashbacks.

Whilst cooking my MRE of beans and sausages, irritating lumps beckoned me to scratch them; the mosquitoes had gotten in. Bastards. Having a wash with unscented wet wipes, checking for nasty bugs as I did, I noticed this morning's air was fresher than yesterday. The sounds of the jungle and river were sublime. I had to suppress my enthusiasm to rush to finish my breakfast and check the next stage of my route. I couldn't wait to explore. Adding the cam-cream on my exposed skin, then getting changed into camouflaged attire, brought back a lot of good feelings. After packing my gear, I swapped the battery in my phone, then texted Ocker the direction I was heading. My plan: to cover at least half the distance to the area and set up a second intermediate LUP.

With all that tea and coffee, standing on the lip of the slab I marked my territory, peering down to the bottom of the raging river. I pondering how much water flowed in twenty-four hours, then smirked at the ease and time I had to think of such facts. One thing I hadn't thought of last night was how I was going to get up back up to the ridge. Possibly it not being such an action-packed, crazy mission really had sent me soft. I thought back to Operation Blue Halo and Operation Last Assault whilst sucking on a boiled sweet. I knew a tiny part of me missed the action, but I tried to kid myself all the same, hoping this wouldn't rear its ugly head.

Choosing the items to leave behind in my Bergen, I then packed the rest in my webbing. After making a second crude ice-axe out of the remaining tree, I turned my attention to my priorities: to find poachers' traps and the camp that threatened the already critically endangered tigers. My aim was to remain unseen, which was the best way since I wasn't armed with my Heckler. A sense of pride filled me at what I was taking on. I was now ready.

Making the first few metres back up to the ridge was precarious, my weight pulling the wooden ice-picks. My rock-climbing expertise kicked in, finding the rhythm that was needed. Ignoring the sweat pouring out of every pore, I stamped on the negative thoughts of the slippery handles and the drop below. I was physically at my best; the extra training was paying off.

Crack!

I jerked forward as my right hand crumpled into the loose shingle where the pick had snapped. Instantly, I dug my elbows in to stop me tumbling downwards. Perfectly still, I slowly peeked at the remainder of the handle in my right hand, then gradually looked up at my stretched-out left hand: I had good traction on that ice-pick. The ridgeline was about three metres away. There was no point looking down. My heart started to race; the noise of the river intensified. I put it down to the adrenalin. I couldn't stay still forever, knowing the sweat had already found its way into my vice grip. Lifting my right hand enough, I let the remaining handle slip through to allow me to stab it back into the earth. Once I had a bit more control over the situation, I started to get back into the rhythm of traversing to the top. I made it.

Following the narrow trail further into the maze of foliage, I thought back to when the improvised ice-pick had broken; it's funny how your life can be defined by a single moment. Thank fuck I wasn't lying dead at the bottom of the river. Reaching what appeared to be the end of the trail, I checked the time: 07.49 hrs. Ahead, a hollow had been made through the thick spiky bushes; it was impenetrable. To the left of this was the sheer drop to the river. The right led off in a less awkward direction down the slope to the jungle floor. It was an easy decision to make. I checked the GPS: five kilometres to target area. Next, I set up the mini-satellite to my mobile and phoned Ocker to give him the sitrep. The signal was poor, but at least I had communication. It rang and rang, until I gave up. I tried again, this time going to voicemail:

'G'day. Don't leave any boring messages, especially if you're a pommy bastard.' Beeeep!

'Ocker, if you're listening, pick up... You're supposed to be on call twenty-four-seven, you wanker. Tell Nico I'm within five klicks of the target area. Get off your kangaroo friend and call me back.'

I waited five minutes for Ocker to phone me—nothing.

With one last swig of water, I stepped down the sandy slope and headed towards the area I was to recce. Not knowing how far the poachers' camp was or if the armed men were in the vicinity, I had to take caution; my stealth slowed the pace. Drawing from my jungle experiences, I tried not to make any trail by breaking branches, and stayed out of the mud pools, so as not to leave tracks.

My senses were still hyper-alert after making three klicks. Apart from me smelling of smoke, other smells started wafting in. Fifty metres dead head, I noticed a movement high in the trees. I froze, just my eyes looking up under the brim of my hat. I waited again for the movement—it did. Through the condensation that dripped from the trees was an incredible sight: the distinctive orangutan. It hadn't spotted me, proving I still had some of the old Elite skills.

I studied the animal in awe as it ate what looked like to be a fig fruit. Its red hair was wet, the hair slumped forward over the forehead of its long narrow face. Another orangutan came from lower in the trees, joining its larger mate. Huddled underneath the new female was a baby. It was all mesmerising. You see it on the TV or in zoological parks, but seeing the beauty in its habitat was amazingly different. However, as much as I wanted to, I couldn't sit here all day in awe.

Deciding not to disturb them, and with the jungle ahead looking almost impassable, I slowly made my way towards the direction of the river. Out of view of the orangutans, I calculated on the map where the higher land contours lay. After a small drink and snack, I headed out with my compass, saving the GPS batteries.

The journey back to the top of the ridge had been arduous, but seeing the river again was spectacular. Weirdly, I felt a comfort being near it, like it was my home. I pondered how long this dream of a mission would last. Fuck; I shouldn't have thought that. Suddenly, a weird scream echoed through the jungle. Automatically, I hunched down, withdrawing my knife. What the fuck was that? It sounded like a cross between a shriek from a fox and a human. My heart was thumping not knowing what had caused such a terrible noise, and why. A low growl sifted through the other jungle life. I remained frozen; my eyes narrowed searching for anything that moved.

Within a few minutes, the jungle birds and creatures came back to life; obviously, I wasn't the only thing to be freaked out by the noises. I was sure the shriek had come from the direction I was heading. Deep down, I was itching to assuage my curiosity. Taking a breath, I began to follow my inquisitiveness by heading through the dense undergrowth. It wasn't long before the path veered slowly in a curve away from the river. At least away from its roar I could now hear more of the jungle.

Below in the distance was another track. Between the trees and vegetation something was sat on it, but it didn't make sense. Another tree had half-fallen onto another, reckoning it had fallen in a recent storm. From its pinnacle point where they had collided, I would have great eyes on the area. The foliage was still attached, so it would easily conceal me. Feeling energised about my new great observation point, I made quick ground towards the tree.

Heights didn't bother me, just as well as I was sat in the slippery canopy about fifteen metres up. With the rope, I tied myself to the largest branch and then secured a good foothold. I had to cut a few of the smaller branches out of the way as they obscured my view. Different insects made their escape as I became king of their kingdom. One creature I didn't want to meet was the king cobra; its venom could potentially kill an elephant. I double-checked the branches in the near vicinity.

The object on the path still looked odd. A chill ran through me as a mass of blood had stained the sandy earth. Opening the webbing pouch, I pulled out my binos whilst still not taking my eyes off the path. Once in focus, the hairs on my arms raised and my gut tightened. I quickly pulled the binos away and checked with the mark-one eyeball, as if the binos had been lying. I refocused the dial, my hands slightly shaking. My mind raced as the reality hit me of what I was viewing: part of a human, the arm and shoulder ripped off. The biggest shock was the tattoos: a yin yang with a Chinese dragon and wind bars. I followed the blood trail, but lost sight of the path due to the complex undergrowth. Something flicked a memory switch. I panned back down the path to view logs set in the path with leaves covering in between. It wasn't obvious unless you had seen this type of trap being set. It was the kind to snare a tiger, the same that Nico had showed me photos of. Obviously it hadn't worked. More worrying were the gruesome remains of Gavin.

I quickly viewed back to the arm and shoulder, studying the tattoo on the white skin; it had to be. What the fuck had he been doing out here? Was that his scream? It replayed in my mind. Was he looking for me? Was he setting the trap? Surely not. Getting into a better position to search further down the trail, I studied the large mass of blood, gore, with other body parts. Ropes had been pegged to the ground. The torso had been dismembered, leaving barely recognisable remains with remnants hanging onto sticking-out bones, like a feast scene on the African plains. Why were there pegs and rope in the ground? I shuddered again when I mentally heard the screaming. I had seen enough. But I still thought on, puzzled as to not what had killed him, that was obvious, but how did it come to this? Instinctively, I checked the way I had come up the fallen trunk, half-expecting to see the killer beast.

Hearing voices brought me to my senses; trees refracted the exact direction. I slowly sank into the foliage, staying perfectly still. I didn't want to be caught out like the orangutans. Occasionally the voices portrayed of more than one person, each time getting slightly louder. My eyes were on stalks searching the dense woodland, like an eagle waiting for its prey. Movement switched my eyes back to Gavin's remains. One by one, four adults stood around looking at the carnage. Then a fifth person the size of a kid bent down. Cautiously, I lifted the binos to my eyes. I wished I hadn't. Three of the adults were Pepen, Rede, and Wayan, their injuries still evident, but wholly pathetic in comparison. The last adult I didn't recognise. When the kid turned around and handed the rope back to Pepen, I instantly recognised him: Setiawan. Nico was in great danger. I had to get a message to him.

Silently, but without wanting to miss the opportunity, I rummaged in the rear pouch, finding what I was searching for: HD Cannon camera. It had been pre-set to silent mode, no flash, and low screen brightness. The lens, like most binoculars, had an anti-reflect cover on. I hadn't taken my eyes off them below. They had started to argue between themselves. Through the viewfinder I kept my finger poised on the button until as they came into autofocus. My lip curled in disgust as they were now laughing. The older unknown man picked up the arm and teased the kid with it. I had the same bitter taste in my mouth after watching three Elkhaba beat the village elder Ghulam Rasool; if only I had the same M16.

They began to follow the trail. As soon as they were out of sight, I quickly chose the photos and put them in a folder. Holding the mobile next to the camera, being paired already, I set the phone to download all the photos. It seemed to take ages; my anxiety about losing them in the jungle grew. Eventually the file went. I quickly followed up with a message to Will and Ocker explaining briefly what the photos were:

'Urgent! Inform Nico not to trust Setiawan. Gavin is dead, used as bait to lure tiger,'—I thought better to add— 'but the tiger is OK.' Time check: 10.27 hrs.

Again, I made sure all my fastenings were secure, making sure nothing could clank together. Tying away the rope and carabiner, I then proceeded to climb down. Rushing, so as not to lose them, I tried to remain quiet and not to slip. I hastily headed towards the trail, staying out of the macabre. A quick glance down had only confirmed that it was Gavin that had been mauled. Motherfuckers. I wanted revenge. Their footprints were easy to see in the disturbed trail of the blood and guts. Unexpectedly, the gruesome evidence just stopped. To my right was an entrance through a bush which led into a tunnel-like hollow. The streaks of blood stained the twigs and bracken; no way was I following. Fortunately, the footprints carried on, but then I thought what a shame as the five of them could have been the next meal.

It wasn't long before I saw the back of Setiawan trailing a stick in the sand, following the others. I slid into the trees until they were out of sight, then crept silently along the edge with the stick's trail leading the way. I had been concentrating so hard that I hadn't noticed how hot and sweaty I was, until now. The heat and humidity had been turned up, the insects multiplying in their thousands. Maybe that's the real reason the rangers never came to this part, making up a load of bullshit about paranormal tribes.

The smell of cooking stopped my progress. I got onto one knee, tuning in. Most of the jungle life had gone quiet, apart from the odd distant bird call. A human odour sifted in, faint, but enough for me to lock onto it. That's why you never brought in soap and deodorant on jungle missions. The rule is: you smelt like the shit you were in, blending into obscurity; you are your own camouflage. There was no need to track the stick anymore, so I snuck into the jungle and found a good place to conceal myself. The vapour steamed up from my shirt collar. The ground was still soggy from a recent downpour; mud stuck to whatever touched it. Even with the non-smelling insect repellent, I had been a main meal for many. Obscuring myself in a bush, I drank some water and then switched on the GPS. Cupping my hands around it, I made a mental note of my position. I wrote down the co-ordinates in pencil on a notepad, which I'd kept in a dry-bag. Every movement was kept to slow and minimal, even crawling out of my hide was at a deathly slow pace.

After what seemed an hour, which was more like half of that, I praised myself for making good ground undetected. A new noise entered the frame as I secretly made my way forward: a blade hitting a tree. My confidence grew knowing I was close, due to the stronger cooking smells and voices. It was short-lived, as curled up close to my face in a rotten log was a snake. This one was slim, about half a metre in length, with prominent black, yellow, and red markings. Its black flat-head lifted and its tongue slithered out. Most snakes were venomous out here. Knowing there were around four hundred and fifty different species, I didn't want to take my chances. It didn't seem agitated, almost shy.

I came out of my frozen state and cautiously backed up a metre, then slowly crawled around to the side. Whilst I moved gradually forward, other thoughts of snakes and spiders came to mind, including furry caterpillars. I remembered a fool who had touched one on training, even though it was forbidden. The recruit ended up missing training due to a severe skin rash; of course, all of us took the piss saying he had caught VD after shagging a monkey.

Locking the thoughts and images away, I got on with the task. The first visual sign was smoke funnelling up in the trees. I began to crawl on my stomach through the damp undergrowth, gently pushing aside any larger twigs that might crack. Just before the final tree, I warily retrieved my binos. Inch by inch, second by second, I tilted my head to the side until I had eyes on. My breathing was slow and steady, not in tune with my pounding heart.

In front was a clearing with huts made from woven branches. The area was similar to the stronghold of the Somali pirates in Operation Last Assault, but hopefully without the firepower; I cringed at this memory. I was laid-up higher than the clearing's ground level, almost at roof height of the huts. The four structures were set out in a circle, standing about ten metres away from my OP. The centre had embers smoking with a large pot in the middle. In the near vicinity, tree trunks had been sliced into sections for seats. They had traces of blood on. On closer inspection bits of fur lay around them. A young male walked out of one of the huts, armed with a meat cleaver. He was covered head to toe in blood. Another man came from the woods to his right. They spoke in their native tongue. It seemed friendly enough until the man smacked the young male holding the clever around the face. Not the best thing to do, I thought. He didn't remonstrate, but instead sulked off into another hut.

Whilst the man waited, he made a call on his phone; worryingly, pacing closer to me. He even seemed to be staring right at me. I squinted, staying perfectly still, mentally preparing myself. The young male with the sore cheek shouted from behind. The man put his phone away and made his way over. He took two skins and checked them over. Seeing the skins of the critically endangered tiger made me swallow hard. What made it worse was he had thrown one of them back at the young man, as if buying second-hand clothes at a car-boot. The buyer placed his goods on top of a wooden crate of skulls and then pulled out a wad of cash, paying the seller. The buyer quickly disappeared back into the jungle. How had this man got in? Even waiting for five minutes, I had never heard a vehicle's engine start.

Whilst I had been watching the camp, with little by little movement I had taken my camera out. I was now taking photos, but lowered the camera when out of the final hut came Gavin's ex-in-laws. Why hadn't they done the unethical tiger skin deal? They sat themselves on the logs. The young male who had taken the money handed Pepen the rupiah notes, who in turn stuffed them in his pocket. An image of the cash left on the shack's bar sprang to mind. They each in turn ladled out whatever it was in the cooking pot into a wooden bowl, and began to feast like a clan of hyenas; even the kid tucked in. Fuck; if that was tiger on the menu.

Pepen shouted to one of the huts behind him. The forth member, the old man, pushed a hunched over figure out of the doorway. When the new bloke was lit up in the sun's rays, I was shocked to see a white man in just his trousers and boots. He was forced down onto a log seat. Instantly, I brought the camera into life. Suddenly, I felt a stinging on my shin. I gritted my teeth and mentally swore. Trying to ignore the hot irritation, I continued to watch, intrigued as to who he was. His beige trousers were as filthy as the grime on his skin. Was that excrement mixed with the dirt? Head bowed, he was subjected to shouting from Rede and Wayan, more than likely feeling tough men as their captive's hands were bound behind him. Maybe a bit of bravado after taking a beating from Gavin.

The old man untied the white man's hands, but the prisoner kept them behind his back. Pepen, with an odd smile, offered the person a bowl of steaming food. The detainee never even looked up, so Pepen shouted at him to take it, but the detainee remained passive. Setiawan stood and started hollering abuse, then kicked dirt over the sitting captive. Again, he didn't respond. Setiawan grabbed the bloke's bearded jaw and lifted his head; the poor sod had taken a beating. If it was me, I would have swatted the kid away like a mosquito.

Setiawan asked him where Nico's camp was. It came to me who he was: Nico's mate, Georges Demblon. Georges didn't reply, so Setiawan threw the hot food over him. Not even a tiny expression showed on Georges' face, whereas my skin was inflamed from anger. I continued to take snapshots as he was aggressively manhandled back to the hut and thrown in. Pepen led his brothers, Setiawan, and the old man into the far right hut, whilst the young male sat and ate his stew. I hope he fucking chokes on it.

Out of the hut came the five of them, all armed with rifles, even the kid had one. Though the weapons looked dated and worn, it was more than I had. Looking at the blue and orange painted stocks, a picture flashed in my mind: the same Nico had showed me in the photo. How ironic that the poachers in the photos now held Nico's friend. The weapons looked like Lee-Enfield jungle carbines, ones I'd messed around with at an army show. The posse were also laden with water bottles, and snares draped casually over their shoulders.

There were no pleasantries with the young male when they left, taking the route north out of the camp. I contemplated what to do next: should I follow them to see where the traps were? Shall I return to my first LUP and upload the photos to Ocker? Perhaps I could rescue Georges. I thought back to when I had rescued Larry from the Somali stronghold in Hordio. Surely this would be easier? Then again, the one remaining guard wasn't stoned or drunk like the pirates, and I didn't have my pistol and Pecheneg.

I decided to take a risk, and slithered a fair way back into the jungle to set up the mini-satellite. The screen showed I had a message.

'Johnny. Urgent! Abort the mission. You need to go home. Will is arranging transport to the airport.'

With the photos downloaded, I sent them with a message asking Ocker what was going on. What was so important that I had to abort? Who was meant to be collecting me? It couldn't be Gavin. Oh shit, I hoped a message had not been sent to Setiawan to pick me up. I had to speak to Ocker, so I plugged in the earphones and called him; it went to voicemail.

'For fuck's sake, Ocker,' I said silently, 'answer the fucking phone. It's a priority one you call me back.'

After checking the time every minute or so for ten minutes, I gave up and put it away. Why wasn't he answering? What was the big distraction for him to leave his post? I decided to at least rescue Georges, and then I would again make contact.

Watching the camp, the remaining young male had finished his food and was now sharpening a knife. Three others lay out on the stump in front of him. I studied his age, size, and possible fitness levels. He seemed relatively easy to take down, but I knew not to become complacent; you would not have guessed Gavin was so lethal. The plan: to keep him away from the huts that may stash a rifle or pistol.

Without taking my stare from him, I crept around to my left, putting a hut in direct view between me and him. The mud slope made it easy for me to quietly slide down. Reaching the wall of the first building, I crouched moved around its left flank. I contemplated the dash across to the next hut, but it was too far a run not to be noticed. Peering further around with the assailant in view, he was approximately five metres side on to me. Should I try to creep further around? He would surely see me if I went to the next hut. Would he turn if I snuck up behind him? Were there any others in the near vicinity? I had to get him to come to me.

'Psst,' I hissed.

He didn't look up.

'Psst. Oi.'

Again, he didn't lift his head.

Less tactful, I thought. 'Oi, fuck-face,' I huskily whispered.

He continued to sharpen his large machete; the sound noisier than my attempts to distract him. Maybe he was deaf. Then I remembered him having a conversation with the skin buyer.

'Bollocks,' I whispered, knowing I had to go in.

CHAPTER SIX

Brazenly, but casually, I walked straight out. He continued to slide the stone over the blade, the sound reminding me of when the Elkhaba were going to sever my head. On my next step he looked up, but I continued to audaciously stroll over to him. His expression was one of shock and disbelief. I knew what I was going to do to him. Suddenly, as if he had read my mind, he leapt up and made a sprint for the hut where the others had got their weapons from. I chased him, managing to get a hand on his shoulder. He tripped over the threshold and we tumbled inside. I saw the elbow at the last moment, striking me hard on the side of my nose. Ignoring the shock, I grappled his arm to the floor. Through the grunts and groans, he continued to thrash his other arm and then kick out. I punched him hard in the back. He yelled before swinging something back at me.

Bang!

The shot lit up the dark for a split-second. I ripped the rifle from his grasp before he had another chance and smashed the butt into the back of his head; he didn't move. I tasted the coppery blood with my tongue as it dripped onto my lips, then stupidly I touched my nose. Fuck; he'd broken it. I cracked him again for good measure; well, for a bit of revenge.

Outside, I checked the area before I ran across to the place where Georges had been thrown in. I skidded to a halt, the dust at my feet clouded over him as he lay on the floor. I slung the rifle sling over my shoulder.

'Georges,' I said.

He didn't remove the filthy cloth from over his head. I took a step closer to lift it. Suddenly, I felt a pain to my ankle as he'd exploded into life. His leg swept past me as I hit the deck. I had no time to think about how awkwardly I had landed on the weapon, as Georges was instantly

47

on top of me. I grappled with his slimy hand that gripped a pointed stick, the tip inches away from my neck, his eyes ablaze.

'Georges, stop. I'm here to rescue you.'

'Who are you?' His accent rich, like Nico's.

I pushed the dagger to the side. With the spit foaming from his gritted teeth, he stared at me, searching my painted face.

'Nico has sent me.'

His body relaxed. I lifted my knee up and rolled him over.

'*Eish*. I could have killed you,' he said remorsefully, tears welling.

'No fucking chance,' I appeased.

I stood up, swinging the Enfield around to my front. I held my hand out to him. Georges' eyes dropped to the weapon in my other hand.

'Listen, we have to move, now,' I said. 'It won't be long before they return.'

'Did you shoot the last fucker?'

'No, but the fucker will wake up with a blinding headache. And you don't mind swearing then.'

He smirked, knowing what I had meant.

Georges grabbed my hand and I helped him up. Like Nico, he was tall and stocky. Our eyes locked as voices sifted into our hut. Sliding back the action-bolt on the Enfield, I was glad to see one was in the receiver. There was also at least one in the mag. Sharpish, I moved to the door aperture. Staying in the shadows I scanned my arcs into the forest where the noise was coming from.

'Georges, on me,' I whispered.

'Well I'm not fucking staying here.'

Now wasn't the time for his shit, so I left it, for now.

I squat-ran out, taking an immediate left. Once at the bottom of the slope, I scrambled up. At the top, covered in the sticky mud, I looked back. The poaching party had entered the camp, sweaty from running. The hut hid Georges as he made a meal of the incline. However, I was in their full view if they looked this way; I gripped the Enfield. As he neared the top, I stuck my hand down and he pulled himself up.

Bang!

The tree behind me shattered, spraying wood splinters. Before the echo had stopped, I had let go of his hand and raised the Enfield.

'Go, go, go,' I said, lining the first ring sight with the open point sight.

As the attacker pulled back on his slide action-bolt on the identical weapon as I had, I squeezed the trigger when his head had filled the sight.

Bang!

He flinched; I had been a hair away from the target. I quickly slid the bolt back and forward whilst he re-took aim; I fired. This time his head exploded out from the back and he fell backwards in the red mist. '*Threat neutralised.*' Another round split the tree to my right, sending the shrapnel into my face; I yelled in pain. I hadn't seen where the shot came from, probably due to the Mk-5 having a flash hider fitted. Sprinting in the direction Georges had run, I rapidly reloaded.

Georges hadn't made much ground, limping badly on his left leg. The thought of helping Ocker through the jungle while being chased by hundreds of Somali pirates came to mind. I grabbed his trouser waistband and pulled him in the direction I wanted to head. Georges resisted; I guessed his idea was to go straight along the narrow path. However, this could lead back to their camp, or make the easiest way for the hunters to track us—too obvious.

Another shot echoed through the canopy. I stopped for a second and took a glance back, shouldering the Enfield. With no signs, I unclipped my machete and began dragging Georges forward again into the thick undergrowth. I only used the machete if I couldn't find a silent way through. I hated that; it made too much noise.

We reached another fallen tree, so I pushed Georges into the void it had left. He was breathing heavily and was covered in lacerations to his bare upper torso. I took aim to the side of the roots, and waited. Georges' rasping was annoying me, so I put my finger to my lips, showing him to shut the fuck up. All the animals, except a few insects, appeared to have vacated. I listened into the silence: twigs cracking and bushes rustling enhanced my vigilance. I scanned my arcs for the littlest movement. My heart was coming out of my chest, the blood was flowing from my nose. Were they waiting for us to make our move? It was now cat and mouse, but they knew the lie of the land better than me. However, I was fully trained.

Slowly undoing the webbing pouch, I took out the GPS.

'You know how to use one of these?' I whispered, close to his ear.

Georges snatched it from me. 'Are you taking the piss?'

'Punch in this coordinate: 0°32'39.1"S 100°23'58.9"E. This LUP is set in the side of the riverbank. Be careful how you get down to it. There you will find rations and water.'

'Where are you going?' he whispered.

I waited for him to set the destination and then asked him to repeat it. 'Now punch in this number: 0°33'23.4"S 100°29'01.2"E. You will find a one-man boat. Wait there for me, but only if it is safe to do so.' Again, I asked him to repeat them.

'Are you not…'

A crunch to my right stopped him finishing his sentence. I swung the Enfield around. My eyes were on stalks. After a few minutes, nothing had happened.

'Why are you not coming with me?' he asked.

'You know where Nico's hideout is don't you.'

'Yes. Why are you ignoring my questions?' He looked worried.

'Something I've learnt from Nico. With you injured and the shit you've obviously been through, you will slow me up. It's best if you head out whilst I distract them and lead them away from you. I will meet you at the kayak.'

'How?'

'Trusted map and compass. If I'm not there by morning, then find Nico.' I put on my best patronising voice, 'Do you think you can manage that?'

'My dad, like Nico's, taught me more than you'll ever fucking know,' he bit back, snarling.

It had worked. 'Obviously not enough, otherwise you wouldn't be in this shit.'

'Fuck off. I should have pushed harder with the stick.' Georges looked fit to burst.

I smiled. 'Now bottle that anger and determination, and take it like smelling salts when the time arises.'

Georges nodded, knowing I had just stirred a bit of the passion inside him. He grabbed my forearm like a fireman's grip and squeezed. He didn't say anything, letting his expression say it all. With that, he took the machete off me and silently sank into the vegetation. Within metres, he had disappeared.

Whilst I thought of how to draw them away from Georges, not having really thought about it before, the stinging came back to my face, my nose throbbed, and my shin burned. Through my facial hair I felt little protruding points that sent sharp sensations into my face. I carefully plucked out the ones that I could grip and examined the tree splinters. It was better than receiving the .303 round. I smirked.

Analysing the map, but keeping an eye and ear out for any trouble, I worked out the best route: basically, head towards the base of the mountains by following the river and then cut across the area where the jungle stopped. I could then travel in an arc back to the lake. The unsure bit: how to lure them away in the same direction, but also to keep ahead of them.

Unclipping the mag, I began sliding out each round, knowing it should hold ten. I was hoping for a full one, except the two that I had fired. Sadly, I only had four left. Fuck. I cleaned them up, then blew out the receiver mechanism, noticing the mag had the same ID number as the one on the black receiver. It was a fantastic weapon. I felt honoured to hold it, knowing possibly a British infantryman had used it in World War Two. Admittedly, it was well worn. The lug that took the bayonet had been broken off. The rifle fired OK, except a little to the left. It was light in weight, about three kilograms. I had read about this weapon years ago and remembered that the best infantryman could fire approximately thirty rounds per minute. In fact, as I relived the part where I had shot the old man, it was damn powerful. However, nostalgia would have to wait. I slapped my uninjured cheek to bring me back to the present.

Digging below the murky, stagnant water that I stood in, I pulled out the rich-black mud. Jesus it stank. I plastered all the showing parts of my skin, not only to make it hard to be seen, but to keep the insects from having me further for lunch. Time check: 11.11 hrs.

As soon as I snuck out, it was as if I was being watched, and I trusted my sixth sense. Slightly crouched, I tiptoed almost back the way I had pulled Georges along. It was audacious, but my thinking was they wouldn't expect me to head back in. My eyes searched around whilst my Enfield swung at a slower pace, listening intently like a burglar stealthily venturing through an occupied house. I stopped and sank low, arching my neck 180-degrees each way. The hairs on my arms stood up, a chill went through me; it wasn't cold. The dull pain to my forehead started. Now I knew I wasn't alone. The unknown escalated my fear. Was I at the end of the hunter's sight? Was an animal stalking me? Maybe the tiger liked the taste of white meat.

I inhaled, slowly exhaling; my heart slowed. Maybe I should head back to the camp and arm myself with more weapons, if there were any. However, the sound of an action-bolt being slowly pulled back sent my nerves into overdrive. Adrenalin surged, telling me to move. I sprang to my feet. Racing through the undergrowth I smashed back anything that got in my way and darted around anything that looked impenetrable. The floor seemed to tug at my boots and entangle my legs.

Bang!

I screamed, but kept running. My right outer thigh was burning with excruciating pain.

'Fuck… fuck… wanker,' I wheezed.

I was also taking a battering to my face and arms as I fought through the undergrowth. My training was screaming at me to turn around and take the fight back to them; however, not knowing where they were, I continued to run. My mind tried to shut down the pain, or was it the adrenalin, or even the fear?

Bang!

The first round had hit the tree to my left.

Bang!

The second, sounding as if it was cutting down the forest, smashed into my right bicep, almost twisting me to the ground. The pain sent spasms through my whole body.

'Shit. Fuck off,' I said.

Strangely, I told myself it was two different weapons that had fired. It didn't fucking matter, I was bleeding, I argued. Rasping, I continued to push through the foliage. The map instantly pictured in my mind. With my left hand, I lifted the clipped-on compass, still charging through. I was on the right direction to the slope, though I seemed to have slowed. A branch cracked behind me, or was it the action-bolt again? Halfway scrambling up the slope, I turned around and lifted the Enfield. I don't know why I was shocked to see my hand was red, it should have been expected. My arm muscle burned whilst taking aim. I tried to breathe slower, suppressing the urge to open fire, sight slightly trembling. The tree in front had started to take my weight; gunshot wounds intensified. As much as I wanted to, I dared not move to check them, or even take my eyes from the threat. A warm feeling flowed down the area in my shirt and trousers.

Slight movement out of the corner of my eye instantaneously made me take aim: six metres creeping through the jungle was Rede. Coming out from behind the largest tree was his downfall. He had now only just spotted me. In what appeared to be a pause, we looked at each other. A tortoise could have walked past, but in reality it had been a split-second. He raised his Enfield, but had a stoppage; it was written on his face, his last expression. '*Threat neutralised*.' I had won the duel.

The tree I leant against shattered. I hadn't heard the shot. I pulled back the action-bolt, concentrating on the chink noise as the shell discharged.

Before it reached the floor, I had swung the weapon forward and opened fire into the dense woodland. I had not locked onto a target, more to suppress whilst I evaluated where it had come from. My left eye was now blurred and stinging. Whoever had taken the shot didn't return fire. Had they run out of ammo? Had I hit them by pure luck? Were they trying to flank me? I rapidly searched to my sides.

My mind told me to rest my body, but instinct must have beaten this as it now screamed at me to move. Finding the energy, I dug deep, sliding up the muddy slope on my arse by pushing my feet in. I reached the top, still scanning my arcs. The roar of the river a long way below imposed its power. It also impaired my tuning in, or was it I was losing too much blood? I used the Enfield to help me to my feet, muttering under my breath about the hurting. Whilst backing up the path, I scrutinised any movement and, at the same time, tried to use the bushes on the edges as concealment. My right leg was soaked, but the feeling stopped when I saw a pair of eyes looking at me through the foliage. Heart fluttering, my finger caressed the trigger, but on closer inspection they were two large bird shits. I let my breath go and continued backwards. I instantly swivelled around when what appeared to be an end of a rifle barrel pointing through a bush, but again, I was wrong; just a branch. I was becoming paranoid. I had to get on top of this and relax; discipline was key to survival. The constant weird animal noises and distractions had drained me. I was becoming light-headed, wanting to rest.

Ahead on the path was a stockpile of large, long logs. The ends had been crudely hacked. I pondered how had they been placed there. More to the point, why? They had been there for some time; the bark had fallen away; insects had found a home. The ends of the stack of logs hung far over each side of the path. The only real way forward was up and over. I had images of the hunters on the other side, so I shook my head to rid the thoughts. I had to remain positive.

Creeping the eight-foot pile, trying hard to keep my footing, the skin around my wounds agonisingly stretched. My senses were in hyperdrive. I nosed the barrel over and followed the sights—nothing. With the fear of a rear attack, I quickly scaled the remaining logs and swung over; pain rippled through me. This side of the logs had a slimy texture and I ungracefully slid to the bottom, gritting my teeth to try to muffle the suffering, but I still gasped.

The jungle had turned quiet and weirdly cold. Time to repair myself, I thought. With numb, bloodied fingers I managed to open the pouch where I had stuffed the medical items. Undoing my wet trousers, I eased them down. The sight of blood didn't freak me out. I had trained as a medic and been in similar situations. Nevertheless, this wasn't meant to be this sort of mission. I mentally cursed Will and Ocker.

Cleaning up the leg wound front and back, I found the entry and, most thankfully, the exit wound. Fortunately, the round had only caught the outer muscle on the edge of my thigh. Fucking shit shot, I thought, boosting my morale. I even broke a smile. The injury still poured blood every time I took off the pad. It was critical I didn't get an infection, so I managed to get some latex gloves on. I poured saline onto the wounds, keeping quiet through the hurt. My expression must have been ugly as fuck. I could hear my old squad taking the piss, making light of the situation.

After dressing it, I injected 10-ml of morphine into my hip and then pulled my trousers up. Next, I gingerly pulled my arm out of its sleeve—excruciating. Maybe I should have waited for the drugs to kick in. Again, I cleaned the area, but this time I had no exit wound. The entry point at the back of my arm was large for a gunshot wound, and it wasn't bleeding much. Probing my fingers into the mass of lacerated skin, a rush of water filled my mouth. I pulled my fingers out and sucked in air. I reckoned the round had gone through a tree, slowing its velocity, altering its shape.

'Don't be such a fucking wuss, Vince. Fucking get on with it.'

I stuck another 10-ml of morphine into my shoulder. Whilst I waited for it to act, I opened my Pelican case and found the lighter. Once lit, hands shaking, I moved the knife blade through it. I was trying not to rush, but my intuition was screaming at me that I would be joined very soon. The tip wasn't totally cooled as I slowly dug it in; the fizzing made me tense. I was holding my breath, and then I let it go with short sharp breaths as I dug deeper. I mentally screamed every obscenity at Ocker and Will for landing me in this so-called easy mission. Feeling the lump under the knife, I twisted it up. Suddenly, the bullet popped out. I sighed and cursed under my breath. Then I swore in my mind for being so loud. The blood flowed down my arm.

With no time to spare, I dropped the knife, wiped my eyes, and then held the unbloodied side of the dressing on the hole. Leaning back with the padded wound on the logs, I fumbled around for the surgical suture kit. Sloping forward, letting the pad drop, I strained back. With blurred vision I pushed the needle through the skin on each side of the wound, tugging it tight with the forceps. This continued until the gaping hole had been stitched. Woozy, I tied off the bandage and rested my head back.

My shin was itching like mad, one that you couldn't ignore. Pulling up my trouser leg revealed a red volcano-shaped lump. Just as I was wondering what to do with it, something climbing the log pile alerted me. I was half-turned looking up when a hand came over the top; I froze. The other hand joined it. Instead of climbing over, the person just waited. My heart was coming into my throat, along with the acid. I glanced down to my Enfield. Making a reach for it, the person hitched a leg over. Before the other leg was over, I grabbed the first and heaved him down. He yelled as he fell. It was the young male I had butted with the rifle. Shocked to see me, he kicked out with his foot, but I blocked it aside. He drew a machete from behind him, like Pepen had. He swung for me, and I jumped back. Following the momentum, I stretched back for the Enfield, but he was coming at me, his charging shriek giving it away. In a blink of an eye, I knew there was no way I would reach the weapon. I had to deal with him the old hand-to-hand combat. I smashed his wielding forearm with a double-block. He must have had a weak grip as the blade hit me on the left shoulder. I quickly struck him with an upper elbow strike under his chin. He staggered back. Really annoyed that I had let the machete make contact, the karate went out the window. I grabbed his shoulders, then ran his face into the logs. As he bounced off, I held the back of his head, smashing it again. He moaned and then went limp.

Still feeling belittled by my poor blocking action, I dragged him to the edge and threw him over. I didn't wait to see him hit the rocks and water below, knowing he would be a dead, but strangely, I didn't have the robotic gaming voice; it annoyed me even more.

'Fuck you then,' I whispered. 'Threat naturalised.' Maybe I'd had too much morphine.

Racing back, I picked up the Enfield and knife and then started to back up with the logs in an unclear vision. It was good that I had kept eyes on, as another head had popped over the top. I took immediate action and fired at him. Fuck; slightly left again. It was enough to keep his head down, so I ran like hell. The other injury pains had subsided, except for a slight stinging on the shoulder. I had one shot left. I cocked the weapon, but the shell did not discharge, so I shook the weapon whilst sprinting. I wondered which one of the in-laws had poked his head up; it wasn't Setiawan. Maybe the lad had stayed at camp due to the intensity.

Once I had made decent ground, I slipped into the jungle, carefully making my way as quietly as possible. As if a kid again, I found a tree perfect for climbing. It wasn't long before I was a good way up it, concealed by its foliage. I scanned the narrow path that I overlooked. My heart slowed, the adrenalin evaporated, and I began to shake. The pain to my shoulder began to hurt even more, especially where the rope was rubbing it. Why couldn't the machete have hit the rope? Lifting the coil over my head, my shirt had a neat slit in it. I opened the buttons and peeked inside, unprepared to see a three-inch gash oozing with blood; it should have been expected. I poured on the remaining saline solution, then put a field dressing on it. Whilst taping it up, I thought of my decision to lead the hunters away from Georges. What the fuck was I doing? I shook my head.

Maintaining my rifle, I wondered if Georges had made it back to the LUP. Call it intuition, training, or luck, but I'd brought the BSA pills with me; I took them. Clearing the shit from my watch face, I checked the time: 11.47 hrs. Surely it had been longer than when I'd last checked, but I suppose time can be deceptive. Why was it so cold for this time of year? In fact, I hadn't noticed before that the jungle was all covered in a black moss. There was also an eerie atmosphere to it as I listened in for the slightest sound, but it was silent: no wind, no animals, or insects. Where were the mosquitoes?

Maybe Ocker could lighten the mood, I thought. The mobile phone had no signal, so I plugged in the mini satellite dish, but it had been damaged. I cursed Georges for leg-sweeping me. Then something shocked me: the time on my phone read: 11.47 hrs. I double-checked. Even without a signal it should have kept the time. I looked at my watch to verify the time again, it also read: 11.47 hrs. Weirdly, the centre two dots were blinking, but the seconds weren't increasing. What the fuck was going on? I was even more confused when again I'd examined the phone, the time not changing.

Trying to reduce my perplexity, I opened the message inbox to see if I had a reply from Ocker, but it was empty. A shadow above cloaked the already creepy ambience. Through the gaps in the canopy, black clouds rolled in. Could it get any worse? I wished I'd not thought that. Someone coughed below and I searched in vain through the gloom. There it was again; I moved my eyes to the noise. In the murkiness, Setiawan was pissing against a tree opposite the one I sat high in. He had an Enfield in his hand. With minimum movement, I sighted him. Squinting, my finger caressed the trigger.

CHAPTER SEVEN

I eased off the trigger; there was no way I could kill a kid who wasn't a direct threat. Where were Pepen and Wayan? Perhaps this was to lure me out of the jungle to attack me. Setiawan was still loitering. I scanned the area, but it was almost impossible to distinguish anything apart from slimy black vegetation. When I looked back, Setiawan had disappeared. How did he get away so quick without making a sound?

Leaving it what I'd thought was ten minutes, as the time still read the same, I checked the map to take a bearing. No matter which way I turned the compass, the needle wouldn't stay still. To keep my spirits up I blamed an electrical storm above; it was all I could think of. From memory I knew I had to follow the river until the base of the mountains.

The morphine was wearing off so I climbed down tentatively, exhausted and in pain. In a crouched stance I moved agonisingly slowly up the slope towards the river. It was like I was leading point-man, always waiting for something to happen. I thought of the poor bastards out in Afghanistan on patrol, knowing any step could hit an IED. Thankfully, I had no problems of that nature, but I had no lads to back me up. I wished Planet, Shrek, and Fish were here to watch my back; a formidable squad in our day. But why was I thinking this now?

Making it back to the path, I checked for tracks before following the river north. If I came across any of the hunters, I had to shoot and scoot; one round had to take down one of them. I began to relax a little as I ventured further. Like before, the ridgeline track ended with a wall of nasty thistles. The only alternative was to head into the jungle. It was time to inject morphine to overpower the ever-growing pain. Whilst administering, I searched the area below. With no sixth sense alerting me, feeling safe, I took the first step down.

Crack... BOOOM!

The close thunderstorm stopped me in my tracks, as if a force was angry that I had taken this route. I shook away the thought of such idiocy. Holding onto each greasy branch as I made my way down, the swaying branches and rustling leaves were rising to a crescendo, rushing through the forest. Suddenly, the wind's howling hit me in a blast of debris. I let go of the branch to cover my face, but slid down the muddy incline, keeping the temptation at bay to grab something, so as not to injure my hands or pull a muscle. At the bottom I quickly stood. Pushing my way through the flying foliage, I found refuge at a large tree. Another deafening rumble raged across the sky, but this time, nearer; each tree nearby appeared to shake. After waiting a few minutes the force didn't relent.

Taking a bearing off the next large tree, I headed out, my arm out in front. Vigorously moving from tree to tree, still hoping the wind and noise would concede, the atmosphere had turned colder, not just in temperature. As I sheltered on one knee, a new noise entered the frame. Bits of undergrowth flew past the trunk. In a state of disquietude, my mind tried to process the vibrations. Suddenly, I was alerted to a large creaking; the crack of the branch was the invite to move. Stumbling forward in a blind panic, I had only just got out of the way of the thump and tremor behind me. I didn't stop, searching for the next salvation.

The next tree was larger in girth. Searching back, the carnage of the huge branch lay on the floor; how the fuck that had missed me was unbelievable. But why did it fall? There were no signs it was a decaying tree and no lightning strike. The recent new noise was now slightly louder than the frenetic storm. I closed my eyes and tried to envisage: a waterfall. Yet, I knew I was away from the river. Curiosity had now taken hold.

Setting off into the headwind, the wet leaves slapped my exposed skin. The clouds above were now sinisterly black, the wind had grown in strength. What a transformation compared to the morning, I thought. My feet slipped and grappled with the forest floor. I was feeling the fatigue of what seemed like pushing a heavy load uphill. With my back against the next oily tree in this oleaginous jungle, protecting my torso but not my shoulders, I held on tight to the glucose tablets. At last, I peeled one out and sucked on it. As I finished it off with a drink of water, I noticed the shredded leaves that flew by were black, like swarms of Gryllidae. Some stuck to my water bottle, glistening in the next lightning show. My feet soaked the vibration of the rolling boom of thunder. In the next flash I was sure I saw the volcanic island in Hordio. What the hell was going on? Peeking around the tree through the hand that sheltered my eyes, I was perplexed at what I saw. Wiping, and shielding my eyes again, I waited for the next lightning strike. The monstrous crack lit up the blackness; the evil heart of the storm was on top of me. I immediately checked the phenomenon that I thought I had seen the first time: a wall of water fell from the sky, like a curtain had been drawn across the forest, wind slightly concaving its appearance.

'What the fuck?' I murmured.

I expected to see a cliff above with the water cascading over the rock-lined edge, but instead there was an ominous black cloud. I double-checked the compass for an alternate route, but the needle was crazily spinning. The torch flickered and went out. I couldn't just squat here, so I checked all my zips and fasteners, then naively pushed forward. Within two metres of the roaring water I became a little unnerved. My hand gripped into fist, the other clenched the rifle; they had become icy cold. This was weirder than the cowboy ranch, wondering what the fuck type of mission I had taken on. The only positive was that the hunters had most probably gone back to camp.

Taking in a deep breath of confidence, I surged into the wall of water. It was freezing. I drew in sharp breaths, followed by the water. A cacophony of sounds resounded as the flow pelted down hard on me, trying to knock me to my knees. I went to pull my hat down, but it had gone. Now through it, strangely, the howling wind had stopped; a little relief. My visibility was down to two metres, the rain still slicing. I looked back, but it was pure blackness. I couldn't even see the wall of water. It was nuts to continue, so I decided to find some shelter, anything to get me out of this storm.

Trudging and slipping, I was wet, numbly cold and had the raving hump. The only optimistic thought was that I couldn't feel my injuries, which was just as well as I was out of morphine. Appearing out of the lightning show was a large tree that had fallen to its death, the mass of roots had left a vacuum. I clambered over to it and slung off my webbing kit at the base. Trying to sit protected by the massive trunk, I rifled through to find my trusty poncho. Tying the paracord wasn't easy, my fingers were numb, unable to believe it was so cold.

Eventually, I sat beneath my shelter from the rain and blew into my cupped hands. The water that had collected above started to pour onto me. This wouldn't do. As if a switch had been flicked, my training took over and I ventured out. I began to cut off thick branches with my saw, sliding as I did. Through the slicing hail, I had formed a makeshift fence against the horizontal trunk by sticking them in the ground, tying them with rope and paracord. It was then back into the witches' cauldron to cut thickened palm-leaved branches, most of which had fallen from nearby trees. Half the time I had to wait for the lightning flashes to see what was what. After weaving them the best I could on top, I retied the poncho over my survival cocoon.

Inside was a stark difference to outside, except for the cold. I had to force myself out to search for the driest wood, but it was almost impossible. I was now wading through pools of muck. The best find was on the underside of the rotten fallen tree. Thrusting my hand into the core, I ripped out the dried shredded innards, along with insects also trying to shelter. Curling around my find like a scared hedgehog, I made my way back. With the kindling sorted, I ventured back out and found varied-sized fallen branches. The rain had eased a little.

It wasn't till I was back in the confinement of my shelter that I took the torch back out of the webbing. Tapping the case, it still didn't work. With a latex glove, I poked it through a twig on the outside curve of the tree under a constant water drip. The blood ran off the outside of the glove, but at least it had started filling. Suddenly, the torch came on; surprised, but feeling safer as it shone. Under the protective light I studied the cuts in my shirt; mostly my forearms. The mud had been washed from my hands and wrists, now showing tiny bites. As I thawed out, the abrasions began to sting and, with the adrenalin subsiding, the wounds increased in pain. I put my hands under my armpits to get some life back to them, bringing back memories of chilblains.

Lighting the fuel blocks was easy as they had been in my dry-sack. Once the kindling had taken hold, I added smaller branches; they fizzed with smoke and steam. It was dangerous to light the fire as it might alert the hunters to my position, but it was a calculated risk due to the storm outside; I had to get warm and dry. It wasn't long before I had a great little fire; maybe small, but it lifted my morale, tenfold. Staring at my billycan of water balanced on top, I moved closer to the heat, thinking back on the challenging and weird events. I had totally lost track of time. My watch still showed 11.47 hrs, as did my phone. The turbulent rain outside had ceased, a creepy silence fell. In the beam of the hanging torch I added three teabags to the hot water. Dazed, I watched the colour turn.

The cracking of a branch close by startled me. Stealthily, I switched off the torch, intently listening. Another louder rustle above alerted my senses. Slowly, I undid the slip knot that held the torch to my knife handle, pulling the blade from the underside of the trunk. I then laid the rifle across my legs. A chill ran through me, not knowing what was above in the trees. My mind raced with different types of animals, and then the thought of armed poachers entered. I clenched my teeth and tightened my grip. The breathing through my nose seemed very loud; I tried to mask it. I had plenty of deterrents here with me, not just my main weapon and hunting knife, but the embers from the fire and the scalding water. I wanted to save the last Enfield round for any counterattack.

A thud on the top of the tree trunk stopped my breathing; I waited. The minuscule light that filtered through tiny gaps was disturbed by a shadow on the other side; I didn't move a muscle. I had one hand on the billycan handle, the other on my knife. If anything pulled back the palm leaves, they would have it. My heart raced. I had to tell myself not to get up and take whatever it was on. I hated sitting here like this.

The silence eventually broke me into pulling back one of the leaves, expecting to see an eye peeking in, but then I squashed the stupid thought. I wasn't in some sort of horror movie. I scanned the whole area with one eye, but only the odd leaf falling caught my concentration. It was a pleasure to see daylight pierce the canopies. Gradually, my levels lowered to something a bit more relaxed. I closed the peephole and let go of the billycan.

After a brew and some scoff, I cautiously crawled out and, stretching, felt that I had commandeered back my territory. Whatever it was had not stayed around. The water still dripped from above, making weird tunes on the ground. Most of the smaller trees had fallen in a criss-cross of mangled trunks. Woven in between these were branches and bushes. It was impenetrable the way I had come.

I was wet through. Steam rose from my clothes as the place became hotter. I looked for the sun, but weirdly I couldn't see it. With no life deafening the area, I concluded that all the animals and birds must have scarpered. Thawing, the shot wounds burned worse than the first time. I found relief in thinking I'd been shot by a World War Two Enfield; one story to tell my kids. Perhaps one day I could sit with my grandchildren in the pub like Weaves had, telling stories of old. I hope my family wouldn't drag me out until I was drunk. The thought of a new family made me more positive. Maybe being broody had stopped me squeezing the trigger on Setiawan. However, I knew I couldn't have slotted him, unless he had attacked. He was just a kid caught up in an adults' mess.

There was no point in clearing up any signs I had been here; time was of the essence to reach Georges at the lake. Now that the electrical storm had passed, I checked the compass over the damp map. Frustratingly, the compass still wouldn't stop spinning. I had no answers to why both my watch and phone had stayed the same time. Even though the map wasn't much good, I could still make out the river, guessing my position. From the glove and water that had collected in pools, I filled my water bottle, then added the purification tablets. Smiling when I had found a small packet of pain-killers, I took two.

With not much to pack, it wasn't long before I was heading in a rough direction to where I thought the river was. The saying, you can tell the direction because of the moss growing on one side, was a load of bollocks, and anyway, here they were black all over. The ambience was almost non-existent, just the patter of drips. My stealthy creeping appeared louder than ever, but at least I could hear if the poachers were tracking. It didn't feel as if I was being hunted. The horrid smelling black mud started to get everywhere; also holding down my boots. The tracks I had left were easy to spot. The heat and humidity were stifling, hotter than Afghanistan.

Sitting on a fallen tree branch, I tuned into any noise, almost wanting to hear something. I fought off the temptation to drink more water. Around my feet a two-foot blanket of white mist was rolling in. There was no smell about it, as I'd considered the possibility of a forest fire. I mean, what else could go wrong?

This time when moving off, I decided to count seconds to gauge how long I had been moving over distance. Like I had Afghanistan it also kept me focused. The trouble was I kept getting images of the past filter in: Haleema, Anoosheh, Kyle, and some of those I had killed. They had totally put me off counting, so I gave up. One thing I did know was that I was as hungry as a rampant dingo's donger. Oh shit, I was now using Ocker's sayings.

Now more than ever, the top of the river's ridge up ahead beckoned me, even though it looked more foreboding than before. I told myself I wouldn't get a drink until I reached the path on top. My energy levels were sapping, my injuries forcing me to stop at almost every tree. Visions of me telling Rabbit that the Afghan village was a lesser distance than what it really was, played out in my mind. We were in serious trouble back then. Why was the past berating me with thoughts and images? Was I becoming delirious with dehydration, or a fever?

On the next rest I smelt the dressings, but no stink registered. Does anything register in this bizarre place? With my head level with the path again, the river roared its power; it was a big relief. Down on one knee, facing the opposite way of the track, I took out the water container. Just as I put it to my lips I spotted movement back on the path. The earned drink had to wait. It was only brief, but I was sure I had seen something. I didn't know if it was human, questioning why my sixth sense hadn't alerted me beforehand. It was time I became the hunter, not the hunted. An idea came to mind so I reached back and pulled out something that I could leave as a sign: the insect repellent's lid. Without taking my eyes off the suspect area, I placed the lid into the sandy path. I hurried off, making sure I made good tracks in the soft sand. The narrow path bent to the right. Now out of sight, I dog-legged back through the jungle. When I was opposite where I had dropped the bait, I hid the best I could, making ready my rifle.

Blending into my surroundings, I waited with the Enfield poking out of the bush. My heartrate had increased. My injuries, again, seemed non-existent, except my blurred one-eye vision. Beads of sweat poured from every pore, my wet finger touched the trigger. Someone had turned up the valve in the steam room; this was getting way beyond crazy. Adding to this unexplainable weather, the mist started rolling in at my feet, warming my shins. In the silence I masked my breathing. A distant sound sieved through the black trees: Wayan walked into my killing zone. He had his rifle slung over his shoulder; it was clunking on something. He was alone, about five metres up the slope. Intuition told me to check to my side. I glanced back to see if he had any surprise attackers, like raptors. Turning slowly back to him, he was studying the lid in his fingers. He smelt it and then looked forward at my tracks.

Bang!

'Threat neutralised.'

Shouting echoed from further back, but I had dumped the Enfield and was now scrambling back up the bank. As I reached the top, I looked for his weapon.

Bang! Bang!

Both rounds had zipped within inches of my head. I didn't have any time to lift Wayan off the rifle.

'Fuck.'

Both weapons cocked behind as I fled for my life, like a chased gazelle. The first round impacted at the base of my spine, sending me stumbling forward. The pain was like being hit with a hammer. Arms flailing, I kept running as I tried not to hit the dirt. Sprinting for my life, I touched where the pain radiated from; the webbing had taken the impact. Bollocks. Was that the end of my spare water bottle inside my billycan? A low branch above my head shattered just as I had ducked under it, sending debris into my eyes.

'Fuck.'

I blinked madly to focus on where I was running whilst rummaging in my side pocket for the carabiner clip. I cursed as I nearly dropped it.

Bang!

Another round flew up the dirt to my left. Strangely, I thought his sights needed adjusting like mine had. I screamed at myself to fucking concentrate. I managed to unhook the rope over my neck whilst at full stride. I fumbled to find an end, all the time not letting it unravel. Each time a shot had fired, the hunter would have had to stop to take aim. The winding track gave me good concealment. I reckoned I had increased the gap between us. I didn't think about my breathing, injuries, or fatigue, but focused on my next escape and evade plan: abseil down the steep gorge to the river and pull the rope back; something I should have done back at the LUP.

Without warning, the paths led out to an opening with an ancient-looking temple in ruins. I sprinted past skulls placed on top of sticks in the ground. They looked ape-like—I hoped they weren't human. The ground below was springy and spongy, like wet moss. A lone tree near the edge screamed at me to use it. I whipped the rope around the trunk, but dropped it as the end touched my hand.

'Fuck… fuck… fuck.'

My hands were shaking picking it up. I caught a quick glimpse of my boots covered in a red liquid. I tied the rope off, but as I stood up, the trunk exploded with the impact of a round. I hadn't heard the shot above the blood pumping through my head. Pepen stood just short of the path where it came out into the opening, his Enfield still aiming at me. He purposefully slowly slid the bolt back. I raised both hands, the rope still in one. My chest was rapidly moving, beads of sweat ran down my face. The pain in my lower back now radiated up my spine. What was he waiting for? He wasn't going to see me beg.

Setiawan came running out from behind him. Coughing, he quickly locked his weapon onto me. A sadistic smile spread across his face as he yanked back the action-bolt. Pepen spoke to Setiawan, who then argued back. I glanced behind them at the decaying stone temple that was swamped by trees. Strange gargoyles were entwined with vines. Should I make a run for it? But I had nowhere to go for cover. I wouldn't survive a jump off the edge. A black rolling storm cast above me. The first heavy drops of rain started to fall onto my hands. The hunters moved into their stance. I raised my hands higher in a plea.

Setiawan smirked and then said, 'You tight fucking English man.'

The roar rumbled through my bones as the streak of colours appeared vibrant against the murky backdrop. Setiawan screamed, his fear intense, but short-lived. Pepen was next to feel the full might of the tiger as it struck him across the face and chest. It then unleashed its teeth into Setiawan's throat. Pepen tried to drag himself away, but he also succumbed to the beast's power as he was leapt on, the jaws of death holding the back of his neck. The tiger slightly lifted his head, its amber eyes transfixing my stare of pleasure and horror. The magnificent colours of its face seemed to move as it proudly panted.

I hadn't realised I had been feeding the rope end through the clip, but the beast knew. The tiger licked the blood from its mouth, egotistically glaring at me, salivating. I was shaking all over and my mouth had gone completely dry, but I had managed to get the rope around my waist; the jungle king knew my next move. It sniffed the air, the long whiskers twitched, appearing relaxed. Was that my que to run? I had to do something. Too late, it had moved into a stalking position, coiled, ready to spring into the murderous. I remembered someone saying to run and shout at a big cat to impose your authority. Fuck that, I thought.

'Stay calm, Johnny, and get the descender out of your webbing,' I whispered.

The big cat's ears twitched.

With my body slightly turned away, I secretly reached back to the left pouch, trying not to let it see. A paw slowly came out of position, taking a tentative step closer; or was it conquering one?

Ten metres…

I couldn't get the fucking popper undone. The other paw slowly felt the ground. As the animal moved forward in rhythm, its beautiful but scary eyes burned into me. This was a majestic predator, but I mustn't become the lower in the food-chain.

Eight metres…

At approximately eight feet from head to tail and weighing in at a hundred and thirty kilos, it hypnotised me to the spot. I had to break it, but I knew it was waiting for me to run. I broke my stare when I glanced at the savaged bodies it had left in its wake. Bingo; I'd found the descender gadget. I slid it round to the front. The beast sank back like a coiled trebuchet, ready to catapult its claws and teeth. I couldn't get the fucking rope through.

'Shit... shit.'

I dared to look down, but heard the tremendous roar, the scuff of the ground. Knowing I had seconds, I made a run for the edge, rapidly entwining the rope around my forearm. I gripped hard with all that my life was worth. Everything you fear about this animal came out. I yelled as I leapt off. A severe sharp sensation to my right calf muscle sent me into a spin. I tensed, knowing what was coming as the wind rushed past my ears. It appeared in slow frame by frame motion, identifying the rocks and debris that followed me down the sheer wall face. Was that the tiger roaring above? A massive pain shocked my body. I gasped for air, but couldn't get any. Strange psychedelic patterns lit up in front of my eyes. Then, the sounds of the river stopped, and everything went black.

CHAPTER EIGHT

Afghanistan; *déjà vu*: blackness as if an evil cloak had been put over me, but instead of branches cracking and ripping, all I could hear was the explosion of water. Like after the Chinook crash, I couldn't see anything. Again, memories of my family and friends flashed through my mind. I knew I wasn't dead. Like before, I also knew what was coming; it did: immense pain flooded my whole body whilst a familiar ringing screeched in my head. A high-pitched noise followed the rhythm of my heartbeat. I found a tiny amount of comfort knowing the Elkhaba weren't out there, and selfishly, I wouldn't have to encounter my dead squad as previously. The pain riddling me was excruciating, beyond my pain threshold. I had no idea what way was up, as if I was floating away. My screams were gargled. The psychedelic shapes started to fade and I began to dream of old times in the SBS.

My eyes suddenly opened. The daylight was a shock compared to the pure blackness. I couldn't remember what was in my dream. The body pain wasn't so bad, but my head felt like it was going to explode. I blinked hard to focus on what was in front; it wasn't working. Into my blurred view came my dangling hand, teasing my mind. Was it the left, or the right? Where was the other? I couldn't answer the simplest questions. I looked beyond the hand to see a mass of grey with patches of white in between, all moving like a kaleidoscope. What the hell was that? I waited for the answer—nothing. Frustrated, I shook my head, but wished I hadn't as mind-blowing patterns lit up my eyes. The agony was so severe that I knew I was going to vomit; I did. My eyes shut of their own accord. The strange world shrank into a dot.

This time when I awoke, I sharply breathed in, unsure to what had startled me. How long had I been out? Again, I hadn't any recollection of dreaming. I had a bit more focus when I opened my eyes, but it appeared darker than before. I was shivering uncontrollably; my teeth chattering sent spasms into my head. I bit down hard to stop it, but a shock from my teeth made me release. Running my swollen tongue around my gums, I located sharp jagged edges and a lacerated inside cheek. My tongue poked right through the injury. The stinging was small in comparison to the rest of my head and shoulders.

Right, Johnny, fucking pull yourself together.

I hadn't heard the voice for ages. Even though it was painful to do, I shook my head to make it disappear. It had to go back to where it had been banished. I started talking to myself, any old shit so it didn't have a chance to interrupt. Opening my eyes, I arched up my neck. I was soaked through from the drizzle and my arm was rope pinned against my chest. I now knew why I was finding it difficult to breathe. I tried to move my swollen red fingers, but couldn't. After resting my head down for a while, the pumping pain continued. I managed to lift my dangling arm up to touch my face; it, too, was wet. Taking my hand away, my palm and wrist were covered in blood; rain began to wash it away. With the cold seeping in further, I would either die of hypothermia or bleed to death. Something had to change.

Searching the ground below, I estimated I was about fifteen metres up, but the light was fading. Looking up the way I had jumped I couldn't see the edge. My knife was missing from its sheath, that's even if I could survive the fall from cutting the rope. Fuck; I was in a bad way. For a second, I wondered if there was any point.

Is that it? You're just giving up? Fucking pussy.

'If you're trying to wind me up, I'm stronger than I was back then, so jog on,' I slurred.

There's a ledge to your right. Why don't you grab it and pull yourself up? Come on, Johnny.

I couldn't be bothered to answer, but turned my stiff neck to the right. There was indeed a ledge about two metres away with a small shrub hanging on for dear life. The shivering had now stopped, but a wave of nausea replaced it. Fighting the battle with lethargy was not the only challenge, in competition was the lack of coordination. Eventually, I managed to lift my arm and feel the jagged wall behind me; it was as cold as me. I dug my fingers in and tried to pull myself along, but my hand felt weird. I heaved my palm in closer to my face: two middle fingers were bent in a peculiar shape. At least the cold was numbing them.

I tried again, but only made half a metre before I let go and swung back.

Is that all you got? Why don't you swing like an orangutan? You're forgetting where you came from.

'What do you mean where I came from?' I mumbled.

The voice didn't reply.

'Do you fucking mean at the beginning of time, or the Special Forces?' My voice had hardly any strength to it.

Agitated, I pulled again and then let go. For a third time I did the same action, and was now within a few inches, but I was fading fast, even though my heart was racing. On the next swing I managed to secure my thumb and index finger on the ledge. Slowly, I dug my little finger in. As I held on, the whole world began to spin. When I opened my eyes, I was swinging to and fro.

'Any... ideas... bright... fucking. I mean... fucking... oh it... I be arsed,' I muttered.

Knowing why my words weren't organised in a simple sentence, I quietly waited for the voice to spur me on—silence. Just take the piss, I thought—nothing. Please don't leave me, but I knew there would be no reply. Shutting my eyes, visions of my family played between the weird shapes. I now got why mum and dad were so upset before I'd left. Yet, I didn't care anymore. A warming dream played out: standing back in the GKR dojo sparring with Trevor. It blended into down the Australian Bar having a few pints with Simon and Oliver. My breathing had become shallow and weak. I found it hard to admit, but this must be it.

★

Startled by being jigged about, the unbelievable pain had returned with vengeance. There wasn't a part of me that didn't ache. A strange hum of chatter came to my returning senses, but I didn't recognise the language. An aroma of sick wafted in. I couldn't move my hands to wipe my sticky, shut eyes. I forced one of them open, my eyelids feeling like the lashes were being ripped off. Through the grime I could just make out that my wrists were bound together. Tilting my head forward so were my feet. Turning my head to the side, I wiped my eyes on my bicep, reminding me of the injuries. Looking back, I had slightly less blurred vision. Where was my shirt? The red-soaked bandages were loosely wrapped. I just wished the pain and ringing would fuck off. My head sharply dropped back and I returned to the blackness.

Strange lights and shadows danced on my eyelids. A new smell hit my nostrils: an oily smoke. As I bounced along, I tried to work out how

I had got here, wherever here was. I asked myself if I was dead or alive, but why would I ask such a thing? Opening my puffy eyes, the skin around them felt crusty. The flickering light ahead was bright orange, sending shadows over the mottled-beige ceiling and walls. I was then shocked to see a white face with big black eyes looking at me, slightly nodding. His expression didn't change. On his naked shoulder was a thick wooden pole that my feet and arms were bound to. I was naked.

'Who the fuck you?' I croaked.

Suddenly, the white face turned almost the other way, then a brown face with brown eyes took its place. Why was this bloke wearing a mask at the back of his head? There was an abundance of shouting around me and, even though I was in pain from head to toe, I still felt a scratch to my neck. The sounds and vision became a mass of indigestible matter. After not feeling any part of my body, which I liked, the motion stilled. More orange lights flickered around me, lighting up silhouettes of people. I couldn't think anymore.

★

A beeping, keeping in time with my relaxed heartbeat, instantly stopped the zombified state I had entered. Weirdly, the pain and coldness had been replaced with warmth. Between the beeps I could faintly hear music. Was that Frank Sinatra? Something touched my arm. What were those weird people going stick in me now? Not wanting to go back to being a zombie, I opened my eyes to confront them. I went to grab the person, but was briskly pulled back. Stunned, a nurse was checking my pulse against her breast watch. She wore a white apron over a grey dress. Her fingers pressed harder on my wrist; my skin was clean and without any injuries. Her large eyes flicked across at me. Another nurse in the identical uniform released her hands from my shoulders and walked away.

'Good morning, sir. How do you feel?' the remaining nurse caringly said.

As she looked up, I admired her soft complexion and blonde wavy hair escaping from her white headdress. I then stared at her large breasts tightly packed under the uniform. The beeping noise became louder and then went into a continuous whine, drowning out the music. Muffled voices droned in the background. I felt weak and sick, and as much as I tried to open my eyes, I couldn't. Shockingly, everything went black. I listened in to the deathly silence.

A massive pain to my chest propelled me forward. The continuous high-pitched tone and muffled voices returned. A shockwave of convulsion tortured through me; lights flickered in my eyelids. The beeping noise became stable again. Where was the music? Gradually, I opened my eyes: the blonde nurse had disappeared. Around the room were many other beds in a neat row, all full of injured people. Apart from me, everyone was asleep. The sash windows were high, without any insulation. The walls had been painted in a heritage cream colour, whilst the high ceiling was off-white. I searched for where the beeping sound was coming from, but although very close, I couldn't find it.

The bloke directly opposite me in his metal-framed bed had his head and arms completely covered in bandages. His chart hung on a clipboard above his head. I instantly looked down at my own bed: the sheets were crisp-white. Peeking under them, I was dressed in a white gown. I touched my thigh injury expecting to find a bandage, but it had gone. Checking my arm under the gown revealed a tiny scar on the back of my bicep. The machete shoulder wound had healed nicely, but I had lost quite a bit of muscle mass. My face was clean-shaven with no facial injuries, but there was a lump in my cheek. I now had straightened fingers. How long had I been out of it? Who had rescued me from death?

A squeaky sound made me drop the sheets and look up. The blonde nurse, along with a brunette nurse, came onto the ward. This new, pretty sister wore a scarlet cape with military ribbons attached. One of them opened the top of the sash window. I inhaled the fresh air, watching the sun make shadows on the bed under the metal-framed window. The birds were singing and there was no sound of congested traffic. As they moved onto the next window, their shoes squeaked on the highly-polished floor. The blonde nurse smiled kindly at me; I smiled back.

'Hi. Please could you come here,' I said, hoarse.

She walked over and then gently picked up my wrist to check my pulse. 'Are you OK, sir?'

'Where am I?'

'You are being well looked after.' She smiled.

'You can say that again.'

She adjusted her uniform down, making her breasts look even bigger. I had a feeling she was flirting.

'What's your name?' I asked.

'Miss Russell, sir. Now, you need to get some rest.'

'What's your first name?'

She looked around in the direction of the brunette and then said, 'Elaine.'

'Well, Elaine, I think we're going to get along fine.' I winked at her—she blushed.

'Sister Russell,' the brunette called.

Elaine quickly took her hand off mine and moved to the opposite bed. That put an end to my flirting, which was a shame as I was just getting horny. At least I knew I was back to the old me. The brunette nurse strutted past, her frown showing her displeasure. What kind of uniforms were these? Where the hell was I? Then the answer came: obviously in a dated Sumatran hospital. I smirked at the mod cons—none. But then I quizzed my thought: why were the nurses English?

The brunette nurse walked around to the man in the bandages and gently shook him. She bent forward and gave him a sip of water and then made her way over to me. The beeping noise picked up pace again, in synchronisation with her walking. She wore a silver medal on the right breast of her cape.

'Good morning, sir. You are up early.'

'Where…'

I was interrupted by a stern voice calling from the end of the ward. Together we looked in the direction. A woman in military uniform stood over someone in a bed. She harshly waved over the brunette nurse. I was glad, as she was cramping my style with the sassy blonde.

'We have a fatality,' the military woman said, without emotion.

I raised my head to get a better look. The brunette nurse hurried to the patient and checked his pulse. I couldn't hear what was being whispered. Both did the sign of the cross blessing and then the military woman pulled the sheet over the deceased head. Was that it? Where was the crash team? Jesus. What type of hospital was this? I sank back into the hard-feathered pillow. I suppose I was, at least, alive.

The military woman marched over, less happy than the brunette. In what appeared to be a World War Two military dress jacket, she had pips on her shoulders. Bouncing on her chest was a row of medals belonging to the same era. Her grey wiry hair made her look older than she was.

'Open wide, please,' she said.

'And what's your name, nurse?'

She abruptly popped a large thermometer in my mouth and then lifted my wrist, feeling my pulse.

'You either call me Matron or Major.'

'I've had it checked twice now,' I mumbled.

She had no expression; deadpan face. The only feminine thing about her was her red lipstick. I went to tell her she needed to brush up on her bedside manners, but I thought I'd wait till she took out the thermometer.

'Where did you learn to be so warm and accommodating, Major Frozen Tits?' I laughed, expecting her to follow the camaraderie.

'How dare you.' Her eyes sharpened through her wiry glasses. 'You will address me as a senior rank. You may have an enigmatic background, but here you are under my command.'

'Where is here?'

She didn't reply, but dropped my wrist and shouted for a sister. The concerned brunette nurse came running over, bouncing in a pleasant way.

'Sister, this is not a school playground,' Major Frozen Tits scalded. 'You do not run even if you hear the sirens. Send a message to Lieutenant Lassen that Corporal Skedgewell has been formally discharged.'

'Corporal Skedgewell?' I quizzed. 'Matron ...' But she had turned her back on me and marched off. 'Major Frozen Tits, you've got the wrong man,' I shouted.

The brunette nurse sniggered and held her hand across her stimulating smile.

'Bollocks to her,' I scowled, but then changed my frown into flirt. 'So, pretty nurse, what's your name?'

'I am Sister Vincent,' she said softly.

'You look so much better when you don't frown. Best not to have a face like a squeezed tea-bag.' I gave her my best smile. 'Hi. I'm Johnny. What's your first name?'

'Helen, sir.'

'Nice name. You're damn pretty, like your friend.'

'Thank you, sir, but I need to help the others now.'

She adjusted her dress down, showing her ample assets, and her white cheeks had taken on a bit of a blush.

'What's a girl like you doing in a place like this?' I cringed at the corniness; my chat-up was shit as it was.

'I work here.'

'So, where is here? And what time do you knock off?'

'Sir, you are in the Cambridge Military Hospital. What does "knock off" mean?'

'Yeah, but where?'

'Aldershot, sir.'

'Aldershot? You mean Aldershot in the UK?'

'Aldershot in England, sir. Now I must go,' she said.

Helen looked down at the far end of the ward. I turned, and there with her hands on her hips was Matron, her beady stare summoning the young sister.

'Sister, I'm confused. How long have I been here?'

But Helen had already made a hasty retreat to carry out her chores.

Over the next hour or so I became more puzzled as to what the fuck was going on. The more I worried about it, the louder and more erratic the beeping became. Where was it coming from? Drained, I shut my eyes and thought back on the events leading up to this strange situation. Images of the tiger's powerful eyes, the dense jungle, Gavin's macerated limbs, and the people I'd killed floated around my mind. I tried to put them into some sort of order.

> *If you could use some exotic booze*
> *Come fly with me, let's fly, let's fly away*
> *There's a bar in far Bombay*
> *Come fly, let's fly, let's fly away*

Right, that's enough, I thought, as the song continued. Opening my eyes, I whipped back the sheets, catching a glimpse of the scars running up my rear calf muscle. The image returned of the tiger swiping me; I went cold. The bloke to the right turned his head to face me, his throat showing the large dressing. I swung my legs over the bed, throbbing where the blood had rushed down.

'You in on this joke as well?' I asked the young lad.

He frowned curiously at me.

'Ocker,' I shouted.

'His name is Private Douglas MacDonald,' a voice said from the bed on my left. 'He cannot speak too well. Took a bullet to his throat. Lucky to be alive.'

I twisted my upper-half to see who had spoken. This bloke had a bandage across one eye, which wrapped around the part of his head. The rest of his face had been mashed and his lips had totally gone, making his teeth look horse-like. His dark hair had been shaven back, almost to stubble, except where the hair had not grown over the white scars. It was bloody convincing.

'Oh nice try,' I said, inching closer to the edge of the bed. 'How much have Ocker and Will paid you guys?'

'Who are Ocker and Will? I have been in here some time, old chap, and have not heard of them. I am Captain Stuart Parmenter, Seventy-Eighth Infantry, Battleaxe division.'

'So, we have an Englishman, and a Scotsman. What's next, a bloody Irishman?'

Weather-wise, it's such a lovely day
Just say the words and we'll beat the birds
Down to Acapulco Bay
It's perfect for a flying honeymoon, they say
Come fly with me, let's fly, let's fly away

With my feet touching the cold floor, I waited for the dizziness to subside. Under the bed there was no hidden music speaker as I'd thought there might be, so I checked the ceilings and walls for further evidence.

'Doug, your typical signs of shellshock,' Captain Parmenter said. 'Skedgewell, you best get it under control or you will end up in Block-D at the Royal Victoria Netley Hospital with Spitfire high-octane fuel pumped into your veins. That is if you get past the firing squad.'

'What the fuck are you on about? And for the record, my name is Johnny Vince.'

'Sure, old chap; anything you say.'

Delicately holding onto the end of the bed, I made my way around to him. Parmenter appeared slightly rattled as I stood over him. Jesus; this makeup is too real. I went to touch his face, but he flinched.

'It is real all right, Skedgewell. Go on, take a bloody fine look.' His only eye welled. 'Biferno, October last year. Stood too close to a tank round as it exploded into the bridge we were trying to build across. Bloody panzer. I deny all knowledge of the rest. I do not want to end up with electric currents passed through my balls. I am hiding the nightmares well, old chap. Best you do the same.'

I staggered back light-headed, but the bed caught me. My mind raced with images and questions.

'You OK, Skedgewell?'

'Hold on. A panzer? You mean a German tank shot at you on a bridge? You sure I'm not in some nutty ward?' I said, starting to doubt my mind.

'Surely you remember the battle of Termoli in Italy? Your SRS unit were there.'

'My what?'

'Special Raiding Squadron... 1-SAS. My Lord, you are a twit.' He scoffed.

MacDonald croaked and coughed. It was the best he could do to share Stuart's amusement—I was at the end of my tether.

'And you're a twat if you think I'm gonna believe we are in 1944,' I said, exasperated.

A silence fell upon the room. Stuart gestured at Doug a twirling finger to his temple.

'I know most British army acronyms, but what is a T.W.A.T? In fact, Corporal, you can address me as a senior officer. I do not like your bloody attitude.'

'Fools rush in where men fear to tread,' Doug mumbled; dribble ran down his chin.

I was about to read both the riot act, putting a stop to this farce, but the sound of a strong walk echoed through the ward. I looked up to see a tall man dressed in army uniform with his chest puffed out, showing off his medals. He was followed by a slightly shorter bloke dressed in US military attire; disturbingly, both World War Two era. My jaw dropped whilst the sound of Blakeys striking the floor became louder.

'I have seen 'em shot for less, old chap,' Stuart whispered. 'You had best tie up your troubles in your old kit bag.'

'Act normal, Skedgewell,' Doug mumbled. 'That is if you want to get out of here.'

CHAPTER NINE

'Attention,' the distinguished-looking officer said. 'At ease, men.'

He dropped his salute. Stuart whipped down his hand. Doug, who only had a stump, followed the action. The Yank, without saluting, went and sat on the empty bed next to the person wrapped in bandages. He looked very familiar, but my mind was foggy. The music had stopped, but the beeping continued. There was a pause, and I guessed they were either waiting for me to speak or salute. I wasn't going to do either.

'Corporal Skedgewell. Apart from you being impertinent to Major Rose, which I shall have to overlook, I have been instructed to have you released back to the frontline. However, I want to be certain you have made a full recovery. Have no doubt, Corporal, what you have survived is nothing less than a miracle from God,' the officer said, having the exact same voice as David McLachlan from the USSS.

I sighed and shook my head, now having the answer: this was a big TV prank. It was too real to be a dream and too big to be a wind-up by Will and Ocker.

'Did you not hear me?' he said.

'And you are?' I said lamely.

The Yank on the bed vigorously shook his head at me, so the officer looked around to see what had amused me.

'That is Major Mark Bugler,' Doug murmured to me.

'Well, Bugler, I know this isn't real,' I said smugly. 'This is just a big TV show and you're all in on it.'

The music started again, but this time one of my favourite bands: Coldplay.

'A television show, Skedgewell?' Major Bugler barked.

The lights go out and I can't be saved
Tides that I tried to swim against

Have brought me down upon my knees
Oh I beg, I beg and plead, singing
'Where are you, Skedgewell?' Major Bugler snapped.
Come out of the things unsaid
Shoot an apple off my head and a
Trouble that can't be named
A tiger's waiting to be tamed, singing
'Corporal Skedgewell,' Major yelled.

The last lyric line resolved it. 'In some jungle cave,' I said, and laughed. 'Most probably in a drug-induced coma from the pygmy tribe.'

The Yank was now swiping his hand across his neck, and then he put his finger to his lips. I nodded at him.

'And who is the puppet with you?' I asked.

Major Bugler looked around and then sharply turned back. 'How dare you make inappropriate remarks about a fellow injured soldier. He is very lucky to be alive. My dear God, man, can you not see he is covered head to toe in bandages? You are not fit to work in the local wash-house, let alone to serve King and country on the frontline.'

The place fell silent, even the music and birds had stopped.

'Tell Major Bugler you are sorry. Tell him you have a lot of anger inside you,' the Yank said in an American-Irish accent.

'And there's the Irishman,' I blurted.

'Corporal, is that all you have to say? I will not be signing your release papers.' Bugler was starting to sound shrill.

Fuck; I wanted out of this nuthouse. 'I'm sorry, Major Bugler. I've got a lot of pent-up anger in me. Please, I need to get back out there.'

'Bloody sharpish, Skedgewell,' he said.

Major Bugler whacked his leg with what appeared to be a horsewhip and then adjusted his medals before strutting back out.

In my place, in my place
Were lines that I couldn't change
I was lost, oh yeah
I was lost, I was lost
Crossed lines I shouldn't have crossed.
I was lost, oh yeah

Stuart and Doug listened intently, as if wondering what was going to be sung next.

'So, you hear Coldplay, too?' I said to them.

'You are never getting out of here,' Doug croaked, and started to cough.

'Corporal, come over here. We need to chat,' the Yank said.

Sighing, I got to my feet and gingerly made my way over to him; the breeze tickled my bollocks in the open gown. I stood at the end of the bed with my arms folded, hoping he was good at reading body language. He looked young, clean-shaven, maybe twenty years old at best. Something niggled me about him, but I couldn't put my finger on it. He took off his hat, showing his gelled-back ginger hair.

'What shit you gonna fill me with?' I asked.

'Tell that lot behind you to mind their own business,' he said.

I turned and looked at Stuart and Doug, who were craning their necks in our direction. 'If I wanted a fucking audience, I would have sent you tickets.'

Both shook their heads and sank back on their pillows.

'Sit down, lad,' the Yank said.

'Look, I don't know what the hell is going on, but I'm not Skedgewell.'

He undid the gold buttons on his thick green jacket. Even though he had rows of awards and honours ribbons, he didn't want to shove the point down my throat, unlike Major Bugler. He rubbed his thin jaw, most probably wondering where to start the conversation.

'I am Command Sergeant Major Timothy McNamara, but please, call me Tim.'

Come on and sing it now, now
Come on and sing it out
To me, me
Come back and sing

'Thank fuck, that's a right mouthful. Tim, let me ask you two questions: do you hear the music and beeping noise?'

He looked around as if trying to hear the sounds, but Coldplay had stopped playing. 'Son, I hear the sweet music of Billie Holiday and Nat King Cole all the time. You gotta hang on to the world you left. But, son, you need to stop looking the fathead in front of the officer.'

'Don't you mean dickhead?'

'I'm not from around your neck of the woods, son, but we gotta be speaking the same language.'

'Hey, you're easier than the Australian pikey.' I smirked, thinking of Ocker. 'Can you stop calling me son or Corporal Skedgewell. My name is Johnny Vince. My mates call me Vinnie.'

'Nice to meet you, Johnny.'

He held out his hand, but I didn't want to shake it, making myself look even more foolish on the hidden cameras.

'So, you believe me then?' I asked.

'All I'm gonna say is, just go along with whatever you see and hear. You don't want to end up in the cranky bin.'

'I thought you Yanks said the trash can?'

'I'm from Ireland and moved to America when I was young,' he said.

'The last question: why are you dressed in a World War Two uniform?' I readied myself for any sign he was in on this joke.

'Son, I mean, Corporal Skedgewell...'

I gave him a glare.

'As you wish, Johnny.'

'I prefer Vinnie,' I corrected.

'I've never liked the nickname Vinnie. We're here to help you defeat Germany. I am here to assist you, Johnny.'

I sharply stood up. 'This is fucked-up.'

The beeping pace increased. Discipline, I thought, and began to slow my thoughts and breathing. Gradually, the beeping levelled out.

'Can you even remember why you ended up here?'

'Sure,' I said. 'I was in Sumatra on a reconnaissance. I had to find the poachers' whereabouts, but it went tits-up. I ended up hanging on the side of a cliff by a rope, that's after I was shot at and clawed by a tiger.'

A few coughs nearby signified muffled laughing.

'A tiger, you say?' he said.

Was that sarcasm? The now familiar sound of Major Bugler shouting interrupted me.

'Listen in hard, son,' Tim said. 'If you want to carry on being khaki wacky, they will section you. Now this geezer Major Bugler, he's gonna bust your chops. We need you right for the next mission. Get your fucking head together.'

'Jesus. Your lingo is worse than Ocker's. And what mission?'

'Look, my time is done here. This chat was between me and you. I will see you at the briefing. Take care, son.'

Tim quickly stood up and embraced me. His fingers squeezed into my back as he held on. With his head on my shoulder, he sniffed. Without a second glance, he marched down towards where the major came strutting in. They didn't even salute each other. That was weird.

Not just the big hug and sorrowful sob, but it felt so real. Now I knew it couldn't be some sort of fucked-up dream.

'Corporal Skedgewell,' Major Bugler barked.

'Stand to attention and salute,' Doug croaked.

Lethargically, I stood and saluted. 'Yes?'

'Name and number?' he asked.

'Corporal...' I paused.

The Major tutted and closed the folder.

'Corporal Skedgewell. 07545885. Special Boat Service. And if you excuse me, I don't use the word sir to a commanding Rupert,' I said, forthright.

You could have heard a pin drop. I stared hard into his piggy eyes.

'Is that right, Skedgewell,' he said.

'I'm different from all of you, that's why I'm in the Elite. You're lucky you got a stand to attention, let alone a salute.'

Bugler's tight lips twisted in a slight wry smile; short-lived, but I noticed it. 'Do you remember what happened?' he asked.

'Oh hell,' Doug mumbled.

'I can't answer that question.'

'Why, Corporal?' Bugler snapped.

'We're trained not to when being interrogated. It's our code of practice. Also, there's the Geneva Convention signing in 1929.'

'I hope you are ready for the Jerries, and I pray Major Andres Lassen is ready for you. Get him out of here,' he shouted.

As he strutted off, Stuart let out his breath. I sat back on the bed, finding it highly bizarre, but amusing. I knew soon this prank would end. Thank fuck.

Once the sounds of Major Bugler's strides had stopped reverberating around the hospital, I looked around the ward. Everyone that possibly could was looking at me. However, the person wrapped head to toe next to me still hadn't moved. Maybe no one had noticed he may be really dead as his acting skills were amazing. Doug broke the silence by clearing his throat. I stared at them; they stared back at me.

A new voice entered the room. We all looked simultaneously towards it. Helen and Elaine both had their arms out carrying something. In front of them strode a middle-aged man, no Blakeys, but his army boots squeaked. He had an air of confidence about him, something I recognised. He looked relaxed in his military shorts, shirt, and beret. He took off his glasses after reading a sheet of paper. Helen and Elaine placed the items of clothing next to me. He kept back with his hands on his hips. Then he took off his beret, rubbing his black short-cropped hair. I couldn't take my eyes off the sandy beret with the winged dagger in his hand.

'Right. Best get dressed, young man, and then follow me,' he said.

'Why?'

'Listen, Pete, I am not happy either for you to be on this mission, but these are my orders. We have some Hun to kill, so get your kit ready. Oh, I found this for you.' He threw me a watch. 'Meet me in the car park.' With that said, he thanked the nurses and walked off.

The Omega watch was very basic: hourly numbers around the outside and two hands. The time read: 11.47 hrs. I watched the seconds hand not move for a few seconds, then weirdly it started to tick. My thoughts processed the images of the last time I had looked at my watch in the jungle; the same time, the same incomprehension. I undid the watchstrap and rubbed the red-stained backplate with my thumb: Peter Skedgewell, love Ray & Dot.

'You are one of them, are you not?' Helen said excitedly.

'Hush your mouth, Helen,' Elaine said.

I looked up and smiled. 'One of who?' However, I knew what she'd meant.

'One of...'

'Helen, we are not allowed to fraternise,' Elaine sharply interrupted. 'You know there are spies.'

'I am only...'

'Would you like help getting dressed, sir?' Elaine interrupted, again.

'Now you are fraternising, or is it you fancy him?' Helen said.

'I'm fine thanks,' I said quietly. 'I want to be alone for a bit.'

'I will wait outside for you. If you need anything...'

'We will both be waiting for you,' Helen finished.

When they had gone, I was left with my thoughts. It was the first time I'd had two beautiful ladies almost arguing over me. My mind was a mess and I didn't know where to start with the questions. There was still a chance this was just one big wind-up. Outside would prove it. I hobbled over to the window, but all I could see was trees and greenery.

Back at the bed, I whipped off the gown and rifled through the clothes for some boxer shorts. However, all I found was a big pair of Y-fronts. I'd also had a glimpse of what was next. Slowly, I put on the brown and lightly tartan-patterned crisp trousers, buttoning up nearly under my chest. There was no belt so I had to tuck the beige shirt in, making my legs look twice the length. At least the brown shiny shoes fitted, and they hid the cream and tan nylon socks. I looked at the tie and laughed. No way was I wearing this brown and green kipper tie, not for no fucker. Lastly, I put on the watch and started to wonder who Peter Skedgewell really was.

'You look spiffing, old chap,' Stuart said.

'Are you taking the fucking piss?'

Stuart became flustered, spitting his words. Doug groaned and lifted himself partly up.

'Do you want to come over here and say that? How dare you speak like that to Captain Parmenter,' Doug said.

Doug lay back and started to gargle. I made a quick exit, but on the way I told Major Frozen Tits that he was in trouble.

Once I had zipped around all the nurses through the maze of wide corridors, I found the main doors. Pulling my trousers back up high, I walked through the exit and down the grand stone steps. This wasn't what I expected, or should I say, what I wanted. There was nothing in any way modern about anything.

The SAS bloke was leaning on a beautiful car door and talking through the window aperture to Major Bugler. I made my way over, admiring the shiny cream paintwork on all the curves, contrasted with the chrome. My stiff shoes played havoc with my feet as they graunched on the gravel. I recognised the chrome jaguar on the radiator. Beyond the Jaguar car were grassy fields and a church way in the background. The most striking aspect was the quiet and the fresh air.

'Nice wheels,' I said.

The SAS bloke leaning through the window sharply turned whilst the major quickly wound up his window. After making a point of revving, the major sped away on the stony drive. The Jaguar disappeared onto the main road, the only vehicle in sight.

'Down the pub for a pint then?' he said.

'Sounds good. I'm amazed you have pubs in this era. So, what shall I call you?'

He rubbed his blue-stain and then his moustache, staring hard at me. 'I do not care about your upbringing or what you have done in your military career, but you do not try to pull the wool over my eyes. Stop acting the twit. I am in charge of you. Do you understand?'

'Sure, if you say so.'

'Bravo. My name is Andrew Graham. You can address me as Sergeant, or in private, Andrew. Now, there is one thing I hate more than the Hun, and that is my visceral dislike for staff officers. Fossilised shit, as the good old giant sloth used to say.'

'The who?'

'The Hun. You know, the Germans.' Andrew placed his hands on his hips, again.

'I meant, who the hell is the giant sloth?'

'My God, Skedgewell, you had better get your tin hat sorted before you get a thrashing.' He looked up high at the building. 'We need to press ahead for that pint.'

As he stomped off, I observed the large clock at the top of the ornate spire. My watch was the correct time: 12.22 hrs.

I followed Andrew around to the side of the wall and was surprised to see two bikes leaning against it. I immediately laughed at the style. Andrew joined in whilst I pushed down on the large spring-assisted seat.

'You thought you were getting a lift with the fossil shit, did you not.'

'Why not just use a fucking penny-farthing,' I said. 'Has it got any gears?'

'Another outburst of profanity. I think some manners are required. And as well, it is the latest model.'

He snatched his bike, huffing as he got on it, and started to ride away. I tried to get my feet on the pedals.

'Where's the basket for carrying the Hovis bread?' I shouted.

CHAPTER TEN

This wasn't a mountain bike in any form, but I had soon caught him up, even after a few big wobbles. With the hospital now in the background, we turned into a road next to a war memorial on top of a grass-banked mound. I didn't have time to take a good look as I had started to gain speed down Hospital Hill. There were no cars, giving the freedom of using all the road. I edged past Andrew, but I got the sense he wasn't happy about this as he tried to pedal faster. However, without gears, his thin but muscular legs couldn't keep up. Somehow he just about managed to get a wheel in front. We raced in and out of the shadows and light formed by the large trees that spanned the roadside. I wasn't going to lose this one.

As we bottomed out on a lesser gradient on the hill, I spotted a woman pushing an oversized pram. Her slim figure was dressed smartly in suit-type attire, with a lovely Victorian-style hat. That lack of concentration lost me the race as Andrew had gone ahead. The sound of his brakes squealing alerted me to apply mine. As he came to a stop, I tried to do a broadside skid, nearly falling off.

'You need to work on your fitness, Skedgewell,' he said.

'You need to work on your banter, Sarge.'

He looked up and down himself. 'My what?'

'Your humour.'

'Bugger off. And it is Sergeant.'

Instead of carrying it on, I marvelled at what was obviously the town. The beeping was at a good rate, but I wasn't sure why it had followed me from the hospital. We were at a crossroads and opposite were areas of kept lawns and flower beds. Strolling on the paths around the area and sitting on the benches were finely dressed people. In the distance were old-style buildings. I spotted a few vintage black cars parked and a dated motorbike with sidecar. It was like viewing an old black and white photo, but all in perfect colour.

Andrew had turned left into the High Street whilst I was still admiring the scene, and he wasn't hanging around. I pedalled with all my strength just to catch him up, but he increased his speed as soon as I came level. More trees lined the litter-free route and we passed what looked like flats on the right. It was only when I saw a few army lads milling around smoking that I guessed the building were some sort of barracks. A few classic cars were parked on the road as we whizzed by, and it was amazing to see no yellow lines.

Andy was now seven metres ahead of me. He took a quick look back, the pleasure written on his face. Suddenly, he veered right, whipping in front of an old black Ford. The driver sounded his horn, the type in dated films. I not only found the horn amusing, but the driver was doing less than twenty, and he was days away from Andrew. In fact, I could have got off my bike, changed a puncture, and then walked across. I waited what felt like a lifetime in the middle of the road for him to pass, only to get a good look at the driver. It was surreal to see such a bygone vehicle looking so young and fresh. The driver even lifted his hand and thanked me; how polite.

After he had driven by, I rode into Pickford Street. Andy was leaning against the wall, fag in hand. The sign above the pub read: The Royal Military. I placed my bike next to Andy's and I looked down at my oil-stained trousers.

'You need to brush up on your driving skills, Skedgewell,' he said.

'You need to brush up on your highway code, Sarge.'

'I am not sure whether to have you down as a twit, suffering from shellshock, or damn right insubordinate. Now, Corporal, it is 'sergeant' in my local. Do I make myself clear?'

He walked past me with a steely glare. I grabbed his arm, but he tore it back and took a step right up close.

'A couple of things, Andy. Respect goes both ways. I prefer if you use my nickname Vinnie or my first name Johnny.'

'Oh, is that right? Anything else?'

'Yep. I've got no money for a round. You didn't leave me any.' I smiled.

Andy slowly nodded his head, searching my face. 'Correct answer, Skedgewell. I will take care of the round,' he said, and turned to go inside.

'One last thing.'

Andy stopped, but didn't face me, instead, he sighed.

'Are you not going to lock up the bikes?'

Andy quickly spun, looking bewildered. 'You, young man, are nothing but a wag. I hope you have some fight left in you.'

As the pub door swung shut behind him, a waft of smoke curled. I looked at my dress code again, feeling as if I stuck out like Jim Carey in the film *The Mask*. All I needed was a yellow, brimmed hat. Taking in a deep breath for courage, I got an unpleasant whiff of nicotine.

There were no roars of laughter and piss-taking once the door had shut behind me. Maybe they couldn't see me due to the amount of smoke. Through the haze I spotted Andy at the oak bar with a few blokes dressed in World War Two military uniform. It was still a shock to see the uniforms of the era, especially a new Navy type. The huddle of men were all patting him on the back and shaking his hand. The barman looked at me and then nodded at Andy. They all turned and stared, so I acknowledged them. This was like going to a new school for the first time. Andy turned back and continued to chat to them, but I watched on. He gesticulated the twirled finger to the temple. I couldn't hear what he was saying, but he had them all in hysterics. My temper began to rise. I wanted to go over and sort their problem, and give them a new one to think about. I released my fists when I heard music: 'You Do Something to Me', by Paul Weller.

'Oh great, now you're playing my wedding song,' I said.

A photo of me and Ella floated into my mind. The only thing anything like a stereo was an archaic radio set in a wardrobe-like unit, but that wasn't where the music was coming from.

'Here you go, Pete,' Andy said, interrupting my thoughts. 'You look like you have seen a ghost.'

I took the pint off him, whatever the drink was, and made my way through the people and smoke to a wooden table. On one side was a wooden bench, on the other were two rickety wooden chairs. I sat on the bench and stared at the dark pint, not wanting to take in anymore of the décor, people, Paul Weller, the annoying beeping, and the weird situation I was in. I wanted this dream to end.

'Put hairs on your chest, lad,' the old lady with no teeth said from the table to my left.

I turned my eyes back without any expression. With my head slightly bowed, I took a sip. Straight after, I screwed my face up.

'What the fuck is that?' I said—the place went quiet.

'Go easy with the language, Corporal,' someone shouted from the bar.

I was about to let rip, but Andy squeezed my wrist.

'Take it easy, Pete,' he said.

Through the sips and grimacing, I began to get used to the strong flavour. I waited till the ambience settled before I started to relax. Holding up the glass, I tried to see if I could see through it, but it was nearly as thick as the smoke.

'What is this, Sarge?' I said.

'You not had Benskins double stout before, or has your memory not come back yet?'

'What happened to Skedgewell?' I asked.

'Ah, my good fellow, Blondie,' Andy said, and stood.

I tried to look around him to see who it was he was greeting. Once they had finished shaking hands, Andy led him to the table. No one else in the pub made eye contact with this skinny, blond, geeky-looking bloke. It was almost they had intentionally turned away from him.

'Pete, this is Private Stuart Saxton, known as Blondie. Blondie, this is Corporal Peter Skedgewell, known as Pete,' Andy said.

I stood and put my hand out. 'I'm Johnny Vince, call me Vinnie. Good to meet ya.'

'Err... it is a pleasure to meet you... Vinnie,' Saxton said, with a surprisingly firm handshake.

'Wey-aye, man. I can hear a bit of the Geordie in you,' I said.

He pushed his thin round glasses further up his slightly crooked nose. 'Haddaway, man.'

'What the bloody hell are you doing in here?' Andy asked.

The pub life stopped. In walked a black man dressed in a smooth double-breasted suit, purple shirt and tie, and a black hat.

'I fought, I passed, I am going,' he said.

'You are fucking not, lad,' Andy said, right in this bloke's face. 'It is a fucking big mistake you coming in here.'

I nearly shouted hooray that someone had actually used the f-word, but it seemed immature given the tense atmosphere. Andy pushed this bloke back towards the door and then took him outside. I couldn't quite understand their raised voices, but got the impression it was leading to a fight.

'What the fuck's going on with those two? Should we not intervene?' I asked.

'It will resolve itself. No need for the Lord's prayer yet.' Blondie took off his cravat.

I noticed his white collar. 'Shit... I mean... you're a vicar.'

'Military chaplain, padre, man of the cloth, Christian. Yes, many names.'

'I wasn't expecting...'

'A Geordie? We are all God's bairns,' he said, reverting to a thick Geordie accent.

Andy came back in, looking riled. He gulped down his pint and told us to stay put whilst he went home and got changed. A few at the bar said goodbye to him before he stomped off.

It wasn't long before the well-dressed black man came back in, squeezing into a gap at the bar. Many harshly eyed him. I was ready to get up if anyone gave him problems for the colour of his skin. He turned around and plonked another pint of goo in front of me and then a small glass of orange juice in front of Blondie.

'Thanks, dude. I'm Johnny Vince, but Vinnie is good. Not Pete, Peter, or Skedgewell. OK?'

'Fine with me, Vinnie. I am Private Benjamin Garvey. My chums call me Benny.'

'Private Benjamin,' I said, and scoffed.

'You have a problem with a nigger in a suit?'

Blondie laughed nervously.

'Oh fuck off playing the racist card on me. I just thought of a film with Goldie Hawn.'

'Do you want fisticuffs outside?' Benny said.

'Bollocks, we'll do it here if you want.'

I quickly stood, knocking the table, slightly spilling the drinks. Benny undid his jacket, but then roared with laughter.

'I am fooling with you, Vinnie.'

'Pure belta, Benny,' Blondie said.

'Bunch of wankers,' I said, and laughed with them.

There was an awkward silence. Benny began thumbing at Blondie, who had a straight face. I guessed Blondie didn't like swearing, or being called a wanker. I went to question why Blondie was in the army, but let it go. Benny offered me a cigarette, breaking the uncomfortable mood. I told him I hated smokers, which slightly shocked him, but it pleased Blondie.

On the next round, I told Benny I had no money. He told me the drinks were free, compliments of Andrew. I guessed Sarge had some big bar-tab going, so I ordered two. I managed to steer the conversation around to me; well, Peter Skedgewell. However, they knew nothing of

Skedgewell's past, only that a band of men had been picked for a special mission. On numerous occasions I had to remind them that I was really Johnny Vince. Blondie was more interested in speaking about God, but in the end, I had to tell him I was a non-believer. The shock on both their faces was as if I was dressed in a red suit holding a three-pronged fork with flames around me.

After a few more pints of treacle we began to talk more freely. Blondie hated my cursing, even more so when I had to explain to them both what certain swear words meant, much to the Benny's enjoyment. The relaxed chat came around to Andy: at the age of four Andy had lost his dad in the Battle of the Somme. Andy had joined the Scots Guards and then went on to join the SAS. He had fought many battles, from North Africa to Germany. Just after Benny had told me Andy's mum, brother, and wife were killed in a German bombing raid, he stopped. Blondie put his hand on Benny's shoulder. Clearly upset, Benny crooked his neck to restore a bit of pride and then took himself off to the lavatory, as he had called it.

I was hanging, Blondie had begun to fuzz around the edges. The smoke had started me wheezing, playing mayhem with my throat, even though I had kept it well lubricated. My cue for some fresh air came when Blondie pulled out a small bible. I hastily made my way through the different types of uniform and berets to the much-needed outside oxygen. The night was eerily quiet, and I was still surprised to see no cars or loads of drunks fighting in the street. My stomach gurgled. The thought of a kebab floated into my mind. Only my bike was leaning against the wall. I was busting for a piss, but couldn't be bothered to go all the way back inside, so I trotted into the side alley. It was only now I paid attention to the beeping noise.

Just as I had nearly finished, I heard some female laughter. Not wanting to get caught, I strained the last and quickly zipped up. Peeking around the corner there was a man and woman snogging; another lady was waiting. Looking as innocent as possible, I ventured out.

'Peter,' a woman shouted.

I turned to see her waving, walking towards me. In the light from the pub was the nurse, Helen. I didn't have to guess who the other woman was, and I was right: Elaine and, surprisingly, Andy. They made their way over. All three were out of uniform and dressed very smart.

'You dirty old dog,' I said.

'The night is young,' Andy slurred.

'She certainly is.' I winked at Elaine, who blushed.

'What are you doing, Pete?' Andy asked.

'I was… erm… just going to go for a doner. I'm bloody starving.' I wiped the drool whilst all three looked at each other.

'Do you mean a lady of the night?' Andy asked—they all tutted.

'No, a doner kebab with extra chillies.'

Andy lit up a cigarette, blowing the smoke my way. I waved it away.

'There's no smoking out here, only in the pub,' I said.

'Right, ladies, it is time to say goodnight. Thank you for a marvellous evening,' Andy said.

'Do you know if there is a Burger King in Aldershot? Or even a chippy?'

'Time you ladies went home rather than listen to this man's nonsense,' he said, and gave Elaine a kiss on her hand.

'Why don't you girls come in for a few drinks.'

A look of horror flashed across their faces.

'It is not really appropriate for these young ladies to go into that pub, Pete.'

'Oh bollocks. Anyway, there's already a woman in there; well, apart from the hairs on her chest from the stout.'

'Corporal Skedgewell…'

'Come on then,' I butted in, linking arms with Helen.

After the initial shock of bringing in these beautifully dressed ladies, eventually the place accepted it by getting on with drinking and chatting. The tension between Benny and Andy was thick. Between the cold stares from Andy, they never spoke to each other. The radio was eventually turned on, the presenter sounding like Mr Cholmondley Warner. Blondie tried to keep the chat on the righteous path. I endeavoured not to speak about anything to do with the war, and not answer questions about Skedgewell's past. I did, however, try to tell them as much about me as possible. Most of it was received with disbelief. I could sense their fear that I had lost the plot. What mostly intrigued Andy was my knowledge of the British Special Forces and the other SF units around the world. I tried to get one up on him about certain weapons that weren't even out in this time. Instead of putting up a defence, he quizzed me more about Germany and Italy.

CHAPTER ELEVEN

Someone banging and crashing woke me up. After a coughing fit, I squeezed open one eye to see where I was; disappointment immediately set in. I was hoping to wake up anywhere but in 1944. I shut my eyes again, wondering if Georges had got back to the kayak, just hoping the GPS's low batteries had held out. Perhaps if I remembered more of my world I would get back to reality. I thought hard of Nico, Gavin, and his in-laws, but I found it difficult to picture beyond. Just as I tried to visualise the events before the mission, a kid shouting startled me. There were another two voices adding to the argument, sounding like Benjamin and Andrew. It was coming from the room above me. The scuffling and quarrel continued downstairs and then the front door slammed. A long sigh came from the other side of the pastel-green door to the room I was in. Then the footsteps plodded back upstairs.

I wasn't as hungover as normal, considering the amount I'd had to drink till I left when the whole pub was singing, 'We'll Meet Again'. I remember an argument outside about us all piling back to Andy's, but I couldn't remember the journey back. Did I ride my bike home? Where was Blondie? What happened to Elaine and Helen? I vaguely remember having an intimate kiss with Helen. I checked the mottled-orange carpet for any ladies' underwear and then looked under the hairy yellow blanket; I was still dressed. Worse, I stunk of nicotine, I could even taste it.

Time check: 12.03 hrs. That wasn't right as it was only breaking daylight. After winding up the watch, I set it to the hideous wall clock: 06.37 hrs. I needed a brew. Sitting up felt shit, my guts were bloated and my head was thick. In front of me was a mahogany coffee table with a large bunch of lilies placed in a crystal vase and an ashtray full of dog-ends. Two mahogany and pink velvet-cushioned chairs sat either side of the table. Blending in with the pale-blue walls were two blue velvet chairs, which had elaborate pelmets running around the base.

The living room door flung open and in marched Andy in his military uniform, his beret tucked in the back of his shorts. He went straight through another door and slammed it shut behind him.

'Morning, Andy,' I said flippantly.

He didn't reply, but started clanging about. He came thundering back out of the room, pulling the door hard shut behind him. What had rattled his cage? Within a few minutes, he was strutting back past me. Again, he pushed shut the kitchen door. I started to get very amused at it all.

'Everything all right, Andy?' I shouted.

Just as I heard some mutterings, the familiar sound of a vintage kettle's whistle started to drown him out. Good, I thought.

First, he brought in a bowl of soggy cornflakes. They were also sprinkled with loads of sugar. I hated soggy cornflakes, let alone any sugar on my cereal. I couldn't think of anything worse, until he banged down the mug of milky tea in front of me.

'Oh great, a cup of warm milk. Did you run out of tea-bags?' I asked.

'Get used to the rations, Skedgewell. Good men have died on less.'

'What happened to the nice name Pete?'

He didn't reply.

After tipping the soggy cornflakes back into the bowl, I used the spoon to hopefully find a teabag in the cup.

'Five minutes before we press on with the objective.'

'And what's that?' I asked.

'To serve our King and country, Skedgewell.'

'As we're in private, Andrew, can you please stop calling me Skedgewell. It's really starting to piss me off.'

'It is Pete, or Skedgewell. Now eat up,' he barked.

'OK, Sarge. By the way, who was the kid, Andy?'

He throatily growled. 'Why the dickens Lassen wants you back in is a mystery to me.'

With his fists clenched, he stomped past the coffee table, knocking it so that the whitey tea slopped over the sides of the mug. This time he banged the front door shut behind him.

I sat in silence, staring at the tea as it made a pool around the bowl, like old murky dishwater. With all the fun last night in the pub, I had forgotten about reality. Why was I stuck in 1944? How did I get back here? Would I ever see my family and friends again? A wave of guilt came over me as I had not thought about them since the hospital. I had to remain in the real world, not get sucked into whatever the fuck I was in. I told myself I was Johnny Vince. In fact, every time I tuned into the annoying beep, I would tell myself that.

Shutting my weary eyes, I tried to focus on Will, Ocker, Oliver, and Mum. However, when it came to Dad, the image was blurred.

'Are you praying?' someone asked.

Immediately opening my eyes, there stood Blondie in the exact same uniform as Andy's. I stood up and threw the blanket at him.

'Piss off, Blondie.'

'I can speak to God with you,' he said softly.

'Listen, Saxton, I don't want to hear the crap that comes out of your mouth. Capeech? And before you ask, that means do you understand?'

'Of course, but when you want to share your troubles, Johnny, my door is open.'

'Well fucking shut it, bolt it, and padlock it, or even get Andy to slam it as he is good at that.'

A small part of me felt good that someone had actually called me by my real name.

Outside, Andy was loading luggage in the boot of an iconic car, the style I had seen in many black and white photos. I walked around the front and read the Austin emblem. It wasn't in the best of nick: a headlight was smashed and a pool of fluid had collected under the radiator. As I moved around to the rear, many dents and scratches were across the faded-black paintwork. Only one of the chrome hubcaps remained. Andy was trying to ram the boot lid shut.

'Been in the wars,' I said, before I had engaged my brain.

'It was the wife's,' Andy said.

'I'm sorry to hear what happened to her.'

'Who the blazing told you that?'

Andy put his face in mine. This was like the early days with Roy 'Rabbit' Franklin, but rather than stoke it up, I had to think quick as I didn't want any more problems for Benny.

'Well?' Andy demanded.

'Some drunk told me last night.'

'Really? Who was that?'

'I didn't get his name.'

'What uniform was he wearing? What did he look like?'

Andy was almost searching my body language and expression for another answer. This wasn't about the death of his wife.

'Answer.'

'Blimey, Sarge, I was drunk. Everything was blurred.' I knew it had sounded unconvincing.

'Have to be careful, young man. Loose lips and all that. Spies are everywhere.' Andy was looking at me differently.

'When do I get changed?' I said, changing the subject.

'Was the person who told you my life a black man, by any chance?'

'No, no, it wasn't Benny,' I said.

'So, you remember his colour then.'

'You really have a fucking problem…'

'I would suggest we do not carry this argument on, but instead, get to the airfield before our flight leaves,' Blondie interrupted.

'Sure,' I said.

I wondered in the silence and malicious stare from Andy if Blondie was embarrassed by our spat, or just trying to be Mr. Nice.

'There will be a new attire for you at camp, Skedgewell. Now get in you two,' Andy said.

He kicked the rear bumper; the remaining indicator fell off it. I was starting to rage inside, the beeping noise picking up pace. After swearing what I thought of Andy, I looked over at Blondie, who nervously half-smiled. I nodded at him and then opened the rear door, loudly creaking. There was no way I could go on like this with Andy. Like with Rabbit, I knew it was only a matter of time before it kicked off, big time.

Along the journey so far, no one had said a word, but I didn't care about how awkward it was. The dreamlike scenery through the nicotine-stained quarter-light window kept me absorbed. There wasn't one car driving at this time of the morning, but then it dawned on me: I didn't even know what day of the week it was; perhaps Sunday. Another point that struck me was the lack of buildings and parked cars. A couple of miles in I started to find amusement in the car's performance: whining and crunching gears, droning engine, and a jolting ride.

'Lovely car this,' I said.

'Thank you,' Andy replied.

Incredulously, I looked at Blondie to see if he had noticed my sarcasm, but he nodded his head to agree. Get me out of here, I thought.

The trip had just about become unbearable, when I spotted the signs at the north gates to Farnborough Royal Aircraft Establishment. Coils of barbed wire and sandbags fortified the perimeter and gates. After a quick chat from Andy and a swift scrutiny from the guard, we were let through. There were quite a lot of staff walking around, some in overcoats, some in overalls. I admired the architecture on some of the buildings, noticing each one was referenced with a Q or R sign.

'Is this where they do all the new design and testing?' I asked.

Blondie didn't answer, seemingly in awe of it all.

'Yes, but it is all classified,' Andy said.

'I read somewhere that they have a vault full of old records and films of everything designed, built, and tested.'

'Where did you read that, Skedgewell?' Andy asked, his tone changing.

'YouTube video, if I remember rightly.'

'Oh, I see.'

'Is that a German plane?' I said, seeing a stripped-down aircraft as we drove onto a large airfield.

'Well spotted, Johnny,' Blondie said, scrambling across the brown PVC seats to get a better look.

'Yes, well spotted indeed,' Andy added, insinuating something.

We drove onto a concrete track and, following it further in, Andy made sure the train-track grooves stayed centre of the car. The brakes squealed as he pulled up on the grass.

'Out. No time to hang around, chaps. Got some Hun to kill,' Andy said.

'Thank fuck,' I said.

Blondie tutted. 'Do you mean you are relieved about killing evil?'

'No. To get out of this shithole car.'

Blondie tutted even louder.

I still found it humorous that the door opened the other way out. I caught a glimpse of myself in the driver's mirror: I still had tiny scars and my nose was crooked. I remembered the wanker that had broken it in the hut. Turning my head, I had a scar on my cheek.

Walking across the massive airfield, dotted around was what looked like the old type air-raid shelters. What did interest me was the anti-aircraft guns dug in with sandbags placed around. I wasn't sure why Andy had parked so far away. A groan behind me made me turn. Blondie was on the floor rubbing his shin. Obviously, whilst he was looking around, he hadn't noticed the knee-height sign, which was now tilted over. I started to laugh. It wasn't that funny, but it pleased the morning's dullness, and the stress of Andy's ways. I gave Blondie a hand up, spotting a small bible on the floor. As he brushed himself down, I handed it to him.

'You keep it, Johnny.'

'You're fine,' I said.

'I would like you to have it. I have many more.'

'Like I said, I don't need it.' I held out his hand and slapped it in it. 'Rather than buy anymore bibles, why don't you spend your money on an eye-test and new glasses.'

I pointed at the sign and laughed. For a moment it seemed to provoke anger in him, staring menacingly at me. However, he patted me on the shoulder, joining in the joke. I read the sign as I straightened it back in the ground: 'No Parking on the Railway Line.' Really? They needed a sign to tell them that?

'Skedgewell. Saxton. What the bloody hell do you think you are playing at?' Andy shouted, marching back towards us.

I turned to Blondie and said, 'If there is a God, ask him to strike this fucker down, now.'

Blondie tried to hide his amusement, but I heard him snigger.

'Saxton,' Andy barked. 'Does my face look gay? Do I look in the mood for jovial jesting?'

Blondie tightened his lips, trying to hide his nervous laughter.

'No, the look on my face should tell you I am bloody stoked. Now, if you two want to stay here and abort this mission, then that is dandy with me. Skedgewell, if you even mutter something, you are grounded. Do you understand me?'

Yes, Sarge… ant,' I said.

My joke about his face looking gay because of his thin moustache would have been brilliant, but having seen how red he was, I'd decided to keep it in.

'It was not Johnny's fault that I looked gay. I was amused that I had tripped over the sign,' Blondie said anxiously.

'I can clearly see that, Saxton. Are you going to be this bloody clumsy with your Sten gun?' Andy slapped him around the head.

Blondie adjusted his glasses.

'Answer,' Andy barked.

'No, sir.'

'No, sergeant.'

'No, Sergeant,' Blondie repeated.

'Good. Because this mission is everything, Saxton. I cannot afford to carry clumsy soldiers who are not up to protecting Great Britain, and to follow orders from the top. What do you think Winston Churchill…'

'Sarge, he only fell over a sign,' I interrupted.

Andy took a step my way; my fists tightened. If he goes to slap me,

I will block it and beat him to submission, I thought. I glared into his eyes—this was becoming too familiar.

'You're not related to a bloke called Rabbit, are you?' I asked. 'Because you're so much like him.'

'It may be a simple sign here, but it could have been a sign for land mines. Or when we are on the run from the Hun, or when we must stay silent behind enemy lines. Apologise, Skedgewell, you scoundrel.'

'For what?'

'Do it,' Blondie whispered.

'Shut up, Saxton,' Andy yelled.

Seething, I stared harder into his cold eyes. They in turn narrowed and glared into mine. He was heavy breathing through his nose. The beeping noise increased.

'Sergeant Graham.'

We were still locked in defiance.

'Sergeant Andrew Graham,' a voice shouted, closer this time.

'You had your chance, Skedgewell,' Andy said. 'Both of you grab the kit bags and follow me.'

Andy turned and walked towards the blokes coming across the field, one of whom was dressed in an RAF uniform, the other in a boiler suit.

'Why did you not apologise?' Blondie asked.

'I hate bullies, and this cunt is really winding me up. I was about to knock him out.'

'He is a what?'

'For God's sake, you need to get out more. It's a harsh swearword.'

'Oh… well, that is why I do not understand. What does it mean?'

'Do you really want to know?' I said, hoping he would say yes.

'Canny. Cannot wait. Haddaway, man.'

I think he meant yes, but Blondie opened the boot lid and started to hand the bags to me.

'Fanny…? Minge…? Snatch…? Pussy…?'

Blondie kept silent with his head in the boot.

'OK. Vagina?'

Blondie began to slightly tremble, and then he stood up and roared with laughter, tilting his head back and holding his ribs as he did. I began to laugh inside. Blondie took off his thin glasses and wiped the tears from his eyes.

'Wey aye, man, he is geet walla one,' he said, still chuckling.

It started me laughing again. 'A what?'

'A great large one.'

I burst out laughing even more, just as Andy shouted. We both tried to hide our amusement as we looked over at him waving frantically for us to come over.

We took a slow walk following them all in the direction of a hangar, at the same time releasing the odd giggle.

'In all seriousness, Johnny...'

'Don't spoil it with the Jesus mumbo-jumbo shit,' I interrupted.

'I was going to say, be careful as Andrew has a few boxing titles. I have seen first-hand how he can knock someone out.'

'Is that why you didn't slap him back?'

'No. I respect him. He maybe a large one, but he has high morals. His country, unit, and boy come first. He has travelled the world, defended his King and country, and made it back. Losing his chums and family has reinforced his mission to beat Hitler. Andrew goes back to the beginning of the SAS with the sloth. Did you fight out in the deserts?'

'Yeah, been to a few. And who is this sloth that you and Andy mention?'

'Haddaway, man. What unit and desert did you fight in?'

'Paras, SBS, and a bit of PMC. Iraq, Afghanistan, Yemen, Somalia, and quite a few other places.'

'I have not heard of any of those places. What is a PMC?'

'A whole load of trouble.'

Blondie turned his head to me as we walked along and then pushed his glasses up, still waiting for the right answer. I was bored of explaining my past to Blondie, who was now cleaning his fingerprints off his glasses.

'Did you say Andy had a son?'

He looked unnerved by my question. 'Let us talk later.'

'As long as you don't try to convert me, dude.'

'There is no chance the Church or God would accept a heathen like you.'

'I thought you said we were all God's children.'

'All... except one,' he said, and laughed.

Blondie put the kit in a pile next to Andy and I placed mine on the stack.

'Thank you, Blondie,' Andy said.

I sighed. 'What's in the hangar?'

As if Andy had pressed a button to answer my question, the gigantic doors started to slide open. I squinted to try to make out the shapes in the gloom. The sun glinted off the glass-domed gunner's front turret; the bomb doors were open.

'Is that a Lancaster?' I said joyfully.

'You ask a lot of questions, Skedgewell,' Andy said.

I couldn't be bothered to answer his dribble, in awe of the Spitfire that was parked next to it. There were a few staff working on ladders around it, the front propeller was off. I wanted to go and touch the planes, help service the Hispano cannon. As the doors clunked to a stop, I could just make out part of a large German wing. The rest of the damaged plane was being disassembled. It was a cross between the US Stealth and British Vulcan. I'd not seen one like this and I started to walk, almost drawn towards them.

'Wow, that's amazing,' I said.

'Where the bloody hell do you think you are going?' Andy said, breaking the spell. 'Just stand to.'

'Blondie, do you have a camera?' I asked.

'This is a restricted area,' Andy said. 'You cannot go taking photos. You should know that. What would you want with photos?'

'Dunno, really,' I said. 'I just thought it would be nice on my wall at home.'

Before the next words came out of Andy's mouth, a small truck pulled out a trailer with what looked like an experimental helicopter on top.

'Who's the Meccano expert?' I said, and laughed.

'This was not built by Frank Hornby,' Andy said. 'This has been transported from the United States of America.'

'I bet it didn't fly here, but came by boat.' I scoffed.

'Correct, Skedgewell.'

'No, Sarge, that was a flippant remark. What the hell is it?'

'It is a helicopter, Johnny,' Blondie said.

'Really?' I said incredulously. 'Cracking, Blondie. Can't wait for the Scalextric.'

'What is Scalextric?' Blondie asked.

'Listen, you two jesters, this is a Sikorsky YR4B. It is being tested here and we have the privilege to use it. This nineteen litre, one hundred-and-eighty horse-powered helicopter travels at…'

I had got bored with the Andy's details; I didn't want to fly in it. 'Please don't tell me we have to fly that thing,' I butted in.

'No. We have a pilot all the way from the United States of America.'

'You can shorten it to USA, Sarge,' I said. 'Is it the same Yank at the Cambridge Military Hospital?'

'Who are you babbling on about, man?' Andy asked.

'Command Sergeant Major Timothy McNamara.'

'Never heard of him. I hope you have brought your hospital medication with you, Skedgewell.'

'I hope the pilot has brought some sick-bags,' I jested.

'Stop acting the twit. Now load up, you two.'

The closer I neared the helicopter, the more dubious I became. The three-rotor-bladed contraption with its odd-shaped glassed cockpit didn't feel me with joy. As the four of us squeezed in, I was the only one who appeared concerned, even Blondie seemed at ease. The controls and instrument panel were basic. As the motors whined, the air was filled with exhaust fumes. Finally, the pilot made a wobbly ascent.

'Did you say this had been tested?' I shouted in the ear of Andy, sat up front.

'This is the test flight,' he said.

Andy lit up a cigarette. Not knowing if he lit up on purpose to annoy me, I leant over to my side to get out the way of his filthy habit.

'Do you reckon this thing is going to make it, Blondie?' I asked.

'I am not afraid to die.'

'I'd rather stay alive.'

He pulled out the bible and handed it to me, I swatted it back.

Really? 'Fly me To the Moon', I thought, as it started playing. Oh this just gets weirder by the hour.

CHAPTER TWELVE

Whilst flying across Britain in this non-state-of-the-art machine, I began to relax watching how unpopulated the world below appeared. Even if we had tried to make conversation, I don't think we could all have heard. Andy and Blondie somehow had fallen asleep. At least I had music to listen to, even though I was getting a bit tired of the same Sinatra and Coldplay. The niggling feelings were now at the forefront of my concerns: what was this mission? Would Blondie, a padre that looked like he would run away from trouble, and Andy, a racist and bully, be in the squad? How would I pretend to be Skedgewell if I met any of his old mates? Surely they would see I wasn't the same bloke.

The pilot tapped Andy on the shoulder, he instantly was alert. Looking back at Blondie who was still asleep, I wondered how old he was; possibly twenty-two. I searched the scars on his arms and scalp, it was only then I saw the top part of his ear was missing. He didn't have any facial hair. His nails were perfectly kept as he held onto his small bible. Did he fall over the sign on purpose so I would pick up the bible that he had dropped? Is he trying to convert me? I had to be on my guard.

Suddenly, the helicopter began to vibrate. It wasn't long before this developed into a serious shake. A pathetic warning sound went off on the dash. Blondie woke up and leaned towards his window. The pilot grappled with the controls, also working his feet.

'What the fuck's going on?' I asked.

'We seem to have an aviation malfunction,' the American pilot shouted.

'No shit,' I said.

'Over there, take us down,' Andy yelled.

The engine seemed to cut in and out, and at times it felt as if we were dropping like a stone. I looked across at Blondie who was calmer than me.

'Got any of those angel wings in your bag?' I said.

'Should have brought your chute from your Parachute Regiment days,' Blondie replied.

'Skedgewell was not in the Paras,' Andy shouted.

Blondie frowned at me.

'Saxton, is that what he told you?'

'Yes, Sergeant. Also fought in Afistan, Iroq, and somewhere else... erm... S... Sum...'

'Come on, Saxton, spill the beans.'

'Sumilia, Sergeant,' Blondie blurted, looking proud after—I shook my head in dismay.

'Utter balderdash,' Andy said.

Here we all were about to plummet out of the sky, and they were having a chat as if in the pub.

'Hey, let's stop talking about me, and sort the little bloody problem of hitting the ground at a hundred miles per hour.'

The helicopter started to veer to the right, the engine and rotors whined. The pilot tried to stop us going into a full spin and, at the same time, he kept flicking a control switch. With another shudder, we began to stabilise and keep altitude, but the clean air around us filled with fumes. Andy patted the pilot on the shoulder.

'Well done, old chap,' Andy said.

That was my chance. 'Yes, well done, old chap, but I would recommend not leaving the Meccano's eight-millimetre bolts and square nuts from the engine mounts. Did this fucking kit not come with a small spanner and instruction manual?'

The pilot couldn't have turned his head anymore if he had tried. I didn't see his expression, but Andy's glare said it all.

'You wanna be fucking thankful us Yanks are here to bail you out,' the pilot said.

'Does your chitty-chitty-bang-bang have any music to drown out the droning? And I don't mean the helicopter,' I said, and nudged Blondie—no one answered.

Jeez, this lot needed a humour transfusion.

As the flight continued, the weather mood changed, along with Andy's. He continued to tap his fingers on his knee and occasionally looked around at me, like he wanted to get something off his chest. Blondie had shut his eyes again, his head gently rocking side to side. Through the rain that had started to land on the front screen, ahead was what looked like a large industrial farm that had been built in the middle of nowhere. The only entry in was through a narrow lane. Different types of fields like a patch-work quilt were as far as the eye could see. There were no forests, just the odd tree. Coming clearer into view were four dark-coloured buildings. Amongst these were smaller units with narrow tracks that ran between.

Shocked at what I saw, I leant as far forward into Andy and the pilot's space as I could, staring at the neat rows of planes. As we neared, I started to count the dug-in AA battery guns. I was put off by another row of larger aircrafts close to a runway. This wasn't a farm, but an airfield. I scoured the landscape, slightly surprised to see no security fences coiled with razor-wire, and manned gates.

We descended lower and banked left over to a large two-storey building. The front screen was getting harder to see out of as the drizzle had become one sheet of water. I was going to ask to put the wipers on, but I doubted it had any, or they would have just fallen off. Instead, I wiped my steamed-up window for a better view. Between the running droplets, I made out the lone wreckage of an old type propelled large plane. I quizzed why I kept saying words like: old, vintage, and dated. Now that I was questioning about this era's terminology, was I now settling in too much? Shit.

Another smaller wreckage caught my eye to the far end of the grass runway, not your concreted, white lined, lit, modern landing strip. The pilot hovered and then nosed the helicopter forward. Was he showing off at the few blokes that had come out to marvel at this flying machine? Or was it he didn't know how to land it?

'Shame we're not in an Apache or a Chinook,' I said—it fell on deaf ears.

On top of the flat-roofed building was another smaller room with no windows, but instead, a door. A large number seven was painted on the side. Telegraph poles had anemometers mounted high, with wires that railed down to further poles. At the front, next to the handrail that ran around the top, was a smaller AA gun, partly covered by a stained tarpaulin. A bloke in a World War Two RAF uniform stood on a gantry on level two, next to a light on a tripod. He waved at us as we lowered further to the ground. It was me alone who didn't wave back.

The landing wasn't the smoothest, but we had made it, alive. Then it struck me: I'd had no bad flashbacks of the near-death Chinook crash in Afghanistan.

'Skedgewell, you are to stay here,' Andy ordered. 'Blondie, grab the kitbags, haversacks, and follow me.'

'Yes, Sergeant.'

Andy managed to give me a dirty look as he aggressively shut his door. What was it with him slamming doors? He and the pilot walked towards two finely-dressed uniformed men, with Blondie struggling to carry all the gear. With the formal pleasantries finished, both officers looked my way. I felt like an admonished kid again, being imprisoned in my dad's Ford Sierra in the service station for fighting with my brother on a holiday journey.

Some other uniformed staff came and greeted them all with handshakes and back-slapping. They helped Blondie with the luggage and then walked off towards one of the large hangars. I was left with the slight wind howling through the gaps, dispersing the fumes. All the military staff had gone back inside. I couldn't see any sign of Andy and his mob. The tinkering sound of the hot metal cooling down kept in tune with the beeping sound. I had become very bored, not even checking the time, something I used to do regularly. Time check: 08.47 hrs. I started wishing for some music, even the same songs.

'Right, bollocks to this,' I said.

I swung the door open. The fresh air was a pleasant change and the rain had subsided. I took in a 360-degree view around me. A few windsocks fluttered in the breeze. I made my way across the daisy-filled wet grass towards the building. Reaching a twin axle ambulance truck, I ran my hand across the wet bodywork until I met the red cross on the side. I wondered if the same crew had managed to save the airmen of the crashed planes that were littered about. A few from inside the control room were watching me as I made my way over to the next vehicle: a truck with a large fuel tank sat over four wheels. I nosed in the open cab and felt the seats and then rattled the gear lever. Drips from the soft-top roof went down my neck. Next to this fuel truck was a trailer with a large tripod and light, the type used to spot advancing German warplanes. These trucks and equipment were awesome. I had to test out the light, I thought.

'Johnny, so glad you made it safely,' someone said.

Slightly startled, I turned to see Tim come around the rear of the tanker. He looked different, but not his clothes.

'Tim. Where the hell did you come from? How did you get here? You look... older.'

Chuckling, he gave me another long hug. 'It's the war, son. Takes it out of you.'

'I didn't see you come over,' I said, pushing him off.

'Because you had your head in the clouds, or should I say, the fuel truck.'

'What are you doing here?'

'Fighting the war, son. Why are you here?'

I paused at his question, then said, 'I'm meant to be going on a mission, but I think I've pissed Andy off.'

'Sergeant Graham? Don't read into him so much. He's a good, solid man, and I would have him fight by my side.'

'Really? He says he doesn't know you.'

Tim laughed and took off his cap; his hair was lighter. 'He would say…'

Brrrring… brrrring… brrrring!

'What the hell is that?' I asked.

'That's the ambulance.'

He cupped his hands around his eyes looking to the sky. I did the same. On the limit of my sight was a tiny dot. I blinked again and focused: a thin line of smoke trailed the plane. A jeep skidded to a halt, with two blokes wearing trousers, shirts, and braces. Both wore their RAF hats tilted. One stood up and searched through his binoculars. Someone shouted from the gantry and I looked up to where it came from. A crowd of onlookers all faced the aircraft.

'This doesn't look good,' Tim said. 'You know what you have to do, son.'

I looked back at the plane, now clearly visible and travelling in fast. Its wings wavered, leaving smoke patterns from two of the engines. I looked back at Tim to ask what he had meant, but he had gone.

'Where's the fire response crew and truck?' I shouted.

'In for a bloody service, my fellow,' said the bloke next to me.

'One bloody fire truck for the whole airfield?'

'The other is being filled now. We only just used it this morning,' the jeep passenger said.

The plane's deep engines could now be heard, along with a drone and spluttering.

'Come on, girl, keep your bloody nose up,' the jeep driver said.

'How long till the fire truck is full?' I asked.

'About thirty minutes, chum.'

'And we just fucking stand here and watch? Why don't we have a few banners and a round of fucking applause.'

'Steady on,' the driver said.

The magnificent beast was now almost touching the grass, but it appeared too fast to stop at the length of grassy runway. I ran to the jeep, started it, and then drove at speed towards the bomber. The shouting behind soon disappeared; I was now transfixed. Almost level, I slowed the jeep and then pulled the handbrake. The wet grass made spinning it 180-degrees, easy. At the same time as drifting backwards, I managed to crank the long gearstick into first and then release the clutch. Pressing hard on the accelerator, mud and grass spewed up. I grappled with the large steering wheel. Traction now on and bouncing in the seat, I went through the gears. I was now just right of the plane at its rear, but it was going a lot faster. I could taste the smoke that poured out as I looked at the RAF markings; bullet holes fanned the brown and green side.

Turf and dirt flew up as soon as I had heard the smash. In what appeared to be in slow-motion, a dark object careered through the smoke trail of this bulk that gouged its way down the runway. However, I didn't have the time or the traction to avoid the collision. Just before the bomber's wheel hit my jeep, the main ram dug in the earth, kicking it upwards. The crashing noise was terrifying as it ripped through the passenger part of the screen, taking it all with it. I open my eyes as I fishtailed through the crater that it had made, quickly reacting by countering the wheels, changing up a gear and flooring it.

More debris flew up. The smoke had worsened so I decided to go further left to protect what was left of my vehicle. Above the jeep screaming its nuts off, I heard an explosion. A light now glowed from the disintegrating plane. Suddenly, something rolled in front of me. I swerved to miss it. Was that a body? The rear gunner's glass had been smashed. Was this done before landing?

The end of the runway was in sight, rapidly along with the oncoming ditch, bushes, and a previous aircraft wreckage. The fire was now spreading; smaller crackles and bangs were going off. A few whizzes overhead made me duck. I'd heard the noises many times before, knowing what they were. A mass of flames rolled in the gouges that were left in its wake. As the object stopped, I noticed his uniform on fire. I pressed hard on the brakes, skidding to a halt. The plane's nose dug in, sending it almost over. As the bomber reached its pinnacle, it stopped for a second, creaked, and then crashed to the earth. I leaped out and slid across the bonnet, the glass on my lap falling into the scrapes. I sprinted to the carnage. The crazy crescendo of engines had stopped, now an almost deathly silence took their place. From the intense heat of the fire in the mid-section came the pleas and screams. It was too hot for me to get to; I felt sick. I tried again to battle the smoke and heat to get to those yelling, but I had to let them go—it hurt. I had lost men before like this.

With the tears streaming, I ran back to the jeep, and I then drove it alongside the cockpit that was sunk into the earth. Rows of bombs and a lady were hand-painted on the side. Standing on top of the bonnet I smashed the glass with the jeep's wheel-brace. The acrid smoke that had been contained now billowed out, along with the hot temperature. Thrusting my arms in, I felt a face. I tried to pull at his shoulders, but he was stuck.

BOOOM!

For a few seconds I watched the grey clouds in the sky, then realised it was smoke. I sat bolt upright, remembering Rabbit's story in the aftermath of the Chinook crash.

The heat from the fire was almost unbearable, and I had to whip my hands away from the hot metal as I climbed back up to the cockpit. This time I hauled myself up and over the jagged glass. I knew I was cut, but I didn't feel the pain. Was this because I was in a dream? My heart was thumping as time wasn't on my side. Kneeling on the lap of the pilot, I had trouble seeing the buckles, not just through the smoke, but my vision had begun to turn white. The beeping was going mental in my ears. I closed my eyes and fumbled for the release buckle.

Click!

Moving almost blind to the other pilot, I lifted the first pilot out the way I had entered. He landed on the jeep's bonnet, relieving my anxiety a little. The beeping slowed. That was it: I needed to relax, slow it all down. I opened my eyes; the white was disappearing.

'Relax, Johnny,' I choked.

Into view came an awful sickening sight. Through the white, pungent haze was the pilot's face with glass embedded in it. He looked no older than twenty-five. I checked his blood stained neck: a slow pulse registered. Even though he was unconscious, I carefully prised back his belts. Sitting back in the other pilot's empty seat, I heaved him over, but he was stuck. I pulled harder, which woke him. The situation soon grabbed him. He began to panic. I thought twice about slapping him as the glass would have gone further in. Instead, I told him to shut the fuck up whilst I released his legs.

Belly-down on the floor, I felt around his legs and feet. Part of the mechanical undercarriage had come through, pinning his leg to the seat; a bone had pierced his trousers. Bollocks; I knew we didn't have long. As soon as I'd thought this, a smaller explosion went off, almost as if agreeing. The pilot started to yank at his leg, going berserk. He shouted that he didn't want to be burnt alive. It was no good whichever way I heaved on the metal and his smashed leg, so I scrambled back up and held his head still. The bell of the ambulance rang.

'What's your name?' I shouted.

'Jameson… Jameson Mullen,' he said, trying to get a handle on his emotions.

'I won't let you burn alive, I've just…'

'Give me your pistol. Let me end it,' he yelled.

'I don't have one.'

'Please, sir, go and get one.'

Jameson felt the back of his hair that had steam rising from it. Petrified, he leant as far forward as he could; heat wafted over me. Again, I bent down wrenched at the obstruction and his leg; bone and tissue coming through the trouser tear. He screamed in pain. My mind raced for answers, but I knew I had to go and get the weapon.

Coughing and tears flowing were now taking over. I leant out the window to see a group, shocked to see me. The first pilot was being loaded onto the ambulance. In a flash, an idea came to me.

'Grab the fucking lifting strops in the back of the jeep and throw them up,' I shouted.

None of them came forward, but instead they all started to quickly walk backwards. Could they not hear me? I hollered again and pointed at the strops. One of the lads held his forearm up and stretched out into the heat. At last he managed grab them and throw them up, but they didn't make it. I cursed. Glancing back at the rest of the burning fuselage, I wished I hadn't. Jameson started to yell.

'Fuck,' I shouted.

The young lad dared to venture in, and he managed to chuck the strops again; on the money. He made a hastily retreat.

Inside, with my breath held, I felt Jameson's chest through the smoke. Looping the strop under his armpits, he suddenly held on tightly to my forearms. I pulled my wrists away, but his grip was too strong.

'Jameson, let go,' I gasped.

Coughing, he dug his fingers further into my skin. I pulled back again, but he wouldn't let go.

'Jameson...'

'Do not leave me to burn to death.'

'One of the lads has brought a pistol. Let me go and get it,' I yelled.

He stared at me through tears, and then released.

In an instant, I was scrambling out and, sliding down the scorching metal, I bounced awkwardly off the hot bonnet. Trying to suck in air, I sprinted around the jeep and hooked the loop over the tow-ball. Sitting with my back off the burning driver's seat, I started the engine, crunching it into gear. Slowly, I let the clutch out. Once the jeep had taken up the slack, I revved the engine, holding the bite. Unbelievably, he wasn't coming. I wasn't sure if Jameson's screams were because of the pulling pains or the fire had taken hold. With no choice left, I let the clutch up and floored the accelerator. For a moment, the wheels spun, but then the jeep shot forward. I tried to block out the fumbling noise behind. After about ten metres, I stopped and switched the engine off.

CHAPTER THIRTEEN

A crowd had gathered beyond the ambulance as I ran back to Jameson. The two RAF blokes who were originally in the jeep had beat me to him. The passenger was throwing up. I pushed him aside to see Jameson not responding. I felt around for a pulse, but as I did, he moaned. Brilliant he's alive, I thought. Looking down at his feet, he only had one. His trouser leg from below the knee was saturated, the blood continuing to seep through. I remembered not having a trouser belt on; also, leaving the kipper tie behind. Bollocks.

'Give me your fucking braces,' I said to the driver.

'Wwwhat?' he stuttered.

'Give me your fucking braces, unless you want him to bleed to death.'

It shocked him into removing his braces. Handing them to me, I used them as a tourniquet. The paramedics arrived and placed Jameson on a stretcher, the jolt waking him. He yelled in pain and then started to cough. Loading him into the ambulance, he stared back at me.

'Better than the pistol,' I muttered—Jameson's eyes closed.

'Do you want a lift back, sir?' the passenger asked.

'You know what, I'll pass on that. Just in case you throw up on me.'

'Oh, as you wish, sir,' he said.

It was meant to be humour as I wanted the lift, but on the other hand, I needed to collect my thoughts.

I trudged away with the fading sound of the ambulance's bell and the noise of the dying wreckage behind me. A few blokes were taking photos of it, more were picking up parts along its landing path. Four other stretcher-bearers were walking back across the airfield, the bodies had been totally covered. Tucking my ripped shirt back in, I was soaked through, muddy, and bloodied. I sat down on the wet grass and stared into nothing. Lying down with my hands behind my head must have looked weird to anyone watching. The images played over and over whilst my body trembled. I'd forgotten to thank the lad who dared to get the strops. What was I thinking getting in that jeep? What a fucking idiot. I began to laugh, a bit like Blondie did when he seemed nervous.

'Johnny,' a faint voice shouted.

I tutted. 'Can't a guy get any peace.'

I delicately sat up. Walking at speed towards me was a bloke in a high-ranking uniform. Behind him, right back at the tanker, was someone waving and sticking their thumbs up: Tim. His actions were exaggerated, appearing jubilant. I lamely waved back at him. The officer walking towards me took a long look back at Tim. Aching and stiff, I stood to greet him. The RAF officer was dressed in a dusky-blue, thick material trousers and jacket, the type that would make you itch. He also wore a blue shirt and tie. Little ribbons and wings decorated the area above his left pocket. Smoke from his pipe wafted around his badged peaked hat.

As he neared, he took off his hat and put it under his arm. His perfectly kept jet-black swept-back wavy gelled hair did not move. He stood to attention and firmly saluted. Just as I went to return the salute, he put his hand out. I didn't know which to do first. Slightly flustered, I shook his hand. His firm grip held on for a bit, then he let go. He handed me a handkerchief from his top pocket and nodded at my hand. The officer removed his pipe whilst I wrapped my injury.

'Corporal Skedgewell. Let me...'

'Please, call me Vinnie.'

A little taken aback, he said, 'Vinnie, I am Wing Commander Kenneth Wilson of One-Three-Eight Squadron. Let me start by quoting success is not final; failure is not fatal; it is the courage to continue that counts.'

'Winston Churchill, right,' I replied, feeling good I knew it.

'Of course,' he said, as if everyone should know. 'Your valiant effort will not go unnoticed. You must have an ability to know what is coming.'

'You mean sixth sense?'

'I am not sure what that is, sir, but you somehow knew I was coming across to greet you, and you knew that you could save those pilots.'

'It was Tim shouting that made me sit up,' I said.

Wilson turned back to me, frowning as if he didn't understand, and then he put his hat back on.

'Do you know whose son Squadron Leader Mullen is?'

'Is he OK?' I asked.

'Oh... yes,' he said awkwardly. 'He will never fly again, but patriotism comes at a high price. You are a brave man, sir. You have saved two of my best pilots.'

He held his hand out, again, and I shook it, again, slightly embarrassed.

'Cheers, Kenny. How's the other pilot?'

'I am not certain. However, mark my words, a little brush down and Wing Leader Earnest Sayers will be bombing again.'

'If it wasn't for that courageous lad who'd dared come near whilst the others stood, we would have all burned. Please make sure he is recognised for his bravery.'

'I will find out who he is and make sure. You are both heroes.'

An air-raid siren sounded in the distance, breaking my awkwardness. Wilson ordered me off the runway and I was to follow him in quick-march.

Following his pacey steps back to the hangar area, I recognised a majestic sound: a squadron of eight Spitfires taxied across the grass towards us. In awe of the spectacle, I stood transfixed. Wilson broke me from the hypnosis by grabbing my arm and telling me to get out of the way. A few on the gantry saluted, the pilots returning the gesture. The rumbling and roar captivated me as the first Spitfire rolled past, only ten metres away. The young-faced pilot saluted at Wilson. I looked into the lad's eyes. Was it fear? Was it determination? Was it excitement? As the last of the fledging men turned next to the smouldering wreckage, I could only imagine what they were thinking. It wasn't long before they were all airborne, the familiar sounds disappearing, along with the tiny hope of returning. I lowered my hand in the silence; thoughts lingered on.

Back at the airfield control building, one of the medics was closing the rear ambulance doors. Slightly bemused as to why it was still here, I asked him why he had not taken the injured pilots to hospital. I was informed that both wanted to see their pilots take off. Another officer opened the glass metal-framed doors and introduced himself as Squad Leader Worthington from One-Six-One Squadron. Again, my hand was shaken; also, I had a few pats on the back for good measure. What spoilt the moment was he told me that he had a message from Sergeant Graham to make my way over to Hangar-1. Maybe Andy would now cut me some slack.

With the rain starting, I opened the small wooden door situated in the hangar's closed main door. Sitting amongst kit was a large group of uniformed soldiers. The place fell silent, the bloke playing the harmonica was nudged to stop. A few coughs and laughs came from around the hangar. I knew I looked like I was the only one who had turned up to a normal party in fancy dress.

'Vinnie,' someone called out. 'Vinnie, how are you doing?'

Between the hordes of kit, soldiers, and smoke, Benny strolled leisurely over. He looked different in his army uniform. Benny put his arm around my shoulder and led me away, the place soon went back to its business.

'Benny, what the hell are you doing here?' I asked.

'Ganged up with Andrew now have you?' he insinuated.

'No. He doesn't intimidate me.'

'I have earned my beret like him, so I am going on this mission. By the way, you look like shit, and stink worse.'

'Good,' I said. 'I mean, good you are going. And when is this mission?'

'We were supposed to be going tonight, but the weather has delayed the raid.'

He relaxed on a crate and handed me a packet of cigarettes. I noticed the Germen advertising motif and writing on the side.

'Take one,' he said smoothly.

'Not for me. I hate smokers,' I said, even though I was possibly the only one in here not smoking.

'Yeah, man.'

'How come they're German?' I asked.

'Shhh. There is a high premium for these.'

His big smile widened, looking even more cool. He definitely resembled Will, I thought.

'Where did you get these?'

'From the American. The Yank got them off some bastard German, apparently after he shot him up.'

'Tim gave you…'

'What the dickens are you doing here, Private Garvey?'

I knew it was Andy who had interrupted me. I quickly shoved the packet in my trouser pocket before turning to see Andy angrily barging his way through people towards us. Benny put the fag out under his boot.

'Oh bloody hell,' Benny muttered.

'Don't worry, I'll sort this. It's about time.'

I blocked Andy's route to Benny. Andy tried to go around me, but I kept in the way.

'Move aside, Skedgewell.'

Play it cool, Johnny, I thought. 'It's Johnny, or Vinnie. When are you going to get that in your thick fucking head?'

Andy took a step back, but I stepped into his space, my lip slightly snarled.

'Oh, now you're listening,' I said.

'That is it, Skedgewell. You are no longer a corporal. You are no longer on this mission. I have had just about...'

'Oh spare me the lecture, you motherfucker.'

Andy, stunned, looked around at the opened-mouthed men behind him. The whole place had gone quiet. He faced me, fit to burst.

'Are you implying that I fornicate with my mother?' he said.

'I'll tell you what else...'

Benny interrupted me by holding my shoulder. 'Leave it,' he said.

'No, people need to know he hates you because of the colour of your skin.'

'You have got it all...'

The jab to my face as I'd looked back to see what Benny was saying sent my head back. Another shock to the jaw sent me to my right and I stumbled to the floor. I'd been wrong about feeling any pain, the spasms had shot through my skull. Not for the first time I felt the coppery taste in my mouth. Through watery eyes, I looked at the blood on the back of my hand from where I'd wiped my lip. Andy was overshadowing me in a boxing defence. Benny went to help me up, but I pushed his hand away.

'Get up, you fool,' Andy said, snarling.

Looking around, it was plainly obvious these young men were wanting to see more action. Why disappoint, I thought, and slowly stood, spitting blood to the side. Andy went into an odd boxing pose, then did a jig like the gentlemanly era. A few of the spectators encouraged him.

'Just give me a second,' I said.

I stretched out my legs and then rotated my arms a few times. After that, I went down in a low sumo-stance, pushing out my knees to stretch my groin.

'Stop acting the twit, you coward,' Andy said.

The onlookers laughed, then a few voices told him to hit me again. After standing and stretching my back and neck, I went into a karate *Sachin Dachi* stance. Tightening my core, I raised my hands, one slightly in front of the other.

'Queensberry rules, old chap,' I said, in piss-take posh voice.

The first jab to the face made me realize I had started to take too much notice of the Red Hot Chili Peppers song that blared into my mind. I closed my guard as another punch came at me. The crowd had started to jeer. Andy took a step back and began dancing around. The next quick session of his boxing, I just calmly blocked with open hands. Andy was getting slightly annoyed. Whether it was because I was just swatting him away, or that I wasn't fighting back, I smiled; it angered him. Encouraged, I started nodding in time to the song: 'By The Way'. I must have looked odd to the others.

Andy's next barrage of strikes were quicker and he managed to get a blow to my gut. Even though I felt the pain, I didn't move. Knowing that he would do it again, I blocked it and then tapped him on his cheek. A few blokes taunted him. Andy danced and darted around even more. With the song now in rocking mode, I put my right leg back into short fighting stance. Focusing on the area in front of me, I blocked his quick left jab, then right jab, but I'd had enough of being the intended punch-bag. Immediately, I struck him in the ribs with a hard *Mae Geri* and, with the same kick, instantly powered a *Mawashi Geri* to his head; the noise was satisfying. Andy staggered to his side, not knowing whether to hold his sore ribs or his head. Following the momentum, I fired a punch to the same side head injury. He managed to get a block up, but not the next one that hit him fully in the face. The soldiers he landed on tried to push him back, but he was dazed. Benny barged me out the way to give Andy a hand up

'Vinnie, that is enough,' Benny barked.

'Thanks, would have been nice,' I said.

Andy tried to get past Benny for some more action, but was held back. I grinned at Andy, infuriating him. Benny was shoved aside and then Andy stormed through the crowd. The door slamming echoed around the hangar; I knew that was coming.

'Vinnie, you had better skedaddle,' Benny said.

'No way. He had that coming. Anyway, where the hell do I go?'

'Home.'

'I'll ask the helicopter pilot to take me to Newquay, shall I?' I said flippantly.

'Be quick as the Yank said he was leaving soon.'

'Oh, I forgot, I can't go home as my parents aren't fucking born yet.'

'Are you OK, Vinnie?' Benny asked.

'Did you mean Tim the Yank, or the Yank pilot?'

'Johnny, what is going on?' Blondie said, holding a bible.

'Do you carry that everywhere? You don't fucking need it. I'm not dead,' I scolded.

'Keep it out, Blondie,' Benny said.

Oh great, Andy has come back for round two, I thought. However, I was shocked to see him strutting towards me with a pistol aimed at my head.

'I do not give a hoot about your bloody military past, but your guttersnipe ways do not fit in here,' Andy shouted.

With the pistol coming closer, the tension rising, I kept quiet. I even pacified my body language, hoping he would stop within a distance where I could force the weapon away, immobilise it, and him. However, he stood still at a three-metre distance and cocked it.

'Well, Skedgewell, say something. Or has the cat got your tongue?'

'No, Sergeant, I'm just wondering what type of pistol that is.'

The men watching laughed under their breath, which wasn't the intended plan.

'You see, Skedgewell, you put a lot of your memory down to shellshock, and...'

'You mean PTSD,' I interrupted.

'What?' he said, thrusting the pistol at me a few more inches.

'Post-traumatic stress disorder.'

'There you go again, trying to make me look the fool. I actually think you are not suffering from lunacy, but you are a German spy.'

The gasps and mumbling orchestrated around the hangar.

'You cock. How the hell did you get to that?' I said.

'Your interest in certain buildings, planes, etcetera. You ask a lot of questions and you cannot explain your past. You do not act like the British Army.'

'That's the dumbest thing you've said so far, and there's been quite a list. Go ahead, slot me, and go to prison for murder. Your lad will be fatherless.'

His eyes intensified. 'How fucking dare you.'

'Sergeant, please do not shoot this man,' Blondie said.

Blondie walked straight out from behind me and into the front of the pistol. Andy's finger seemed to squeeze the trigger.

'He is a good man,' Blondie said.

'Move it, Saxton,' Andy barked.

'No, Sergeant, I will not. Skedgewell may be troubled, but he has done no wrong.'

'I will put a bullet in you, then this spy.'

Blondie held his small bible to his chest. With his other trembling hand he held up a small wooden cross. The situation was at the pinnacle. Everyone was like statues. You could have heard pin drop.

'Move,' Andy said.

'I am not afraid to die for doing what is right.'

I disregarded the next track of the Red Hot Chili Peppers and ignored the ever-growing pace of the beeping. My mind was racing on what to do when Blondie got shot as I believed Andy's emotions would do it. Should I say something to try help the situation? Should I push Blondie aside and go for Andy? If I got shot in the face and died, where would I go? Back to... I couldn't think of the answer.

'Sergeant Graham. What the fucking hell do you think you are doing?'

Everyone turned like a mob of meerkats to see a higher-ranked officer coming in fast like the eagle, holding a stick under his arm.

'Oh dandy, fossilised shit,' Andy mumbled.

'Drop the side-arm and head up to my quarters,' the officer said.

Andy quickly stared back at me, but didn't lower the pistol; instead, his fingers re-gripped it. The officer smacked the cane into his own palm.

'Do I have to ask twice, Sergeant Graham? Do you want me to remove you?'

With the air stifling with anticipation, Andy uncocked the pistol, swung it down, abruptly holstering it. I let out a small sigh of relief.

'Yes, Mullen,' Andy said.

'You can address me as Lieutenant. My office, now,' Mullen barked. 'Peter, please give me quarter of an hour with Graham, and then please come and see me,' he said politely.

I nodded an acknowledgment, and then watched them march to the end of the hangar. Andy slammed the door behind him. Benny barged my shoulder and made his way past.

'What's up with Benny?' I said.

'Leave him to simmer down, Johnny,' Blondie said. 'I will go check on him.'

I held Blondie's arm back. 'Thanks, dude, but you're a dickhead for putting yourself in front like that.'

Blondie frowned inquisitively, then he smiled. 'Dickhead?' He scoffed. 'Andrew would not have pulled the trigger.'

'I think you're blinded by faith on that one, Blondie.'

'The Lord may work in mysterious ways, but Andrew is as protective over his men as the Lord is as protective over you and I.'

CHAPTER FOURTEEN

The hum around the place wasn't as friendly as when I had first walked in. Between the muttering and the blokes going silent when I strolled near them, I tried to keep the cold stares out of focus. I moved towards the piled kit at the rear of the hangar. There was a lovely smell of oil in the air. On one of the crates near the back was the iconic Bren, set out on its bi-pod; it was brand new. I fiddled with the trigger and then put my fingers in where the mag went. On the next crate I lifted one of the lids that wasn't nailed down. Inside were freshly made Sten guns, a film of grease on the holed barrel. Further wooden boxes, all serial marked, were stacked high. I was tempted to open more.

Looking at the back of the heads of some of these young men playing cards or reading, I wondered how many would be joining me and Blondie. I doubted Andy would be allowed to stay on the airfield. If I had expected him to pull a pistol and possibly kill either me or Blondie, then I wouldn't have wound him up so much. It now appeared a lot of people thought highly of him.

The harmonica started playing, taking my mind off the issue. A young man in a blue baggy boiler suit came from behind a pile of boxes, checking off the numbers as he did. He glanced at me, but then looked back at his clipboard.

'All right?' I said, trying to make at least one mate.

'Shhh.'

He went back to checking the list. I walked around the back of him to see what was on his clipboard, but he held it to his chest. He moved away over to the next crate stack, tapping his boot on the bottom one. Tutting, he shook his head, his perfectly gelled black hair not moving, but ash dropped from his fag.

'What's your name?' I asked.

He sighed. 'Word is spreadin' around about you bein' a spy and all that.'

'Do I look like a fucking German spy? It's like me saying you're Scottish instead of a Londoner.'

'Known for gettin' a few fings.' He exaggerated his wink at me.

'Don't tell me, your minder is Terry McCann.'

'No. The trouble and strife keeps me in check,' he said seriously, smoke puffing out from the corner of his mouth.

'So, what's your name?' I asked again.

'Richard Mead.'

'Big arsenal of weapons in here. This is going to be some mission.'

Richard put his fag out on the crate and stuck the butt behind his ear. 'Listen, me old china, I ain't supposed to tell ya this, but this ain't earmarked for the likes of you.'

'What do you mean?'

Richard came close and shiftily said, 'I can't give ya the brass tacks, me china, but you and the raidin' party are at the bottom of me list. However, with the right amount of bread and honey, I could see ya gets some stuff.' He rubbed together his thumb and index finger.

'Are you saying that none of this fucking stock is for us?'

'Don't get yourself in a two and eight, but you ain't 'avin' any of these men either. It's gonna be a right load of pony for you lot... unless.' He rubbed more vigorously. 'Couple of Lady Godivas might help ya.'

'Is that so?' I said. 'Well shove it up your bottle and glass, you slimy Hampton Wick. I'll come and half-inch what I want. Now, where's Lieutenant Mullen's office?'

I wasn't sure if he was a little taken back because I knew my cockney rhyming slang, as me and Will used to have a right laugh over it, or if he thought I was going to tell Mullen about him. Richard brushed the front of his overalls down where I had pushed him, looking me up and down in disgust.

'Gordon Bennett, me old china, no need to get ya Isle of Wight's in a twist. I was just tryin' to 'elp. Through the door and up the apples.'

That's another friend made, I thought, and sighed.

Just before I knocked on the office door, I put my ear to it. I was a little disappointed that I hadn't heard Andy getting a bollocking. My knuckles hadn't quite reached the door when I thought: what am I doing? What is the reason I need to go on this mission? Will I find a route back to 2015? Should I just steal a vehicle and head back to Newquay? I stood there for a little while, contemplating it further.

As soon as I had knocked, I was asked to enter. Mullen was speedily folding maps and shoving them in his desk drawers. His bald head and pips caught the reflection off the single lightbulb above. It wasn't like McLachlan's office in Washington DC. Apart from a photo of King George IV and another of Winston Churchill, his office was bland. I stood at the desk waiting whilst he removed his holster and peaked cap. He hung his jacket on a coat-stand, his green shirt neatly pressed. He was a little chubbier and had stubble, compared to those skinny clean-shaven blokes I'd met so far.

Loosening off his green tie and undoing his top button, he then thrust his hand out, leaning forward. I shook his firm handshake, but released quickly from earlier cuts.

'Sorry, old chap, been one of those bloody mornings. I am Lieutenant Mullen, but as this is an informal occasion, please, call me James.'

'Same name as your son, almost. I bet that's caused some problems around here.'

'Far from it, Peter. Please, take a seat. About saving Jameson's life. I owe you... my wife and I owe you... a lot of people owe you a big plate of gratitude. Yes, he will never fly again, and will complain for years about losing his leg, but without your heroic actions, he would have...' James cleared his throat as he'd clammed up. 'Anyway, thank you.'

'No worries. I hope both pilots receive the care and counselling they deserve.'

'Err... yes, quite,' he said, puzzled. 'Now, how about a drink to celebrate?'

Blimey, this is informal, I thought. 'Is it a pint of that black goo?' I pulled a grim expression.

'I am not sure what that is, Peter, but I have a reserve for a special occasion.'

James pulled open the drawer to his right and then placed two tin cups and a single water bottle on the green-leathered inlay table.

'Don't tell me that's water in there,' I joked.

'Better. It is camel piss.'

He poured out the two glasses, similar to brandy, and he handed one to me. He took a large sip, scowling after.

'Fuck,' he said.

'This isn't going on my résumé, is it? I'm already a German spy, and I don't want to be known as an alcoholic as well.'

'No. Records of this meeting are not being compiled. Top secret, old bean.'

After downing mine, it left an after-taste that I couldn't quite get my head around. James laughed at the reaction on my face.

'What the fuck is that?' I wheezed.

'Surprised you do not remember. Suki... remember now?'

'I bloody will now as it tastes like...erm... more like goat's piss than camel's piss. I fucking hate it.' I put the tin cup in front of him, nodding for some more.

He leant forward and topped it up. 'Good man.'

'I also hate goats,' I admitted.

'Why?'

'The Middle-East are training them to sniff out Special Forces.'

James laughed. 'Well, they will never be invading our country with their goats.'

I scoffed.

'Enjoy your red wine and rum. Cheers,' he said.

Yeah, cheers.'

'You are now in charge of this mission. Anything you need, and I mean anything, you come and ask me. I will see to it.'

'What do you mean, "now in charge"?'

'Put your feet up, Peter.'

I lowered the cup, trying not to screw my face, then put my feet on the table, like him.

'Sergeant Graham has been RTU'd,' he continued.

'I don't think that's wise, James.'

'I have every bit of confidence in you. Your modesty in your outstanding record of accomplishment with the regiment is what I have been warned of. You, my dear fellow, are the right man, the only man, to lead the Special Raiding Squad.'

'I don't really give a flying fuck for your opinion as you hardly know me.'

James spluttered his drink. 'Just like Paddy.'

'Paddy who?'

He smiled. 'Only a few are not scared of big old Paddy Mayne.'

James poured the last of the suki into my cup, clinked his mug on it and then he pushed it my way. Looking more serious, he took his feet off the table and said it was about time I knew the mission I had agreed to. I didn't remember agreeing to it.

I was to lead thirteen men in three groups to parachute behind enemy lines: slightly west of Bayeux, France. When I asked why we could not all parachute in one plane, I was told putting all eggs in one basket would jeopardise the mission if that plane was shot down or malfunctioned over the sea. I now wished I'd never asked. One of the three squads had to succeed before Operation Neptune could take place. Once we had all met at the rendezvous point, the first squad led by Lieutenant Peter Weaver would stay hidden, the plan being as a reserve squad, or to attack any German troops who may give chase on our withdrawal. Weaver would have mortar and airburst shells at his disposal. The other squad, led by Captain Martin McConnell, would seek and destroy a bomb dump.

I was to lead the remaining squad to a secret German communications building to destroy all the equipment. This was the highest priority. Any member of any squad had to abort the orders if their mission was compromised. They had to sabotage the radar communications. One point James had mentioned went against my morals: any injured or dead member was to be left; in James' words, "Keep going and finish the job, no matter what." James told me not to return to the Normandy beach, and repeated the point.

With the missions briefing finished, I sat back whilst my mind churned over the details. James sat back and waited for my questions.

'Operation Neptune, you mean D-day?' I asked.

'Yes, this is a combat attack. The more you make the Jerries battle-worn, then the more British and allied forces will survive. There will be no time to bed down for the night.'

I sharply inhaled, then exhaled. 'Fuck me. This is going to get messy. And the thirteen men, does this now mean twelve as Andy has been binned?'

'Your maths is very good.'

'What are the plans to get us out once we've done the business?'

'Can you elaborate on "the business"?'

'Yes, mallet the fuckers and destroy everything.'

'After you have done the business, you head back to the rendezvous.'

'Then what?'

'Hide there until you are found. I trust you have the ability to scarper and hide if the rendezvous is compromised. It will be every man for himself.'

'Found by who?'

'An LR group will pick you up and support you to find French, British, or US troops holed up in the fight.'

'What transport do we have?' I asked.

'None. You are on foot.' He opened the left drawer next to him. 'I want you to study these maps. The positions are marked. You will all receive a copy.'

Taking it from him, he then handed me a few black and white aerial photos of the area. I quickly scanned through them.

'Is this it?' I asked. 'There's nothing but forests, fields, ditches, and the odd building.'

'This was the only reconnaissance pilot to make it back. Think yourself lucky we have these.'

With the photos and maps laid out on the table, James went over the marked positions where the strategic targets were meant to be, and then the best area for the LZ. The bomb dump didn't look like an ammunition holding, and the suspected communications was outlined marked as a field. I mocked the photo of the field, saying there was nothing fucking there except maybe the odd hiding wood mouse. James laughed, then showed me the five tiny dots on the photo, believed to be sentry towers and a mast. It was my turn to mock, but I soon stopped when he told me that a recent raiding squad of six 1-SAS were killed before they had even got near it.

Remembering what the cockney inventory bloke had said about not having the stocked weapons or soldiers, I asked for a list of all the weapons and kit that had been put aside. However, I was informed I would see the inventory at the next meeting; also, where I would meet the other squad members. I quizzed him further on what type of weapons and explosives were ready for us, but he stayed silent. Rather than trying to flog a dead horse, I decided to learn about the new members. The only information James would divulge was that the band of men, who would be under my command, were a new bunch of recruits that had recently passed selection. All had a pedigree background from another tough unit, but none of them had been behind German lines, but then neither had I.

A new song played out and I found it difficult not to tap my hands and feet whilst studying the maps and photos. The phone rang, taking James' confused stare off me as I had started to sing the words. Why the hell was Adamski-Killer playing? I tried to concentrate on what James was saying on the phone, guessing he was speaking to a senior rank. James put the black receiver down and grinned at me.

'What?' I asked.

'That was your old chum, Anders. Said he cannot wait to meet you.'

I stopped jigging. This was going to be impossible to blag as he was going to see I wasn't Skedgewell. I'd already be accused of being a spy. Shit.

'What's wrong?' James asked.

'When's he going to be here?'

'Anders, Roy Farran, and Paddy Mayne will arrive tomorrow morning. They have to sort their own missions out with two and 1-SAS. You do not look pleased. In fact, old chap, you have gone white. You know all three, therefore it should not be a problem. I do not believe there is any rivalry, well, except the healthy type.'

Fuck; three of them, I thought. Should I tell James the real story? 'Listen, James, I've been through a lot, as you know.'

'Bloody miracle.'

'To be honest... erm... look...'

'What is it, Peter? Spit it out, young man.' He searched my face. 'Peter, look at me. Whatever is troubling you, you can tell me. My gratitude for saving my son's life is beyond my words.'

I sat firmly still and looked him in the eyes. Do I tell him? I thought.

CHAPTER FIFTEEN

I asked James to sit back down in his chair. He first looked at his watch, tutted, and then did so. My chest was burning; I put it down to the suki.

'I can't remember my past, well, apart from a few recollections,' I lied, trying to look sorrowful. 'I've been on a hell of a journey, and apparently the medication and the PTS... the shellshock, has robbed me of the events.'

'And you want me to tell you what happened.'

'Yes,' I cried out. 'Nobody has told me.'

'I can inform you what happened leading up to the attack and where you were found, but we have no information on what happened to you in between. Only you know that, Peter.'

He opened another drawer and pulled out a bottle of single malt Old Taylor whiskey. I sat forward and he added a small measure to my tin cup.

'Just the one,' he said. 'We are not rolling out the barrel on this. I think you might need it.'

I drank a tiny sip, keenly ready to listen. At last, who was Peter Skedgewell?

'After succeeding the SAS from the commandos, you were assigned with L-detachment on a mission in the bluey to...'

'A what?' I asked.

'Bloody hell, Pete, I have not the time to remind you of every slang word. L-detachment, organised by the Phantom Major himself, ran into some trouble across the North African *desert.*'

'Sorry to ask, but who is the Phantom Major?'

James sighed. 'Woe is me,' he muttered, and looked at his watch. 'David Stirling. Now do you now remember his nickname from the Jerries. Splendid. Now let us move on. The SRS must have been compromised, as the Luftwaffe had sent out two Messerschmitt to seek and destroy. The aftermath of the strafing runs was desperate, to say the least. Many were killed. Amongst the pandemonium, you grabbed Welshy and lured the aircraft away by heading off in the jeep. Bravely you returned fire from the mounted Vickers. We now know from the intelligence office that one Messerschmitt had crash-landed. Returning that evening, those who were still uninjured helped you and Welshy assist those clinging on to life. The rest were mopped up. You buried them there.

'In the early hours of the morning you all fled back to safety in the two jeeps that had survived. But you came under attack from a long-range Jerry group. Outnumbered, with very little ammo and two further dead, you ordered those still alive to take the injured and flee on the jeeps. Welshy made it back with the others. He said the last thing he remembers is watching a red Very-light illuminate the marauding Jerry positions. Then he heard the furious firefight, turning back to see tracer rounds lighting across the blue.'

James gulped down his whiskey and then poured himself another, but not me.

'After the Hurricanes had made the area safe, our LRDG went out a month later. The Jerries had not collect their dead. Somehow, you did a fine job, mostly with frags. With no trace, we assumed you had been killed and swallowed by the moving sands, or escaped, becoming lost at your peril.'

'What about being captured?' I asked, tapping my empty cup on the table.

'You have obviously forgotten the Kommando Order issued by the Führer.'

I stayed silent, nodding at my cup.

'All saboteurs, whether in uniform or not, are to be shot. That will be the same rule for this mission, Pete, so remember it. By the way, your mate Welshy was shot on the next mission.' He looked at me to see if he had stirred any memories.

'Did Welshy die?'

'I am afraid so, Pete.'

'Did he get a medal?' I said, waving a finger at my cup.

'Err... I am not sure.' He looked a bit embarrassed.

I leant forward and poured myself a drink. 'Where did you find me?'

'Headquarters received a telegram saying a Peter Skedgewell had been found in a hospital in Malta. You had been looked after there for two years. With no dog-tags or military clothing, the only ID was the watch.

Fortunately, the British had left a few military personnel to guard the docks. By chance, one of the chaps broke his leg falling from a crane. It was him who started the process after seeing your engraved military watch. We did send one of the troop out to identify you, but he said you were in such a bad way that it was hard to tell. How you received so many gunshot wounds, broken bones, severe lacerations, and a fever to top it all, is anyone's guess. I am amazed the hyperthermia, hypothermia, or dehydration didn't kill you first.'

'Must have been trained by the best, but not the SAS, the SBS,' I said, making light of it.

'Ah, the camaraderie between two rivals. I see your survival as a phenomenon. One day when your memory does return, make sure you come and tell me, for the history books of this regiment.'

Still baffled as to how I had got from the jungle to here, I asked, 'What happened next?'

'Six months later you ended up in the Cambridge in Aldershot. The nurses have done a splendid job over the eight months rehabilitating you. I can reiterate, it is a miracle from God. I even believe that you were sent here to save my son and Wing Leader Ernest Sayers.'

Wanting to tie lose ends, I said, 'What about my family?'

'In time I am sure you will remember. However, for now let me say you were an unwanted orphan. You had gone through a troubled life, until you were fostered.

'Is that who Ray and Dot are, my foster parents?'

'Yes, Raymond and Dorothy. And how you have come through after your dead foster...' He stopped and grimaced.

'It's OK.' I pretended to appear disheartened.

'You saved a lot of chaps in the blue.'

'I was just doing my job. Anyone would...'

'Job?' he butted in. 'Do not let Sergeant Graham hear you say that. It is about protecting Great Britain from any invading country. You know what the Germans will do to his lad if they invade?'

I paused for thought. 'Why just his son?'

'His boy has a mental problem, you know, the ugly type one. I think a few call it mongrel. Andrew has done well to bring him up. He will fight till the ends of the earth to protect him, especially from the Jerries. I only met ...'

'You mean Down Syndrome? Anyone that called my kid ugly or a mongrel wouldn't fucking see the light of day for a fucking long time. What's wrong with this fucking society? It's not a fucking problem.'

'Peter, calm down. I meant nothing by that. You are acting the nuisance like Graham.'

I stood and put my fists on the table and said, 'I want Sarge back. I don't want him to be returned for something I started.'

'What do you mean, started?'

'I didn't realise he was so patriotic and was a single parent bringing up a Downs son. I have kind of been pressing his buttons, and him thumping mine.'

James frowned. 'Pressing buttons? Never heard of that saying.'

'It's slang I picked up in hospital in Malta. It means creating a very strong emotional reaction in someone.'

'Oh… but where are the buttons?'

'Look, it doesn't matter. I would rather have him by my side on this mission.'

'I am afraid it is…'

'You said anything, right?'

'Yes, I did, but he has become more than a nuisance. In fact, I would say his troubles have now obscured his mind.'

'He has big bollocks, sometimes needed for the job. Yeah, he can be a wanker at times, but we can all be, sometimes. Plus, if it goes noisy or tits-up, I know he won't cower.'

'What strange words…'

'If he isn't in the squad, then you can fucking return me.'

Leaning forward, I slowly placed the empty cup in front of him, not releasing my glare. James slowly nodded his head.

'They told me you were uncouth, and that you do not really care for us officers. I think you said we were, "stick-in-the-mud toffs". I believe you are perfect for the position.'

'Well don't be a fossil shit, and agree it. Get him back.'

James smugly smiled as if he had known I would ask for Andy's return. He reached over and picked the large black receiver off the telephone base. He then dialled a number. I found it amusing watching the dial slowly return. After a quick impetuous ordering, he replaced the receiver, pushing the telephone away from him.

'Done,' he said. 'Is there anything else? I am a bit pressed for time.'

'Have you ever thought about fitting magnified scopes on all your main rifles? Or night-vision goggles that can pick out a laser beam from your main weapon?'

James put his fingers together under his nose, clearly thinking; I became excited by the look on his face.

'What about a camera that could pick out thermal heat source?' I continued. 'Imagine a sniper rifle that could fire a round eleven hundred metres. Or a missile that could follow a laser-guided sight from a man hidden in the field.'

'Or send a man to the moon and back?' he said, and smirked.

'Yes, it has… I mean, it will happen in nineteen sixty-nine.'

'Hmmm. OK, Pete, time for you to go. I have other more important duties to carry out.'

'I've got so many other ideas that will help.'

'I hope we can pick up the conversation if you return as I am keen to hear more. Just be careful who you tell. Some already think you are covertly, no, blatantly working for the Jerries. I mean, is that where you were all this time?'

'Oh yeah, having a few pints of Heineken with Hitler over lunch of bratwurst. Don't be such a bellend.'

'Is that one of your slang words from Malta? What does it mean?' he said.

'It's a church bell thing. Ask Private Saxton.' I tried hide my enjoyment.

'I will. Now, I need you to find Captain Martin McConnell. He will show you to your bunks. Get changed and go and find intelligence officer Krycler. Ask him to brief you further on all the mission details. Meet me at seventeen hundred hours in Hangar-2. Dismissed.'

'I need one more favour… please?'

'No. Dismissed, Skedgewell.'

'I didn't hand the pistol to your son or leave him to burn,' I said, crossing the line.

James glared at me with immense hatred, but then he scoffed. 'I think I know why Lassen wants you back. What is it?'

'I can't meet Paddy, Farran, or Lassen. It might, no, it will provoke my stored-away damning memories of the blue. If that happens, I won't be focused on this mission. I'll end up at the Royal Victoria Netley Hospital with Spitfire fuel pumped through my veins, or my bollocks wired up with electrodes.'

'Do you know how hard that will be?'

'Do you know how important the success of Operation Neptune is?'

'I will do my best, Pete. Now fuck off.'

'I like you, Mullen,' I said.

Shutting the door behind me, I thumped the air. With a little spring in my step, I headed back downstairs and found the cockney. I asked Richard where I would find Captain Martin McConnell. He frostily told me that Martin had a worse humour than mine, and Martin was in the bunkhouse. Before I left, I asked Richard where all the soldiers had gone. Most of them were billeted in the local village because the missions had been stood down due to the weather. Brilliant, a local pub, I thought.

Once I had found the correct corrugated-roofed domed building, I opened the green metal door and wandered in. With only a ceiling fan for decent air circulation, it was hot and musty in here. Seven empty pairs of metal bunk-beds lined the windowless curved walls. The thought of sleeping off the alcohol was inviting. Except for one bed, the rest were laden with kit-bags. Where was everyone? At the end of the building was a door, so I followed the wet boot prints over to it. I knocked, which was unlike me, but something didn't feel right. The dull pain to the right side of my forehead started, something I've not felt since whatever it was I was in. I tapped on the door again.

'Captain McConnell?' I asked.

The door swung open to a stocky, tanned, young bloke.

'Captain McConnell?'

'It is very nice to have met you,' he said drolly. 'Your music beats keep up with Beethoven in my mind.'

'What music? Or did you mean the beeping noise?'

'Your door knocking,' he said, with a deadpan face. 'Lovely tune.'

'What's your bloody name?'

'Do you have a harder question? That one I know,' he answered slowly and seriously.

'Are you taking the fucking piss? I don't suffer fools.'

'I like your shirt.'

'What?' I looked down at it. 'You're fucking nuts. Right, are...'

'No, no, no, thank you,' he interrupted.

'Huh?'

He boomed with laughter as if I had told him a funny joke, then stopped dead. 'My name is Martin McConnell, that is if you were still unsure,' he said in a monotone voice.

I sighed. 'I've been told by Mullen to meet you for new clothes and to show me my digs.'

'What strange words you conjure up. I have been ordered to show you to this seat.'

'Oh yeah, and who was that?' I said, thinking it may be Lassen, Mayne, or Farran that could have arrived early.

He slowly exaggerated showing me the chair behind a desk. I walked past him, keeping a wide berth, then sat down on the metal folding chair. On the table was a comic. I turned it over to see the front.

'Superman,' I said.

'I have other hobbies... Captain America... friendships... killing.'

Smirking at what he'd said, I studied the number twenty-three edition with Superman swimming in the crosshairs of a German U-boat. It felt as if a bit of normality had returned: a superhero from my era. I began to flick through the pages. Martin just stared.

'Where did you get this?' I asked.

'It was not off the two Grossdeutsches Nazis on the front. Do you know them? Oh dear, I am letting your secret out,' he said oddly.

'You've been hanging around with the sarge a little too long. I'm not a spy.'

'Curiosity killed the cat, but for a while, I was to blame.'

Martin didn't show even the tiniest bit of facial expression, and then he did a bow like a geisha girl and backed out the door, clumsily closing it with his foot.

I sat there half-amused, half-baffled, as to what he was all about. Was he on drugs? Did they have weed back in 1944? Maybe he'd had too much suki. He did appear to speak very slowly, almost a slur at times. He was muscular, broad, with a shaven head and wide jawline, like the actor Matt Damon.

Whilst waiting for the mystery guest, I took off my muddy shoes and rank ripped shirt. I had forgotten about the packet of cigarettes, so I threw them on the table. Sitting in the pure silence, I had begun to get impatient, the heat not helping. Just as I sighed again, a door slammed, dust off the single lightbulb floated down. Footsteps became louder, more than one person. Low voices murmured. Unsure why the beeping and headache were increasing, I was then startled when the room's light bulb went out. The dull pain to my forehead was now bulging. I slightly leant back in the chair as a very tall, muscular bloke had stood in the doorway, silhouetted by the light from behind. A further two heads appeared to the side of his broad shoulders. This huge bloke slapped an object in his other hand.

'Time to kill me a spy,' he said in a deep Scottish accent.

'Planet,' I shrieked.

Gasping for breath, I stood and shoved the chair back, but I fell over it. The beeping increased to its highest rate yet, my eyesight becoming blurred. Gripping my chest, I started to shake in a mess on the floor. With the gloomy corner of the room turning white, the beeping noise became one continuous high-pitched piercing tone. I was suffocating. A shocking agony surged through my body. I tried to yell out in pain, but heard nothing. Another powerful spasm contorted my body. Then there was relief as the pain subsided. Through the white blurred image, someone came into view. The beeping began to slow. A muffled voice called out my name. Mum, is that you? I didn't know if I'd said it or thought it. The person disappeared, the white slowly gave way to an inky-black.

In the background, voices were arguing about how I wasn't supposed to have been beaten up. I slightly opened my eyes, head resting on my folded arms. The light was on, my breath formed a dampness against the table. The Scottish voice was identical to that of my fallen mate: Robert Archibald. I tuned into the other two. They were my dead squad members: Tony Fisher and Gary Harding. The hairs stood up on my arms. No, they were dead, I was wrong. No, I want it to be them, I argued back. But why were they here? Perhaps I will look up and see that I'm back in 2015. No, they were dead then. Then it struck me: I would open my eyes to see myself somewhere in 2013. I had blacked out after the Chinook crash; the rest had been a dream; they had been alive all this time. I sneered at the thought that since the crash, my life had been a dream. The room had gone quiet; my mocking had alerted them.

CHAPTER SIXTEEN

Martin was ordered to go and find Sergeant Graham. I peeked up over my forearms and first eyed my old mate, Gary. My heart fluttered whilst my stomach did somersaults. He was how I remembered him, except a little less rugged. He still looked a brute you really wouldn't want to mess with. Although only five foot ten, he was poking my best friend, Rob, in the chest, ranting at him. I smirked, having remembered Gary was brutal in unarmed combat. However, prodding the colossal Rob was lunacy. This argument, and seeing his stocky stature with a large almost overhanging forehead, flat nose, and intimidating eyes, proved Gary had not changed.

The wonderful idiosyncratic sound of the Spitfire retuned overhead. I hoped those brave men had all made it back. Lifting my head further, I then sat back and folded my arms. I was covered in sweat. Tony was reading a book: *The Constitutional History of Modern Britain 1485 – 1937*. He was still as handsome as ever. Overwhelmed with emotion, I just wanted to get up and embrace them. They needed to know I had missed them.

'Here, lads,' Tony said, after looking up at me.

'See. I told ye I had not given him a heart attack,' Rob said, and backhanded Gary in the chest.

Gary picked up an iron bar from the floor and said, 'You may not be dead now, but you will if you do not spill the beans.'

Hearing their voices again brought a wave of relief and pleasure. I couldn't help but grin. Rob threw the German cigarette packet on the table. He smugly nodded at me as if they were mine, and I was a German spy.

'Look at him sitting there all gay. Maybe a stiff old whack to the head might wipe that smile off his face.'

'That's a bit homophobic, Gary,' I said.

Gary lowered the weapon and looked at Tony for some answers, but Tony just shrugged.

'Yes you, Gary Harding, from Hampshire. Ferocious in a firefight, bordering lunacy, but always the first to chip in at the bar, and always making sure your mates are OK.'

Tony and Rob turned to Gary, who looked bewildered.

'And you, Tony Fisher, from Dorset, who does nothing but read, almost a human encyclopaedia.'

Everyone faced Tony.

'You prefer brains over brawn,' I continued, 'and you use your high IQ and good-looking babyface to lure the ladies, of which you have notched up many. However, your downfall is the fact you can't handle your drink.'

Tony went to say something, but was speechless. He and Gary then turned to Rob, waiting for what I had to say about him.

'Lastly, Robert Archibald. At six foot ten you are an aggressive Scotsman from Darvel in East Ayrshire. The army is your life. You hate your Scottish heritage having the piss taken out of. You are very well respected by those around you.'

'See,' Gary blurted. 'The sergeant is correct: he is a spy. How would he know all that?'

'Perhaps he works with the British intelligence office,' Tony said.

Both looked at Rob for answers, or was it the deciding vote? I abruptly stood up, knocking over the chair. Simultaneously, they took a step back. Gary tightened his grip on the bar.

'Listen,' Gary said, snarling. 'We have knowledge of your kicking style fighting. I am going to smash your face in with this and then break your bones.'

'It is a form of fighting known in its earliest stage as Okinawa. Back in China in ...'

'Be quiet, Wordsworth,' Rob interrupted Tony. 'How did ye know where I lived, Skedgewell?'

'Actually, Tony,' I replied, ignoring Rob's question, 'my style is GKR Karate, founded in 1984 by Kancho Robert Sullivan. And that's a fucking shit nickname, Wordsworth. I prefer Fish.'

'I do not give a damn what you think. Let me just put a bullet in his head and leave him in an unmarked grave.'

'No, chaps,' Andy said, entering the stalemate.

'But, Sergeant, ye said...'

'I know what I said, Jock,' Andy interrupted, 'but that is an order.'

'Jock?' I said, and laughed. 'Is that the best nickname they can come up with?'

'I'll twist...'

'Ye fucking balls off,' I stopped him. 'I've heard it all before, Rob.'

Rob looked shocked. 'Are ye reading my mind, laddie?'

Just as I was about to answer, Blondie came skidding in, knocking into Gary; if looks could kill. Behind Blondie stood Benny. The atmosphere was now divided as Blondie and Benny had stood next to me. Benny picked up his German smokes, as he had called them, and made a point of telling me not to steal them again. I returned the smug look to Rob, proving they weren't mine. Now in the doorway stood Martin with a new young lad. More began to join them in the background.

'Right, lads, it's about time I told you who I am,' I said, trying to cut the tension. 'Let's go sit on the bunks with a brew.'

'We take our orders from the sergeant,' Tony said.

Wanting to keep Andy in the loop, I said, 'Sergeant Graham, do I have your permission?'

He acknowledged me with a tiny nod and said, 'I guess it would be proper to hear what Skedgewell has to say.'

'I bet that is a relief for the plucky little priest,' Gary said.

Everyone else laughed, except me, Benny, and Blondie. Benny held Blondie's arm as he went to remove his glasses. Andy caught my glare and, reading it correctly, Andy ordered everyone into the bunkhouse. With the room empty, Andy deliberately stood in the doorway.

'I do not want Private Garvey on this...'

'And I thought you were going to thank me, Sarge,' I interrupted. 'I don't want to hear another word about Benny from your lips. Got it? Good.'

Eleven young men, some of whom I had not been introduced to, were sat sharing the bunks. Andy eventually joined us, sitting next to Gary, who gave him a pat on the shoulder. Fetching the chair from the office, I placed it at the other end and sat down. I didn't really know where to start. Then an idea came to me whilst I looked around at the expectant faces: alcohol.

'Gary, who's missing?' I asked.

'Peter Weaver.'

'Go find him.'

'Bugger off, Skedgewell,' he said.

'Right, let's cut the fucking shit here. I've been put in charge of this mission. If you don't believe me, go and ask Lieutenant Mullen.'

They all turned and looked at Andy.

I continued, 'However, I need Andy, sorry, Sergeant Graham, to be my 2-IC.'

'A what?' one of the new blokes said.

'Second in command. And your name is?' I asked, but he didn't answer.

'It is true, chaps. Now do as your commanding officer says,' Andy ordered, without looking at me.

'Why do I have to find this fellow? I want to listen in,' Gary said.

'Stop your moaning,' I said. 'Whilst you're searching I want you to borrow some whisky or suki. I'm sure you could do that, as I know what you're like, Gary.'

Gary quickly made his way out of the door. I then asked each of the remaining blokes who had not been introduced to me to stand and make themselves known. First to stand was an athletic, tall bloke with cropped black hair and a moustache.

'Hello. My name is Corporal Charlton,' he said in a rich Devonshire accent. 'David 'Geordie' Charlton. I am from Somerset and joined the...'

'All right, Geordie, we don't want your whole life story,' I interrupted—a small murmur of laughter rose. 'At least you're more Geordie than Blondie over there.'

'Haddaway, man,' Blondie said.

'Right, in order as you go around the room.' I nodded at next bloke.

'Private Jeffrey Moline.'

'Nickname?' I asked.

'I don't have one, sir,' he said in a high-pitched but husky voice.

I tutted. 'Don't call me sir. Bear with whilst I think of one.'

I looked at his large forehead, dark bushy eyebrows, and wavy hair, trying to think of a character he reminded me of. I'd not done for that trait ages. I smirked when I thought back on Nico's and Ocker's wind-up name for me: Tom Hardy.

'I got it,' I said. 'Kauf. As in Andy Kaufman.'

Everyone looked stumped.

'Next,' I demanded.

'Gunner Scott 'Tommo' Tompkins,' he said proudly.

'Rifleman Stuart Crawford,' the next said half-heartedly.

I smirked at his concern of hearing his own nickname; the rest waited.

Apart from his round face, flecks of grey hair, and northern accent, I didn't have a lot to go on.

'I'll come back to you on that one, Crawford. And you?' I asked, pointing at the youngest.

'Private Alek Sagar,' he said quietly.

'Come out. I can't see you behind the man mountain,' I said.

Robert stood, his height towing over Alek as he came cautiously out like a kid about to be reprimanded. I cupped my hand behind my ear.

'Pardon?' I said.

'Private Alek 'Trigger' Sagar. Ready for duty,' he bellowed.

'Jesus,' I said—Blondie sighed. 'How old are you?'

'Nineteen,' he said, his voice deeper this time.

'Really? When were you born?'

Alek rubbed the bodged attempt that someone had made at a crewcut, thinking.

'Well?'

'Nineteen twenty-five.'

'Hmmm,' I said.

'I am ready to kill,' Alek said.

'What's with the name Trigger? Been down the Nags Head with Del Boy and Rodney?' I joked—nobody laughed.

'I am the best marksman by far,' he boasted.

'Can you even lift a rifle?' Benny mocked.

'I am not fucking scared. I will fight any of you men.'

'Sure,' I replied. 'When Gary gets back we'll all line up, and one by one you can beat the fuck out of us.'

Everyone mocked by laughing, except Alek, and Andy who had not showed any pleasure so far. Alek leant down and whipped something out of his sock, brandishing it around tip first. He reminded me of Kyle 'Chav' Slater in Operation Last Assault: fearless and full of enthusiasm.

'Who fucking dares to step forward, then?' he said.

Rob grabbed the young lad's wrist and held it high. Alek punched Rob in his stomach. However, unfazed, Rob's hand came around, almost whooshing as it did, and slapped Alek around his face. Then he turned Alek's wrist and ripped the knife away. Alek continued to fight back, so Rob threw him to the floor. Alek was straight to his feet with his hands up for a fight. It was comical to watch, in a weird way, but no doubt this young lad had plenty of throttled mettle.

Rob strode over to me and handed me the dagger. I studied the seven-inch double-edged blade and then tested the sharpness with my thumb. I gripped the heavy handle and waved it about. Alek was still as angry as a Pitbull having had his nuts yanked.

'Fairbairn fighting knife,' Tony said. 'Developed by William Fairbairn and Eric…'

'Trigger said his brother gave it to him before he went to do his duty again, but he never returned,' Rob spoke over the top of Fish.

'Killed loads of Germans and Italians that dagger,' Alek boasted, crooking his neck.

I walked over to him and presented the handle to him. 'Excellent. Make sure it's only the enemy you use it on, because if you fucking pull it again on any of us, every time you sit down after you will be reminded of the point.'

'If you poke the rattle snake, it will bite,' Alek countered.

I tapped him on the shoulder and said, 'Feisty fucker, but don't bring it to a firefight, use your rifle instead. Keep it for cutting your bacon and eggs. Welcome aboard. Fancy a new nickname? Chav?'

'No, I bloody do not.'

'Shame, Trigger,' I said.

'Let us get this party swinging. Pistol packin' mama,' Gary sang.

As Gary continued to dance with delight, he waved two bottles of whisky. Out from behind him walked someone new, his eyes a crystal-blue.

'Hello. I am Peter Weaver,' he said. 'Apologies for being late. I went for a good run.'

'Weaves,' I said, stunned.

'Err… yes. Who the devil are you? And it is Lieutenant Weaves.'

'This is the first in command,' Andy said to Peter.

Peter saluted. 'Sorry, sir.'

'We don't use that fossilised shit in here, do we Sarge,' I said—at last, a wry smile from him. 'Right, listen in. Gary, fill up everyone's mug. I'm just going to have a private chat with the lieutenant. I want you all to get to know each other's nicknames. We have, Geordie, Blondie, Fish, Planet…'

'Planet? It's Jock,' Rob interrupted.

'Not anymore.' I continued pointing at them. 'Benny, Tommo, Shrek…'

'What the bloody hell is Shrek?' Gary said.

'An infamous ugly, green ogre.'

Gary moodily took a step my way.

'But feared by many, tough as nails,' I added.

He relaxed and nodded in glory.

I then looked at Martin who was reading a Batman comic book. This one was proving hard. The rest of the group waited.

Still reading, Martin said, 'Why would a bat and a robin be friends?'

'Spike Milligan,' I murmured. 'Right, this is Spike.'

'Nocturnal versus daylight,' Spike continued. 'It would not work.'

'Anyway, moving on,' I said, staring at Andy—his eyes sharpened. 'Churchill,' I blurted.

Andy proudly nodded.

I continued to point. 'Kauf, Trigger, and finally... Stuart... Crawford. Erm... let me think on that.'

Crawford looked relieved.

Holding Weaves by the forearm, I led him into the back room. The others started chatting between themselves. I closed the door. After releasing him from my embrace, of which he had gone rigid, I thumped him on his arm. Weaves looked at his arm and then curiously at me.

'Weaves, it's me,' I said. 'Remember our chat in the Australian Bar? Actually, thinking about it, you wouldn't know.'

Weaves looked flummoxed.

'Then why are you here? Why would you meet me in the Australian Bar in Newquay? Is this why I have come back? To meet you?'

'Shall I get that?' he said apprehensively.

I took my hands off the table and looked up. 'Huh? Get what?'

'The knock at the door.'

There was a second knock.

'Yeah... yeah, sure,' I said, shaking my thoughts.

A young man saluted and then told me that I had to be with the intelligence officer in Block-D in ten minutes. Weaves asked how many spitfire pilots had returned, and was disheartened to find out that we had lost four. I thanked them both and asked them to leave the room. A few seconds later, I took in a sharp breath, mentally preparing for the bit I dreaded: telling the group who I really was.

CHAPTER SEVENTEEN

The burning whisky didn't settle the anxious moment. In turn, I looked at the eager faces. Blondie was rubbing the crucifix hung around his neck.

'Before I start, who believes in the God Almighty?' I asked.

Blondie was the first to thrust his hand up, appearing fit to burst with joy. A few of the others, a little apprehensive, slowly copied.

'Well, if you have any belief in this mysterious character, then you will have no problems in accepting me,' I said, grasping at straws.

'Does that mean you have faith in the Lord?' Blondie asked jubilantly.

'No. Load of bollocks.'

Blondie miserably lowered his hand.

'I'm not Peter Skedgewell,' I admitted.

Apart from Andy's groan, I waited for any other reactions. Benny and Blondie had already heard my news, but I was unsure how convinced they were. The quiet room was killing me.

'My real name is Johnny Vince,' I continued. 'I was in the SBS. However, I quit it, something that I deeply regret. Instead, I became a PMC. That's a private military contractor, a mercenary as some call it. Now here's the thing… I'm from the future.'

'Utter bollocks,' Andy yelled.

'I understand your scepticism, Churchill, but it's true.'

'You may be in charge, Skedgewell, but surely…'

'If you want to stay 2-IC, Churchill, then let me at least bloody finish,' I interrupted.

'Yeah, Churchill, let Vinnie finish, man,' Benny said.

From the look of things, Churchill was going to go into another rage at Benny. I took another sip of whisky and then quickly got their attention.

'I'm not sure why I am back here in 1944. In 2015, I was tasked by Will and Ocker for an easy mission in Sumatra. However, as per usual, trouble seemed to follow me, but this time I didn't want the action.'

'But that is seventy-one years of history gone by,' Fish said.

'What was the mission called? How did ye get back here?' Planet asked.

Churchill sighed and put his head in his hands; I couldn't quite understand his mumbling.

'Unlike Operation Blue Halo and Operation Last Assault, I didn't bother with a mission name. There was no need. Ocker had said it would be "a piece of piss.".'

'Who are Ocker and Will?' Kauf asked, still frowning.

'Ocker is an Australian pikey, and Will thinks he is a lookalike for the actor Will Smith.'

'What is a pikey?' Shrek asked.

'And what films has Will Smith been in?' Tommo questioned.

'Oh for heaven's sake.' Andy lifted his head from his hands. 'How can you be taken in by such trickery and deception?'

'Shut up, Churchill, before I make you,' Shrek snapped.

'You would not last one round with me, Harding.'

Shrek thumped his fist into his hand. 'Step outside, old man.'

'Lads… lads. Shut the fuck up. Now that's an order. I don't want to have another interruption off any of you. Got it?' I sighed.

'What he is saying to you right now is happening. It is what he is about to say next that is not,' Spike said.

Mentally cursing, I then wondered if this band of blokes with the mission ahead was some sort of punishment. Spike had returned to his comic.

'Thanks, Spike,' I said sarcastically. 'The Sumatra mission was tasked to track some poachers, and…' I stopped. 'No, no… No,' I said, waving my finger at Fish who was about to ask something. 'I became the hunted,' I continued, 'and after being shot, my nose broken, bitten, injured by splinters, and clawed by a tiger, I ended up jumping off a cliff to survive. Trapped by the rope with broken fingers and a busted head, I was suffering from blood loss and hypothermia. Basically, I was a dead man.'

Blondie thrust his hand up.

'If it's a question about did God intervene, put your fucking hand down,' I said—he did.

There was an air of disbelief rising, so I took off my sweaty nylon socks and trousers. Almost naked, I pointed at the scars.

'Look,' I said.

'I heard that your injuries were from fighting the Hun in the blue,' Churchill said.

'That's the story of Peter Skedgewell. For the very last time, Andy, I am Johnny Vince,' I fumed, the beeping increasing.

Andy glared.

Crawford, who had remained quiet, gingerly raised his hand. 'What happened after you died on the cliff?'

At last, someone with some sense, I thought. 'I don't think I did die. Well, I might have. All I remember is some weird blokes in masks carrying me, and bizarre lights and shapes. I guess now it was the mysterious tribe. When I awoke from whatever was happening, I was in the Cambridge Military Hospital in 1944.'

Crawford rubbed his chin—hopefully believing me.

'I know, mad hey? Well, that's it,' I said, massively relieved.

Planet was the first to raise his hand, whilst the rest of the group's cogs worked away. Then all the hands shot up, like kids desperate to give the answer to a teacher's question. I should have expected this, but hadn't. I gestured for them to lower their hands, like a teacher would. Yet, like naughty kids, they kept them up high.

'Look, lads, I am already late for a meeting with the snot-head.'

Trigger immaturely giggled. 'A what?'

'The intelligence officer,' I answered. 'Right, no more questions for now.'

Groaning, they all put their hands down, except Planet.

'This better be good, Rob,' I said.

'Ye said a lot of personal information about me, Gary, and Tony back in the office. How did ye know all that if ye were from the future?'

Churchill nodded his head in agreement as if I had been caught out. I had to tell the truth, but kept it short.

'Back in 2013, I was tasked to lead Operation Blue Halo with a bunch of SAS and SBS, but it went drastically wrong. The Chinook came under heavy fire.'

Kauf put his hand up, but spoke before I'd agreed, 'What is a Chin...'

'A big fucking helicopter,' I butted in. 'It had crash-landed with our RAF crew. You, Gary, and Tony were on board. Due to the skills of the pilots, I survived, along with one pilot, my rival, Roy 'Rabbit' Franklin. The rest of the escape and evade was hell.'

That was me done; time was ticking for this meeting. There were no more questions, which was good, as I was becoming emotional talking about the horrific crash.

'Why was he called Rabbit?' Tommo questioned, without putting his hand up.

I glared at him. He raised it. I ignored him. 'You've got all the info, so no more,' I said, voice wavering.

'How could we be onboard as we were not even born?' Planet asked.

'I don't know why you three have come back in time with me. I've not figured that out yet.'

'What happened to us?' Shrek asked.

Andy groaned, tilting his head back.

My eyes uncontrollably welled. I cleared my clammed throat. 'None of you made it, but I did try to save you guys.'

Blondie put a hand on my shoulder and said, 'Best you don these, Johnny.'

He handed me a neatly folded pile of army issue clothes. As I placed them on the floor, I tried to disguise wiping a tear; also, coughing into my hand, trying to hold it together.

'I have also left behind my mum and dad, brother, and good friends,' I said.

'Stiff upper lip, old chap. We all understand,' Blondie said, a little patronising. 'Now, go and get kitted up and see the snot-head,' he said, easing the situation.

'Cheers, Blondie,' I said quietly.

Stuart Saxton was turning out to be quite a rock, much like my blond-haired brother Oliver. Walking through the lads, I made no eye contact. It was a surprise how much emotion I still had bottled up about those tour events and losing my squad.

Whilst quickly getting dressed amongst the low chatter, Churchill came over and stood with his hands on his hips.

'My questions have not finished,' he said coldly. 'Very soon, I am sure these decent men will see you are a liar, as I do. I am not sure if you are a spy, a cad, or a lunatic, but I wish now I had left you in Aldershot.'

'Whereas, I now think you're a tremendous bloke, but slightly tainted by your strong patriotism and morals. But then, after losing your family and looking after a son with a genetic disorder, and as a single father, who wouldn't be?'

Churchill looked as if he was bubbling inside.

Not wanting to have a drawn-out argument and possibly another fight, I quickly made my way out of the dormer, not having a clue where the hangar was.

At the first overhang from a roof, I sheltered from the rain. To my shock, Tim had walked through the wooden door. He pulled his collars over the neck scarf. His face had become more wrinkled and he had lost his tanned complexion. He blew into his cupped hands, I noticed brown spots on them.

'Tim,' I said.

'Oh, hi, son. How's you?' His Irish-American twang wasn't so evident.

'I'm OK,' I lied. 'How are you finding the base?'

'Bloody freezing today.'

'You sound and look different.'

'Must be getting the British influenza, son.'

He pulled up the scarf around half of his face and then put his hands in his pockets. It wasn't that cold, but the awkward silence was. I thought of a way of catching him out.

'I've been put in charge by Colonel Mustard,' I said.

'I still like your humour, son. Are you sure it wasn't Miss Scarlet with the candlestick? I had heard James Mullen has put you in charge; congratulations. I must fly, son. You take care of yourself.'

'Where's Block-D?' I asked.

'Right here, son.'

Tim opened the door he had come from. Something didn't sit right with him, but I also had a good feeling about him; it confused me. Tim kept his eyes on me as I went through. I turned around to say goodbye, but he shut the door, his whistling fading away.

The warm air in here had a strange aroma, like a paraffin heater. The first brown door on my right had a sign: Simon Krycler Intelligence Officer. I went to knock, but then if he knew his onions, he would know it was me. I waltzed in. Simon looked up from his desk, pushed his glasses up his nose and then placed his measuring instrument down.

'I did not expect you to knock. I had been informed of your ways, Corporal Skedgewell,' he said. 'Cup of tea?'

'Do you know what, that would be a bloody great. I've not had a decent brew for... years.' I scoffed at the truth.

Simon went out the back. To me he looked very similar to the USSS agent Ronaldo Gomez, although a little younger. I thought it was best not to call him the nickname 'Jeremy', as I had Ronaldo.

Around the room on the walls were maps of France and Germany. Other rolled maps lay on oak desks. On each table was a pull-chain lamp. On top of one of the wooden sideboards was a strange machine. Closer inspection revealed ten dials each containing letters and a row of large buttons at the front, like those of a typewriter. It was too tempting not to touch.

'Leave that, Skedgewell,' Simon barked.

I whipped my hand away. 'What is it? Some sort of enigma machine?'

He handed me a china cup of milky tea and said, 'It is a Cryptanalysis. A paragon weapon of the war.'

'Ah, the only weapon to beat Superman. Someone really has to stop old Lex Luthor.' I laughed. 'And what's this contraption? A decoder?'

'No, that is a squeeze box. It was confiscated from one of your lot as it drove everyone insane.'

'What does it do?'

'Are you being a fool? It is an accordion.'

'Oh.'

I walked on to another strange upright machine. It had about a hundred dials set out in rows of ten; orange, red, green, and yellow. I looked around the rear to see loads of cables plugged into circuit boards. With Simon breathing down my neck, I dared not play with it, as hard as it was not to.

'Wow, this is cool,' I said.

'Please do not interfere with anything,' Simon grumbled.

'A bit high-tech for this year. What is it?'

'This is the latest Bombe. Please may we get down to the mission details,' he said anxiously.

'Like the ones in Bletchley Park? Did your lot get the German version from the U-boat?'

'How did you know about this? Have you been in the SIS?'

'No, I wasn't in MI5.'

'That name has not been made public. It is classified.'

I turned to boast about what I knew, but stopped as Simon was scribbling notes. I'd had enough of being labelled a spy.

'What the fuck are you doing?'

Simon whipped his book behind his back and said, 'Nothing, dear chap.'

'Is that right,' I said, knowing he was making notes on me. 'Write this down: Command Sergeant Major Timothy McNamara. He is your German spy.'

'Are you informing me you know this man?'

'Do you know him?'

'No.'

'His ways are slipping, so get him on your radar. Now let's stop with the trick questions and get down to the task.'

Simon slipped his notebook inside his tweed jacket pocket and then walked to a desk. On top was a map stretched out with paperweights on each corner.

'Bring your tea over here,' he said.

'I've a dairy intolerance, forgot to mention it,' I said, looking at what resembled a cup of Horlicks.

'What is a dairy…'

'Krycler. Is that a Jewish name?' I interrupted.

'That is correct, pronounced Crys-ler.' His eyes narrowed. 'Do you have a problem with Jews?'

'No. Do you want to smash the German motherfuckers as much as me?' I smiled.

'Yes, I was a precocious, solitary boy.'

I didn't want to go into what had happened to him or his family. I had probably seen more images than him, but only on photos and film.

Simon gave me a large magnifying glass whilst preparing the information. Pulling the lamp chain on and off a few times annoyed him, so I stopped. Over the next hour we studied what little maps and photos there were. I quizzed that he trusted some of the intelligence received from the undercover gypsies that roamed the area. Mocking further about all the telephone wires and copper transistors being stolen, that piss-take went down like a shit sandwich. We studied intercepted German codes and possible areas where the SS Panzer divisions would be located. The details of our objectives were very sketchy, including the answers to all my questions about number of guards, dogs, infantry, security, and armoured vehicles. Once the information had been locked and stored in my mind, I was handed three smaller scaled maps in clear plastic, and then informed each squad would only get one map—fucking ludicrous was my reaction.

The next stage whilst having a cup of black tea was the weaponry list. A flashback to Ocker and Kyle getting a boner in the ops room in Operation Last Assault made me chuckle, which didn't please Simon. My amusement was short-lived when I started reading the inventory. Finished, the Girl Guides would have been better tooled up. Seeing Simon chuffed with the inventory, I went into a rage, telling him he had to be at the next meeting with my men and Mullen. After seeing the band of SAS men and their arsenal in the hangar, we were being short-changed, no, robbed.

The good news: the mission had been stood down tonight due to bad weather. This gave me and the lads more time to prepare at least the basics. The bad news: this only left us tomorrow night for insertion. I now knew today was the fourth of June. Then the most damning update: the three Halifax bombers would have limited crew and no gunners. We would also not have an escort of Spitfires due to the loss this morning. I threw my toys out. Simon explained that all resources were on other missions, Operation Overlord using most of it.

Another genius diversion, as he'd called it, was Operation Titanic. This mission would see the deployment of five hundred dummy parachutists dropped, deceiving the one hundred thousand-strong German defenders into believing large forces were invading. The idea was to draw the enemy away from the main areas. I questioned why five hundred real troops couldn't be used as a dummy couldn't kill anyone and, once a few had been found, word would soon spread.

Simon quickly moved on to informing me that misleading information of false missions had been sent out, and had been intercepted by the Germans. Also, there would be a vast amount of French Paratroopers to assist in Operation Samwest. Furthermore, 1-SAS, B Squadron, would seek and hamper the 2nd SS Panzer and German reinforcements heading to the Normandy beaches in Operation Bulbasket. I had heard somewhere before about Bulbasket, but with all the new data coming in, my mind was fuzzy. What I did know was that I had this terrible gut feeling that I was to lead in inexperienced men with a lack of decent firepower, little intelligence, and no backup into an area swarming with heavily defending Germans. Were we just a decoy mission to draw the Germans away? Perhaps the real dummies. Had our mission details been purposely leaked?

As Simon piled copies of the details and maps, I thought on: was this why Skedgewell had been brought in, to use his experience? Maybe according to the records he was still missing in action. It was strange how I was put with a group of men who had never met me. Were these top SAS blokes, Lassen, Mayne, and Farran really visiting this airfield? Had Andy really been so much of a nuisance that he was to be killed off? Did Mullen know I would ask for Andy back? Was Mullen giving me the royalty treatment because he was in on it all? Could I really have anything at my means? Time to put it to the test, I thought.

'Right, Krycler, I want you and that cockney Richard Mead making the inventory list in Hangar-2 at 17.00 hrs. Got it?'

'By Jove, dear chap, that sort of request is not...'

'Listen, egg-head, if my request isn't met, then you can tell Mullen to return the lot of us. Or maybe put us in front of a firing squad, we would have more of a fucking chance.'

I grabbed the notes I had been making, and his that he had been writing on me, and then slammed the door behind me; Sarge style. Time to rally the troops.

CHAPTER EIGHTEEN

Slightly opening the dormer door, I eavesdropped on the mood, disheartened to hear everyone jovial and laughing. So, they didn't believe my story. But then, did it matter if I held their respect. Shutting the door behind me, I was confronted with most of them playing cards around Crawford's bed. A haze of smoke wafted around the ceiling fan. Tommo was on the closest top bunk staring at a poster. He whipped it down when he saw me.

'All right, Pete... oh, I mean... what do we call you?' Tommo asked— the rest looked on.

'You can all call me Vinnie, or boss. What you got there?'

Showing me a poster of a stunning woman posing in a black velvet dress, he said, 'She is a beaut. Would not stop a pig in an alley. They say she is coming to England next year. Reckon she will get hitched to me.' He kissed the poster.

'Yeah, but who is she?'

'You find your own woman, boss. Margie Stewart is mine.'

'Not if I get to her first,' Fish boasted.

'You carry on dreaming, Fish,' Tommo bantered.

'Right, listen in,' I said. 'I've just finished a meeting with Krycler, and it sucked.'

'He sucked what?' Kauf asked.

'Not going all homosexual on us, are you, Vinnie?' Benny said, and nudged Blondie.

'Not as gay as you bunch,' I said.

'Nothing wrong with gay rhythms, Vinnie,' Churchill said. 'I could do with some melodies.'

Shit me. That's the first time he had referred to me by my real name. Churchill put a hand behind his head on his pillow and took a long drag of his cigarette. Had he had too much whisky? Whatever it was, I hoped the contentious twat had disappeared and we could now get on.

'What time is it, Churchill?'

'The time is 15.50 hours. About time you disposed of that watch, Vinnie.'

'Thanks, Sergeant. Wake me in an hour.'

I made my way to the empty bunk at the end of the room. After kicking off my boots and socks, I laid my head on the hard white pillow, staring at the metal springs above. The green blanket itched my skin. It was nice to hear the light banter and card game continuing. With my eyes shut I visualised all the maps and photos, but it wasn't long before the slow beeping became louder than the atmosphere. I was exhausted, mentally mostly, and I yawned.

'Johnny... Johnny. Rise and shine, Johnny.'

'Fuck off, Blondie,' I said, rolling to my side. 'I'm trying to grab some sleep.'

'The meeting with Lieutenant Mullen started ten minutes ago.'

'What?' I yelled.

I quickly sat up, scraping my head on the metal frame above. The place was quiet. Observing the room, all were crashed out on whatever space they had found.

'Why the fuck didn't one of you wake me earlier, Blondie?'

'I am afraid to say they have all had too much alcohol.'

'And you?'

'Sorry, but I was reading the bible.'

'Help me get them up. Mullen will go nuts if we're late,' I said.

Quickly putting on my socks and boots, I rapidly tied the laces. Blondie went around and shook the lads. I tried to think if I'd had a dream, but couldn't remember. It was like I'd just shut my eyes for a few seconds. We were all late, no one was moving, my fretfulness levels rising. I went to the bunk opposite and ordered Shrek to get up, but he didn't respond. The chorus of snoring and heavy breathing continued to bounce off the corrugated walls. Blondie looked less worried than me, and he shrugged.

'Right you lot, get up,' I yelled—nothing. 'What the fuck are we going to do, Blondie?'

'We could ask the Lord for some divine intervention,' Blondie said, nudging my elbow with his bible. 'You know it will work.'

I was fit to burst, when I heard a small chuckle from close by. I snatched the bible and threw it at Trigger—on target. He lifted his face from his pillow, still laughing. The whole place erupted with laughter.

'Oh fuck off,' I said. 'Yeah, very funny, but I'm not praying. Best you lot get a bloody move on because we're late.'

'But it is only a quarter to five, Vinnie,' Weaves said.

I grabbed Blondie's arm and looked at his watch, and then said, 'Wankers. You know I'll get you lot back.'

'Right. Come on you 'orrible lot, let's be 'aving you,' Churchill said, impersonating Richard Mead—terrible.

Following Churchill on the way to Hangar-2, Shrek told us to wait a minute, and then he ran into Hangar-D, clutching the empty whisky bottles. He soon reappeared with a satisfied grin. Even though it had stopped raining, the clouds were getting darker. Churchill held the door open for me. Inside was cooler than the other buildings. The lights were off, some of the metal-framed windows had been blacked out. At the far end, light seeped under a door in the centre of a partition. As all the boots thudded and squeaked on the floor, a pungent smell hit me, burnt and rotting. Trigger was retching, and I turned to see what they were all viewing. At the very outer wall under an open metal-framed window were the charred remains of RAF heroes and a heap of plane wreckage. Churchill put himself between the carnage and Trigger to block the distressing sights, and then Churchill placed his arm around him.

The fourteen of us trundled through into the classroom without knocking, and then sat on the seats at the tables. In front of the oversized map on the wall sat Richard Mead and Simon Krycler, both appearing sheepish. The lads stared at them. I sat on the edge of the desk at the front of the class. Slowly, the adults turned to kids, until the headmaster, James Mullen, strolled in, a cane under his arm. He plonked down a pile of maps, photos, and notes next to a stack already on the table.

'Afternoon, chaps,' James said.

'Afternoon, sir,' the lads responded.

'As you know, Skedgewell has been put in...'

'It is Vinnie, sir,' Planet interrupted.

James glared through the peace. 'As you know, Skedgewell has been put in...'

'Who is Skedgewell?' Fish asked.

James smacked the cane on the table. 'One more outburst and that imbecile is demoted to their original unit.'

152

'Great. I always thought lady luck had a grudge against me,' Spike said sarcastically.

'Dismissed, Captain McConnell. We need some discipline in here.'

Spike lethargically stood up. Suddenly, the rest of the lads did, too. The pride ran through me. James turned to me with a slighter shade of red showing.

'They now prefer to use my nickname Vinnie,' I covered-up, and shrugged. 'Do you want me to address them?'

James snorted through his nose, then smiled. 'Your charm has worked. I told you, you were the right man for this mission, codenamed Operation Condor.'

'Sorry, James, but that operations name has been used in the Special Forces,' I bragged.

James turned to Krycler.

'It's no good looking at Simon for conformation as not even the SIS would know,' I said.

'Where would this have taken place?' Simon asked me, pen and paper ready.

'Afghanistan. We had to go in and destroy the force that had ambushed the Australian SAS.'

'What year?' Fish said, scribbling notes.

I looked at the faces of those stood in front of me, contemplating my answer. Did I continue the trust I'd built with them of who I really am? Or did I ruin my chances of running this operation with the likes of Mullen and Krycler by exposing about the future?

'I'll fill you in later, Fish, but for now, what's important is you all sit down and respect Lieutenant Mullen by shutting the fuck up.'

I winked at the lads, without letting those behind me see. James waited for them all to sit, and then he stood back around the front.

'Now, Skedgewell, known to you all as Vinnie, is leading Operation Condor. I will leave it to him to brief you.'

Was that it? I thought, as he sat back down.

First, I ordered Richard to fetch a round of coffee, then prepared my speech, 'Right, listen in, lads. All of you have been trained to a high standard, so I'm going to skip the pretence that I know more than you how to stay alive. However, it's my job to keep you lads living, so listen to me now, and in the field.'

Simon handed out the pens and paper. Whilst I waited, I got the photos and maps into order.

'I'm going to keep this brief as I want to do some weapons training,' I continued. 'And to be blunt, we haven't much intel to work with.'

'But we know how to use our weapons,' Trigger pipped up—the others mumbled their agreement.

'Trigger, are you fucking familiar with a Bren or a Vickers?' I said. 'And to strip it down and clean? If you are, when was the last time you trained hard with it?'

Trigger looked down at his blank paper, admitting his submission—the reality was: I needed a quick lesson.

'Planet, I see you nodded,' I said. 'Do you fucking know how to use every German, French, and Italian weapon?'

'No, Vinnie.'

'Crawford, you stupidly grinned in agreement. Do you fucking know how to drive the enemy's armoured vehicle and use it in an attack?'

'Sorry, boss.'

'The fucking firepower of us as a unit is reduced by every member not content with his weapon,' I said, finishing my rant. 'Simon, get me all the info on every enemy weapon and transport,' I ordered—Mullen answered Simon's stare with a nod. 'And whilst you're earning your wage, Simon, I want you to find me as many German weapons as you can. Are you fucking writing this down?'

He started making notes.

I now had everyone's attention and, more critically, the Head Shed was listening. I sat back and scrutinised the lads, thinking of a mission name. Richard was back with a tray and was now handing out the black coffee.

'This mission is called Operation Poppy Pride,' I said.

Ignoring the coughing from James to get my attention, I handed out a map in a plastic wallet to Shrek and Weaves, still cringing there were only three. With the identical map, I held up mine and began to talk about the 'ground': the area we would be dropped into. On the larger detailed map pinned to the backboard, I pointed out the layout. Once they had stopped taking notes, I moved onto the 'situation': the Germans and their allies that we would be up against, including what the enemy intentions were. I reiterated the 'Kommando rule'. As well as borders, I showed the towns and where friendlies could be reached. I repeated that we were not to head to the Normandy beach.

'I want you to know the area like the back of your hand, with or without the map,' I said. 'If you don't, you could die. Next, the 'mission': your mission is to deny the German's resupply and destroy their main communications.' I held up two aerial photos and waited whilst they all got theirs to the forefront. 'This is the ammunition store, and...'

'Don't you mean bomb dump,' James interrupted.

I sighed. 'This is the bomb dump, and this is the suspected area for the radio mast. Somewhere close by is the enemy communications bunker. Study the area well, in your sleep if you must. If not, you might die. The LZ will be this area. We will re-group here, the first RV.'

Showing the targets on the map again, I had to gesture to Churchill to put down his hand, but he kept it high. I knew he wanted to know the attachments and detachments, and who was in charge.

'A-squadron...'

'You cannot have A as it has been used,' James interrupted me. 'Or, B, D, and L detachment.'

He was grating on me, so I thought I'd take the piss, 'F-squadron will remain at the first rendezvous with a mortar and a heavy-machinegun. You know the defensive drill. U-squadron and K-squadron will take this route to the second RV.'

Repeating the positions on the map, I waited for them to spot the prank. Only Fish smiled to himself—FUK squads it is was then.

'Once in position,' I continued, 'we'll radio in with a sitrep. Two from F-squad will move up to the second RV with another heavy-machinegun.'

Whilst taking a break of coffee, I eyed Richard to make sure he was writing down every weapon I had spoken about. I waited for everyone else to finished making notes.

'U-squad will head to the bomb dump and observe, whilst K-squad move to the comms tower,' I said. 'Each squad confirms they're at the location. If our communications fail, we attack both targets dead on 00.00 hrs. Once the objectives are executed, return to the second RV. F-squad will cover the retreat. If anyone gets split, meet the remaining squads at the first RV. This becomes the ERV. We stay here and become a defensive group until its clear to move. What we need is three...' I stopped, having spotted Shrek drawing on his map. 'What the fuck are you doing, Shrek?'

He looked confused. 'I am marking the points on the map, Vinnie.'

'You fucking dickhead,' I raged—Shrek appeared ready to launch at me. 'If you get caught, you'll show all the points of attack and retreat. Have you forgotten your basic training? Fucking memorise it. Who else has marked their map?'

Shrek looked around, going red as the others took the piss out of him. He then snapped his pen, reckoning that was my neck he was thinking of.

'Simon, get this moron another,' I ordered. 'Right, 'enemy forces': the number of enemy is uncalculated, but there will be thousands in the area. We must remain undetected. If you can avoid a firefight, then do.'

'What happens if we cannot?' Tommo asked.

'Only if you are compromised as the enemy, shoot first, shoot straight, or you will die. Right, 'squads': Geordie, Trigger, Tommo, Crawford, and Weaves are in F-squadron. Spike, Benny, Shrek, and Kauf are U-squadron. That leaves me, Planet, Fish, Churchill, and Blondie in K-squadron. As for another detachments joining, it's just us. But remember, we are a killing force like no other.'

'I want to be in U-squad,' Churchill moaned.

'He can swap with me,' Shrek said. 'I do not want to be with Spike, he is suffering from madness.'

'I tend not to think about it too much,' Spike said.

'I can't have you with Benny, Churchill,' I argued.

'I only want to be in charge. Look after them all,' Churchill pleaded.

'No. Shrek, you are 1-IC of your squad, and, Weaves, you are 1-IC of yours. No questions.'

'That is an array of nicknames you have going on there,' James whispered. 'Have you got one for me?'

'Not quite yet,' I hushed back.

'Well, think of one soon, Skedgewell.'

'OK, 'commands': there are no higher or lower ranks between us, just those in charge who make the final decision. You all have an input. If command is lost, use your skills and discretion.'

The chatter between them increased, especially the objections from Churchill, Weaves, and Spike. I knew James would be beaming behind me. I looked at my watch, thinking of all the studying we still had to do.

'Oi,' I shouted. 'When I want your fucking opinions, I will ask.'

Everyone went quiet.

'Good. As I was about to say, until we are inserted and form into our squads, I will remain in command, until that time.'

'Yes, boss,' they all said.

'Lastly, 'signals': we synchronise our watches before, and at the RV. Each member has a handheld radio, and we set...'

'We only have four available,' Richard butted in.

'For fuck's sake,' I mumbled. 'Each squad sets the same channel. Any questions?'

'What happens if one of those who are in command gets killed?' Kauf asked.

'You do not go back for that man,' James barked.

'What?' I said, abruptly turning.

'You get on with the job. You leave that man where he is, come what may.'

'What happens if he is badly injured, sir?' Crawford asked.

'If that man hinders your progress, then you leave him with his sidearm. If he is close to death, then you end it for him. Now they are my orders, which by the way, overrule anyone else. Do you understand?'

'Yes, sir,' Churchill said, forthright—the others mumbled it.

'What happens to our bodies?' Blondie asked.

'The French SAS will mop up,' James said nonchalantly.

'What guns do we have, boss?' Trigger asked.

'Good lad,' I said, 'I'm glad you brought that up. According to Simon, we each have a Colt 45, and a further ten Sten sub-machineguns between us.'

Weaves stood, scraping his chair. 'But there are fourteen of us. That is barmy. We have no chance,' he said, gesticulating in dismay.

'What about all the crates of Thompsons and Brens in the hangar?' Benny yelled.

'If ye think I am going without a Vickers or Bren, then bollocks, think again,' Planet boomed.

It wasn't long before everyone was shouting. I looked at Richard, seeming to have shrunk. James looked uncomfortable. I bellowed above the racket, asking everyone to quieten down.

'I totally agree with you lot,' I said. 'I'm not a pistol lover, especially as a back-up weapon. We're not here doing the circuit or some undercover work in a pub. If you want your chances of staying alive higher, you need another rifle or a light-machinegun. Or for close quarters, a sub or a shotgun.'

The approving became loudly vocalised. I faced Simon and Richard, then James, gesturing for all of them to listen to the lads' response.

'Unless you want a mutiny on your hands, then I would take note,' I said softly.

James looked at the lads' harsh faces and said, 'Agreed.'

I covered my mouth with my hand and whispered, 'We should have been fucking armed to the teeth in the first place.' I smiled back at the lads. 'Right, Churchill, get a list of everything we need.'

'Right away, boss,' he replied, excited.

'James, I know that we can't get an escort of fighter planes in, but what about parachuting three jeeps in first before we jump?'

'I am sorry, Skedgewell, but some things are out of my hands. We have no jeeps here, let alone any rigging and parachutes left.'

'Can't we steal a few from another mission?' I asked.

'No. And that is the final word on the matter.'

'Sir, what about if we get the French SAS to leave three at the first rendezvous,' Churchill said. 'We could make a great escape.'

'Bloody champion suggestion,' Blondie said, returning to his thick Newcastle accent.

'Sergeant Graham, you know how dangerous that would be,' James said. 'Then there is the time to get the message out.'

'You could make communication with the French SAS, Intelligence Officer Krycler. It's what you are paid for.' I gave him an icy glare.

'Well... yes. I suppose I could make contact... at least.'

'That's the spirit, Krycler,' I said.

'What about the mines, boss?' Tommo asked.

'I have always wondered why people were worried about mines, but then it hit me,' Spike said.

All the lads began groaning and laughing, resulting in throwing stuff at Spike, who sat there deadpan.

'Steady on, chaps. Now stop larking around,' James said.

'We don't go unless we have three armed jeeps,' I said.

James sighed. 'See to it, Simon,' he ordered. 'Lance Corporal Mead, please hand me the haversack.'

Richard scraped his chair back and leant down behind him. He then passed a beige bag to James. The lads looked on. James handed a maroon beret over to Crawford, first.

'Chaps, please wear these with pride,' James said. 'I wish you the best of luck, men. Your country and I are proud of you.'

'Hold on. Why are we not wearing our sandy berets?' Churchill questioned. 'We have all earned them.'

'You are going in airborne,' James said.

As James went around with the berets, he saluted and shook the hands. Finished, he pulled me to the door.

'After sabotaging the German lines of communications and the destruction of the bomb depot, I want you to harass as many Germans as you can. Do not bloody balls this up. Good luck, Peter. May God be with you all.'

I held on tight to the hand that he held out and said, 'If my requested weapons list gets seen to, we won't fuck this up.'

'I am finding your attitude a...'

'One last thing,' I interrupted.

'I think I have heard that before from you, young man. I think you can now start addressing me as an officer.'

'James, I want to take the lads down the local pub tonight, but I have no money. Can you lend me some?'

'Bit of Dutch courage, hey.' James pulled out some folded large white notes from his trousers and reeled off one. 'Here you go. Do not go overboard on the alcohol.'

'Of course,' I said, hoping.

Turning to the lads, he said, 'Your attitude should warrant you to open fire to kill, not wound.'

When he had left, I went back into the main room. The lads were crowded around Churchill and Richard who were discussing the latest list. Just as Simon went to leave, I grabbed his arm.

'Make sure those jeeps are there,' I said.

'I am going to make the communication right now, Skedgewell.'

'Fancy a quick pint tonight?'

'I cannot. My wife and I are celebrating our wedding anniversary.'

'Fancy leaving some spirit behind the bar for the lads. Go on, remember when you were young, free, and single.'

Simon looked at them and then delved into his pocket. Eventually, possibly begrudgingly tight, he unfolded a large blue and white one-pound note.

'Wow, thanks,' I said sardonically.

'Destroy the Germans.'

I let the chatter go on a bit before I asked Richard to bring the list to me, and for Churchill to come to the front. I led Richard back into the dark, smelly hangar and then showed him the banknotes.

'Right, Richard, do you want to earn a bit of the pie and mash?'

His eyes lit up. 'Yes, governor.'

He went to take them, but I whipped them just out of his reach. Instead, I handed him my personal list that I'd made earlier.

'You cross me and I'll make sure you're on that fucking plane, and

I'll feed you to the Germans myself. Do you fucking understand me, Richard?'

'This geezer can get ya anyfin'. I'm known for it. Just the other...'

'Do I have your word?' I barked.

'Yes. My word is my bond.'

I gave him the money and told him to find me tomorrow.

CHAPTER NINETEEN

The lads were sat studying as I entered. Churchill stood up and folded his arms, ready. I nodded at him to carry on.

'Firstly, I am not going to need this,' Churchill said.

He ripped up a small red book. The others watched him toss the two halves into the air. Looking at the half that lay at my feet, I wondered why I hadn't received a *Notes for Instructors* booklet.

'There is no rulebook on this mission, boys,' he continued. 'You kill, you sabotage, you cause mayhem, you show no mercy. We have earned our bloody places in the SAS.'

He tossed his maroon beret like a Frisbee. Trigger tried to catch, but missed.

'But not just in this regiment. We, this small but courageous Special Raiding Squad, will go down in history. Our code of remembrance is to our forefathers: Lest we forget. My fellow men, look around. There is no fear in this room. If you do not have the confident ego to become the Phantom Major's Elite, then fucking go home.'

Churchill pointed to the door; nobody took their eyes off him.

'I swear I will do all in my power and honour to protect you from what lies ahead. Some of us may not return, but until our very last breath, we will endeavour to defend our monarchy, our nation's people, our country's flag. It is your duty. Whatever happens, many more will follow in your lion-hearted footsteps.'

Churchill paused; perhaps letting it sink in. Everyone's demeanour had changed, including mine. He cleared his throat.

'We shall go on to the end. We shall fight in France, we shall fight on the seas and oceans, we shall fight with growing confidence and growing strength in the air. We shall defend our island, whatever the cost may be. We shall fight on the beaches, we shall fight on the landing grounds, we shall fight in the fields and in the streets, we shall fight in the hills.

We shall never surrender.'

The silence was electrifying; I didn't want to break it. I had a lump in my throat. Furthermore, how could I follow that? I went over to Churchill and placed my hand on his shoulder, but strangely, he turned and stared right into the depths of my eyes. He then grabbed both my shoulders.

'Nicely put, Sergeant Andrew Graham,' I said.

'Please leave Benjamin behind. I will tell him, if you cannot. Please, Johnny.'

'Right, lads,' I said, leaving Churchill, 'I won't keep you long. Tonight we are celebrating down the pub.'

A big cheer sounded, all except Blondie, who'd managed a fake smile.

'Our commanding officer is buying the rounds,' Benny said exuberantly.

Further shouts of joy resounded. Churchill sighed and then left the room.

'I want you to enjoy it, get pissed, get off with the ladies,' I said— Blondie looked awkwardly around. 'However, in the morning I want you all up at seven a.m. Have a hearty breakfast. Do not shower, do not...'

'No more pretending to play in a German U-boat that has been hit?' Spike interrupted—we were all processing what he had said. 'It was a magnificent joke,' he said sorrowfully.

The first chuckles came in, and very soon everyone was in stitches, except Spike who'd remained deadpan.

'OK, lads, the point being that the Germans won't be using aftershaves and perfumes. Nor will you. You are all to stay clean-shaven using only hot water, especially that seventies moustache, Geordie. I want all those with untidy hair to have it cut.'

'What about our face paint camouflage, boss?' Crawford asked.

'No, leave the cam-cream off. Who speaks German?'

'*Jawohl, mein Führer*,' Shrek said, looking pleased.

'Typical of you, Shrek,' I said. 'Anyone else?'

'*Perfekt*,' Kauf said.

'*Parlo correntemente italiano, tedesco e francese*,' Fish bragged in an exaggerated Italian accent.

'What the fuck did he say?' I asked.

'He said he cannot drink more than one glass of scotch without falling over,' Planet said.

'No, I did not,' Fish said, above the laughing. 'I actually speak fluent Italian, German, and French.'

This encouraged the laughter.

'What are you laughing at, four eyes?' Fish retorted.

Blondie quickly stood up, fists clenched, and said, 'I see through the eyes of the Lord.'

'Oh, you speak God bollocks.'

'Hey, Fish, leave it,' I reprimanded. 'Take your intel and notes, then head back to the bunk house. I want you all to discuss the plans. At eight o'clock we get ready to head down the local for a few drinks.'

Back in the dorma, the professionalism was rewarding as we all bounced ideas and questions off each other. Even the stroppy Churchill joined in. Simon came in with a stack of notes and photos of enemy weapons, vehicles, and uniforms. What they had been trained in so far came out of them, and a few arguments as well.

'Last one down the pub buys the first round,' I said—I'd never seen people get changed and a room clear so quick.

Travelling in a sidecar wasn't my idea of fun, and I felt silly. Did Spike have a stupid grin like Wallace? What was worse than having been persuaded to get into the black Triumph sidecar, was being without a helmet. Spike was fearless as he pushed it to its max around the greasy tarmac country lanes. We had left later than the rest, but at this rate we weren't going to make it alive.

Just after we had slid around a blind corner, ahead was a twin-wheeled truck, the backwash of water from the trees spraying into my face. Coming up at speed, I read the number plate of this American school bus styled truck: RAF 31436. From the rear window, a commotion of faces appeared. Trigger stuck his fingers up, further childish gestures from the others followed.

A plume of exhaust smoke billowed, and the truck began to gain distance. Through coughing, I managed to shout at Spike to catch up, but there was no way we would be able to overtake. The front of my wedge-nosed sidecar was almost under the truck's high-backed bodywork, as Spike had peeked around the side to pass. The lorry braked; my heart ended up in my mouth. Spike suddenly opened the throttle, and I leant over to miss face-planting the corner of the truck. Through the spray, a small part of lane had widened, like a place to let traffic pass. After seeing the angry faces in the side windows, I looked forward again to see the lane converge back into one. Both vehicles were travelling at full speed. Spike was gaining the lead, but I knew we wouldn't make it. I screamed at Spike to stop, but instead, he kicked down a gear, the motorbike screaming its nuts off.

The truck became that close, I could have banged on Shrek's door to tell him to let us through. It had to have been *him* driving. Even in the last dying metres, Shrek did not ease up. We jolted in the muddy ruts. A slight clink at the back and I knew we had passed, but we began to fishtail. The sidecar lifted off the wet tarmac and then impacted back down. Shrek was right up close. The engine seemed to roar at me through its grille. The truck was that close, again, I couldn't see Shrek to tell him to fuck off, even though I shouted it. The truck's brakes squealed. For a moment, all the road noise stopped, but then I shook forward as we landed, Spike quickly regaining control. I glanced behind to see the truck take the brow of a hill on a blind bend, Shrek only just slowing down.

Outside the Lancaster Inn, I had to prise my fingers off the front of my mini cockpit. The truck tried to skid to a halt, but ended up careering into the rear garden. Thank fuck it was a rainy evening. The shirt Benny had lent me had now soaked into the trousers that Blondie had given me to wear. Getting out wasn't easy. Had I swollen? Annoyingly, after all the dangerous and desperate racing to get here first, Spike just sat on his large black saddle. He greeted the rest of the lads who jostled and jeered as they went by.

'Why the hell are you just sitting there, Spike?' I said.

'What is the rush? The boss always pays.'

'So why were you bloody driving like a lunatic?'

Spike smiled. 'I was not. Shrek was on the accelerator. Feet are just shit hands.'

He left me there trying to work out what he had said. In fact, thinking back, everything he said made perfect sense. He was actually very clever, in his own way.

A resounding cheer boomed as I walked in. Geordie and Crawford started to thump the table for their drinks. Planet walked by and back outside. With the amount of banter that had started to fly around, the old couple quickly made their exit. The pub was totally different in decor to the one in Aldershot: the furniture and decorative items had an art deco theme. The pub's best transformation was the person behind the bar: the barmaid. She had that 1920s' chic style, with her red lipstick colouring her plush pouting lips. She had thin eyebrows over her bronze eyeshadow, all enhanced by the long black eyelashes. Her green and gold headband kept back her delicate, wavy hair. My gaze travelled onto her slender figure and sufficient breasts in her matching green and gold embroidered dress. Wow.

Annoyingly, Fish was now propping up the curved-edged bar, chatting to her. Play it cool, Johnny, I thought, and not your shit chat up.

'Good evening. Fourteen pints please, my good lady.'

'You are not going to cause any mischief tonight, are you…' she said, with a slight Liverpudlian accent, and pausing for my name.

'Major Vince, but please, call me Johnny.'

Fish spat his beer back into his glass.

'And no, we're a fine bunch of lads. Well, except Private Fish here who can't handle his drink, and has a penile dysfunction.'

'That must be hard for you, Private Fish,' she said.

'That's not what his wife says,' I said.

'You have not a chance, Vinnie,' he whispered.

Fish knocked my head forward into my beer as he went past holding his pint. Wiping the froth from my lips and nose, I stared at the barmaid's long slender arms as she poured yet another pint; this ogling went on till she had almost finished.

'What's your name, love?'

'Barbara Peet. You can call me Babs, not "love", that is, once you have paid for the drinks. That will be one pound and twelve pence.'

She rested her wet hands on her hips, waiting. I noticed Churchill wasn't at the table, but at least Fish was on his way back to collect more pints.

'That will be one pound and twelve pence,' she repeated.

'Fish, where's Churchill? I need him to pay,' I whispered.

'I can only apologize for this cad's dishonest conduct,' Fish said loudly. 'This despicable rogue always follows us around trying the same old trick that he is a major in the army. He has no intention of paying.'

'Dad,' Babs yelled. 'Dad, we have another traveller who thinks he does not have to pay.'

Fish winked at me. Through the entrance behind her stood a humongous bloke in trousers and a vest, his bald head showing in the grand mirror. The dad raised what appeared to be a long pheasant gun. He cocked the hammer.

'Now, my little gypsy friend, pay the lady,' he said in a thick Liverpool accent.

I quickly looked at the lads for some help, but they all appeared amused, as if watching a play. Be brave, stand your ground, I thought, and took a sip of my beer whilst he continued to aim his weapon.

'Oh put it away, fat man,' I said.

'There is one thing I loathe as much as a Kraut, and that is a thieving rotten gypsy,' he said spitefully. 'I am happy to share your brains for the crows in the morning.'

Hmmm. OK, not that brave, I thought.

'Let me pay, and at the same time, please let me buy ye two good people a drink,' Planet said in a charming voice, like Sean Connery.

I looked around, shocked to see Planet in a green suit. He looked like a walking army marquee. Planet put two one-pound notes on the bar.

'And what about this scallywag?' Babs asked.

'I sincerely hope he has not offended ye,' Planet said. 'Please, accept my deepest apology if he has. Even us brave servicemen must mix with the gypsies. This scoundrel is coming to the frontline with us. I will endeavor to keep an eye on him.'

My jaw almost hit the floor.

Planet loosened his purple cravat and then forcefully grabbed me by the collar, pleasing Babs and her dad. He then dragged me to the tables where the lads sat, pushing me hard into a seat, spilling my pint on my trousers. The rest of the lads sniggered.

'Now, be a good gypsy and sit there,' he boomed.

With the pints shared around, and with Planet back at the bar, the humour turned about me being a gypsy. Babs walked elegantly across to the corner of the room and lifted the lid on a highly varnished unit made of yew. The distinctive scratching played out before the big band tune. I immediately recognised the song, but didn't know who it was. Fish supped his pint, looking very relaxed; perhaps pissed already.

'Fish, who's this playing?' I asked.

'Glen Miller. The song is: "In the Mood".'

'Cheers,' I said.

'Military man like us. He joined…'

'Someone get Fish another half to crash him out so he shuts up. I am trying to listen to the song,' Crawford said.

The group went quiet as we all enjoyed the music. Churchill strolled in. He and Planet shared the story of me trying unsuccessfully to chat up the barmaid. They both brought over a tray, each with fourteen large scotches on ice. I began handing out the drinks.

'Sorry I am late,' Churchill said.

'Where have you been?' I asked.

'Out of the base I can do what I want, Peter.'

He slammed a glass in front of me and then Benny. I took in a deep breath, and then sighed out at his mood.

'Cheers, everyone,' I said, and took a long sip. 'Planet, why are you wearing a parachute as a jacket?'

'What?' he snapped.

'I mean it's so fucking big.'

'Tonight, the enemy will not be using the Hindenburg Zeppelin,' Kauf added.

'Could wrap up a lot of that haggis shit in that,' Trigger joined in.

'Does ye want that penknife shoved up ye arse? Don't take the piss out of me roots, lad.'

And so, it continued into the night with more drink flowing. Shrek was the one who paid for the rounds; a great mate. It wasn't long before Trigger had slumped onto the table, even before Fish has started to slur. I was getting concerned at Trigger's immaturity. Was he really the age he said he was? Was he even old enough to join the army? If he wasn't, he had passed and fooled everyone. He certainly had the bollocks when rattled. I made a mental note to research him tomorrow.

I was glad that Blondie was sober as he had kept checking on Fish who had regularly stumbled out to be sick. Blondie had also continued to give Trigger some water. No one spoke about Operation Poppy Pride, and nobody had brought up my past, which was just as well as the alcohol was obscuring my memory. It was amazing to be back with the SF lads, especially Fish, Planet, and Shrek, teaching them new words and sayings, piss-taking, laughing; like old times.

'Check you are in position, see your gun is all right, wait until the convoy comes creeping through the night,' Churchill began a drunken chant. 'Now you can press the trigger, son. And blow the Hun to kingdom come, and Lilli Marlene's boyfriend will never see Marlene. Back to the rendezvous we will steer...'

The others joined in hollering. I left for a piss.

Staggering out of the toilet, trying to get my flies done up, Planet and Babs were having an intimate dance to Vera Lynn's 'White Cliffs of Dover'. How he could still stand, let alone dance, with that amount of scotch he had drunk? The cigarette smoke had lessened due to those who had crashed out. Blondie still sat like a spare prick at a party. Benny had disappeared.

'Where's Benny?' I slurred.

'He went out the back with a couple of burly blokes,' Blondie answered. 'Said they could sell him a stash of cigarettes.'

'Where's Churchill?' I asked, slightly concerned.

'He left when you swayed to the convenience.'

My conscience was slapped for some reason. I waded through the strewn chairs and tables that were holding up the lads. Finding the door that led to the rear, I yanked it open. In the fresh air and shadows of the back alley were two figures kicking and thumping a mass on the floor. I took a step forward after seeing Benny's beat-up face.

'Oi,' I yelled.

The two thugs faced me, panting heavily.

'You're gonna pay...'

As my face hit the ground, the pain seared through the back of my head and down my neck. A pair of shoes ran past my blurring vision. Blinking hard, I tried to get up, but collapsed. A warm feeling ran down my ears and neck. The thugs continued to hit Benny, who was less than three metres away. There was no groaning from him, just the striking sounds, muffled with the ringing in my ears. I tried to yell for them to stop, but my voice sounded weird. The next shout wasn't mine. Opening my eyes and seeing Blondie with his back to me, shocked me into sobriety. The nauseous feeling returned as the thugs stood tall. Blondie's thin round glasses landed in front of my face. However, all went darker than the situation I was in.

CHAPTER TWENTY

The electric guitar rocked into life. I squinted at the white pillow and then shut my eyes. The beeping, something I hadn't really paid attention to, was now very loud. Then I realised it was the first song that I had heard for nearly twenty-four hours. Why had no songs been played? Was it a message trying to tell me something? The latest tune was on the tip of my tongue, but I just couldn't say the name or the artist. To stop the music and beeping enhancing the hangover, I stuffed the pillow over my head; I wished I hadn't. Taking it quickly off again, I touched something tightly padded around my head. Blondie, I suddenly thought, and opened my eyes, startled.

'Benny,' I said.

I ignored the pain and wooziness as I'd sat bolt upright. Lying on his back in the next bed was Benny, his face and body bloated and battered. His fingers were crossed across his chest, his knuckles showing abrasions. I knew I had seen someone close in this state before, but the music and hangover were playing havoc with my memory. I calmly called his name. One of his puffy eyes slightly opened and his red eyeball took a side glance at me; a tear ran down from his inflamed eyelids.

'You look worse than me, Vinnie,' he mumbled, touching his swollen lips.

'Who were those wankers last night?'

'It does not matter.'

'It fucking does,' I snapped. 'Who whacked me from behind?'

'I am not going am I.'

'You know who it fucking was don't you.'

'Telling you is not going to heal me in time, is it.'

'That's enough of that pussy talk. You're in the SAS. A couple of Tic-Tacs and Gaffa Tape and you'll be fine.'

I unwound my head bandage and threw it away, and then tore the pad from the matted hair. The rock music was echoing in my head, along with the pain. The door to this new room opened and in came Crawford, looking like a bag of shite. He slumped back against the wall.

'Morning, boss,' he said quietly.

'Where's Blondie?' I asked.

Crawford held his palms up as if I was being too loud, and whispered, 'He has gone for a morning run.'

'I got it,' I blurted.

'What?'

'Your nickname: Rose.'

'As in the rose of England?'

'No, as in Axl Rose; Guns N' Roses. I've got the name of the song at last,' I said.

Crawford was confused.

I stood up, swaying, and said, 'Have you seen Churchill this morning?'

'No. Is the mission still on, boss?'

'Try and bloody stop me, Rose. Get Benny back over to our quarters. I don't care who tries to stop you, you see to it personally that everyone meets me there in an hour. I'm off to find Blondie.'

Outside the medic block, the sun was beating down on the early dew. Against the wall was someone's pushbike, so I grabbed it. As my feet grappled with the pedals, one of the medics shouted for me to get off. My barrage of abuse left him rooted and I rode passed him. My fuelled anger encouraged me across the grass runway towards a lone figure jogging around the perimeter bushes. Blondie was wearing white shorts and vest, like those in the film *Chariots of Fire*. I shouted at him to stop as my wheels were getting bogged down by the thick, wet grass. He stopped and faced me with his hands behind his back. I threw the bike over, but was sick, head pounding. Turning back to him, his face was lowered.

'Morning has broken,' Blondie said.

'Who the fuck butchered your hair?'

'What do you mean?'

'Hope you didn't pay for that haircut. What happened to your lip?'

'Shaving with no soap, Johnny.'

'Bollocks. And the razor gave you a black eye. Show me your hands.'

'My hands?'

'Yes, you know, the things on the end of your fucking arms.' I went to grab his arm, but he pulled away.

'These are God's healing hands.'

'Saxton,' I bawled.

Blondie showed me the palms of his hands. I turned them over, noting the red marks and skin loss.

'And as a Christian, you also fist fight,' I said.

'If Christ did not ask me to intervene, the world would be full of evil. Everyone would be taking lumps out of each other. No one would learn.'

'Then why did the Almighty let me get a whack, and Benny?'

'How…'

'And what about the poor bastard Halifax crewman who burnt to death?' I interrupted. 'Hey?'

'How much of that was human fault? Why should God take the blame for the wars that take place? Is it he that stands in front of you when you shoot?'

'No, but then how can you kill a man under his religion?' I knew I had cornered him.

'I am his soldier, a bearer of arms to fight the evil.'

'Ah, but what happens if you come across another Christian facing his weapon at you, a German Christian?' Got ya, I thought.

'Those Germans that believe in the twisted cross are not real Christians, but possessed by an evil. Contrary to the non-believers, we do not walk around with a halo and a big wooden cross. However, to kill another opposing Christian will stop many more deaths.'

'It seems a lot of battles are fought…'

'Did God hit you over the head with that pole?' he sternly interrupted.

'You saw who fucking did it, didn't you.'

'Please stop swearing at me, Johnny.'

'Who was it? Who were those thugs?'

'I did not see who hit you, but the pole was on the floor. As for the two who beat up Benny, they learned their lesson.'

'Who helped you tackle these pikeys?'

Blondie started to jog away. 'God.'

'Where are you going?' I shouted.

'To pray for good weather for tonight.'

'I want you back on your bunk in forty-five minutes.'

He put his hand up to acknowledge.

I picked up my bike and wiped off the vomit.

After riding around the airfield base asking anyone if had they seen Sergeant Andrew Graham, I started pedalling my way back to our dormer.

Around the last corner an arm came out and grabbed me off the bike. I apologised to the seething medic and his angry mates. Reaching our corrugated shack on foot, my head was still banging. The heat wafted out as I entered. Everyone but Churchill and Blondie were sat in just their shorts, all taking on water. Benny was sat up against a stack of pillows, his arms and legs were puffy and bruised. There was an air of uncertainty as I stripped off. I noticed the blood stains on the back of my shirt.

The door swung open and slammed shut, just enough to feel a bit of fresh air. Blondie looked at the door and then turned back, worried.

'Johnny, Mullen is on his way down and he is really not happy. He says two bottles of his finest whisky have been stolen from his office,' Blondie said.

'I hope you made up some cock and bull,' I said.

'He did not give me the time. He also wanted to know what a bellend is. He said you said I would know.'

I whispered what it meant in his ear. The colour drained from his face, almost matching his sweaty white vest.

Shrek held the playing cards across his eyes as James made his bolshie entrance. Everyone else stood and saluted. I stepped forward, thinking of a way to stay on the good side of him as he looked really pissed off.

'What the bloody hell happened last night?' he barked.

'Just a bit of Dutch courage, sir,' I said meekly.

'Really?' he shouted. 'And I suppose the police chase of a motorbike and sidecar, and the crashed RAF transporter, had nothing to do with you fucking lot.'

'I made sure this lot were in bed by ten,' I lied.

The rest of the lads all nodded, like toy nodding dogs—pathetic.

'And what the fucking blazing happened to Garvey? And you, Saxton?' he raged—both looked at me.

'Me and Benny had a drunken fight over the barmaid, and sadly, Blondie accidentally got in the way and copped one in the face. That's why we left early. We know nothing of a police chase and a crash,' I said—the dogs continued to pathetically nod.

'Is this correct, Saxton?' James asked. 'Let me remind you, you are a man of the cloth.'

'If I tell the truth, does this mean the mission is off?' Blondie said, submissive.

'It certainly does. I have had enough of you bloody rabble.'

'Good. Then, Geordie nicked the keys and Shrek drove the truck. After a loony race with Spike and Vinnie on the motorbike, Shrek crashed into the pub garden. Vinnie upset the landlord, who then threatened him with a shotgun. They all got very drunk. I had to listen to some outrageous foul language. Fish did nothing but vomit, and I had to pay the barmaid for the damage. Benny and Vinnie had a big fight with some gypsies in the alley, but I alone beat them up. Planet fornicated with the barmaid, whilst I kept the landlord talking. I had to drag all of them onto the RAF bus. Trigger was out cold. Spike and Vinnie, both very drunk, out-ran the police. Shrek, even more drunk, drove us all back, using the sandbags around the control building to stop. So, please return me as I do not want to go to war with this lot.'

James appeared flummoxed. He looked around the room at the lads' bowed heads, but then the first giggle came out.

'Jolly good try, Saxton. I never had you down as a wag. Very humorous, but you still are going on this mission. Just for a second, I did believe you, but it is far too ludicrous, especially from a padre. One last question, Saxton: where is my prized whisky? Who is the culprit?'

Oh shit, I thought.

'That is easy, sir,' Blondie said. 'The empty bottles are in Intelligence Officer Krycler's office.'

'Are you sure? Under the eyes of the Lord?'

'I swear on the bible, that is where the empty bottles are.'

'I think Simon has a drinking problem,' I said, miming drinking with my hand to my mouth.

'Thank you for being so honest, Saxton,' James said. 'Chaps, all be in Hangar-5 at eighteen hundred hours dead on. We have a green light.'

'Yes, sir,' everyone answered—the jovial mood had ceased.

'All except you, Lieutenant Weaver,' James said. 'You are being pulled off for Operation Bulbasket. Get your kit over to Hangar-1.'

'But, sir, I want to...'

'That is an order, Weaver,' James barked. 'Right, carry on, chaps. I need to find Krycler.'

In the silence that followed the door closing, Weaves went over to his bunk and started moodily stuffing all his kit into his bag. I went over to him and patted him on the back for a bit of morale. His tearful crystal-blue eyes locked onto mine.

'Do not lose any of these fearless men,' he said. 'Make sure you all get home safe.'

'That's it,' I said excitedly. 'Weaves...'

I paused as I couldn't tell him that Operation Bulbasket was going to go drastically wrong. His nerves, and the other men he would surely tell, would get the better of them.

'When the time is right, make sure you bloody run, and just keep running. Use your sporting stamina.'

'What do you mean?' he asked.

'Look, don't worry, but if you do this we'll meet up in the distant future. I will make sure Planet, Shrek, and Fish will return this time.'

'This time?' he said. 'I reckon that knock to the head has not helped your already befuddled mind.'

'No, it's clear: I mustn't let them die. What you said in the Australian Bar meant Planet, Shrek, and Fish here in this era, not the ones in Afghanistan.'

'I hope Churchill is wrong that you are a looney.'

The sorrow of losing such a great asset to our mission was etched on the faces of the lads, all shaking his hand before he went. Standing where James had stood, I got their attention from the thoughts they were wrapped up in. It wasn't just that fact we were a man down, but tonight we were being dropped into the hornets' nest. I instructed all of them to find cockney Richard, grab as much kit as possible off him, and then find a part of the airfield to set up a firing range for weapons testing. I asked Trigger to find Simon and remind him of the enemy weapons he was supposed to get. The morale had lifted as I made my over to my bed.

With everyone legging it out the door, Planet sat next to me on my bunk, which was a squeeze.

'What happened in that room?' Planet asked.

'You mean in the alley?'

'No, in the room where ye were going to get a damn good pummelling off us. Was it a heart attack?'

'I don't know, but whenever the beeping noise goes wild, which is linked to my heart, I go into a spasm.'

Planet listened in. 'What beeping noise?'

'You won't hear it, like the music. Another song from the past, no, the future, is now playing, but again I'm having problems with the title. It must be the knock to my head.'

'Ye are a mad mofo,' he said.

Planet smacked me on the knee, and then he left. I rubbed the sore area. Shit, I thought, what other words have I taught them from …? My thoughts had drawn a blank. What year was I from? Anxiety surged through me as I tried to remember my family's faces and names. I quickly undid the watch and threw it on the bed, looking away from the inscription.

'My name is Johnny Vince,' I said. 'My brother is… Oliver. My mum is… Joanne, and my dad's name is…'

I hit my head for the answers.

'Fuck,' I continued. 'Move on, Johnny. I was born by a beach. Oh shit, what was the name? Why am I bloody forgetting?'

The beeping noise picked up.

'Am I married?'

I checked my wedding finger for the slightest mark, and I then shut my eyes to try to picture the images of my past. I couldn't remember.

'Bollocks.'

Was it that the further I remained in this time, the more I forgot?

'Who the fuck are my mates? How did I get here?'

I dropped my face in my hands, my breathing now rapid.

'Yeah, go on then, have a fucking spazzy moment. Just take me away from all this. I want to go home.'

I quickly lifted my head, realising what I had said.

'But then I leave my mates here, and they need me. And what about the importance of this mission I have been given?'

I dampened down my levels of fear, taking slow breaths in and out.

'But I could die and never get home and see my family.'

I felt sick.

'Are you all right, boss?'

I peered around the side of my bunk to see Kauf and Geordie standing there, both looking slightly unnerved. Kauf came over and patted me on the shoulder.

'How long have you two been there?' I asked.

'Do you want to get it off your chest?' Kauf said. 'I have also lost my family. I was only thirteen.'

'My family are not fucking dead. I just can't remember them all,' I said.

'Your memory will come back, it is the healing process,' he said.

'Anyway,' I said, 'what are you two layabouts doing back? You want to clean the latrines with a toothbrush?' Shit, I was starting to talk like them.

'Stop being a pussy dickhead, Vinnie, and get your lazy minge out of bed,' Geordie said. 'You are coming for a run with me, you ginger twat.'

Geordie legged it out the door, Kauf hot on his heels. I laughed at Geordie's misuse of words. I must have used them last night in the pub, as I was not ginger. Running after them, I yelled abuse; also giving them extra duties for their insubordinate behaviour.

CHAPTER TWENTY-ONE

Me and the lads had done a half-decent job at setting up a testing range in an outside high-walled disused coal storage area. There were three alcoves, each about ten metres in depth and six wide. As the items I'd requested were being collected from my little thieves, it began to look like a scrapyard. At the back of the first alcove we positioned a few crates and poles, placing our maroon berets on top. We left Benny to draw faces on with white paint that he had stolen. He had remarked that I was a racist for not letting him use black paint, which everyone else but me found the funny side of.

In alcove-2, Planet had ripped out and carried back furniture from the vacant building next to us; well, I hoped it wasn't in use. Once we had set up a makeshift HQ in it, Planet heaved into place some large pallets that he had acquired. Coming across the field at speed was a jeep, closely followed by a troop-carrying truck. Just as the jeep stopped, the truck crashed into the back of it. Trigger got out holding his neck, and then he kicked the door of the truck, ranting. Shrek debussed and couldn't stop his hysterics, but then the pushing and shoving started. Rose was first over to calm it down, and it wasn't long before they were all laughing at the damage vehicles. More piss-taking continued against Crawford's new nickname, calling him daisy and little flower. This started the heated pushing and shoving again.

After helping them unload further crates and weapons, including some battered German rifles and machineguns, we sat in the beautiful sun, looking over the enemy diagrams of weapons. We then stripped them down before reassembling; it was very easy work. From a large market fruit-box, Tommo handed out bottles of cold Worthington's beer and doorstep cheese sandwiches with lashings of buttered bread. I didn't ask where Shrek and Trigger had stolen all their booty; however, I did say one beer each—much to their annoyance.

First to take the piss out of the construction in the alcoves with his sarcastic dry wit was Spike. After a bit more banter, Kauf asked why the last alcove was empty. Before I could tell him that I had run out of ideas and objects for target practice, Shrek had jumped up and started to run back to the truck. With a crazed look in his eyes, he headed towards the empty coal bay. Just as the vehicle entered, it turned sideways, the front slamming into the dividing twin wall. We all stood fearing the worst as steam poured out from under the bonnet. Yet, the large door was kicked open and Shrek jumped down, smiling at us, trying to look innocent as the blood ran from his nose.

'Ye crazy mofo,' Planet shouted.

'A what?' Trigger asked.

'Oh, I forgot, ye passed out after one shandy.'

'Piss off, Planet. I heard you missed most of the conversation because you were up to your neck in clunge.'

'What the fuck is clunge?' he asked.

Geordie leant forward and whispered in Planet's ear.

'Ye bastard,' Planet raged.

As the big frame chased Trigger across the airfield, I ordered everyone to load up with a British machinegun. Rose was the most familiar with the Thompson and Sten, so he was tasked to remind the rest how it stripped down and reassembled, finding great pride in the role. Whilst he did, I went further out and set up the Bren and Vickers. Planet, out of breath, was returning across the field. I ordered him reacquaint himself with both weapons.

On my return we loaded up. Set back from the first alcove, we took it in turns from prone, kneeling, and standing to fire at the objects. It wasn't long before everything was obliterated in the first alcove. As cocky as they were, I asked them to assault alcove-2, all except Planet, who I'd whispered the secret orders to; he could hardly contain himself.

With just our sub-machineguns, we got into our squads and headed towards the target. Unbeknown to them what was coming, Planet opened fire, sending rounds spewing above and to the side of us. A few shit themselves, almost, and dived to the ground. A couple laid on their bellies and faced the threat, then started to simulate a leap-frog attack. I had made good ground, hiding behind the truck, with Fish and Shrek now behind me. Once the incoming had ceased, I asked everyone to come in for a chat. Planet received a barrage of abuse as he walked in. I ordered all to shut up and then explained it was better to find a scrape in the ground, any cover, and then work out a counterattack. Sometimes you fire, your mate goes, then fires as you go, as soon as you have had a threat can get you killed. That is, unless you have an armoured vehicle to take immediate action.

Just as we were about to do it again, but with someone else using the Bren a litter further out this time, an ambulance and jeep came racing across the field. James jumped out of the pursuing jeep, followed by Wing Commander Kenny Wilson. After a little heated discussion, James returned with the ambulance, whilst Wilson sat watching. I handed him one of the hidden beers.

After a few mock stages with the Bren, we all sat together and learnt about that weapon. Trigger wanted to train with the Colt-45, but I didn't see the point in it. In fact, I saw no reason bringing them. I'd rather take extra ammo, grenades, and a rifle. To keep the momentum going, we swapped our weapons for the German type. With certain objects placed around the tables and chairs, the attacker had to walk through the stacked pallets and hit each target. After we had moved the objects, we did the same again, and again, and each time they got better and better. The adrenalin was pumping.

A crowd had gathered behind Wilson, whilst we practiced live firing extracting a pretend wounded man, taking two to help Planet from the alcove. We then tried with the enemy weapons. They were good and fired OK, making us more aware of the enemy.

Taking on some much-needed water, the others began to open the other crates. Shrek wanted to make the last alcove as if we were hitting a German troop carrier, but I drew the line at adding the spectators in the truck. Instead, we placed some of the broken poles as rifles, poking them out of the truck's tarpaulin side. To finish it, we positioned the last of the crates and pallets, adding mess plates and saucepans as heads. We set a fire-position just on the perimeter of the field and began to move and fire with the Lee-Enfield. Planet, who made the Bren look smaller than it was, took the sling off his shoulder. To the right of us he lay prone with the bipod out, stock tucked firmly into his right shoulder. Once it was cocked, he took aim on the offset sight and then fired a controlled burst as we charged down the left flank. It made mincemeat of anything it hit—bloody awesome. However, perhaps a little too zealous, as the truck had caught fire. Shit. We're in big trouble, I thought.

The rest of the lads were pissed off that they didn't get to have a go. They vented their anger at Planet who had returned with a big grin on his face. He quieted everyone down and gave us some further tuition, including its pros and cons.

The sound of a siren whizzed by. I felt a little guilty as the crew were now wasting their water on the burning truck.

'What's next?' Shrek asked.

'The Vickers,' Planet said, picking it up.

'That is a nice target,' Shrek said, pointing at the fire truck.

'Hey, boss, pick someone else. I am just as good with that as him,' Tommo bragged.

'Bollocks are ye,' Planet said.

'Happy to fight you...'

'Where's Trigger?' I interrupted the testosterone fuelled spat.

A stack of empty beer bottles on the crate exploded. I dived to the ground. Another round took off what was left of the truck's mirror. It must have been close to the firemen leaving the airfield; I don't even think they had realised. Raising my eyeline above the grass, the others cautiously got up from the little they were hiding behind. Another shot hit one of the saucepans. I stood up and searched the whole area. From the control tower's roof, someone stood in front of the large number seven, waving. It had to be Trigger.

When Trigger had returned, with a bucket load of confidence, he gave us a short demo on the rifle, scope, and maintenance. He even let us all have a go. After, this led the desperate Tommo grabbing the twin Vickers mounted on the jeep and pummelling everything that was left in every alcove—we loved it. With still too much testosterone, I had to think of more situations. Hoping the French SAS were preparing their jeeps with mounted weapons, and good amount of fuel, I decided we should practice our shoot and manoeuvre in our jeep. We needed to be ready for our escape once the mission was complete.

Whilst we had another drink break, the growing crowd wanted more. Strangely, well, no more than normal, Spike had been sledgehammering a long length of angled iron into the ground. No one had a clue what he was doing as he tugged at the strop loops that he had placed over the iron. He then began to run around in a circle, stopping to pull on the strops. Many in the crowd started laughing, that was until Tommo and Rose wandered over and told them to shut the fuck up or they would be the next target. It was then I knew we were coming together as a unit: a band of brothers.

Parking the jeep next to the pole, leaving the engine running, Spike tied off the steering wheel. He fastened the strops through the open door and onto the seat, shutting the door after. Spike sat in the seat and let out the clutch. The jeep went around in a circle. There was a scramble to pick up the weapons. Spike casually jumped out and walked back, gesticulating to put everything down. I was horrified to see Shrek put down a green rocket launcher, and its projectile.

Whilst the jeep continued its never-ending path, making deeper ruts in the grass, Spike lifted the lid off one of the crates and grabbed out an object that I didn't recognise.

'What the bloody hell is that?' I asked Fish.

'Lewes bomb. Created from mixing diesel oil and Nobel 808. It was invented by Jock Lewes from L-Detachment. Been a lot of sabotage to the Germans since 1941. Each bomb can have a timer...'

'You're boring me now, Fish,' I interrupted.

I went over to take a closer look at the green mass, and then I leant forward to smell it: almonds. Spike gave me a look as if I was mad and snatched it away from my nose.

'This is a bomb,' he said slowly. 'This is a pencil detonator. Do not get it damp.'

With that short speech, he broke the timer. Rapidly after, he ran through the cloud of exhaust fumes, keeping at speed with the jeep. After placing the explosive, he sprinted back to us, but didn't stop.

'Take cover,' he said lamely.

No way, I thought, and hid behind Planet who had curled up behind a wooded slatted crate.

BOOOM!

The shockwave was followed by bits of debris hitting the wood. Through the ringing in my ears, the sound of an engine screamed. Coughing and spluttering, Planet pushed me off him.

'Forwards into battle,' Spike shouted.

'Was that an instant fuse?' Geordie yelled, picking his face out of the grass.

'I must learn my colours,' Spike said.

The jeep had stalled and now lay smoking about twenty metres away. Only the side had been ripped out, the door lay in the opposite direction. Spike took a bow at the jeering crowd. From the audience strode Churchill, my eyes narrowing as he casually clapped. He patted Spike on the back.

'Bloody good show,' he said.

'You wanker,' I ranted.

Grabbing him by his shirt, I thrust him back, but he tried to put up a defence, asking what I was doing. I gave him a short sharp punch to his stomach, and then I pushed him to the ground. Churchill puffed in and out. I clenched my fists ready to strike. Rose tried to calm me, but I pushed him aside.

'Now it's your fucking turn,' I said.

'Hold up, boss. What the dickens have I done to upset you? I thought that was all behind us.'

'The only thing behind me was you striking me with that fucking pole. I'm gonna bust you up like you had those thugs do Benny.'

'Boss, I have no idea what you are babbling on about. I left the pub early. I did not feel well, old chap,' he said.

'So why hide all morning, Andy?'

'I have not been. I managed to persuade Mayne, Lassen, and Farran to stay down the pub. I knew you would not want to meet them, therefore I got them boozed up. What a racket. That Mayne can't 'alf hold his drink.' Churchill slowly got to his feet.

I grabbed him again, fist back in chamber. 'You're lying.'

'I was under Lieutenant Mullen's orders,' he pleaded.

'Where are they now?'

'I left them at the pub to sleep it off. Ask Mullen or Planet's girl.'

'Oh fuck. Lieutenant Mullen is on his way over,' Benny said.

Running across the field was James, looking more fuming than me.

'Oh my Lord, what happened to you, Benny?' Churchill asked.

Benny pushed away Churchill's sympathetic hand and walked off.

'Let me deal with Mullen,' Wilson said.

'Cheers, Kenny,' I said.

The lads had wanted me and Churchill to make up, but I kept my distance. Meantime, Shrek had volunteered a spectator to come over. Shrek handed over his pistol to the bloke and instructed the man to point it at Shrek's face, but the volunteer refused. Shrek grabbed the bloke's hand holding the revolver, cocked it, and aimed at his own face. Shrek began shouting at the helper that he himself was a German prisoner and was to be escorted away. The bloke holding the Colt-45 started to jostle Shrek back, even hitting Shrek between the shoulder blades. Somehow, I knew what was coming, and it did: in a split-second Shrek had disabled him to the ground and had a knife at this poor bastard's neck. Shrek came over and gave a little talk about what had happened, and how. The volunteer moped back to the exuberant crowd.

The show went on with two further non-volunteers. Both had to pretended to be German guards, both holding readied rifles. They didn't end up any better. The last, and by far the most menacing-looking, was an RAF mechanic. He was given a knife and ordered attack; his mates jeered him on. It was quite a battle; in fact, Shrek's opponent was taking it too seriously. But in the end, the mechanic was battered.

I ordered the crowd to disperse. We sat and had one more beer. Something niggled me in the back of my mind, feeling I had been through this all before, but something was missing. Further doubts crept in that we hadn't trained for something. I shut my eyes and looked at the sun, then it came to me.

'We need to practise in the dark,' I said.

'We do not have the time,' Rose said.

'We need to simulate the targets we're going to hit at night. Right, everyone up and grab anything that can be used to black out the windows of that building.' I pointed to where Planet had got the furniture from.

'Hey. Where is my squeeze box?' Spike blurted.

The lads sniggered and then pointed to the shattered remains in the alcove.

'I could not play it anyway,' Spike said drolly.

In just under an hour we had blacked out all the windows with the truck's wet tarpaulin and further bits of scavenged wood. In a locked storeroom, after Planet had kicked in the door, we found what appeared to be parts of a funfair, and more tables and chairs. In each room we set the furniture under the glow from either a lightbulb or a lantern. One of the rooms was left completely dark, except for the light emitting from the hallway. Outside, I instructed no one was to enter this area of the field, or they could die.

First up I called in F-squad: Geordie, Tommo, Rose, and Trigger. I instructed them to fucking ammo up and then enter the lower rooms and kill any Germans. Looking bewildered at me, I explained that they had to shoot each chair after an explosive entry, the chairs being the enemy. Before they started, Tommo asked who now led the squad since Weaves had gone. Geordie seemed the obvious leader, so he was appointed—he relished the challenge. Once kitted up, I asked them to jump up and down. They all got a roasting for their equipment making a noise.

Inside, watching from the rear, they causally went forward, all looking the same way. Geordie opened the door and peeked around.

'Stop. Stop,' I yelled. 'You're all fucking dead.'

The embarrassment and confusion showed on their faces. I ordered them back outside. This time I instructed them how to watch the corridor and, after a silent countdown, how to enter the target room with balls of steel. On their next turn they were better at the task going down the corridor and breaching the room. However, none of them had shot the enemy in the room; instead, they'd shouted, "You are dead, you are dead.".

'Stop. Stop,' I bawled. 'You're all fucking dead.'

'Again?' Tommo said.

I pushed him up against the wall, putting my arm across his throat. 'Are you taking the fucking piss? You only die once.'

'No, boss, I meant, do we do it all again?' he spluttered.

Fuming, I ordered them out, giving the whole squad a bollocking in front of the others, telling them to actually fucking shoot next time. Rose asked what would happen if they shot each other. I told him that person would not take part in the next stage, but go home in a body bag.

Looking even more serious, their senses hyper-alert, the entry was awesome. After they came out through the smoke, I inspected all the bullet holes in the chairs. The ego had grown between them. Geordie had led brilliantly.

'Not bad,' I said. 'Just one problem: as soon as you had gone through that door, you were more of a target than whoever was inside.'

I walked over to two crates and took one frag, leaving behind the incendiary grenade. On my return I held out a grenade.

'This time, throw a frag in to stun,' I ordered.

'But what about if there are hostages?' Blondie asked.

'I'll admit, on your previous breach any hostages would look different compared to the German uniform. However, in my time, any terrorist, insurgent, or nutter would be dressed almost the same as who he held captive. A stun grenade might not stop someone running out or returning fire, and you wouldn't have time to tell who the enemy was.'

'But the frag might kill the hostages or even one of us that might be captured,' Blondie argued.

'It's highly unlikely a frag will kill, more just incapacitate, but let's practice it,' I demanded—they did, and it worked well.

Next, I shouted for U-squad: Spike, Benny, Shrek, and Kauf. Before I took them in, I gave them a briefing and a re-enactment with what had happened to F-squad. I was dubious about Spike, but he changed in stature once he was going down the gloomy corridor, weapon tucked in his shoulder. Each man knew what his role was in that silent squad. After the explosive entry I told them to wait outside. Whilst they were gone I changed the layout. All the lads were buzzing outside, saying what they had done and how they went about it, and especially where the Germans were. I instructed K-squad to get tooled up ready for their turn.

After praising U-squad for how brilliant and accurate they were, I sent them back in, but without a grenade. They were far too relaxed and, not surprisingly, they had immediately opened fire, shooting at where they thought the Germans were situated. Each one of them got a smack around the back of the head and told they were complacent, and, all were fucking dead. Holding Kauf back whilst the rest sulked off, he agreed to my request to secretly tell K-squad the new layout of the room. Whilst he went outside to play the ruse, I stayed back. After removing all the Germans, I ordered K-squad in, the smugness written over their faces. It was even better when they had finished, all dejectedly walking out of the room. I had my best smug face on, as they had shot at nothing.

This exercise went on for the next hour, but we had changed the rooms, lighting, and mixed the squad members. The squads had to act a man was down. Whilst getting him out of the building, the other members fired live rounds close by, inside and outside. We even moved onto the next floor, with the staircase having chairs as German targets, even though we had obliterated nearly all the chairs. I was impressed with them all.

At the next briefing outside, they were all lively. This time, I said they would have to go in singular. Shrek was first to volunteer. He quickly got loaded up and went in, whilst we all reloaded and took on some water.

BOOOM!

The shattered glass and debris billowed out from the upstairs window, followed by a harsh smoke. Fuck; that was a prosperous grenade. Had he picked the wrong one up? All of us sprinted into the building and up the stairs, but at the top was Shrek, grinning wide.

'Burnt and suffocated all legs off the motherfucking Kraut chairs,' Shrek boasted.

'Outside, the bloody lot of you,' I ordered—the laughing stopped.

Under the warm sun rays, Shrek stood his ground at the front of them, his hands on his hips. I casually walked over to them. He clenched his fists.

'What the fuck was wrong with that?' he said angrily.

'Nothing,' I said—he relaxed. 'Oh, except you've just killed a hostage or your wife and kid. How the fuck are we supposed to enter after throwing a phos? You only use that type if you know what's in the fucking room, only to flush the enemy out that hasn't had his lungs burnt.'

Shrek stepped in my space, showing he was serious. I had a feeling he had not excepted me as a leader.

'You wanna argue some more? Maybe a bit of hand to hand?' I asked.

Shrek put his nose on mine and squinted. Planet joined him, staring hard at me and, knowing who would be next, so did Fish. I took a step back.

'Anyone else want to join these in a fight?' I asked. 'Who thinks I'm too hard on you lot?'

A few mumbled they were tired and hungry, as I'd guess they would.

'Bollocks are you. You've fucking passed selection. You're fucking supposed to be in the Elite. Man the fuck up.'

'Sorry, boss,' Rose said.

'I'll tell you what, we'll have one more exercise in this building. Let's call it the killing building.' Something triggered a memory. 'No, as we're all one big family, let's call it the killing house. Then after, you can all beat the shit out of me and then go back to your bunks for a rest. Agreed?'

'Seems like a plan to me,' Shrek said.

Everyone nodded, except Blondie and Rose.

I instructed them to stay outside whilst I made some alterations. From the side storage shed, I bust off the lock with the sledgehammer and then dragged around two high-pressurized gas cylinders that I had spotted earlier when foraging. I made sure the inquisitive lads saw the danger labels on the side. Inside, at the top of the stairs, I placed a German chair. Back in the watchful eyes I grabbed the tin of white paint. Their concerned silence was electrifying. On the last trip outside, without saying a word, I picked up the broken beer bottle glass and some small pieces of jeep wreckage. I placed them in a discarded cardboard box, then smiled. The lads became even more restless when I took a grenade and Thompson with me.

'What do you need all that for?' Shrek asked.

'You now know the layout of the whole building. In two of the rooms there each will be one highly explosive cylinder. Make sure you aim straight, or you will die. In the third room will be some Germans, but also some British being interrogated, marked with a white 'x' on the chairs. In the last room I will be sat in the chair. For an extra bit of fun I want you to synchronize your watches and plan to hit the four rooms simultaneously. Shrek, you choose the squads. If I hear the slightest noise before you breach the rooms, I will return a hail of lead down the corridor. Oh, and be careful where you walk.' I shook the intended objects in the box.

'Are you fucking joking?' Churchill asked—my glare gave him the reply he didn't want.

'What is the grenade for?' Shrek asked, intimidated.

'Well, just in case you lot still hate me and want to slot me, I'll drop the grenade and take you to hell with me. Don't forget to synchronize your watches.'

I left them taken aback by walking into the building, chuckling at the choice of words "slot me", knowing it was from my previous life.

Sitting in the chair against the far wall in the silent gloom, I held onto the grenade in full view of whoever came through first. Of course, I didn't really have the pin out, I wasn't that stupid. But then it dawned on me after I'd thought of my past: I had not wanted for any action, until now. Oh shit; I hope this doesn't end up badly.

CHAPTER TWENTY-TWO

Spread between the wreckage, some of those who lay face down were breathing heavy, whilst a few that sat up were motionless against whatever had taken them. Littered around were the weapons and clothing of these once active men. The odour of smoke had disappeared, but I could still smell and taste cordite. My own body had gone into shutdown-mode as I shut my eyes at the heat. As I questioned my actions, a new sound entered the ringing in my ears: a muffled cry. Opening my eyes, there was a mass of blurred lights. Human forms were sat around looking at me. It was a lot colder and the beeping noise and music seemed clearer, louder. Suddenly, the music stopped. A hand squeezed my aching fingers. Was that Ella? Without warning, all went a stark-white. Was this heaven?

I had not realised the time whilst we had all been lazing around in the sun after the training. Once the last exercise had finished, I was looking forward to telling those that had scaled the stairs that they had been killed by the German chair at the top. However, Rose had left a knife sticking out of the back of the chair. The lads had performed excellently. Thankfully, I was in one piece and the building hadn't got wrecked with the gas cylinders. Unbelievably, though, Shrek had tested the bazooka on the building.

A rumbling made me sit bolt upright. The lads all sat up from their sunbathing to see what had made the new noise: a twin propeller beast manoeuvring out of the hangar. The vibration ran through the ground, seeming to rattle in my chest. The sun glinted off the windows of the gunner's viewing cockpit. Another two were taxied into position. An air of anticipation went around us. We all stood up, my heart beating fast. A different look swept across the other faces. I put my shirt back on.

'They're not Halifax bombers,' I said.

'They are the Armstrong Whitworth Albemarle,' Fish said nerdy.

'Originally designed as a medium bomber, but never really proved essential. These have been loaned by RAF Brize…'

I glared at him—he shut up. 'Right, you lot, grab your main weapons and kit and get back to the barracks.'

'What about all this mess?' Trigger asked, shattered.

'The French SAS will mop up,' I said, impersonating James.

Even whilst the lads quietly sorted their personal kit, everyone kept an eye on the planes being loaded. At least we now had the right tools for the trade.

Everyone sombrely walked off, the excited and brazen mood had changed. Blondie tucked in his shirt and then picked up his haversack.

'Blondie, wait here a second,' I said. 'You seem to be best mates with Trigger, right?'

'No more than the rest. He is interested in the Lord, though. He wants to pray with me.'

'I need you to befriend him more. I need to find out his real age as I don't believe he's nineteen.'

'But why would he lie?' Blondie said.

'It might be something to do with his brother recently being killed by the Germans, or wanting to prove himself to his parents. Maybe he was bullied at school.'

We started to walk to the bunkhouse. Blondie pushed his glasses up the bridge of his nose.

'So, you are not scared of dying either?' he said.

'Why do you say that?'

'You sat alone in the killing house in the dark with a force that could easily have killed you. You must have trusted God for faith.'

'Not really. I just trusted you lot not to make a fucking mistake. Talking of the big man in the chair, what's heaven like?'

Blondie stopped and held my arm, looking excited to the point of tears. He quickly whipped out his bible and said, 'So, you are starting to believe. Do you want to pray with me?'

'Bollocks. I just want to go back to heaven and ask them to play different a type of music. I mean, why play my dad's favourite music?' The reality struck me, now knowing who loved these tracks, and I quickly walked off.

'You are a complex man, Johnny,' Blondie shouted, not best pleased.

Back in the dormer, the tense silence was crippling as we all sorted our own kit. The rosy colour from the beer and training had disappeared.

Little snippets of recollections came to mind of my recent operations. Maybe the knock to the back of my head was wearing off. Was Churchill lying about the alley incident? But why were a couple of thugs beating up Benny?

Siting on my bunk, I shook my head in disbelief that we were going to war without sophisticated target-identifying equipment, hi-tech communications, state-of-the-art weaponry and explosives, but most importantly, no body armour or highly trained medics with full trauma kits. But then, these brave blokes knew no better. A part of me wished the future memories would fuck off. My hands had started to tremble.

I let everyone leave first and then took a long look at their personal possessions on each bunk. A few had photos of their loved ones. Letters were enveloped and addressed to Mum and Dad, and other people. A lump came to the throat. I scoffed at the comics, playing cards, pin-up girls, and then sniggered at the whisky bottle tops under Shrek's bed. Weaves' bunk was the only one that was made. I hoped we would all have a few beers with him on our return. Twelve heroes and me under the watchful eye of the nation, the top brass, and all under my wing. The whole situation had become daunting. I'm not sure why, maybe for luck, even though I had never been superstitious, I put the watch back on. Perhaps I did it for comfort, or even as a tribute to Skedgewell.

Inside the hangar, all the lads' complexions seemed to have drained of colour. Richard and two of his mates came over, dragging six large bags, the staff not even battering an eye. They knew what Richard was like. Yet, Richard wasn't his jovial self, but sincere, reserved. He told me that he had got nearly everything on the list and that he had tried his best. Once he had dragged the haul over to the quiet lads, he wished us all the best and then made a hasty exit.

'I hope you have some girls for the flight.' Rose said—Blondie sighed.

'Just some sailors for you, Rose,' I said, adding banter.

'I am no bum bandit, as folk used to say from your era,' Rose retorted.

'No, just a knob jockey,' Geordie said.

With the insults and jokes rousing them, except Blondie, I opened the first bag and pulled out the first object: a German infantry helmet. I was in awe of it, but looking around at the rest, they were not impressed.

'Are you trying to jinx us?' Tommo snapped.

'Sometimes you have to think outside the box.'

They all looked at me, mystified.

I sighed. 'OK, you have to adapt to your scenery. Think about it, this may be another way through the German lines. How else are we going to get past the guards to the ammo facility?'

'The what?' Trigger asked.

'The bloody bomb dump,' I snapped.

I chucked the helmet to Kauf and started to pull out the next bit of kit. As if it was a hot piece of coal, Kauf quickly passed it onto Trigger, who then tapped it.

'I am not going to miss this in my three-point-five scope. Trusty Mark-Four Enfield. Bang,' Trigger said.

After he had smacked the helmet, I envisaged the same weapon being fired in the Sumatran jungle. I held onto my bicep as a weird pain made me shudder.

Rummaging further, I began to throw aside the equipment not required.

'Bin the respirators, Hexi-stoves, and anything else that will slow us down,' I said.

'Respirator? Hexi-stove?' Trigger quizzed. 'You mean gasmask and Tommy cooker.'

Planet gave him a cuff behind the ear.

The rest of the bags contained more helmets and a German officer's hat, about which everyone argued over who was having it. The next bag contained some German trench coats and the iconic Luger pistol and holster, something I had not added on my list. I asked the lads to strip out of their British Army uniform and put on the black trousers and shirts. Confused at my request, I clarified that wearing the British combat uniform could compromise us, getting us killed, especially with the Kommando rule. Furthermore, we could now blend into the shadows, rather than stick out like a beige dog-turd on a highly-polished black granite floor. The other idea: we could be gypsies or French refugees on our escape. Once dressed, everyone cursed Spike for asking if they were going to a funeral.

'What are the small plastic bags for?' Trigger asked, the clear bags trembling in his hand.

'That is your body bag for your scrawny self,' Geordie joked.

'That's your dry-sack,' I said. 'All important stuff you want to keep dry must go inside it.'

'Like Spike's humour,' Tommo chipped in.

My nerves were mounting as the lads were now assembled in a row, the beige harnesses were being double-checked. Only two from each squad had the small parachute first-aid pack strapped on, the cylindrical kit bags clipped to each man's leg. The instructor adjusted each man's helmet and, once done, he tapped the top. One of the Airborne lads came up to me and first put on the deflated lifejacket. This didn't fill me with joy. Next, he started to fit the green packs. I looked at the big red pull lever, and then I tightened the harnesses a bit more. The bloke adding more equipment sensed something. He handed me two booklets: *Emergency Uses of the Parachute*, the other a *Log Book*. He told me to make sure I read one, and that I came back to fill out the log book. He smiled and winked at me.

Babs, who was wearing a lovely long dress, had been escorted in. She embraced Planet in a lingering kiss. I looked on, wanting some of her affection, as did the others. An order went out to get into our sticks, but as the lads rallied into their lines for each plane, someone shouted my name. At the far end in the shadows a lone figure stood silhouetted. I told the Airborne sergeant to give me a second—he was displeased, to say the least.

As I closed in, the bloke stood with his head slightly bowed and with his hands in his pockets.

'Tim, is that you?' I said.

'Yes, son.' He didn't even look up, as if hiding his frail form and aging complexion.

'You don't look well.'

'Good luck, son.'

'You can't keep up this pretence forever: your accent, your looks, your evasiveness. You see, Tim, you're either a spy, or a wannabe... a Walter Mitty.'

'You're wrong on all counts,' he said aggressively.

'You failed the test: I'd mentioned Colonel Mustard, yet when you had replied with Miss Scarlet with the candlestick, I checked with Fish when the game Cluedo had been released. He told me he'd never heard of it. I knew I was right. So how the fuck would you know of such a game?'

'Tell Fish he is wrong. The game is from the States. There it's called Murder. We played it in the shelters.'

'Skedgewell. What the dickens are you doing over there? Stop larking around and get your sorry, pathetic self over here, now.'

I turned to see a moody James standing with the Airborne unit. The lads were marching out towards the aircraft. Damn it, I wanted to do a speech to them before we boarded. I looked at my watch, which had stopped.

'We'll carry on with this on my return, Tim. What's the exact time?'

Tim placed a hand across his watch. 'It doesn't matter, son. Take care.'

Tim walked off with his head still slightly bowed, heading out of sight through the hangar's metal rear door. Heavily loaded, I made a wobbly run past the curious lads and James, my bulky gear nearly tipping me over.

'What were you doing over there? Having a toilet?' James asked.

'Yeah, too much fine whisky, sir.'

'I take that as jest,' he said. 'Have you thought of a nickname for me?'

The Airborne lads next to him waited expectantly, but I hadn't thought of one since he last asked.

'Well?' he asked.

'Fuck knows,' I blurted.

Making a short wiggling beeline run out of the hangar, I was puzzled as to how James couldn't have seen Tim talking to me. As I reached Blondie by the tail of the aircraft, he awkwardly turned to say something, a look of urgency across his face.

'Don't ask now, I'll fill you in later,' I said.

'I need…'

'Where's Churchill?' I interrupted him.

'Saying his good lucks, Johnny.'

I spotted Churchill and Benny embracing each other. Was this them making up? I hoped so. Seeing the lads embark, a wave of guilt overwhelmed as I hadn't given them a morale-boosting speech. I made a mental note to do it at the first RV.

By the time I had turned to see what was on Blondie's mind, he was being vigorously pulled up from the small dropdown foot-ladder and then through the large opening door. It was if the crew were saying, no changing your mind now, lad. Before my turn, I stared at the large yellow, blue, white, and red RAF roundel painted next to the door. Someone behind squeezed my shoulder and then patted it. I half-pivoted to see Churchill. Trying not to let him see my nerves, I pulled a crazy face at him.

'Let's go slot some motherfuckers,' I said.

A big grin went across his face, his helmet straps could have almost broken.

The initial take-off was as bumpy and noisy as I had expected. Once we had hit altitude, the tension rose, the temperature dropped. I sat close next to Planet. Opposite were Churchill and Fish. I was going to tell Planet to get out of the seat closest to the glass turret that had been modified into a tail ramp, like I had in the Chinook, but I decided not to. Surely lightning couldn't strike twice. A whiff of sick was evident, but I didn't ask. Blondie told me he wanted to get closer to God, so he took it upon himself to go up into the top empty mid-section gunnery viewing dome. Maybe we didn't need the gunner crew on board. Perhaps the Germans never flew their fighters at night. Possibly this was what Blondie was praying for.

With the odd swathe of moonlight, I looked at the white faces around me, but nobody made eye contact. I began to think about what lay ahead, trying to stay positive, turn any fear into aggression. However, I knew we were being immersed into the deep end, no, the abyss. The longer I looked into it, the harder it stared back at my soul. It wasn't that I didn't believe we could carry out the mission orders, but was aware of the colossal challenges that lay ahead, especially with the little intelligence and backup. But then, joining the Elite, you knew it wouldn't be easy.

Blondie sat next to me, bible in hand, his weapon in the other. He swallowed hard.

'Blondie, you look like a fox who has just heard the hounds. What's up?' I said, asking the plain obvious.

'I have found out how old Alek is. He is only fifteen.'

'What?' I yelled, not expecting this. 'What the fuck? Only fifteen? Why didn't you tell me?' I stood up, knocking Planet as I did.

Blondie stood as well. 'I did try to, but you interup...'

'Bollocks, Saxton. You should have shouted over me, or even stopped him.'

'I tried...'

I didn't listen to what he had to say next, I was making my way up to the cockpit, passing the navigator who was busy studying a map. I tapped the pilot on the shoulder. He unclipped his half-face mask and lifted his goggles. It was a lot colder in here.

'Who gave you permission to be up here?' he asked.

'It is fine, Billy,' Wilson said. 'This is the man that saved Mullen and Sayers.'

'Fine show,' Billy said. 'William May. Call me Billy. Nice to meet you.'

'Johnny Vince. Likewise.' I shook his cold hand whilst staring into the black blanket and bright stars. 'I need to get an urgent message to the pilot that's flying F-squad,' I ordered.

'Kenny, have you told Skedgewell that he and his men's wages will go towards paying for the annually RAF fete items, the ones they destroyed in the coal bunkers?' Billy asked.

'Did you not bloody hear me?' I said.

'What is your problem, chum?' Wilson asked me.

'One of my men, Trigger, I mean Alek Sagar, is underage. You need to take him home.'

Wilson undid the neck of his thick woollen flying jacket. 'As much as you saved Wing Leader Sayers' life, I do not think he will just turn his aircraft around.'

'He has to. Order him,' I pleaded.

Billy scoffed, then lit up a cigarette. 'He is not the first young man to go into battle.'

'He's fucking fifteen, you dickhead,' I said.

'You will be taking the quick route through the bomb doors in a minute.'

'Fuck off.'

'Chaps,' Wilson barked. 'Leave it there. That is an order. OK, Skedgewell, I will radio Sayers and order him not to let Sagar drop.'

I nodded my appreciation at Wilson, but gave the back of Billy's head a dirty look. There was a bit of an awkward silence, nevertheless, I wasn't leaving until I heard the message.

'Wing Leader Sayers, over?' Kenny mumbled into his mask.

Thud!

I managed to just about stay on my feet as the aircraft shook. Calmly, the pilots relayed messages to each. Further short sharp thuds with orange flashes surrounded us, followed by dark-grey clouds. Looking through the glass panels directly at the front of the nose, a swarm of what looked like a thousand fireflies made their way up to us. Wilson, who seemed unperturbed by the number of tracers and airburst, pointed at me to go to the rear. He then ordered the others to gain altitude. Just as I was hastily making a retreat between the plane shaking and the chaos, Billy said that Sayers had taken a hit. I scrambled back past the navigator who was still looking through a viewfinder. I spotted a glow in the distance, and it was growing.

The explosions and tracers seem to be directed at the increasing light. The mysterious blaze lit up the side of the Albemarle's wing and fuselage. Suddenly, the wing disintegrated. The hulking shape began to twirl into the black below, lit up occasionally by the enemy airburst. I was ordered in level tones to get everyone ready for immediate drop. Racing back through the fuselage, trying not to get snagged, the moon's light showed up big holes in the sides of the aircraft. The crew member at the rear was pushing the basket crates to the edge of the open tail, flashes casting his shadow on the inside. A wash of air slightly pushed me back as the dispatcher opened the door, the horrendous noise intensifying. I screamed at the scared faces of the lads to get up, my high-pitched voice out of breath.

In a line, all holding each other up as the aircraft shuddered and rocked, we were clipped on. Everyone gave their static line a tug; I copied. Bits of metal burst open from the belly; the navigator was now a heap of mess on the floor. Out went the baskets first. I looked back to see the dispatcher push Planet out and, like a train, we shuffled along. I watched Blondie get shoved, knowing I was next. In the next moment, the dispatcher was violently shoved back against the other side of the fuselage, his lower legs completely gone. As I jumped for freedom, I noticed the gaping hole by the side of the exit.

Being sucked out in the turbulence, I quickly checked the canopy above. The vast night sky above lit up like an orange sun for a few seconds. Was that the plane I had just left? I searched the noisy blackness above for both aircraft, but couldn't identify anything, other than the flashes and tracers. Below, I explored the darkness and streaks for any sign of life. The smells and sounds were frightening—and I had thought this was freedom from the plane. It would be a miracle if I landed intact, let alone alive.

Then descended the silence, except the fluttering of the canopy above. In the unnerving chill I saw the black and white photos of F-squadron: Corporal David Charlton, Rifleman Stuart Crawford, Gunner Scott Tompkins, and the youngest, Private Alek Sagar. Rage flooded me, but then a wave of uncontrollable guilt. I wiped the tears that streamed down my face. Fuck; they were all so young. Why oh why did a boy of fifteen want to join this madness? And what about the brave RAF crew and pilots? Had it been worth me saving Wing Leader Sayers? I hoped in the time that he was alive after, that he had got to see his loved ones. Did U-squadron's plane make it? My stomach knotted at the thought of losing more lads, especially Shrek. Was I going to find bits of my squad attached to the chute's harnesses? I looked across the night sky, the stars being obscured by thick smoke. Had Kenny Wilson and the surviving crew made it? I kept an eye on the inky-black below, just hoping it wouldn't be long before my feet touched the ground so I could forget about the horrors above. But then, what lay below?

CHAPTER TWENTY-THREE

Luckily, the ground that had come up in the dying seconds was very soft. Next to a large hedge in what appeared to be a ploughed field, I quickly pulled in my parachute. With the air depleting from it as I lay on top, I stopped and tuned in. Silently, I reeled in the fifteen feet of rope with my kitbag attached to it. In a way, I wished NVGs had been invented, but then, the downside was that I could be seen.

After a few minutes, I laid down my Sten and slowly and quietly took off the parachute gear. In the rut next to me I hand-shovelled the dirt over the top of the equipment. Sporadic gunfire in the far distance stopped me, the unnerving silence enveloped. With the hiding finished, I fought off the negative thoughts of the others that hadn't made it. With just the sound of my own breathing and beeping, I tucked down low, turning on the DB-flashlight. With the red torch filter selected I checked the time: 21.16 hrs.

Making sure all my weapons were ready and everything was secure and wouldn't rattle, I double-checked the bearing against the map. Shutting the flip-up cover on the compass, I was quite a way from the LZ. I prepared to move out, when suddenly, a black object to my left about thirty metres back caught my attention in the rutted field. I pulled my Sten into my shoulder. Creeping along the right-angled hedgerow, upper right arm level with the stock, I sighted the object. Further up, another mass moved. I froze, finger caressing the trigger. Tip toping, and now within ten metres, I realised the mass was a parachute. Rapidly, I returned my eyes to the first object. Was that a body?

It was a tricky decision: to either venture out from the shadows into the direct moonlight, or to leave the unidentified object. However, the squad member could be alive. And even if he was dead, it would compromise the mission if a German patrol came across the field. Squatting as low as possible, I stealthily moved towards it, checking the surrounding perimeter. Foot by foot, lifting a over the ploughed soft ridges, I discovered it wasn't a body but a smashed basket. Further parts were scattered, but the main twisted mortar stuck out. Laying down, I then dug out some earth until the mortar was about level with the ploughed field, all the time keeping vigil. Next, I cut the lines and wrapped in the shredded parachute. How I survived the incoming was a miracle, and I hoped I wasn't the only one. Once the chute was buried the best I could, I did a quick search for anything of value, but it was fruitless. It was very hard not to search the rest of the area and beyond for my squad, but my directives were to reach the RV.

Navigating through the soft soil with the load wasn't done with finesse, but a little time later I found the farm gate. Fortunately, it was unlocked. After checking the narrow tarmac lane, I scurried along the shadow of the hedge. Because of the high moon I wondered if had been a good idea not to wear any cam-cream. Even through the water that had collected along the side of the lane, my boots seemed very loud. Unexpectedly, in the distance was the sound of artillery sonic booms, followed by rapid gunfire. I hoped any Germans in this area would now be going to assist that battle, making our task here easier.

A guitar started to play, followed by more instruments, taking my mind off the firefight. Tucking into the hedge, I listened to the song that had been playing in my mind, not having heard it before.

> From up above I heard
> The angels sing to me these words
> And sometimes in your eyes
> I see the beauty in the world

I knew it was Chris Martin singing the song, but wondered if the lyrics were some sort of sick joke or a message from one of the lads shot down. Had they made it?

> Oh, now I'm floating so high
> I blossom and die
> Send your storm and your lightning to strike
> Me between the eyes
> Eyes

I believed each song that I subconsciously played had something to do with what was happening, trying to tell me something. Bloody hell, now I was going mad.

> Sometimes the stars decide
> To reflect in puddles in the dirt

When I look in your eyes
I forget all about what hurts

A dog barking close by brought me back to my senses. Even without washing or using any perfumes, I knew it could pick up my scent, as I hadn't blended into the surroundings. My eyes were still straining as they had not adjusted the forty minutes to the dark. Quickly, I squat-ran across the lane and waded into the ditch on the other side, the high foliage stopping me jumping the stonewall. The cold water was only about two feet deep. Just as I was about to make a dash to my left through a broken part of wall into the woodland, I spotted a glow; I froze, time froze. Slowly submerging like a crocodile, I kept one hand on the bank. With my eyes and nose just out of the black murkiness, I watched the radiance of the cigarette, seeming to move from left to right.

Wham! Nostalgia, fear, and excitement all hit me at once, the beeping became erratic. No more than ten metres in front of my watery trough were two iconic German soldiers sharing a smoke. Watching the ripples on the surface in front of my nose expand further, the mutt on the lead came closer. I slowed my breathing, almost holding it. Many reactions screamed through me: run, go underwater, do not move a muscle, attack. Were my eyes lit up like headlamps? Should I close them? Would I be able to get up with my weapon in time? Would it work now that is was wet? What I did know was that my heart was coming out of my throat. Adrenalin surged through me. Training, I thought, getting a grip.

Fuck. Why had they stopped? At least they weren't looking my way or on the ground for any tracks I may have left. I studied the field cap on the soldier on the right whilst he took a piss into the ditch, the mutt watching him. Clearly visible was the army's eagle, swastika, and cockade on a grey patch on the front cap's crown. Matching the colour of the hat was the grey-green double-breast-buttoned shirt, and trousers. He turned and took back his Panzerfaust-60 of his mate. Simon Krycler had warned me about the one-shot anti-tank weapon. The soldier adjusted his main rifle that was slung over his shoulder, and then he wiped the tips of his high black boots on the back of his legs. I guessed this infantryman was only about eighteen; yet, with the kit strapped to his back, ammo pouches, egg grenades, and the infamous stick-grenade, he meant business.

As they carried on walking closer, their boots seemed louder than mine had. The evil twisted cross became more intimidating. I wished I had learnt German at school, thinking maybe I could glean some info on where they were heading. The other solider had the standard German helmet and blue-green uniform, including a stick-grenade poking out of the top of his high boot. He flicked the fag away, fizzing close to my head. I wondered if they had watched it fly away. How much of my backpack was stuck out of the water? I mentally cursed for not slipping it off first.

It wasn't till the voices and footsteps disappeared that I let go of the tension. Lifting my mouth above the water I breathed a sigh of relief. Using my hands on the bottom of the ditch I pulled my floating body along to a small culvert. Slowly, I turned back and got onto one knee, thinking how close that had been. Twenty seconds or so later, I would have been seen opening the gate. Instead of focusing on the worry, though, I turned it into a massive positive.

The metal grid that the water ran through was partly blocked with twigs and foliage, so I lifted myself out of the water. It poured from my body in tune with the culvert. An image instantly came to mind: a TV advert of a Royal Marine lifting his head out of a lagoon. At last, more recollections from my past were returning.

Making as little noise as possible through the forest came naturally. Every now and then I checked the map in its waterproof cover against the compass. Even though June, it was surprising cold, and it didn't help being soaked through. Time check: 21.51. Before I made the last stage towards the RV, I scanned the area, but it was pitch-black, not even the moon made its way in. Knowing that the lads were probably on edge, I secured the torch to my buttonhole and turned it on, using a green filter.

Dead on where the first RV was, no one was there. My gut turned and heart sank. The sliding action-bolt behind me kick-started my heart. Slowly turning with my hands and weapon slightly raised, I gulped. Out of the shadows came Fish; I relaxed.

'Thank the Lord you made it,' he said.

'Why wouldn't I, it's me who's in charge.' I smiled.

Pulling him close for a hug, I patted him on the back, not wanting to let go.

'Haddaway, man, it was my message to God that saved your backside.'

'Blondie,' me and Fish said together.

Blondie came out of the bush and joined in our delight with handshakes and slaps on the backs.

'Champion,' he said.

'I see the wind rush hasn't helped your hair,' I said.

'I is all up a height, man.'

Blondie tried to brush the chopped bits forward. Me and Fish looked at each other not knowing what he had said, but it didn't matter, we were overjoyed, and I loved his rich accent more than ever.

'Great to see you, chaps. Now give me and Spike a hand with this lot,' Churchill said.

It was fantastic to see them both. Further congratulations followed, but they still found it awkward me giving them a manly bear hug.

Churchill and Spike had found two baskets of ammo and weapons, and amazingly, had dragged them all the way here unnoticed. The euphoric mood was all the greater because, apart from the odd cuts and bruises, we had all made it with no serious injuries. To add to the elation, Shrek appeared; however, it was short-lived when Shrek broke the news that Kauf had smashed into the trees, having plummeted to earth when his parachute had caught fire. You could see the burning images in Shrek's eyes as Kauf had screamed past his own descent. Without showing any lack of compassion for Kauf, I gave Shrek a massive embrace, happy that he had made it.

In a defensive position, we told our sides of the story: Shrek said that he had cut down Kauf and buried him the best he could, leaving Kauf's helmet over the makeshift grave with the name 'J. Moline' carved with a knife. Any chance of the unknown soldier not happening was agreed before we had left, even though we were completely sterile of ID. Fish bowed his head and cleared his throat...

> 'We laid him in a cool and shadowed grove
> One evening in the dreamy scent of thyme
> Where leaves were green, and whispered high above –
> A grave as humble as it was sublime;
> There, dreaming in the fading deeps of light –
> The hands that thrilled to touch a woman's hair;
> Brown eyes, that loved the Day, and looked on Night,
> A soul that found at last its answered Prayer ...
> There daylight, as a dust, slips through the trees.
> And drifting, gilds the fern around his grave –
> Where even now, perhaps, the evening breeze
> Steals shyly past the tomb of him who gave
> New sight to blinded eyes; who sometimes wept –
> A short time dearly loved; and after, – slept.'

Fish looked up.

'Thanks, Fish,' I said. 'I'm not sure if you know, lads, but Geordie,

Tommo, Rose, and Trigger didn't make it. Their plane was shot...'

'They could have baled out, boss,' Churchill interrupted.

'There was that Yank who lived after getting shot out of a bomber's gun turret. He fell to the ground without a parachute,' Shrek said, looking at Fish for some backup.

'This is true. Alan Magee fell four miles in nineteen forty-three. They reckon...'

'Lads,' I said, stopping Fish. 'I know we have to remain positive, but I saw the plane explode in a fireball and it went spinning out of sight.'

'But you did not see if anyone baled out before it hit the ground,' Shrek said, hoping.

'I really do doubt anyone survived. We need to be realistic about what lies ahead. And with Benny and Planet missing, and Kauf dead, we have to decide whether to continue.'

'Benjamin will show up,' Churchill said.

'And Robert will,' Shrek added.

'I hope you prayed for them with your God bollocks,' Fish said.

Blondie shot to his feet and said, 'You would be a smartarse, if you were smart.'

Fish grabbed Blondie by the shirt, and I sensed that Blondie was going to head-butt him.

'Anyone got any scotch for this party?'

'Planet,' I quietly shrieked.

The damaged radio-comms was dumped to the floor. I quickly ran over to him and shook his free hand. He winced in pain and held his shoulder. I grabbed his head and stared up into his eyes, but my words didn't come out. The rest of the lads crowded around showing their jubilation at the silent party. Planet, ignoring the fuss, placed the Bren on the floor and took off his huge backpack.

'Where are the others?' he asked.

'All have passed over to the other side, except Benny,' Blondie replied. 'We have no idea yet where he is.'

'Defected to the Heinies, hey. Fucking traitors.' Planet grinned.

'I meant the other side, as in heaven,' Blondie corrected.

'Ye don't say,' Planet said sarcastically—a chuckle went around us all.

'What's a Heinie?' I whispered to Fish.

'It is what the Americans call the Germans.'

'Poor old Weaves missing all the fun,' Planet added—Blondie sighed.

'Any of that whisky survive?'

Shrek delved into his kitbag and pulled out a half-bottle of Scotch Whisky, unscrewed the cap and then went to take a swig.

'Bottoms up.'

'No way,' I said, snatching it from Shrek's pouting lips. 'You need to be a hundred per cent on the ball if we are to get out of this shithole of a mess.'

'But, Johnny, it is only right we each take a swig to celebrate the lives of our fallen,' Blondie said—everyone nodded in agreement, like the dogs, again.

'Even you, churchman?' I said.

'If there was not wine at the last supper, I am sure whisky would have been, so I will go first,' Blondie said.

'Aye, and it would have been Scottish, like Jesus was.'

I released my grip. Shrek handed it to Blondie who was still baffled by what Planet had just said. He then took a tiny sip; a silent cheer went up. After the rest had all had a large swig, I took a little one and then tipped the rest out—the look on their faces.

'In Flanders fields the poppies blow...'

'Not now, Fish,' I said. 'We'll let Blondie say a prayer later, but first we need to decide a plan to retreat to the jeeps.'

'Retreat?' Churchill said incredulously. 'We are not a bunch of yellow bellies.'

'I've checked the area designated, and the French never left the vehicles,' Planet said.

'Fuck,' I hushed

'Or Krycler never got the message through,' Fish added.

'The main comms to HQ is knackered,' I added. 'Who has the other handheld radio in your squad, Shrek?'

'Kauf had it, but it was missing on him,' he said reluctantly .

'Bollocks,' I whispered. 'We are five men down and one missing in action. It would be suicidal to carry on to the two targets without any further backup.'

Churchill's eyes narrowed to a steely glare and he said, 'Benjamin might be here soon.'

'And where's the rest of the gear? We've got one fucking walkie-talkie between us,' I kicked the busted radio, 'and no armed jeeps for a decent get away.'

'Perhaps Krycler got mad because of my stupid joke with the empty bottles,' Shrek admitted.

'Conceivably, I should have told the truth to Lieutenant Mullen,' Blondie said.

'Let's not get all negative, lads,' I said, 'it's the first mindset change about survival. However, I don't think we should carry on.'

'I want this to go to a vote. You called it a Chinese parliament, or something,' Churchill said.

Let's give it fair analysis, I thought. 'OK, Churchill. Who the fuck wants to carry on Operation Poppy Pride on the limited manpower? What prick wants to carry on with no mortar and gunner team at the first RV. What dickhead still wants to go into this mental mission with no comms, knowing they are low on resources and have no means of a quick exit plan if it goes tits-up?'

Their hands shot up simultaneously—I smiled.

'I believe God thinks he is the Lord,' Spike blurted.

'What?' I said.

'Blondie asked if I believed in God,' Spike said slowly.

'That was way back before we practised the final exercise in the killing house,' Blondie said.

'Same difference,' Spike answered.

'Man, ye are a bellend,' Planet said.

I started off the quiet laughing as Spike had pulled a face. The rest joined in. It was a surreal moment: here we were behind enemy lines, all enjoying the banter, with alcohol-fumed breaths.

With the time ticking on, I asked Blondie if he could save his prayer for later. We had to discuss an emergency plan and get all the kit ready. After everyone had put their own ideas and views forward, it was decided that we would all hit the first and second target together.

Under low lights from the torches, we ate cold, salty bully fritters, oatmeal biscuits and, oddly, tinned herring. I was damn thirsty after. As we all got our water bottles out to wash it down, especially the oatmeal that had stuck to our gums, Churchill started to hand around some tablets. When I quizzed what they were, he seemed taken aback that I had not seen them before: Benzedrine tablets, or bennies as he put it. They were to keep us awake and alert. With a big grin on his face, Churchill started to pass around the legendary beret, boosting the morale.

Without knowing the internal layout of each target and the outside security, the brief plan for executing the attack was a vague. We did, however, make sure that all the pencil fuses had stayed dry in the dry-sacks. Each man had the same amount of ammo and weapons, except

Planet who wouldn't let go of the Bren. We studied the routes on the map. I had to convert from the usual kilometres to miles. It was decided that Fish, in the absence of the perfect German-speaking Kauf, would take the higher commanding German officer's clothes as he spoke the most fluent German. Plus, he knew French and Italian. Shrek objected, even more so when I handed Fish the Luger. We hid the gear that we didn't require under the hessian and soil, and buried deep our food waste.

The exciting part was opening the wicker-styled baskets, similar to oversized picnic hampers, which had been dropped with us. Churchill opened one, whilst I unlocked the largest one. I pulled out a pump-action shotgun.

'Oh yes, now you're talking,' I said. 'Fucking ammo up, lads.'

The lads left Churchill and crowded around me. Shrek poked his head through the wall of defiance.

'Hey, that is mine,' he said.

'Bollocks is it,' I said. 'Anyway, it has my name on the side: Model 1897 Winchester.'

'Bugger off, you bastard,' Shrek said, and returned to help Churchill.

With the weapon firmly in front of my knees, I unloaded the rest of the ammo, explosives, det-charges, and cortex wire. Lastly, I gave the shotgun's bayonet to Shrek as a consolation prize, knowing he would tell me to shove it up my arse—he didn't disappoint.

Once everything was unloaded and shared out, I ordered everyone to check their main weapons. I picked up the spare Sten machinegun, turning the magazine chamber to the side and slotting in a magazine.

'What are we going to do about Benjamin?' Blondie asked.

'What do you mean?' I said.

'We cannot just leave without him.'

'Do you want to wait, or go search for him?'

'No. We head to the bomb dump,' Churchill stepped in.

I moved the cocking handle back and forth a few times, ignoring Churchill's growing mood. With time speedily ticking, I looked at my watch.

Bang!

'Jesus Christ, boss,' Churchill said, still hunkered.

'Why the fuck wasn't the safety catch on?' I said, trying to blame someone else for my fuck-up.

As the smoke wafted through the light emitting from the torch, Churchill snatched it from me. 'The slide back is the safety catch, you fool. Everyone fucking knows that. It is so easy to snag the cocking handle on something and engage it without knowing. Jesus Christ, boss, you could have shot one of us.'

Blondie raged, 'Andrew, do you know the real significance of the words you bandy around?'

'What the bloody hell do you mean, Saxton?'

'The inappropriate usage of the words "Jesus Christ".'

'Shut up, Blondie,' I snapped.

'Took the words right…'

'Shhh. Both of you shut the fuck up a second. Listen,' I said.

Someone slightly west of us was shouting. Everyone immediately turned off their lights. I whispered for everyone to grab their kit and to silently follow me.

Occasionally, I stopped where the moonlight shone in a clearing on the forest's floor. Every time Spike had tapped me on the shoulder, I knew everyone had caught up. The only noise was from the leaves that sometimes shivered on the trees. At the next wall of bushes that surrounded the clearing, I waited for another shout, and when it came, it had a German accent. A scream echoed into the night; my hands tightened on the shotgun. On my belly I crawled up to the natural ditch that had formed in front of some bushes. With only the breathing of the others, I peered through. In a grassy clearing about the size of half a football pitch was a tall German officer. He stood next to two lit large lanterns, reflecting off his shiny-black trench coat. He kicked something on the ground, a moan followed. He looked around in a 360-degree circle.

'British soldiers,' he yelled. 'Your time is up.'

'What does he mean?' Planet whispered in my ear.

'I don't know.'

This time, the officer bent down and picked up something, his peaked cap lit up in the light. Then he started to violently punch what was in his hand. Fuck; it was Benny's head. Benny's head and shoulders were thrown back to the dirt.

'Come out and I spare this man's life,' the officer shouted.

CHAPTER TWENTY-FOUR

Spike was already aiming down the sight of his Enfield.

'Take the fucking shot, Spike,' I whispered.

'No,' Churchill said.

Churchill pushed down Spike's rifle. Planet nudged me and I slowly looked back to see another shadow holding what appeared to be a candle. The enemy officer forced Benny sit up and then harshly held Benny's puffy eyes open. He picked up the lanterns and walked around in a circle. Benny's eyes stared this way with a look of complete sorrow. Could he see us? If not, could he sense we were here? Was he asking why we were not taking the shot?

The officer took a few large strides back; I lost the sight of Benny's eyes.

'Slot the motherfucker now,' I growled low.

'Wait,' Churchill whispered.

An evil jet of death spewed out, lighting up the area in which the German infantryman stood. In the sickening screams, Benny thrashed around in a ball of flames on the ground. Horrified, I watched the officer smile. As I pulled my shotgun around in a blind rage, Churchill jumped on top of me, holding his hand across my mouth. More hands restrained my intense anger. Through the fingers around my face I peeped to see the flaming body of Benny still urgently rolling. Why were they fucking holding me back? Why weren't they helping Benny?

A hand was taken off my face and Churchill came eye to eye, putting his finger across his lips. I thrust my arms out to try to grab him, but again, I was overpowered. Spitting vengeance at him, I was silenced with a hand tightly across my mouth. I knew it was Planet's, just by the size of it. I was at the stage I could have bitten it, when he released his grip, the weight from my legs and torso lifted. Benny was now smouldering like a solid statue. I quickly sank back into the ditch and grabbed Churchill as he crawled away. With my dagger out, I turned him over and put the tip to his throat. His eyes were raw with tears. He waved at the others to let go of me.

'Go on, do it,' he hushed.

'You fucking racist scumbag,' I whispered.

'You know nothing. You never listen.'

I pushed the tip further forward; he arched his neck back. Blondie held onto my shaking hand and pulled the blade back. Churchill began to sob.

'Why did you let him die?' I asked.

'I let you live, you all live,' Churchill said.

'What?'

'Vinnie, be quiet, look,' Shrek said.

Laying alongside Shrek, peering through the bushes, a German jeep equipped with a mounted heavy-machinegun was coming into the clearing. The headlights lit up the German flame-thrower and officer. I hadn't noticed the track leading in. From the outer edges, concealed in the bushes and trees, many forms started to emerge. One by one they all walked through the beams to view the charcoal remains. After watching twenty German soldiers gloating with pride, I shook, my head buried in my hands.

When the place was quiet, I lifted my head in the eeriness. The only signs of such evil brutality was the weird shape of the smouldering mass on the floor, and the putrid smell. I needed to speak to Churchill, I thought. Sitting there alone was Blondie. He half-smiled at me, tears under his glasses. He knew I was stuck for words.

'Judging a person does not define who they are, it defines who you are,' Blondie said softly.

'I didn't know it was a trap,' I said.

'I am not judging you. You saw what your eyes believed, but if you knew that Benjamin was like a brother to Andrew, you would not have judged.'

'Brother? What do you mean?'

'In the fire that consumed Andrew's mother's house, he was overpowered by the smoke trying to save his family. Benjamin saved Andrew and his son, Arthur. Benjamin became the carer and best friend of Arthur. However, when Benny joined the army and then passed SAS selection, Andrew tried everything to stop ...'

'I get it now, Blondie,' I interrupted.

Blondie came over and put his arm around me, I lowered my head.

'I'm sorry,' I said. 'I thought Andy just didn't want him on this mission due to the colour of...'

'Maybe I should have insisted that you listen, and not let you interrupt me.'

'It's not your fault, Stuart.'

'Neither is it yours that he has gone to heaven.'

'I can only now look back and say others tried to tell me. But why didn't Andy tell me? Especially when I'd mentioned his son's condition.'

'Because you made me so fucking angry that I wanted to kill you.'

I looked up: Andy was front of me. I lowered my stare and said, 'I'm so sorry, Sarge. I... I...'

'Sarge? I prefer Churchill. Now, are you going to get your sorry backside up and go join the rest who are keeping eyes on the Hun?'

Churchill held his hand out and pulled me to my feet, but without making eye contact. He shouldered his Enfield and then cocked his Sten.

'Do you want me to come with you?' Blondie asked.

'No. You go with the boss. And pray for Benjamin. Any fucking Hun left out there is going to wish they had left.'

Once he was out of earshot, walking brazenly across the open space, I told Blondie to go as I wanted to stay guard; it was the least I could do. The hardest thing was watching Churchill go down on one knee and uncontrollably cry over Benny's charred remains. With his compact shovel and bare hands he scraped back the soil. It was heart-breaking, but as if a punishment to myself, I made sure I endured. I felt the same pain as he replaced the earth, Churchill leaving a small item upright in the soil. Before he saw me on his return, I made my way the route that Blondie had taken.

Planet was waiting for me further in the dense woodland. I only had noticed he was behind a tree after he had given sharp flashes of green light. Reaching him, he lifted my drooping head by the chin.

'Are all ye English men such clunges?' he said.

I smirked. 'That's pussies.'

'Aye. That indeed ye are as well. Follow me.'

We cautiously made our way through the woodland until we found the rest of the lads keeping watch in between the bases of trees. Spike was first to sneak over, and he held my forearm for a few seconds before letting it go. That simple touch and look boosted my self-esteem. He whispered that Shrek had gone forward to check out a track that led around a field to a farmhouse.

Just as Churchill crept out from behind us, Shrek made a slight noise a little way in front; only tiny, but it alerted us. Thankfully, Blondie and Fish had their weapons scanning. We all moved to Shrek's direction.

'If you two have stopped your daisy-picking in the woods, you may want to listen in,' Shrek bluntly said—me and Churchill were the only ones not to smirk. 'To the south of the track is a big load of fucking trouble: a whole SS panzer division.'

'Are you kidding us, Shrek?' Fish asked.

'Of course I am not.'

'But you would not recognise a tank even if it had ran over your dense head,' Fish said. 'Can you even count to ten, let alone ten thousand men?'

'Wordsworth has now turned into Lou Costello,' Shrek said. 'You really need to lose a bit of those saddlebags.' He slapped Fish's cheeks—this time, we all found it funny.

'Carry on, Shrek,' I said.

'As I was saying, there are a fucking load of Kraut tanks and infantrymen about half a mile up the road. They are all wearing the SS Panzer uniform and very heavily armed.'

'How many men?' Fish asked.

'Nine thousand, nine hundred and bloody ninety-nine. Does it matter? There are six fucking tanks. And if you start going on about tank stats and SS uniform facts, I am going to deck you, as Vinnie says.'

Whilst they were having their squabble, I had got out the map and compass.

'We're about here,' I said. 'The farmhouse isn't on the map, but it's in the direction we need to head. Let's do a quick recce on it and then restock inside; maybe grab a quick brew.'

'A recce?' Blondie asked—the others looked on.

'Bloody hell. It's an informal term for reconnaissance.'

'What does that mean?' Fish said.

'It bloody means to get eyes...' I stopped when I had seen the covered smirks and nudging. 'Piss off.'

'Oh, I forgot to mention, we cannot go right down the track as two Krauts are patrolling it,' Shrek said. 'But I have a plan.'

'I'm not sure what's worse, you nearly forgetting to mention the guards, or your plan?' I said.

Close to the farmhouse, we hid, watching the two Germans having a cigarette. Shrek snuck off in a trench coat and helmet the way back towards the mass of SS and tanks. What the hell was he doing? I should have questioned his plan. My anxiety started to grow, and I was sure I wasn't the only one. With visions of Shrek coming around the bend in the path with hundreds of Germans and six tanks chasing him, I quietly put the shotgun down, bringing around my Sten, calmly releasing the cocking mechanism forward. The others, almost soundlessly, made their weapons ready.

The guards suddenly looked up the track. Fish and Spike were zeroed in on them. Planet swung the Bren around to the left, but lifted off his sights at the same time as me. Wobbling left to right coming down the track was a German infantryman on a bike. Just as he rode past us, he fell off his bike. The two Germans walked at a fast-pace up the track. The drunk on the bike lifted his head and winked at us: Shrek. What the fuck was he playing at?

He staggered towards the other two, who then slung their rifles over their shoulders. Looking a bit envious that they'd not had such pleasure, they then began clapping at Shrek.

'*Hast du eine Zigarette?*' Shrek slurred.

'*Tauschen Sie gegen etwas Alkohol? Ja?*' one said, the other nodding.

Shrek staggered closer, putting his hand inside his overcoat, and said, '*Sicher, meine Kameraden.*'

'*Wo hast du…*'

Shrek sharply kicked the first German hard in the bollocks and, in a swift movement, struck the other in the throat. The hand that had struck pulled back, and the soldier went to the ground holding his neck, blood oozing through his fingers. The first guard lifted, still holding his groin. Shrek moved around the rear of him, held the German's mouth, then plunged the knife through the base of captive's shoulder and into the neck. Everyone raced out and dragged the bodies back into the woods. I kept my arcs scanned the way Shrek had ridden.

'You all right?' Blondie said.

'Yeah, sure,' I said.

A part of me was slightly revolted by what I had just seen. However, when my mind wandered back to my war zones, was it any different to all those I had slotted? But these weren't terrorists, I told myself, but young men. Though, there was the same intent and contempt in what they had done to Benny.

'Boss… boss?'

'Huh?' I said, shaking my head.

'We are heading to the farmhouse. Did you not hear Blondie tell you?' Churchill asked.

'Yeah, but I just wanted to make sure we weren't being followed,' I lied.

In the main courtyard, many tracks had churned the gravel. Larger trails had cut across the field. The large main door to the rendered-stone farmhouse was left open. The kitchen area was partly lit with candles and lanterns, the smell of wax and oil filling my nostrils. On the stone-tiled floor were loads of dirty boot marks and, as I stared closer, trails of blood. Shotgun ready, I slowly eased around the corner, but the carnage stopped me. Amongst the strewn personal items and smashed furniture were two bodies; blood pooled on the joints between the slate floor. The one who lay face up looked in his teens, his clothes riddled with puncture and exit wounds. Slouched against the fireplace was an elderly man, also peppered, a smashed glass of wine near him.

Blondie put his bible away and glanced up, pain in his eyes. Shrek came through and placed a blanket over each of them, gazing unhappily at the two covered bodies.

'Churchill, lock the front and rear doors,' I ordered.

'Yes, boss.'

'I suppose this is the father and son,' Shrek said. 'The mother is lying naked in the ditch where I found her bike.'

'You don't think those two young infantry men did this, do you?' I asked.

'No. It is more than likely the bastard SS. But the Germans and Nazis are all the same.'

'They're not,' I said. 'Some young Germans don't carry out the orders of the CO. Those that do commit such war crimes will get their comeuppance in later life. I know this for a fact.'

'If they dodge my bullets, that is,' Planet said.

'You could not get down and return fire with that erection you have had since the pub,' Fish said.

'Hey, do not speak ill of my Babs,' Planet snapped.

'Who said it was your girlfriend that gave you the little hardon? Thought it was the dad in the vest,' Spike said.

'Bollocks,' Planet snapped.

'It did me,' Spike said drolly.

'You must get lonely with just the stags to keep you company in the Highlands,' Fish said.

'Now ye have gone too far. I am going to have to rip ye balls off and shove them up ye arse.'

'She was kind of sore on the eyes,' Blondie said.

Planet grabbed Blondie around the throat and said, 'Says the fucking nun.'

'I think that was a compliment, Planet. Put him down,' I said.

Blondie nodded vigorously.

'Oh.'

Everyone laughed as Blondie choked, rubbing his throat.

'Right, get a brew on, Spike,' I said. 'The rest of you upstairs and watch the windows. Lights out and no smoking.'

Churchill came back in and said, 'There are no locks on any doors.'

'Well slam them shut. You're good at that.'

Whilst I sipped on the sweet tea, I worked out the route to the first target: the bomb dump. Spike had also brought us all fruit, eggs, bread, and salami. I gorged from the stockpile that I had made on the wooden floorboards. Apart from the odd battle somewhere in the far distance and the annoying beeping, all was quiet, until Shrek sat next to me.

'Blondie says you have rebuked me for slitting the Krauts,' he said.

'I've got no axe to grind.'

'Nice evening, Vinnie. You will not have to add your quinine this time.'

He's fishing for something, I thought 'What's quinine for?'

'For malaria.'

I cracked another egg and swallowed the contents, and then stuffed in some salami. Shrek pulled a disgusted face, and then he checked the coast was clear.

'Can I ask you a man-to-man question?'

'Sure.' I burped, banging my chest. 'Excuse me.'

'Are you really not Peter Skedgewell?'

'Shrek, what do you think,' I said, mouthful of a juicy apple.

'It is the strangest story I have ever heard. I am shocked that they did not carry on the British etiquette in the future. You fucking eat like a horse with no lips.'

'Thanks for the chat,' I said sarcastically. 'Now go back to your observation post.'

I took up position at the front window, laughing inside at what Shrek had called me. Looking out to where the SS were supposedly camped, I had no visual of anything but the tranquil moonlit landscape. I rested my chin on the low-level window frame. As soon as the new tune came into my head, I recognised it, finding it hard to resist tapping my hand.

I wanna dance by water 'neath the Mexican sky
Drink some margaritas by a string of blue lights
Listen to the Mariachi play at midnight
Are you with me, are you with me?

After a few seconds, the outside fields turned to a shimmering sea. I was now sat watching from the Fistral Beach Bar. Lena was dancing merrily on the warm sand. I had forgotten about Lena up until this point.

I wanna fall like the Carolina rain on your skin
I wanna walk a little too far out on that limb
Take you every place I've been and never been
Are you with me, are you with me?

I craved a pint of Korev as I watched the pint glass bubbles rise in the rays of the sun.

We can chase the wild dreams, live like crazy
Love me baby, come on, come on, come on
Just throw your arms around me
We can run like we won't run out of time

A scuffle behind me brought me back.

'What is it, Planet?' I asked quietly.

'Sorry, Vinnie, but ye need to come down and see what I have found.'

'What is it?'

'I found a girl next to a dead dog in the ox shed. She didn't want to leave her pet. The farm animals have all been hacked. The Heinies must have ate well.'

I stood up. With one more look out the window to see my homeland as the music played, sadly, it had all gone.

After giving orders for Fish to take my stag, I followed Planet downstairs into the living room. On the oak table was a frightened girl, no more than fifteen years old. I asked Planet to go back upstairs to my OP. Spike was bandaging her left leg, which was swollen below the knee, blood staining her dirty bare foot. Through her muddy, ripped nightgown her body trembled. Spike lifted her head, tears dripped off her grubby chin. I moved to block her view of the blanket-covered bodies.

'You're OK with us. Nothing's going to hurt you,' I said softly.

'She does not speak English,' Spike said.

'*Salut*,' I said—her expression acknowledged what I had said.

'Ask her what happened to her,' Spike said.

'That's all the French I know.'

Spike frowned at me.

'What's up with her leg?' I asked.

'Bullet wound.'

'*Ils ont violé ma mère en face de moi,*' the girl sobbed.

'Spike, ask Fish to come down to find out what happened, then get everyone together. It's time to move out.'

Bang… bang… bang!

Fish had opened fire upstairs. I flinched as the glass in the front window smashed, the curtains moving, dust falling.

CHAPTER TWENTY-FIVE

Upstairs, the majestic sound of the Bren was squeezing off a few bursts. More incoming rounds hit the wooden beams, sending splinters over us. Spike partly cover the girl.

'Watch the fucking back door,' I yelled.

'What about the girl?'

Damn it, I mentally cursed. 'Get her under the table and hold that fucking rear door and window. Churchill, get...' I didn't need to tell him; he had already taken the brave position by the front window aperture.

The firing had ceased on both sides, so I ran upstairs. First, I checked on Blondie, who was watching the rear garden. In the next room Shrek was knelt in a tin-bath, aiming down his Enfield. Whistles started blowing outside.

'Come on, Kraut, just stick your bloody head up again,' Shrek said.

Kneeling on the other side of the bath, I cautiously peered out, but could see jack shit in the dark. I pulled out the heavy binos and focused in—not exactly powerful.

'These Krauts move around in a huddle,' he said. 'You see? It is like watching a group of eight men on marching drill. Why do they all charge around and blow whistles?'

'I can't see them, Shrek.'

Bang!

'Got the bastard. You will not see him again,' Shrek said. 'Why hide behind a fucking bush?'

'Yep, just PIDed them.'

'Pardon?'

'Positively identified them.'

'Oh, I say,' he said in a gentleman's accent. 'Well, here you go then, chum. Slot them is the terminology you use.'

He handed me the Enfield. Resting the wooden end on the ledge, I looked down the metal sights.

'Come on, old chap, take a shot at the one poking his head around a tree,' Shrek said.

Bang!

'Oh dear, old boy, you missed. Did you not go to the funfair as a kid? Try again. Give you a monkey puppet if you win.'

'Fuck off, Shrek. Your stupid voice is putting me off.'

Bang!

'*Threat neutralised.*'

'Hey. Threat neutralised. Threat neutralised,' I boasted. 'I've not heard that gaming voice in ages.' It was nostalgic.

Shrek snatched back the Enfield and said, 'All right. It is not a bloody game.'

'No, you don't get it. Every time I kill I get this silly gaming voice in my head. It was when I used to play the Xbox as a teenager.'

'You are a fucking lunatic.'

We both ducked as the frame around the window disintegrated. The mirror on the back wall shattered. Shrek popped his head up, quickly returning fire. Skidding on the glass, I then dashed to Planet and Fish. They had both set up an array of further weapons and ammo neatly around them. Moving to the right window next to Planet, I looked with my binos at three dead infantrymen on the path. Planet and Fish both fired on the cavalcade of advancing troops. Tracers zipped from both sides. An incendiary grenade fell short. Fish boasted he'd got him before it had left the German's hand properly.

'Are you actually going to hit anything, Rob?' Fish asked.

The Bren spewed out its death. 'What, like those bastards setting up a machinegun post. The ones ye missed.'

'Bugger off,' Fish said. 'I am still mopping up the shit you missed.'

Bang, bang, bang, bang!

Fish slapped another mag in his Thompson.

The incoming rounds had increased to a terrifying rate. Everything around us in the room was getting mashed up, with bits of plaster and stone being blown in and out. Amongst the cacophony I heard a new sound. Because of the wall and window being peppered, I moved back to Shrek. He was brazenly still firing shots in between the incoming hail of lead. Trying to find the best position directly away from the window, I eventually managed to raise the binos.

'Out,' I screamed. 'Out now.'

I grabbed Shrek out of the tin bath and, seeing the concern on my face, he followed me out. Almost pushing him down the stairs, I yelled at Planet and Fish to immediately evacuate. Blondie was grabbing his gear as I went in his room, but I still hollered at him to move. Trying not to panic, I shoved them all down the stairs.

BOOOM!

The house shook on the foundations it sat on. I started to cough with the dust that circled me, but breathing in was hard, the weight on me was suffocating. My ears were ringing. A muffled voice shouted. I opened my eyes to see whatever it was on me being pulled off, rubble fell from Planet's back and head. Blinking the grit away, I saw the horror of what the tank shell had done: the side wall where Shrek had been was now blown to bits. In the escalating fear of another strike, I took hold of the hands that reached out. Blondie moaned as I got off him, one of his lenses was cracked. Spike had shouldered his Enfield and was now stood at the rear door. With his Sten covering the back garden he ordered us to move, then pointed to the woods.

Everyone sprinted across the rear garden. Debris fell from their clothes, leaving a haze behind. I waited for Churchill to back up to me as he was still watching the front door. Once he had run past, I threw my kit back over my shoulder and followed him, clutching my two weapons. The outhouse shed was now ablaze. Suddenly, I bumped into Spike, his Sten hitting me in the gut.

'What the fuck are you doing? Go,' I said.

'The girl.'

'Fuck,' I said.

Spike barged his way past. I went down on one knee and scanned the area. The seconds went by, seeming like an eternity.

At last he came out with her over his shoulder. Letting him get ahead, I watched for any unwanted followers and then made a dash for it.

BOOOM!

The pressure staggered me forward, the crashing of the building echoing around me. I lay flat on the ground. Returning to my knees, my ears were pierced by a high-pitched tone. Bricks and tiles started to land close by. Spike had returned and was helping me up. He told me there was no need to yell, his voice muffled, as I had asked him where the girl was. I guessed what he said next was that he had taken her into the woods. How long had I been on the floor?

The muted sound of mutts barking made me scramble back to my feet, and I was quickly chasing Spike. Bollocks; I'd left my weapons. Even though I hated enemy mutts as much as goats, I turned around and ran back. I ducked after I'd heard the first incoming whizz past, the weapon's crack echoing. In fear, I rummaged under the bits of roof tile and bricks until I spotted the wooden pump-action part of the shotgun. The rounds were getting closer, and so were the mutts.

In the forest, I tried not to trip whilst I blew the shit off the shotgun's chamber. In a maze of trees and bushes I couldn't see any of the lads, but at least the incoming small arms fire had stopped. Then a new sound made my ears prick up: a familiar whining sound.

BOOOM!

Fuck; now they were sending in mortars, but at least the first explosion was close to where the garden ended. I pushed through whatever came in front of me, twigs and spiked foliage lacerating my hands and face. My heart was pumping with my short sharp breaths, the familiar white edges closing my view; I had to calm down.

Unexpectedly, Fish and Shrek popped out from behind a tree on each side, and Shrek's muscular arms dragged me in. I was heavy breathing, and I was given a smack around the head. Disgruntled, I looked up: Shrek's eyes were wide, his finger over his lips.

Bang! Bang!

I quickly sank onto my belly, raising the shotgun, only to see one Alsatian dead whilst the other limped off.

Bang!

Shrek had put it out of its misery.

'Best move. There will be others,' he said calmly.

Just as I was squatting backwards, weapon raised, a scream bounced off the trees from my right, sounding like the girl. Shrek sprinted first, and I was rapidly after him. A way behind us, Planet let off two burst rounds from his Bren, the mutt's shriek warning me there were more coming. Whipping away the branches, more shots and explosions echoed around the forest. The screaming suddenly stopped; a new yelp cried out. Clearing the next bush aside, I noticed Shrek pull back on his weapon and then thrust the bayonet back into the mutt. One evil beast came from the side and sank its teeth into my webbing, vigorously shaking and growling. Instinctively, I punched it on the nose, but this made the enemy rage further.

Bang!

My ears were ringing. I sharply turned to see Blondie holster his Colt. The dead mutt, its teeth still showing, had some sort of backpack on. Shrek picked up the girl who had been heavily mauled.

'Go, go, go,' Shrek ordered.

I wasn't sure of the reason we had to get the fuck out, but I was sprinting behind Blondie's skinny frame; he could run like the wind. The sound of a Sten firing came from somewhere deeper in the forest, it had to be Spike.

BOOOM! BOOOM!

More explosions sent a shockwave through the ground, the sound vibrating through the trees. The mortars had landed approximately where we had shot the first mutts. Fuck; Planet.

BOOOM!

The explosion from where we had just come from sounded different, and deadlier. I looked over my shoulder to see the bush on fire. How did the mortar team know where we were? I doubted they had sent spotters in after us, unless the Germans didn't care about killing their own troops.

Churchill came running towards me and, stopping suddenly, aimed down his Enfield's iron sights. He fired three shots, we all dived to the ground. Was he trying to take my head off? Had he lost he mind? I automatically checked my ear, as the rounds felt that close.

'What the fuck are you doing?' I said.

'Look,' Churchill said, and nodded.

On the floor, no more than five metres from where Shrek was picking up the moaning, bloodied girl, was one dead beast: a Rottweiler.

'That is going to piss off the *SS-Oberst-Gruppenführer*,' Fish said.

'Saves him feeding his dog those shitty Hun sausages,' Churchill said—we all laughed.

'Bratwurst, actually,' Fish said, killing the moment.

I put my fingers through the mutt's teeth holes in my webbing. 'That was close. How the hell did you miss me, Blondie?'

'Because it was not a Christian dog,' he said—further explosions stopped the mockery.

'There is another farmhouse just beyond the river,' Churchill said. 'The dogs will lose our scent if we cross it. Plus, the tanks will not be able to cross it.'

'Where's Planet and Spike?' I asked.

'There is no time to search. We need to press on.'

'It's not like fucking pressing on for that pint, Andrew,' I ranted.

'We do not go back for anyone. We need to complete the mission.'

'Bollocks, Andrew. You may have had that rule instilled into your brain, but I haven't. Right, Blondie, you come with me. Between the rest of you, carry the girl to the farmhouse. If me or Blondie haven't arrived half an hour after you have arrived, then finish the objectives.'

'No, boss, it is essential we all go together,' Churchill said.

'On me, Blondie,' I ordered.

'Champion,' he said.

Shotgun cocked and out in front, I slowly squat-moved through the forest. The deathly silence was intimidating, as if at any moment the jaws of death would strike from any angle. Blondie was about three metres to my side. With every footstep on the pine needle floor, I scanned my arcs. In the area where we'd found the girl, a mash of fur and blood had collected on the branches and trunks. The crater was about a metre wide and two feet deep, and the bush that the girl had laid in had burnt away.

'How did the mortar get on target? Was it luck?' I whispered.

'Did you not see the device strapped to the dog's back?'

'Yeah. Was that an explosive?'

'The Russians started to use the idea first to blow up tanks. Looks like the evil has caught on,' Blondie said, looking around, unnerved.

'Fuck me. That's grim.'

A moan of pain filtered through the bushes. For a moment me and Blondie locked our wide-eyed stares. Without the starting pistol we raced zig-zagging through the trees with our weapons at hip level. Lying there in a twisted heap four metres from a crater was Spike. I told Blondie to keep watch whilst I cleared the dirt from his body and face, gently turning him over. His shirt was shredded. He wailed in pain, then gritted his teeth. Between his hands he was holding his guts in.

'Fuck,' I said. 'Blondie, give me a hand here... Blondie, stop staring at him and fucking help me.'

'I do not want to fly again,' Spike said.

'Save your strength,' I said.

I wasn't sure if he had meant the plane that had flown us in, or flying through the air from the explosion. Blondie gently helped push his innards back and then covered the area with dressings. Blood rasped through Spike's clenched teeth.

'Do birds have a fear of walking?' Spike murmured.

I looked up at Blondie. This time, we didn't laugh.

After patching up the rest of his neck and facial wounds, we carried him back towards the river. Every now and then I looked over my shoulder, not just to see if we had any unwanted guests, but to see if Planet was around. The nearer we got to the river, the sicker I felt. Spike was unconscious, but at least he was rasping.

The river's current wasn't fast, and it was only about five metres across. The problem was: how deep? Also, the bank on the other side was very steep. As we rested, strange noises from the forest spurred me on to think of a plan. Spike had become as white as the moon.

'Psst. Oi, cocker.'

Turning the shotgun to the person beyond the river, I was relieved to see Shrek and Fish in the shadows, the white dust having been washed off.

'Get in the water and help carry Spike,' I ordered.

Like in a crowd at a rock concert, we manhandled the main man over our heads. Blondie had drips of blood on his face. Once Shrek and Fish had waded neck height to the bank, I swam the remaining distance, making sure I washed off the remnants of blood. Blondie footed me up the bank and, like in the early days of over-the-wall training, we all pulled each other up. Lastly, Shrek pushed Spike up the bank whilst we carefully heaved, Spike's groaning making it harder.

We tabbed as quick as we could the last half-kilometre, all taking it in turns to help carry him. My anger was intensifying towards Churchill, but I had to temper it as he had been through quite enough. In times of anguish the littlest thing can seem magnified.

At last we made the sanctuary of the farm. It was an impressive house made of flint stone and a thatched roof. It had no animal sheds, but a smaller stone-walled building to the left, like a guest house. Churchill was at the window with his weapon raised. Before I shut the heavy oak door, I stared outside, wishing that Planet would appear. Should I go back? Would that risk the lives of the others or Operation Poppy Pride? Fuck the mission, I thought. Come on Planet, where are you? But I could see nothing but the evening shadows. I closed the door and bolted it.

This farmhouse was a lot grander inside: plates, cups, and ornaments were laid out on a French dresser. Churchill came up to me as I smelt a jug of milk.

'Is it off?'

'Not like your attitude, Andy,' I grumbled.

'We are on the brink of failing this mission, our duty, and our homeland that prepares its soldiers to invade. We have come so far, and some have paid the ultimate price,' he said.

I felt guilty as I pictured the black and white photos of Private Jeffrey Moline and Private Benjamin Garvey. I went to apologise, but the girl's cry and Spike's wailing had interrupted me. Where was the music to drown it out? When would our luck change?

'Go check the other building, Churchill.'

'Yes, boss.'

CHAPTER TWENTY-SIX

The outbuilding had no occupants, but instead loads of crates and bottles. Where were the owners? I really hoped they all had got away unscathed. Against Churchill's objections, Blondie had lit the fireplace upstairs. All the doors were locked, the windows barricaded. We all shivered in the front bedroom, not knowing if it was the come-down from the adrenalin, the shock of what we had been through, or our wet clothes; perhaps all three. Churchill had taken the girl upstairs and placed her in the opposite room. At times the girl let out a twisted scream of pain.

Lying closest to the heat was Spike. We huddled around him, the orange and yellow flames reflecting in our distant eyes. From the expressions, I guessed the others were also craving for some of Spike's dry wit, but it never came. Blondie slightly lifted Spike's head and gave him a sip of water. I knew it wouldn't be long before someone uttered the expression, 'the elephant in the room', I thought.

'Is Rob dead?' Shrek asked.

And there it was, I thought. 'We couldn't find him.'

'How hard did you fucking look?' Shrek said.

'Harder than you fucking did.'

'Chaps, the girl is in a bad way,' Churchill said, choked. 'I cannot watch her suffering any further.'

The girl screamed again from the other room.

'The dogs have ripped her to shreds. We need to end her suffering,' Churchill said.

> *That's life (that's life), that's what people say*
> *You're riding high in April*
> *Shot down in May*
> *But I know I'm gonna change that tune*
> *When I'm back on top, back on top in June*

'That's life,' I mumbled.

Churchill glared at me. 'What a bloody awful thing to say.'

'No, no, I meant the song I can hear.'

There was a heavy silence, the only sound was the wood crackling on the fire. I studied their faces to see who would end her suffering, but each one bowed his head, refusing to meet my eyes. The girl was crying, again.

'Help her,' Spike mumbled.

'I will do it,' Shrek said, and waited for an agreement.

> *I've been a puppet, a pauper, a pirate*
> *A poet, a pawn and a king*
> *I've been up and down and over and out*
> *And I know one thing*
> *Each time I find myself flat on my face*
> *I pick myself up and get back in the race*

Nobody had said a word, so Shrek got to his feet, a wet residue covering the floorboards. My nerves jangled and I swallowed hard. All our eyes were averted from each other's. Blondie closed his eyes, holding Spike's hand. He started mumbling the Lord's prayer. A part of me wanted to hear him say it aloud. The girl stopped screaming and was now breathing hard and fast. Why was Shrek taking so long? Jesus. How could I think such a thing?

Bang!

We all jumped. The muffled shot echoed around the room.

Shrek returned, trying to look dignified with his head held high. He holstered his pistol, feathers had stuck to the barrel and his arm. He was the only one who could have done it.

> *That's life (that's life) that's life*
> *And I can't deny it*
> *Many times I thought of cuttin' out, but my heart won't buy it*
> *But if there's nothing shakin' come here this July*
> *I'm gonna roll myself up in a big ball and die*

'Thank you, Gary,' I said quietly.

The rest, one by one, muttered their thanks. Spike managed to raise his bloodied thumb. Shrek sat back in his spot by the fire, the floorboards dried from the heat.

'A faint heart never fucked a pig,' Shrek said meekly.

'Where did you learn that, Shrek?' I asked.

'Rob said it to me on training. Why?'

'Did Rob have a brother?'

'Yes. His name was...'

'John,' I butted in. 'Everyone called him Archie. Broke his leg and arm in parachute training.'

'How the blazes did you know that?' Shrek asked.

'I've just sussed it: my mate Planet told me of his great-grandad that used to say that same thing.'

'Are you talking of the Rob in the future, or the one now?' Fish asked.

'The one in my world,' I said. 'Anyway, Rob even wrote it in a book he gave me for my birthday. I've used it when things have hit the wall. Rob had told me how his great-uncle and his two best mates had died in Germany in World War Two. That's you lot. You see, I am here to save Fish, Planet, and you Shrek, not the ones from the future. That's what Weaves had told me in the Australian Bar.'

I nodded, feeling I had not only explained myself well, but realised why I was 1944. However, searching the lads' faces, I wished I had shut my big mouth instead. The ambience in the room had darkened. Shrek's eyes had narrowed.

'So, us three are going to die?' he asked.

'What about the rest of us?' Churchill said. 'Did the great-grandad mention if we made it, or died?'

'How did Weaves know about all this?' Blondie asked.

Fuck it; I'm digging a hole, I thought. 'Look, no one else is going to fucking die. We'll wait out till the morning, and after the major battle on the beach we'll make our way to our troops.'

Everyone had the thousand yard stare, except Churchill.

'Are you saying that Operation Neptune is a success?' Churchill continued. 'That we win?'

'All I can say...'

'If that is true, then why the fucking hell did we come on this mission?' Churchill butted in.

Like at the bunkhouse, the lads all nodded—not at all pathetic this time. Whilst they waited for my answer, I thought hard how to defuse the growing tension.

'Well, Skedgewell?' Churchill said.

I sighed. 'Maybe you lot did carry out the mission on the ammunition store...'

'You mean bomb dump,' Fish said—everyone sharply turned, frowning at him. 'Sorry,' he said.

'As I was saying, maybe you lot did carry out the mission on the

German bomb dump and communications. Perhaps it was called Operation Condor, and some of you lived. Possibly if we sit here it won't matter, and our invading troops will do well.'

'But possibly more will die because we sat on our backsides,' Churchill argued. 'Maybe we will not defeat the Hun because we became yellow bellies.'

Shrek stood up and kicked the metal-framed bed, then ranted, 'Damn fucking right. I am no coward. In fact, I want to kill more Krauts. I vote we carry on till the bitter end. All those in favour?'

Churchill's hand shot up. 'Young men, never give up. Never give up. Never give up. Never, never, never-never-never-never.'

Fish raised his hand. 'I would rather die fighting, than die a coward.'

Blondie provoked his bible. 'I am not afraid to die. I cannot wait to meet God.'

'Blondie, are you crying because of your shit haircut?' Spike muttered.

Blondie wiped the tears from his cheek. An encouraging laugh went around the room as Blondie began to push his hair down. Shrek added a joke about combing it with a hand grenade. The banter picked up pace, and before we knew it we were all taking the piss and laughing.

When it had calmed, Spike had his eyes shut, breathing shallow.

'What about you, boss? Where is your vote?' Churchill asked.

'Boss now, is it?'

'Apologies,' he said.

'Who dares wins, is my vote,' I said.

'Do you remember the first SAS motto for the flaming sword by Bob?' he asked.

'Are you trying to fucking test me again, Andy?'

'No, boss, I was just bloody asking.'

'Oh please tell me,' Fish begged.

'Great Scot. A fact that the half-intelligent Tony does not know,' Churchill said. 'It was 'seek and destroy', but Stirling preferred his own motto.'

'Thank you, Churchill,' Fish said.

'Pleasure,' he replied.

An uncomfortable quietness followed. Was it because we had all just sealed our fate? Was it because Planet wasn't here to make the choice? Maybe if he was dead, that was a good thing.

'I think it's only fitting that Blondie here says a prayer for the fallen before we head out to do battle,' I said.

Excitedly, Blondie pulled out a piece of paper from his dry-bag. With shaking hands he opened it and cleared his throat.

'Oh Lord, who didst call on thy disciples to venture all to win all men to thee. Grant that we, the chosen members of the Special Air Service Regiment, may by our words and our ways dare all to win all and, in doing so, render special service to thee and our fellow men in all the world, through the same Jesus Christ Our Lord, Amen.'

'Amen,' they all followed.

'Lest we forget,' I finished.

Whilst Blondie began to flick through his bible, Fish handed around some billycans of rice pudding that he had been preparing.

'Do we beat the German invasion? Win the war?' Fish asked.

'I shouldn't tell you this as I don't want us to go in without your fearsome aggression and bollocks of steel, but yes,' I said.

'Does that twat Hitler die?' Churchill asked.

'Normally, I would complain at another uncouth reference to a vagina, but in this instance,' Blondie said, and grinned.

'He committed suicide on April 30th, 1945,' I said.

'Utter balderdash.' Churchill stomped out of the room.

'I think Churchill has kept back a silver bullet for Hitler. He wants to make the kill,' Fish said.

'Silver bullet for the evil, like the evil Count Dracula,' Blondie said proudly.

'Ah, but Hitler never bit on meat. He was a vegetarian,' Fish said gloatingly.

'Actually, Fish, your fact is wrong. Although he liked a diet of vegetables, he loved German sausage and ham,' I corrected him.

'I bet he liked a sausage,' Shrek insinuated.

'Where did you read that, Vinnie?' Fish said.

'From the future.'

I held up my fist and, with the other hand, pretended to wind my middle finger up. Fish frowned, puzzled.

'What are you doing?' he asked.

'Just telling you silently that I have one up on you; fuck you.'

Spike started to cough up blood, his fingers ripped at the dressings. I held his bloodied hands back as he started to groan louder. There was an urgency in the room.

'Finish me, Shrek,' Spike gargled. 'Give me some dignity. Do not let the bastard Germans kill me.'

'They won't kill you,' I said.

'They have. I am dying,' he muttered.

'I'm with you,' Blondie said.

Spike turned his head to the side, spitting more blood; someone was sobbing. I released my grip from his and tried to have a peek at his wounds.

'Fuck,' I mouthed.

'I want a British bullet to send me to heaven,' Spike mumbled.

We all looked at Shrek who was wiping the tears from his face.

'No. No, I cannot do it. I am sorry,' Shrek said.

He walked out of the room, and I'm sure he wasn't the only one who wanted to leave this dreadful scene. The expectant eyes turned to me, but I looked down at the spoon in my cold rice pudding. Fuck; I had no answers for Spike. I needed to change the mood.

'Right, we need to blacken our faces. The Germans know we are close in the area, so ditch all the spare uniforms and items we don't need. Anyone got any cam-cream?'

'You told us not to bring it,' Churchill said.

'We could burn off some wine corks in the embers, and with some cold charcoal black our faces,' Fish said.

'I knew there was a reason you had come,' I said.

'Was not for his shooting skills,' Blondie said, and laughed exaggeratedly.

'Bollocks, bible basher. What have you killed? Satan the dog,' Fish bantered.

It was nice to see Spike chuckle and smile; we all needed that. Maybe we could leave him here and then return after the completed mission.

'Fish, go tell Shrek to find some wine,' I ordered. 'He seems to have a nose for alcohol.'

'Sure, Vinnie.'

It wasn't long before Shrek had returned, slightly embarrassed that he had left the room shedding tears. With everyone back in the hub, we took it in turns to black-out our faces. It didn't go down well that I would only let them take one gulp of red wine to celebrate the lives of the brave young men we had lost, enforcing it on Shrek that it did not mean one gulp for *every* man lost. Blondie even tried the bread and wine holy communion shit thing.

The kit we didn't require was hidden. Spike was carefully placed into bed with water and rice pudding in his reach. I threw a crochet blanket over the blood on the floor. Those who wanted a smoke, I let have one. Even Spike took some much-needed drags. Blondie left us and said a prayer over the girl. With the remaining sat on the bed or chairs, ready to go, there was an awkward tension.

'What about Rob?' Shrek asked.

'We have to leave him,' Churchill replied.

'But he may only be injured,' Shrek said.

'Injured, mortally injured, it doesn't matter. Our objective is to press on.'

'Oh fuck off, Andy,' Shrek said. 'Would you want to be…'

'Lads,' I interrupted. 'Shut up. Let me think.'

The candleflames flickered in their whitened eyes against the matt-black faces, all wanting to know my decision.

Knock… knock… knock!

'*Öffnen Sie die Tür.*'

The candles went out immediately, the weapons were silently cocked.

'What did he say?' I asked.

'Open the door,' Fish replied.

The door banging become louder.

'*Ist jemand zu Hause?*'

Once Fish had translated that the person wanted to know if anyone was home, I whispered to Shrek to go look, but not get us compromised. Heavier thumps and shouting came from the rear door. I knew the bolted oak doors would be impossible to kick in, but with enough force the windows would give way. Maybe if we stayed quiet they would go away, even if the smoke from the fire could be smelt; it had been a risk we had to take.

Spike was biting down hard on a rag, squeezing Blondie's hand. The trepidation was killing us. Shrek returned and made safe his rifle.

'Three Krauts heading back south across the field,' he said quietly. 'I have lost sight of them through the first hedge.'

'Right, time to head out,' I said. 'Make a mental note from your maps of the next destination: the bomb dump. If we get split up, this is where we RV. Synchronise your watches to… 23.20 hours. Any trouble, make every shot count. Fucking ammo up.'

'I am staying, Johnny,' Blondie said—Spike smiled.

'What? But if they come back…'

'I cannot be killed, Johnny,' he interrupted, strangely calm.

'Have you had too much fucking plonk, Blondie?' Shrek asked.

'I am a Christian, and guaranteed eternal life.'

'Bollocks,' Fish said. 'And what about Spike? He is no Christian.'

'Exactly. That is why I am the right man to stay behind. Trust me, I am God's soldier, and the first evil motherfucker that comes through that door will meet his maker. Now fuck off, you lot.'

Blondie pushed his broken glasses up his nose, broadly smiling. I wasn't sure if the silence that followed was due to Blondie's colourful language, or that he wanted to remain.

'Are you sure?' I asked weakly.

'Two requests: one, not all Germans and Italians agree with the Nazis. Take Dietrich Bonhoeffer, for example. Secondly, if I do not return to England, even though I will be watching over you, please tell my family and friends that I love them.'

'Once Operation Poppy Pride is complete, we'll all return and pick you both up,' I said.

'Hear, hear,' Shrek said.

Blondie gazed at our faces and said, 'Best you ugly bunch go. I will pray that you find Robert.'

In turn, they all shook Blondie's hand and patted him on his shoulder. Spike was given a gentle tap on his cheek. He smiled and nodded, rather than opening his eyes. Just before I left, now alone, Blondie grabbed my arm.

'If you get back to your other family and friends, please let my future relatives know I was a Christian serving our King and country.'

'This isn't the end. Keep some of that wine for me. You're a top bloke, Stuart Saxton, like my blond bro, Oliver.'

'Thanks, Johnny. Do you want that bible, now?'

I laughed and gave him a hug. Releasing him, I looked down at Spike and held his blooded hand.

'This journey wouldn't have been the same without your humour and courage, Spike. I'm looking forward to some of the funny shit that comes out of your mouth once we've finished the objectives.'

'This is serious shit we are in,' he muttered. 'Some of the paratroopers back at the base confided in me that that were scared of heights… not me, I'm afraid of widths.'

I left, ensuring they were safe and that we would be back.

With the back door unlocked, we all made a point of checking our compasses. Annoyed that I had left my Sten behind at the other farmhouse, I made ready the shotgun and then squat-ran across the grass to the woods. As I checked to see everyone was following in a spread-out single file, I heard the distinctive thud and then the whistle. Down on one knee I checked the lads as they went past: Shrek... Fish... Churchill.

BOOOM!

The farmhouse had taken a direct hit to the side elevation, but the stone appeared to withstand it. Suddenly, the thatched roof exploded, an orange fireball rose, scattering debris with it. I tried to return, but something was stopping me: Churchill.

'Blondie,' I screamed. 'Spike.'

BOOOM!

I flinched as another direct hit had impacted on the thatched roof, now raging with fire; my stomach knotted. I yelled, trying to break free. Close by automatic gunfire echoed into the tragedy.

'Boss, we need to go,' Churchill said.

Just as I shoved him and Shrek off, I was horrified to see Fish facing the woods with his hands up. Meandering through the trees were three nervous German infantrymen, all bearing their hate and weapons on us. Then, the iconic helmets and uniforms moved towards us.

CHAPTER TWENTY-SEVEN

The nostalgic German uniform feeling had very quickly eroded. I slowly raised my hands above my head. The infantryman at the front was the same as the one I'd seen taking a piss in the ditch. Where was the mutt? Shit. Had we killed it in the forest?

'*Leg deine Waffen nieder. Schnell, schnell,*' the infantryman said.

'I am not putting my weapon down,' Churchill growled.

'*Jetzt,*' the infantryman said, pushing into his rifle. 'Now,' he translated.

'And I'm not picking your brains up,' I whispered. 'Do it. We might be able to talk our way out of it.'

'Like Benjamin got out of it,' Churchill said.

That one hurt, I thought.

'I'm sorry, boss,' he said, placing his weapons down.

'Don't be. I deserved that low blow.'

'I mean, I am sorry for hitting you with that pole.'

'He can suck my dick,' Shrek blurted, snarling at the German.

'You're supposed to be playing the grey man. Now put it down,' I said.

'What the hell is a grey man?'

The older German soldier signalled his weapon. Shrek sighed and then placed his weapon on the floor.

'*Bewegen Sie über es,*' the German barked at Fish.

Fish slowly backed up towards me and Churchill. My mind began to wander as I listened to the flames and destruction behind me. I tried to shake off the horrendous thoughts of Blondie and Spike.

'*Geh auf deine Knie,*' someone yelled.

'Do not let him ask you again, Vinnie,' Fish said. 'Get on your knees.'

'Tell him we are just French farmers,' I whispered.

'*Pardonnez-nous. Nous sommes de simples fermier,*' Fish said—they all laughed.

'*Nein, nein, nein.* You are Phantom Major SAS,' he said to us. '*Sie sind Phantom Großen SAS,*' he interpreted for his comrades.

His men leant harder into their stance.

Churchill got off his knees and said, 'I take it this is the end then.'

'I told you we should not have put our weapons down,' Shrek said, also standing up.

Getting up, I swallowed the acid in my throat and thought about pleading, begging. 'Tell the German cunt to fuck off,' I said—the lads laughed.

Fish stood tall and boldly said, '*Verpissen Sie Nazi-vagina.*'

The rage almost exploded out of the German soldier's hat.

I proudly smiled. 'I'm sorry, Andy, for thinking you were racist and a bully.'

'Forget it.'

I made hard eye contact with all of them…

The squad leader took aim…

Fish grappled to hold my hand…

I grabbed Churchill's, and squeezed both…

We shook with the amount of deathly fire put down.

Opening my eyes, pulling my grip away from the lads, I then held my hands on my chest. Another burst spewed into the already riddled bodies on the floor. Shrek picked himself up and we all stared into the hedgerow to our left. Emerging from the shadows was a large silhouette with a weapon, almost smoking from the end of the barrel. I tried to catch the others as the rest had sprinted across. Even with our emotions running high, Planet just shrugged it off, making a quip about the Scottish saving our arses, again. He then asked why we all looked like Golliwoggs.

Part of the house imploding stopped our delight, guilt replacing it. The clunking of tracks and roaring engines of tanks in the distance took our attention from the house, which had become a grave. Scrambling back to our weapons, also picking up of some stick-grenades, we sprinted into the woods. I questioned how long we could outmanoeuvre the SS, infantry, and Panzers. How long before another squad member's death?

We tabbed at speed through dense woodlands and then across marshy fields, taking it in turn be point-man. I hoped Blondie had escaped and was in hiding, and if Spike had died, that it was instant; I pictured the horrific scenes. The only relief from these harrowing thoughts was being startled by objects that looked like the enemy. A new tune played:

'Land Down Under' by Men at Work. I grinned when I thought of my Australian mate, Ocker. It overpowered the negative feeling of the plain-crazy mission that lay ahead with just the five of us. Then my heart sank, remembering Ocker had messaged me in the jungle to abort the mission to return home. Home; where was home now?

To keep my spirits up, I watched the large backpack of Planet who had taken point-man, his Bren still in his hand. Never in my lifetime after the fateful Chinook crash could someone have said to me that I would meet up with these men again, even though they were the relatives. The similarity was indescribable. Just as I smirked thinking it would be amazing to meet Roy 'Rabbit' Franklin, it occurred to me how similar some of these other blokes were to my other mates from the future. Was this a coincidence?

Planet had stopped and got down on one knee behind a stack of hay. I crept low up to him, the others joined, all catching our breath. Planet stared hard into my eyes.

'What is it?' I asked.

'Where is Spike and Blondie?' Planet asked.

'Blondie volunteered to stay back and protect Spike from any Germans that might come into the house.'

'Why? What happened to Spike?'

'He took a lot of shrapnel from either a mutt exploding or a mortar. It was very close to where we had left you. He was in a bad way.'

'Were they in the room where the mortar struck?'

I nodded.

'Spike… nuttiest fucker I'd ever met. But strangely, he had the same morals as us. I miss him,' Planet said, trying to disguise a tear. 'Blondie… such a heart of gold for a deadly killer… so brave… so brave. Big balls for a little squirt.'

'Everybody is a squirt compared to you,' Churchill said.

Planet scoffed. 'What happened to the girl, Churchill?'

'She…'

'She outran the lot of us, even with that bullet wound,' I said, stopping Churchill.

Shrek nodded his appreciation to me for not telling the truth.

'She is most likely now hiding, safe and well,' I added.

'That is some comfort, I suppose,' Planet said, and he had the thousand-yard stare, but began to chuckle.

'What?' I asked.

'Do ye know what Spike said to me? If we dressed army ants as rice, we could invade China.' Planet tried to hold back his deep laugh—it was infectious.

'Very funny man Spike,' Fish said.

'That night at the pub with all of us there was fucking ace,' Planet continued. 'God damn, I miss all those poor bastard lads.'

'It's good you don't forget them,' I said, and squeezed his muscular shoulder. 'But we need to move out and find the bomb dump.'

'That is the bomb dump.'

He pointed over the haystack. Lifting slightly over the bales, at the far end of the field was a road with a ditch on one side. The only building looked like some sort of cattle shed, but there were no signs it could be the target. Planet opened the top of his backpack.

'Before ye ask,' Planet said, 'identical layout of buildings, including the stack we are now behind.' He handed over a crumpled reconnaissance photo.

'I bloody told you not to bring any of this shit,' I said.

'Yeah, cheers, Planet,' he said, impersonating me.

'If we had been found with it, it would have compromised the mission,' I said.

'Last time I saw, ye had ye pants around ye ankles and were about to get spanked by a load of Heinies.'

'Yeah, but if...'

'Oh, and thank you, Planet, for taking care of the German mortar team that killed Spike and Blondie,' he said, trying to sound English, 'just before I saved ye fucking arses.'

'Fair point, Planet. Good job,' I said, having now remembered the machinegun fire before the Germans came out of the woods.

'I do believe that was an apology, and praise,' Churchill said.

'Jesus. I actually think there is a God,' Fish said.

'Vinnie, are you handing out any more of those apologies and thanks?' Shrek asked, all upbeat.

'Bollocks.'

We all laughed under our breath.

Scanning the area with the binos, I was drawn to new cables compared to the existing old ones on a telegraph pole. The cables spanned the field and, where they met another wooden pole, they spread out in different directions.

'Right. I want us to get a closer look. The only real cover is that tractor,' I said.

'That will not even hide your fat backside, let alone the rest of us,' Shrek said, nudging Planet.

In the still of the night, one by one we made a low run over to the ditch in front of the tarmac track. With the water backed-up by grass and foliage, I was the only one who knelt in the piss-smelling water, much to the enjoyment of the others.

'Do you need your Mae West, Vinnie?' Fish whispered.

'My what?'

Fish smugly wound his middle finger up at me and said, 'A life jacket.'

'What ye doing, Fish?' Planet asked.

'Just a little bit of revenge.'

'Be careful, Fish, Vinnie may have a heart attack,' Planet added.

'Planet, you need to blacken your face,' I said.

'With what?'

I pointed at the cowpat.

Through the binoculars, I focused on both tall wooden sentry towers. Even in the black of the night I could see the heavy-machineguns, but at least they weren't manned. I questioned why, but then wished I hadn't. We couldn't afford any further fuck-ups, especially with the high body count thus far. Quickly turning the binos around to my right, after hearing an engine, I came full on with a pair of headlights. Slightly dazzled, I sank into the stagnant water, my shotgun resting on the bank. I shook my head, as Fish wanted to turn and see; we couldn't afford to be compromised.

Lying there like abandoned turds, we watched the truck take a jerking, clumsy turn to its right and then across the field towards the building. I dared to lift my head up further, my heart skipping a beat having spotted the German swastika on the side of a khaki-green half-track vehicle. I could hear Blondie's voice telling me of the twisted cross. The top gunner spun around in his turret, I slightly lowered back. Another truck came around the hedge onto the road heading towards us, the headlights shimmering off the murky water. My heart started to race in tune with the beeping, so I slowed my rate of breathing.

Twenty metres…

Surely they could see us…

Fifteen metres…

Shrek slowly took his Enfield off the bank…

Ten metres…

Planet made his Bren ready…

Seven metres…

Fish's face darkened, he was still facing the wrong way…

Five metres…

The truck's brakes squealed to a halt, the warm fumes rolled in, the engine's hypnotic idle making time slow down. I held my breath for a second, ready to burst into action as there were a lot of panicked German voices. A door creaked open and then slammed. Here we go, I thought; Fish's eyes saying the same. I told my shoulders to relax, breathing out gradually and quietly as they did. Fish was itching to turn and look, or was it attack? I gave another tiny shake of the head. The engine suddenly revved, gear clunking followed. The heat warmed my neck and face as the truck drove by. Fish's eyes squinted, going slightly left to right as if reading an autocue. How many infantry men had he counted?

After what seemed to be a lifetime, the engine was killed and then more metal creaking and slamming continued. Fish nodded at me. Slowly, I turned around in the slosh. With my eyeline level with the road, the last of the infantry piled out the back of the dusky-blue transporter. A total of eighteen men started to walk towards the large building. A pair were ordered to take each sentry tower. Fuck.

'Plan E, then,' Fish whispered.

I frowned at him. 'E for efficacious?'

'E for emigrate,' he replied.

'E for let us exit and get the fuck out of here,' Planet hushed.

We all looked the same way as a creaking had caught our attention. Two men in officer-type uniform closed the rear door to the half-track and walked off to the building. I waited till they went inside and then told the lads to come in closer. Once I had guessed why they had refused, I moved out of the stinking water and went over to them. Time check: 23.36 hrs.

'I've got a plan, but after I tell you, you have a choice to go for it, or we can retreat,' I said. 'Planet, you follow the ditch down to the start of the track, then cut across in the blind rear view of the half-track.'

'What if the gunner turns around?' Planet asked.

'Slot him before he does you.'

'Past that armour protecting the turret, Vinnie?' Planet quizzed.

'Once you have reached the vehicle, dead on midnight I want you to set the explosive to the track with a dry fifteen-minute pencil fuse.'

'Oh, the track. Not the rear door?' he said sarcastically.

'Once set, take the cortex wire and set the charge on the telegraph pole, then wait in hiding.'

'Where shall I hide?' he asked, looking back.

'Far enough away not to get blown to bits,' I said—Fish and Shrek sniggered.

'Seems like I am doing all the shitty work,' Planet moaned.

'That is because you keep disappearing when there is trouble,' Shrek said.

'Ye potato-munching twat,' Planet grumbled. 'Don't ye forget I killed the mortar team and infantry at the farm.'

'Did the full of haggis shit dickhead learn "Ye potato munching twat" from you, Vinnie?'

Sensing this wasn't the time, I replied, 'Right, switch on. Shrek, Fish, you two will follow me in the opposite direction through the ditch. We'll then dart across to that tractor, the one you said won't hide my fat arse. Let's hope it covers all three of us from the left sentry tower.'

Planet sniggered.

'Once there, Fish, you will sneak up to the troop-carrying truck. Dead on twenty-four hundred hours you will also set a fifteen-minute fuse. Once set, you take a wide route out of the field back to where Planet will be hiding with the det-cord.'

'What if someone is still in the truck?'

'Deal with him silently, Fish,' I said. 'Shrek, you will follow me through the hay barn to the left side of the building. You will double-back and deal with the sentry guard with your knife. Once executed, you will man the tower's weapon, just in case it goes tits-up.'

I waited for his questions, but he just grinned with pleasure.

Churchill had stayed silent till now. Had the death of Benny got to him? He had not been right since it had happened; who could blame him. No doubt, if we pulled this off, we would all have terrifying memories to deal with, but he had to switch on.

'Churchill, thanks for coming back and stopping me re-entering the farmhouse,' I appeased.

'I didn't come back. It is instilled in me not to on this mission. We cannot fail.'

'Oh, I thought you came...'

'No. I was next to you when I merely stopped you. What are my orders?' Churchill spoke in a monotone, almost robotic.

'Churchill, the right sentry tower is a no go as it's in full view of the half-track gunner. However, the sentry is blinded to the other tower, the tractor and truck, and the rear of the half-track. I want you to stay here and cover us. Planet, give him the Bren.'

'No fucking way,' Planet scowled.

'That's not open for fucking debate. Swap weapons.'

'Where are you going, boss?' Churchill asked.

'I am going to find another way in and set a fifteen-minute charge on something explosive.'

'I want to come with you,' Churchill said.

'No. One last thing, lads: if it goes noisy before the charges are laid, add the shortest fuse you can and get the hell out. Any questions?'

'What happens if one of us gets injured or pinned down, with or without the Lewes bombs set?' Churchill asked.

'You help that person and then get as far away as possible. We'll meet at the next Target. If not, fight to the death. Fucking ammo up, lads.'

CHAPTER TWENTY-EIGHT

Coming out of the wet ditch and squat-running to the tractor, I felt very vulnerable in the open, even though I had made sure the vehicle blocked the view of the sentry and half-track gunner. Once we were all huddled behind the front one twin-wheeled green tractor, the smell of cow shit filled my nostrils. Shrek hid his smile as he looked at my stodgy boots. How come I was the only one covered in shit? I didn't enjoy Shrek's quip about it soaking up the cow piss.

Shrek stood half-up behind the large rear tyre, slowly resting his weapon on the metal seat, sighting the sentry tower. I laid under the main body, scanning my arcs, then watched the feet of Fish making a dash towards the German truck.

'Fuck,' Shrek whispered.

I switched my view to the lone infantryman walking back from the building. Even though I knew all our weapons would be sighting him, I glanced at Fish who looked concerned sat in the shadows, Lewes bomb already in hand. Time was balanced on a knife-edge, but twenty seconds later the passenger's door opened and closed. A cigarette glowed from inside, slightly relaxing me.

With the new problem, myself and Shrek made a wider circled advance to the hay barn. Once inside the pitch-black shed, a putrid smell whacked my nostrils. Feeling the stacked hay bales as we pushed on, tears welling, I found the flooring different underfoot. Just as I looked down at the rotting human bodies, Shrek shoved me forwards at a quick pace. It wasn't till we got to the end of the building that I quietly let go of my breath. Seeing the mess on my boots, I began to retch, as silently as possible.

With the clock ticking, we had no time for such pleasantries, so we ran over to the side of the cattle building. Less than ten metres away was the tower, cigarette smoke billowing. Shrek grabbed my hand and shook it.

'Remember, no rule book,' he mouthed.

'Remember, by strength and guile.'

As soon as he drew his knife, I began to run the other way. I stayed tight to the wall, out of the moonlight. After checking the rear field was clear, I found the metal door. Adrenalin surged through me, virtually telling me to kick it open and burst in with shotgun raised. Instead, bottling the enthusiasm, I peeked through the gap that I had opened, spotting my watch: 23.57 hrs. Three minutes to set the charge. Fuck. I rapidly went through, making sure my foot stopped the door slamming, shit dripping onto the floor. The ridged concrete floor had remnants of what used to be here: hay and muck. Amongst the debris were leftovers of what it now was used for: oil, nuts and bolts. Beyond the shotgun sights were racks of boxes, all with the German eagle over the swastika emblem.

Laughter from a nearby room made me swing the shotgun around to the left. A glass-panelled low-lit room hummed with noise. My boots squeaked on a newly patched floor as I backed up against the far wall—cringing. At the end of each stacked aisle, my heart pounded as I had to make the three metre dash across the open. On the last aisle I was directly opposite the canteen room. Cigarette smoke billowed from the open top window. What I saw next shocked me even more: a vast area stacked with bombs. The array were either loaded in specially designed shelves or on their ends, hundreds and hundreds, different sizes and shapes. Around the edges was further racking with crates piled to the ceiling. Some of the wooden boxes had Italian writing printed on them.

Once I had seen it, I knew the place for my explosive: the largest bomb. Even though I knew it was crazy to go out into the open, I couldn't resist it. Suddenly, a bell sounded, making me jump. I tucked back behind the stacking. The wide doors began to mechanically slide open. The laugher and chatting from the smokers room became louder. The infantrymen came out, stretching, and made their way over to the far crates. The smell of nicotine wafted over.

'Bollocks,' I muttered.

With the large doors fully open, a forklift truck was started. One of the officers carrying a clipboard began shouting orders. I needed to get to one of the bombs; any type would now do. Two soldiers came over to the first row of bombs and hitched the chains around it. My heart sank when the target truck that was outside reversed up to the entrance. I quickly checked the time: thirteen minutes to detonation. Would the

Germans load that truck and leave in time? If I left now and they did, then I wouldn't have completed my objective. However, if I didn't find somewhere to place the explosive in time, then I would be mincemeat.

I couldn't see the Lewes bomb that Fish had set. Maybe it had fallen off, but then, the right sentry guard would have spotted it. I hope Fish had the common sense to place it on the inner chassis.

Now that the truck was being loaded, I prepared the charges, but incredulously, the pencil charge was a five-minute fuse. What the fuck should I do? Do I dare to sit here until ten past midnight? Think, Johnny. Automatic gunfire reverberated from outside to inside our building. Was that the Bren or the German *Maschinengewehr-42*? I instantly recognised the shot of an Enfield. The heavy-machinegun stopped, but then pandemonium erupted. Like poking a hornets' nest, loads of infantry swarmed around, grabbing what weapon was nearest. Sparks lit up from the truck, bits disintegrating. The German who had jumped from the forklift fell back in his red mist. With the cocking of weapons and shouting, the Germans returned fire, the noise deafening. A group of three sprinted out the main doors, but just as they headed right they were mowed down. An image of Shrek behind the heavy-machinegun in the tower flashed into my mind.

Pinned down, the soldiers resorted to throwing grenades. A part of me was bloody annoyed at how stupid the lads were for hurtling a load of rounds into this ammunition store, with me in it. Fuck it, I thought, and put down the shotgun. Under my muddy boot I crushed the end of the thin copper tube containing the cupric chloride, breaking the glass vial, releasing the liquid contained inside. After making sure I could see right through the inspection hole next to the brass safety strip side, I knew the countdown had begun, so I removed the brass safety strip. Inserting it in the explosive, I crept as quickly as possible through the maze of bombs. I placed it on the largest, about two metres in length and as fat as an elephant's gut.

Creeping back, there was a lull in the battle. Back in the relative safety of the racks, I turned to see the main doors closing, with the truck inside. Fuck. I glanced at my watch; a waft of almonds rose.

'Shit, time to go,' I said.

The hairs on my neck raised as I'd heard boots squeaking behind me; a shadow appeared. My shotgun was between me and whoever was behind. I sharply turned and tried to grab the weapon, but at the last second the bayonet thrust in at lightning-speed. My reaction blocked it, but the searing pain in my upper left thigh had told me not good enough. With an aggressive look on his face, the soldier pulled it back out; the searing pain shot up to my bollocks. His bayonet reflected the light as it came back in. I launched, double-palm thumping him in the chest. As he went over, he grabbed my shirt and then lifted up his boot, flicking me over. I managed to spin around and kick his rifle into the aisle. Like an angry gorilla he jumped on me and started pounding my face, the coppery taste filling my mouth. Even crossing my forearms, he succeeded to get one through on the bridge of my nose; the crack, meaning one thing. The blows started to rain down on my gut, so I lifted my legs up. The air was sucked out of me by a hard punch to the side ribs. I coughed the blood into his face. His fingers dug deep into my leg wound; I screamed. Out with the karate, in with the street fight, I thought.

Uncrossing my forearms, I wrapped my hands around the back of his head, pulling him in, butting him, and then I bit his nose; he yelled in pain. I kneed with as much angered force right between his legs; his eyes wide. Now it was his turn to suck in air. I shoved him back, but he landed close to his rifle, his hand flapping to find it. Side-stepping him, I dashed to my shotgun, grabbed it, and in one flowing movement I faced him. Incredibly, he had managed to take another thrusting run at me, bayonet at throat height.

Bang!

The force from this close range blew him off his feet. '*Threat neutralised.*' Weirdly, the place had gone quiet, like the whole world had eyes on me.

Slinging my pack on, I limped down the side wall. The next poor bastard in front never got to see what propelled him against the wall in his red mist. '*Threat neutralised.*' With the new shouting behind me, my heart was coming out of my mouth. Slamming the door behind me, a hail of bullets penetrated the metal door. I placed the shotgun under my arm, making a mental note to add a sling. Unclipping a grenade, I primed it and tossed it overhead behind.

Around the next corner on the right flank of the building, running at full speed, I heard the explosion and then the screams.

'Fuck,' I said, seeing the half-track in front.

Rasping and spitting blood, I changed direction to the furthest left of the field towards the hedges. The gun turret followed. My mind screamed at me to dive to the ground, but my legs took over and just kept running.

Bang… bang… bang… bang!

My head sank into my shoulders on hearing the deep sound of the heavy-calibre gun. With no body parts missing, I turned slightly to see the long single AA gun recoil rounds away from my sprint direction. Looking back further over my shoulder, the wall of the building shattered onto those unfortunate to be dead on the ground. Further rounds thumped out.

Stupidly, I wasn't watching where I was running and my foot slipped, bringing me crashing to the ground. Hurrying to my feet, I noticed a figure running towards me: Planet. Facing the shotgun back the way I was heading, I made up as much ground as I could. Once out the main gate I headed across the dirt track, jumped the watery ditch, and flew into the dark woods. Close behind me was Planet, his feet thumping, the branches breaking, his breathing quicker than mine, like the Giant was after me: Jack.

A new person running parallel caught my eye: Shrek, as fearful as me and Planet. Something was wrapped around his hand and he had no weapon. We weaved through the trees that quickly came at us in the gloom. As if in a race, the time getting nearer, it became a challenge to see who crossed the line. Desperately, I checked back for Fish and Churchill, but couldn't see them—too dark. A shock wave vibrated through my feet and up through my body. I dived into the soft moss at the base of a tree, hitting my forehead on the bark. Planet and Fish ran past, and I'm sure I heard them laughing. Then an almighty explosion's sonic boom erupted.

I quickly crawled around the other side of the wide trunk and hid. The other two picked themselves up and scrambled to the safety of another tree, eyes wide with confusion. Further massive explosions ripped through the forest, with inharmonious weird lights and sounds. Further high-powered bursts exploded.

'How much fucking explosive did ye lay?' Planet said, flinching.

'Move,' I yelled, as bits of hot shrapnel burnt through the canopy.

'Arghhhh,' Planet screamed.

Planet franticly patted the back of his neck whilst pushing through a bush. Shrek joined in knocking the smouldering metal off the top of his backpack. More hot and twisted bits rained down on us. Some of the bushes had caught alight, the smoke making it difficult to see where we were running. The crackles and explosions didn't relent, wave after wave, the sonic booms shaking the earth. I wasn't sure if it was the wind pushing us along or the blast rings.

A small stream of water ahead fizzed and crackled. Planet stopped and scooped up a large handful of water, dowsing his neck. He looked seriously pissed off with me, but I couldn't stop the laughter as I tried to get my breathing down.

'Let us pray that fucking half-track comes and lands on ye fucking head,' Planet said.

Still laughing, I headed further into the woods.

With the orange night glow dying down, along with the destruction, I stopped and leant against a tree. Shrek and Planet stood facing me, and they slung off their gear. We were breathing hard. Shrek took a long gulp from his water bottle. It was a while before Shrek spoke.

'That was fucking fun.'

'Fun?' I squealed.

'What in God's name was that all about?' Shrek asked.

'What happened to the fucking fifteen fuse?' Planet said.

'I only had a number five in the bag,' I said.

'We could have been blown to bloody smithereens,' Shrek gasped.

In the same piss-take voice Shrek had done on me in the farmhouse bathroom, I said, 'Oh, by Jove; smithereens.'

'Why didn't ye wait till nearer the detonation time?' Planet asked.

'I tried to, but then you twats started fucking firing at where all the ammo was held.'

It was their sniggering that got to me first...

'Yeah, you can fucking laugh, but that could have been it for me,' I ranted.

Their mood heightened into laughing and holding their sides...

'Piss off. I had to fucking fight my way out whilst you lot were pissing about outside.'

It didn't calm them...

'Fuck off. Bollocks to you both.'

'Have you seen yourself?' Shrek said squeakily, between laughing.

I looked down at my shit-stained and pissy trousers and shirt. My hands and shotgun were covered in shit, mud, and leaves. Planet handed me a mirror from his side pouch. Jesus, I thought, looking at my reflection: nose clearly broken, the blood staining my teeth, chin, and neck. The rest of my face was covered in all sorts and my hair was stuck up like Laurel's from the old films. I handed the mirror back, trying to hide my amusement.

'Thanks for the make-up mirror,' I said.

We all slumped to the floor and I began to tremble. A distant smaller explosion erupted, but none of us took any real notice. As soon as I saw the blood dripping from the rag around Shrek's hand, I looked at my own leg wound.

'What happened to your hand?' I asked.

'Lost three fingers, but have two more,' he said.

'We all need to check ourselves over for injuries. Get stripping,' I ordered.

My leg wound was full of mud and shit. Under the only torch working I cleaned the stab slit with river water from a billycan, trying not to gasp the pain. I guessed Shrek was not trying to show his pain either, as Planet had finished wrapping the last of his bandages around Shrek's remaining index finger and thumb. With the two of us patched up, there was no cream for Planet's large neck burn; instead, he opted for a wet ripped-off shirt sleeve tied around his neck.

A twig breaking to our side alerted us. Shrek was the first to pull his Colt out of the holster that was on the floor. Me and Planet desperately searched for ours, having forgotten the first defensive drill. Fish walked into the small clearing and lowered his Thomson.

'Tony,' we all said together.

'Am I interrupting something? You homosexuals want to carry on in private?'

'I think Planet is the drag queen as he has the make-up mirror,' I said.

'A what?' Planet said.

'Wasted joke; never mind,' I said.

I went across to give Fish a welcome embrace, but he took a step back.

'No thanks, Vinnie. You look like shit.'

That started the other two laughing, again.

Fully clothed, we handed around the last of the water and rations. Whilst we cleaned our weapons and re-stocked the mags, I told them what had happened to me, but had left out the part where I had planted the explosive on the largest bomb in the factory. Next, the others summarised their stories: Shrek had dealt with the sentry guard. The soldier in the truck's passenger seat had slid across and reversed the truck into the building. The primed Lewes bomb was firmly placed on the underside of the chassis. If the driver had put his headlights on, he would have exposed Fish lying flat on the ground. When Fish had eventually made a break for the tractor, the right sentry guard opened fire. According to Shrek, the trail of bullets followed Fish's feet all the way to the tractor. Planet shot the sentry, but this alerted the gunner on the half-track, who spun around and started firing aimlessly into the field. Planet snuck in the back and shot four rounds into the gunner.

Meanwhile, Churchill had laid down a barrage of fire into the building. It was Shrek in the left tower who had opened up on the Germans that tried had to flank, but he'd lost three fingers on his left hand whilst fleeing. Shrek was more annoyed that his Enfield had been smashed out of his hand.

All in all, apart from the injuries, and now the lack of ammo and rations, it had gone surprisingly well. Fish didn't have a mark on him, whereas we looked like bags of shite. The det-charges and cortex wire never happened, but with that amount of explosive destruction from the ammo dump, I doubt anything close by was still standing; I could still smell the carnage. Even though the banter carried on for a bit, one burning question was evident; you could sense it. The answers came when I had eventually asked where Churchill was. No one had seen him since he'd stopped firing the Bren.

Staring into nothing, there wasn't a part of me that didn't feel fatigue, but at least the 'stay awake' tablets were keeping me sharp. Black and white images of Private Stuart Saxton and Captain Martin McConnell filled my gaze. I thought clearly about what lay ahead, and even though my boots were on and ready, I had changed my perception.

'Lads, it's time to abort. The risks are too high,' I said.

'Trigger was a great shot with his rifle. Some marksman,' Fish said.

'Had an aggressive heart. And Gunner Tommo, no fear in him,' Planet added.

'The best support to have, those two,' Shrek said. 'Rose, Kauf, and Geordie were really switched on for this mission as well.'

'Quite flabbergasted by how tough and mentally balanced Blondie was,' Fish continued. 'And Benjamin, I hope he didn't die in vain.'

'Totally agree. I bet they would love to be here now, alive. I know Spike had a different mind, but when it came down to it, he...'

'Yeah, yeah, I get the message,' I interrupted Planet.

'What do you mean?' Fish said. 'Rule Britannia, Britannia rule the waves. Britons never, never, never shall be slaves.'

The others started whistling.

'We've hardly any ammo left,' I said.

'Could have made a nice bazooka bomb if you had managed not to drop that Panzerfaust-60, you dickhead,' Shrek said.

'I never even picked it up in the garden,' I snapped. 'And you don't even have a main weapon.'

'Oh yes, I remember now, you couldn't bend down to pick it up from the dead Kraut as your pants were filled with shit.'

'Oh bollocks. If you…'

A new hum and mechanical noise had interrupted me. Further sporadic firing echoed into the night. The SS group had found a way over the river and were probably wondered what the fuck had happened at the farm. Nevertheless, what were they firing at? Had they found and killed Churchill? My nerves were fraught with the thought.

'Lads, I need to go back and scan the outer area for Andy,' I said.

'We all go then,' Planet said—the others agreed.

'No. I'll take Planet with me. You two head out to this new RV.'

'But…'

'No buts, Shrek. That's an order,' I said.

Planet grinned stupidly at Fish and Shrek.

'Give us an hour to return to the RV,' I added.

'And if you two do not return?' Fish asked.

'That decision will be in your hands.'

With our packs now on, I ordered everyone to put on their sandy berets. According to the map we had run off course when making a flee before the mighty explosion, almost back to the second farmhouse. With the new route for each group calculated, we synchronised our watches and then we set off. Planet started a strong tabbing speed through the woods, with me in tow. I gritted my teeth to hide the pains, mainly from my thigh.

CHAPTER TWENTY-NINE

Even though we had purposely taken a south west direction back to the bomb dump, the carnage that littered the forest floor was far and wide. Maybe it was a blessing that it had rained here for some days prior, otherwise we could have been chased by a raging fire. It wasn't long before we found the main road that left the farm. Although we were set back two hundred metres on the wood's edge, the devastation was unparalleled to anything I had witnessed first-hand: a huge crater was where the buildings and fields were once sited. The trees that led into the wood had been flattened. It reminded me of the aftermath of the Lochnagar mine crater on the 1916 Somme battlefields. Everything that had thrived in the near vicinity had disintegrated. My thoughts for Churchill turned dark.

'I think that thwarted any resupplies,' Planet said.

The field opposite us had been churned up, the tank tracks turning west. Perhaps the Germans thought we would have mined the road on our escape.

'Best we head back to the RV,' Planet said.

'Let's stick to the road's treeline. It will be quicker, and I'm getting pissed off with being Robin Hood.'

'Do ye not mean Little Red Riding Hood.'

'Ye fuckin' read as well, Mr. Wolf,' I said in my best Scottish accent.

'Ye are right, ye German is fucking shite.'

Two miles down the road, we were amazed we had not encountered any enemy, especially after the huge explosions. We had also not come across Churchill. I tried to block away the negative emotions. Planet stopped suddenly and then he waved me into the trees. Both of us concealed, he positioned his ear towards whatever had spooked him.

'What is it?' I whispered.

'I think I just heard voices.'

'Think?'

'I am not certain.'

I tuned into the cold morning air: water running. Even with the binos I couldn't see beyond the opposite hedgerow and the bridge.

'Do you want to check the area?' I asked—it was a stupid question.

At a stealthy pace we squat-ran over to the bridge, hugging into the brick wall. Peering over the flint stone edges, the water ran down a slope with a series of wooden blocks in a chicane, capturing the debris and slowing the speed. At the end was a metal grate packed with woodland foliage. With the Germans in the area, I knew why it had not been cleared for some time by the staff.

Beyond the grate was a huge reservoir, a lone funnel stood high in the middle. The metal ladders that scaled the side were rusted. Beyond this was a concrete wall spanning the curve of the reservoir. Insects darted over the still, moonlit water that the wall retained. At the furthest left was a small cottage-type dwelling, and to the far right was a small single-storey building. I handed the binos to Planet. He lifted them for a while, studying the blackness.

'Was that a tank turret beyond the cottage?' I whispered.

'I am not sure. The only way to know is to get closer. If it is, there will only be a couple of Heinies.'

'Don't ever underestimate the enemy,' I said.

'We can't just leave the Heinies with a tank, they could follow us. What are we going to do? We could blow the reservoir dam.'

'I've not got a radio to call in 617 squadron,' I said sarcastically.

'Aye, shame. Would have been great to watch. Best we head to the RV.'

I sighed in despair. 'I'm curious to see what's in the storage building. Maybe there are some German weapons and explosives stockpiled. We could do with some when we hit the radio mast and comms room.'

'More likely to be stored in the cottage. Perhaps they have left the tank behind for some reason. Can ye drive one?'

'Sadly, I can only drive an eighties Pak Suzuki Jeep, but I am shit-hot at racing a Nissan Bluebird across the Afghan desert.' I scoffed at the thought.

Planet stayed deadpan.

'Right, you recce the cottage and I'll head off in the other direction to check out the storehouse.' I looked at the time. 'Make it silent and quick. You haven't long before we need to head back to the RV.'

'What happens if we get into trouble or do not meet back here?'

'Just head for the RV and wait there for a while. Even though its desolate here, don't wake the fucking neighbourhood with your Bren.' I grinned.

'Bollocks. Ye know I have swapped it.'

'We can't afford any compromises. Use your knife if you can.'

Planet took my shotgun off me and headed back to the treeline; I was slightly confused. Thirty seconds later he was back, empty handed.

'Ye are not to be trusted with that pea-shooter, and ye might move quicker without it.'

'Then in that case, go and hide my pack,' I ordered, looking smug.

'Aye,' he growled, and snatched my beret off. 'Ye won't be needed that either.'

Planet snuck off, muttering. It was a good idea to go in light, and to hide our gear in the woods, but time was ticking. Planet returned, his forehead sweating.

'Anything else, mofo?'

'Aye,' I said, taking the piss. 'You can camo-up your bare arm.'

'What with?'

I nodded at the muck caught in the trap.

Planet sighed. He then handed me a Fairburn fighting knife and said, 'Look after it. It belonged to a courageous young lad.'

I thought of Trigger. 'How did you get this?'

'I took it off him, telling him he could hurt himself. I wish I had not.'

'Bellend.'

Planet stared at nothing, before retrieving his own knife. He then moved down the embankment.

'Mind you don't cut yourself,' I said quietly, but I don't think he heard me.

Creeping quickly on the steep, stony reservoir bank wasn't easy or quiet. The sound travelled across the water, or that's how I perceived it. It didn't feel right to be without my main weapon, and the closer I got to the building, the more the mood heightened. At the base of the outer wall facing the water, I hid between two wooden barrels. I searched for Planet across the reservoir, but he was invisible. Just after I checked the Colt's magazine, something caught my eye at the water's edge: a floating corpse. Facedown, it was impossible to tell gender and age. Scanning the bank further, I counted another five bodies; one, a naked woman.

Silently, I skulked around the building's side. A light shone through small opaque glass windows. Down on one knee, on the edge of the brick wall, I furtively glanced around. A scuff to my rear made my hackles stand up; I knew someone was behind me. Stealthily, I reached down to my Colt, but a cold sharp point pricked the back of my neck. Touching my Colt, the point then dug in further, breaking the skin. I lifted my hand away, showing that I wasn't going to risk it. The bladed instrument released its pressure, blood droplets ran down my neck.

Head slowly turning, heart and beeping racing in tune, I had to stop as the bayonet was almost touching my eye.

'*Heben Sie Ihre Hände,*' another voice said from the barrels.

So, there were two, I thought. Bollocks. They must have come out of the building and headed behind me. Had they seen me coming? Shit. Had they seen Planet?

'*Heben Sie Ihre Hände,*' he said aggressively.

'I don't speak German,' I said in my best French accent, and then raised my hands.

'Yet, you knew to raise your hands,' he said, and laughed.

'I am a simple French gypsy,' I pleaded.

My Colt was abruptly unholstered. A short while after, I heard the water splash.

'*Steh auf,*' said the person behind me.

'Stand up,' the other German said.

Getting to my feet, hands raised, I turned around and was confronted by two oily-faced German soldiers showing no fear, but they held their rifles meaningfully.

'Throw your knife into the water where your English gun lies,' he said.

'*Französischen Zigeuner. Lier,*' the other German said, and laughed.

'My comrade says you are not a gypsy.' He joined in the amusement. 'Throw your knife.'

'But…'

'*Rapidement,*' he interrupted. '*Ou nous vous tuerons.*'

Bollocks; he spoke French as well, I thought. There goes my ruse to be a Frenchman, dumbfounded what he had said. Just before I threw the knife, I thought of Trigger and his brother. What a waste.

As soon as the splash happened I was prodded with the bayonet to move around to the front. The other solider kept his distance. There was no way I could take on the first soldier without the other German shooting me. Perhaps I could grab the first soldier and use him as a shield. The scenario playing out in my mind was abruptly interrupted as I had been shouted at to open the single door in front of me. The sharp jab moved me forward. Opening the door, a stagnant odour wafted out. Inside, my eyes secretly scanned for a weapon of some sort. Again, I was prodded along. Four large metal padlocked tanks stood against the back wall, all with smaller interconnecting pipes. Being yelled at and spiked to move to the wall, yet again, was pissing me off.

The first soldier gave his comrade his rifle and then fumbled in his pocket. It was then I noticed a large spanner on the tall, green generator at the end of the room; that was the weapon I needed. The second soldier, after looking at my idea with the spanner, turned back to me. He menacingly gripped his rifle, showing me not to try it.

The metal lid was lifted on the first tank, condensation droplets dripped into the black water. I tried to see what the smelly water was that sat several inches below the edge.

'*Entrez dans.* Oh, no French.' They both laughed. '*Holen Sie sich.*' Oh, no German.' Again, they found this highly amusing. 'Get in,' he barked.

'*Alik allanh. kobl mo'kherti,*' I said.

A stalemate arose. I wasn't sure if what I'd said in the little Arabic that I could remember was even correct. However, thinking I'd said for them to "fuck off and kiss my arse", had made me feel good. The bayonets were thrust forward.

'Get in. *Jetzt. Schnell,*' he demanded.

I stood my ground, not wanting to get in the murkiness. Both raised their weapons

'Then you die.'

I nodded at them, knowing at least I had the choice.

The cold water stank as I gingerly swung a leg over. Bits of black stuff rose to the top, like pine needles. On the edge, both legs now in, the water sloshed through the joining meshed pipe. Suddenly, something hard hit my back, and the next thing I was splashing around in the water; there was no bottom. I turned to see the lid slammed down, the fear resonated in my water chamber. In complete darkness I calmly began to tread water, but the panic levels rose when the padlock was added. Their banging on the top, almost for good luck, started me yelling at them. However, the door to the building was shut and the jovial voices disappeared.

Whilst I hung on with my fingers in the narrow pipe, my eyes slightly adjusted to the dark. A little positive was the light in the room had been left on, shining through some of the holes from missing bolts. In the warming beam I looked at my watch, but it had stopped, obviously not water-resistant.

After swapping hands, shouting, and even trying to push the lid open on numerous occasions, I was beginning to lose faith in Planet finding me. I couldn't blame him as I had said to give it ten minutes before heading to the RV, reckoning I had been in here about an hour. The strong fumes inside had started to play havoc with my breathing, and I was now becoming lightheaded with nausea. Even changing grip with my prune-like fingers was a big effort. The air from the other tank was no better as I tried to find some way of getting some fresh oxygen. Occasionally, the water level would rise above the seven inches, frightening me into lifting my mouth to the ceiling. As the time went on, negative thoughts began to enter my mind. Many times I had shouted for help, each time with less effort, blaming the vapours. I couldn't hold on for much longer.

The first foul-tasting water seeped in, not even realizing I had shut my eyes. Frantically, I kicked my feet and shook my head. Getting my rapid breathing down, I shut my eyes again. Thoughts of those at the RV getting on with the mission entered my mind. The water around me swelled up again, but this time, more powerfully. I held my breath, tightening my eyes.

'Are we gannin yem, man?'

The water dripped from his blond hair, and glasses. He winked at me in the light beam.

'Blondie. How the fuck did you get in here?'

'God's divine intervention.' Blondie smiled, lighting up my tomb.

It was joyous to see him; my heartrate had lowered. I changed my numbing grip.

'Your bible is going to get wet,' I joked.

'Wey aye, man, but you had your chance to have it.'

'Did Spike make it?' I knew the answer, though.

'His soul did.'

'I'm sorry what happened to Spike.'

'They shall grow not old, as we that are left grow old. Age shall not weary them, nor the years condemn. At the going down of the sun and in the morning. We will remember them.'

In the silence that followed, the water dripping stopped.

'How did you escape?' I asked.

'That does not matter right now. How long can you tread water for?'

'Not much longer, but I have no options to get out.'

'Are you not curious how I got in here?'

'Yeah, but fumes are clouding my mind.'

'Think about it. This water is being pumped from the reservoir into this tank. Its then filtered into the others. Take a deep breath, Johnny.'

'Cheers, Blondie. I'll buy you a pint of goo at The Royal Military.'

'Champion.'

I took a massive breath and opened my eyes: Blondie had gone.

The sludge at the bottom of the tank funnelled into a pipe, and the water became less thick. Following the tunnel blindly, I had begun to get the chest pains that told me I needed a gasp of air. It had got to the stage that I was grabbing the metal joins to help me get along the narrowing pipe. I had no way of knowing which direction was up, or down, or even if I was going the right way, but so far I had not felt another directional pipe.

The air started to push out from my tight lips. Had it been a minute? My head and lungs were going to burst, but I fought on for the last ten seconds. Eventually the water above was lighter. Silhouetted objects were in front of me. To touch, they were cold and slimy as I desperately pushed them aside. I coughed up the water as I'd gasped the simple air of life. A euphoric wave immersed me as I held onto the metal ladder, the moonlight on me. A white object popped up alongside me. Seeing the corpses appear, I quickly thrust my way up the rusty rungs. On the top platform I rested on my back and got my breath back. The beautiful stars lit up the sky; a meteor flashed across the inky-black.

'Thank you, Blondie,' I said.

The cottage and surrounding area were desolate. The German tank that I thought I had seen was not there, nor was Planet. As stealthily as possible I climbed down and swam back to the metal grate, trying to ignore the recent images of dead bodies. I took a hard look around before climbing out.

At the weapons hide the Sten had gone. I questioned why Planet had left my kit. Maybe he knew that I wouldn't be far behind. Perhaps it was a sign he had made it back here, and not an enemy soldier who would have taken everything. The map was still dry enough for me to work out the route to the RV, even though the water had started to stain it. Whilst working out the direction, I wondered why the two Germans didn't search me for the map and other objects. I thought back on their age, dirty and oily faces, and leather-like uniform. I reckoned these were the tank operators, the tank that had been next to the cottage.

CHAPTER THIRTY

Travelling alone felt a bit intimidating. Every time I had stopped to check my whereabouts, I became further vulnerable. Nearing the RV I snuck in the woods, taking my time moving. Just as I was about to do a low whistle I was grabbed from behind and pushed to the floor. A hand was quickly placed across my mouth, a determined pair of eyes glared at me, but softened when his smile beamed. Shrek withdrew his knife.

'You fucking stinking pikey,' he said.

After a good bit of quiet joking with him, he took me further in to meet the others. Most pleased to see me was Planet.

After I'd told them the story, further insults came about me reeking, but the banter was a great relief. I didn't tell them about Blondie. Planet told me how he'd found nothing in the cottage, and that the tank was inoperable. He had waited an extra five minutes by our concealed weapons before heading off to the RV. He said he knew I would make it, but he still appeared a little ashamed. Now that Churchill was MIA, Planet would still not forgive me for making him swap his Bren. I was more annoyed that I had lost Trigger's knife; I didn't tell Planet, not yet. We were all low on ammo; however, we had a good number of grenades remaining, including a few German stick-grenades. It was time to assault the last target.

On the next rest, under complete darkness as the only torch had failed, we passed around the last two water bottles. I wanted to ask why I was the only one seeming to struggle with my injuries, but thought better of it. Planet needed a shit, and I pondered why as my stomach felt shrivelled.

'Ye need to blacken your lily-white English skin,' he said.

'With what?'

Doing up his trousers, he pointed at his feet, and he then grinned.

I looked at the deposit on the floor and said, 'Fuck off.'

A faint dog bark quickly got us to our feet and we set off at a faster pace. Through what seemed to be an everlasting mishmash of trees and bushes came a welcoming site: the forest's edge. Hunkered behind the treeline we took a much-needed rest. The others pulled out some felt and started to nail this to the underside of their boots. I asked them what they were doing: making them quiet for the next raid. Without any of my own, Fish handed me some.

After fitting it, I handed the dregs of the water bottle to Planet, telling him to put it over the drying cloth around his neck; instead, he drank it, then tossed it behind him.

'Three things,' I said. 'One, don't fucking leave behind signs that we could have been in this position. Two, keep the fucking container as we might find a fresh water source. And thirdly, how come you lot aren't in any fucking pain?'

'Did ye cockney chum not hand ye any syrettes?' Planet said, and grinned, knowing.

'No. What's that?'

Planet took off the lid exposing a hollow needle. He threw me the small tube, similar to a miniature tube of toothpaste.

'I think Richard said something like, "Make sure the Hampton Wick don't get any unless he is white bread," Planet said in a terrible Londoner accent.

'That is "brown bread", you cock,' Shrek said, trying to impersonate better.

'What is cock slang for?' Planet said.

'It is not slang. You are just the biggest penis, ever,' Fish said.

'At least I know which hole to put it in,' Planet said.

'So what is it?' I asked.

'It is morphine, Vinnie. Looks like ye could do with some.'

'Smug bastard,' I said, and injected it into my leg.

'Smug *Scottish* bastard, to ye.'

'Do not worry about pinning it to your collar,' Shrek said. 'By the time we are found, we are going to be part of the dust, anyway.'

'Talking of that, if I die are you also going to tell my family in future about me?' Fish asked.

'And mine?' Shrek added.

'Was it you that gave your future squad the same daft nicknames then, as you gave us in the bunk house? Were they similar us?' Fish asked.

'Fish has told me the reasons why ye have come back to 1944,' Planet said. 'What are my future cousins like? Were the stories about us dying in battle, brave and disturbing?'

'None of us are going to die,' I said, feeling warm from the drug. 'I'll tell you something else: the year I left, the world still remembered those that had fought and the fallen in both great wars. Every day on websites, such as Twitter and Facebook, you will find those that pay homage.'

'Webs and Twitter? Are you talking spiders and birds?' Fish said.

'Do you mean our faces are on books? Are we heroes?' Shrek asked.

I sighed and raised my eyes. 'Yes. Let's just say you're heroes.'

'Good, because if we were sent to do our duty to kill the enemy, and protect those whilst they slept in their British homes, then I would expect to be remembered,' Fish said.

'With regrettable disgust there was one British Marine who killed a terrorist...'

'A what, Vinnie? Terrorist?' Shrek asked.

'A sick lowlife, cock-scum, goat-fucking coward. Anyway, let's crack on.'

'No, finish the story of this hero soldier in the future,' Fish demanded.

'In short, he and his men had engaged the Taliban terrorists. An Apache was called in...'

'An Indian?'

'For fuck's sake.' I sighed. 'No, Fish, a helicopter with more sophisticated gadgets and weaponry than anything the British Army, or any other army of this era, has. Anyway, under a lot of battle fatigue, and with some of his squad injured and killed on the tour, this marine killed the prisoner.'

'So what?' Planet said. 'Anyone in a war that goes against me, especially if they point a gun at me, will be killed.'

'I agree. How many had this farm animal molester killed before he was shot?' Shrek asked.

'What happened to this marine when he returned home?' Fish asked.

'He was court-martialled and sent to prison for murder,' I said—silence followed.

'Oh you nearly got me with that jest of a story,' Shrek said.

'As if the Prime Minister of ye time would allow that. Imagine if good old Winston did that,' Planet said.

'Yeah, nearly had you. I said I would try to get my own back after you lot made me think I was late for a meeting with Mullen.' I laughed with them, but inside, I was crying of the truth.

'You know Churchill still does not believe a word you say about the future. He thinks you are still Skedgewell and should be locked up in an asylum,' Fish said.

Planet quickly cocked his weapon and raised it to his shoulder. In an instant we were all on our stomachs facing at whatever he had seen; my arms bristled. A green light flashed three times from inside a hedgerow, but I had to rapidly blink to keep my focus.

'Churchill,' I mumbled.

'It might not be, it could be a trap,' Planet whispered.

'Only one way to find out,' Shrek said.

He crawled backwards. The light flashed again. Shrek would have to make some distance to get around the other side of the hedgerow. In the prone position I was beginning to feel tired. Enjoying the moment I shut my eyes, only for a second.

'Boss... boss, are you dead?'

Immediately opening my eyes, I focused on Churchill's lacerated face. Shocked, I turned over and rapidly sat up. Around me was the relief on everyone's faces.

'What happened?' I asked.

'You fell asleep. Thought you were dead, old chap,' Fish said.

'No I bloody never,' I snapped. 'I was resting my eyes.'

'Do not think so, Vinnie', Shrek said.

'So, what happened?' I asked again.

'You have been asleep so long we are now back in 2015. The war is over,' Shrek said.

'Who needed him anyway?' Planet joined in.

'I meant, what happened to Churchill?' I said.

'I pulled him out of the bush at knife-point,' Shrek boasted.

'Oh for fuck's sake,' I said, as Churchill sat next to me. 'Churchill, tell me what happened at the *farm*.'

'After laying down suppressive fire on the Hun in the building...'

'Yeah, the same fucking building I was in with the bombs,' I pointed out.

'Anyway,' he nonchalantly continued, 'I came under a lot of fire from behind. After dealing with them, and knowing we did not have much time left, I retreated to a safer point to cover your withdrawal.'

'What attack from behind?' Planet asked.

'The squad of eight Hun started taking shots at me in the ditch. Stupid fuckers were hiding behind a hedgerow. I did see you making a run for it. You all looked scared that something big was going to happen, so I ran along the main track and ended up here.'

'We never saw you,' Fish said.

'I do not like your tone, Private Fisher.'

'I do not give a flying shag, Churchy.'

'OK, rein it in lads,' I said. 'That's flying fuck, Fish,' I whispered in his ear. 'Whatever happened, it's damn good to have you back with the Bren.'

'Are ye OK, Vinnie? Ye seem to be slurring. How is the beeping noise?' Planet asked.

'What size morphine did you give him?' Fish asked, picking up the tube. 'That size is for near death. Bloody knock out a fucking rhino.'

'Had no effects on me,' Planet snapped.

'What the devil happened to your sleeve, Planet?' Churchill asked.

'What the fuck's it got to do with ye?'

'I'll be fine,' I said.

I had gone beyond caring about the bickering and I shut my drooping eyes. Their voices started to mellow into the background. A handful of tiny objects were put in my mouth, followed by a water bottle. I swallowed the water and shook my head.

As the maps were brought out, the conversation started about where the communications building should be. The beeping picked up an erratic pace, slowed down and then sped up. I felt weird, but energized. It wasn't long before I vocally took over the meeting, also snatching Planet's reconnaissance photos. Scanning my binoculars, I relayed what I saw, but was ordered to slow down; it irritated me. We had to get the job done before the invasion started. Hastily, I told them to grab their gear and follow me across the open field to the next gate in the hedgerow. To me this gate looked out of place. I didn't care for their objections and I ran out of our hiding. Had I just shouted "Forwards"?

In double-quick time and ease I had made the gate. The others were struggling to reach me. Hurriedly, I scanned the open field with binos: a bank surrounded the field, like a medieval settlement that had succumbed to time's erosion. In the middle of the pitch the grass grew in patches; too grid-like for my liking. On each corner of the large area were the broken reminders of sentry towers. To the right of the raised bank was a lone shed, about the size of one of those toilets you could hire for a building site. I laughed, then told the others that was the clue, but I wasn't sure why there was such a look of disbelief. Were they scared to go into battle? Were they planning a mutiny? Perhaps they were the real German spies.

I wiped the sweat pouring into my eyes and then refocused the binos: a primitive track beyond the mound stopped in the field. In the middle of this open grassy arena was a vacant German outpost with a sandbagged defence. In the distance was a German officer's patrol car and a petrol bowser. The beeping had now become distorted. Just as I thought about the danger of the lads turning their weapons on me, I spotted a large antenna.

'Bingo,' I said.

'Boss, keep your voice low,' Churchill hushed.

'I'm in fucking charge, Sarge,' I retorted. 'Just remember that, you lot.'

I quickly pulled my shotgun around to the front to show them. Why was my mind so empty? I looked to the warm, fuzzy stars.

'I need some rock music,' I blurted. 'Come on, get me in the mood.'

'Are you OK, Vinnie?' Shrek said.

'Are you ready, Shrek? Or have you gone all chicken shit on me?'

'Chicken shit? Damn right I am fucking ready. Let me neutralise some threats.'

'Hey. Fucking find your own catch phrase. Yeah, you can give each other that look, but I know what's going on here.'

Their silence showed me I had won their respect.

'Right. Here's the plan: we enter the underground bunker through that shed.'

'And what is next?' Churchill said.

Was he mocking me? Who the fuck does he think he is? Does he think I haven't the bottle? I wiped my forehead, letting my mind process the answers.

'Answer,' he asked.

'Give me a minute,' I said, but a second later, I asked, 'How many Lewes bombs do we have left?'

They started to search.

'Hurry up. You lot should bloody know.'

'None,' Planet said.

'Fucking ammo up,' I ordered.

I started to load up as much ammo as possible, and then I took Fish's Thompson off him. A little surprised, he watched me unclip the shoulder sling and then clip the strap onto the shotgun's trigger guard. More bewildering to him was that I didn't hand his Thompson back. I can take what I want, I thought, and slung the shotgun over my shoulder.

'Is anyone else very hot?' I asked—no reply.

They were all scared, I could sense it. Secretly, I wiped my perspiring hands down the front of my shirt. Did they need a rallying speech, I thought.

'Good question, I replied.

'No one asked...'

'We don't need insubordination, Planet,' I barked. 'We'll just go in and annihilate everyone and everything. Make sure your grenades are accessible.'

'Your plan is a bit vague,' Churchill said.

'Well, the Chinese parliament is shut, harder than you do doors, Churchill.' I hysterically laughed. 'Give me your Colt, Planet.'

'Bollocks.'

'Are you guys going to join his side in a fight?' I said. 'Kill me and take the glory?'

'Here ye go.' Planet slapped it my hand. 'And, Vinnie, slow down. What the fuck is wrong with ye?'

'You're forgetting something, Planet,' I said.

'I think we know ye are in charge.'

'My beret. And hand me that mirror.'

Once he had gingerly handed me the items, I made myself look good in the mirror. The sound of distant tanks rolled in. Who had alerted them? One of my men?

'That's treason,' I rapidly said.

'What is?' Churchill asked.

'Right. Let's go,' I ordered.

Again, I was the first to make the sprint to the shed, but was confused as to why the others went on their stomachs in an all-round defence. I stood and searched the fields to see what they were viewing. My sixth sense was not battering my judgement, but there was no need for it, I argued, I had been here in this position for many hours.

'I've changed my mind,' I said, out of breath. 'I will sneak in alone first, then you rabble follow after a minute or so.'

Shrek stood up, and for some reason pulled me to a crouch with him. He came close to my ear.

'That is crazy, Vinnie,' he whispered. 'What happened to the explosive entry? It was what we trained for in the killing house.'

I pushed him away, the feeling of him being too close had set me on edge. I tried to think of the killing house training, but it was a blur. I focused on my watch, but it hadn't started since the water tank. The hot air blowing in from the neighbouring Afghan desert suddenly stopped. Fuck; it was cold, and I began to shiver.

'Right, chaps,' I said, as the spiffing officer I'd been tasked to be, 'I'm going in.'

CHAPTER THIRTY-ONE

Yanking back the wooden-slatted door, on the floor was a sealed metal hatch, like one you would find on a submarine. Keen to get on with the task, I placed down my Tommy and then ripped the wheel around. Hot air rose as I lifted back the hatch. No Germans to kill, I thought. Rather than use the metal ladder, I jumped down, parkour style. The drop was longer than I had thought, but without the expected pain I was quickly up from my roll to my feet. Even though the soles of my boots didn't make a sound, I wouldn't have cared; feeling invincible was rushing through me. Even the beeping noise and my heartrate were calm, but it was a shame that no Glen Miller was playing.

Quickly striding through the concrete hall, my ears pricked-up further than my already heightened state.

Brrt... brrt!

The German whirled around and fell back down the stairs, his blood following in the same direction. *'Threat neutralised.'* The gaming voice sounded posher that me; it annoyed me. Marching on through the cordite haze, I peeked over. Heavy boots echoed in the confined stairwell and then a hand appeared on the railing leading around the bottom of the stairs.

Brrt... brrt... brrt... brrt!

The guard behind the first also fell under the weight of the first German. *'Threats neutralised.'* More footsteps and shouting echoed through the ringing in my ears. Shrek was right: you could always hear them first. Tugging hard on the grenade that was clipped to me automatically released the pin, and I lobbed it down.

'Bewegen, bewegen. Schnell,' a voice yelled.

BOOOM!

I turned my face away from the upwards blast of smoke and debris. You didn't move quick enough, I thought.

266

'Into battle,' I heard.

Was this me? Still in that pompous voice; I liked it.

After adjusting my beret, leaving the dying screams, I moved down the stairs. Reaching the bottom level I turned through the smoke to rapidly go down the next set of stairs, Tommy not even raised on my shoulder. I was very relaxed. Shredded bodies were strewn around. It was difficult telling how many were dead, so I entered a bullet in each head. '*Threats neutralised.*'

Ignoring the blood-splattered walls, I hurriedly stepped over the carnage into the first clear area. Just as I brazenly walked across the gallery-type landing, a hail of rounds smashed into the corner of the wall. I sharply turned away, leaving my back to the wall; my beret had nearly taken a round.

'That won't do,' I said.

Yelling from the stairway behind alerted my relaxed state. Ah, trying to flank me, I thought. I went into overdrive.

Brrt... brrt... brrt... click!

The concrete had smashed where the rounds had penetrated through him. '*Threat neutralised.*' However, the next soldier managed to side-step his comrade who had fallen to his death.

Bang... bang... bang!

Replacing the Colt, I rushed over to the lower level stairs, making sure he was dead. '*Threat neutralised.*' Slapping in a new Tommy mag, I pushed it hard into my shoulder. Casually walking out side-on I suppressed the group of four at the far end of the landing. Reaching the square concrete pillar, I quickly changed the magazine, tossing the empty over the three-foot wall that surrounded the whole gallery. In an instant, the sharp pillar corners and the far wall soaked up the German hail of lead; the noise was exhilarating.

Into view came Fish and Shrek, followed shortly by Planet. Who invited them? I frowned my displeasure. Fish took up position at the smashed corner, taking a quick look around the edge, but probably wished he hadn't as further rounds hit the same corner. I laughed, much to his annoyance. Shrek covered the stairs going down to the next level, having swapped his Colt for one of the dead German's semi-auto *Gustloff Volkssturmgewehr*. Whilst Planet made his way towards Fish, I guessed Churchill was guarding the way in. Why weren't any of them sweating; it was so hot on this level. Fish pulled out his Colt, ready.

'Hey,' I shouted. 'That won't do, old boy.'

I threw him his Tommy. Churchill eventually joined us. I hoped he was better than this rabble, but not as good as me, I thought. Planet moved to the corner and sunk low behind Fish.

'Planet, suppress the bastards then,' I ordered. 'Follow me, Fish.'

Without even waiting for Planet to unleash the Bren, I calmly walked across to the next pillar. At the same time, I unclipped the two sling ends off the shotgun's trigger guard. The Bren unleashed its deathly evil as I reached the next corridor that opened out into a room; it was very dark inside. My arm swung across to stop Fish entering.

'Hold on, laddie,' I said. 'Could be Germans in there.'

Unclipping a grenade I tossed it in. There was a split-second of horror on Fish's face. I tucked into the wall.

BOOOM!

Turning the shotgun around over the balcony wall at the view below, I spotted Fish getting up off the floor.

'Forwards, Fish. Kill the bastards then,' I said.

'You can stop the fucking annoying voice, Vinnie.'

'It's Major Skedgewell, you scoundrel.'

'What the fuck is wrong with you?'

The Bren stopped, but Shrek was now firing his German machinegun in the same direction. Below us were two other floors, the ground was a mass of Germans scurrying around. Some of the cowards were taking cover behind the labyrinth of tables and equipment, like a swarm of locusts in a vivarium; us being the bearded dragons. What a fantastic analogy, I thought, and patted my shoulder. Fish had found some targets inside the room. Churchill started firing down on the stairs.

'Grenade,' Shrek shouted.

BOOOM!

I ducked behind the wall as a vortex of debris flew towards us. Shrek darted across to me.

'Good man,' I said.

'Threats neutralised,' he said.

'I've warned you about that, Shrek,' I reprimanded.

Spanning across the open area below, from side to side were two steel beams. Centred was a thick wooden plank section with a generator on it. I hitched up onto the wall and jumped down to the timber section, grabbing the cables with my other hand; the rush was amazing. The wood beneath splintered from incoming as I made my way around the edge. With no fear, adrenaline surging more than ever, the thin steel beam appeared a piece of piss to take on. Not even focusing, I ran across it, ignoring further zipping rounds. The floor below had four Germans sneaking towards the staircase that led to the level where Churchill was guarding—that won't do. Momentum stopped me pulling the shotgun around; I was committed.

The first soldier managed to look up, but both my feet planted into his face, his head breaking my fall. His comrade to his right turned with his weapon, but I butted him in his face with the shotgun and he stumbled back. Pirouetting around a 180-degrees, I swiped out my foot, contacting the back of another attacker's leg. His weapon fired as he landed on his back. Treading on his neck, I front-kicked the remaining German straight in his chest.

'Should have cocked your rifle before going into immediate action, old boy,' I said.

Enjoying his screams as he went over the wall, a dull thud to my calf muscle made me look down. A spurt of blood followed his dagger out. I stopped his hand, turning the point at his neck and then pushed down, hard. '*Threat neutralised.*' At double-speed, I charged at the German who had now let go of his busted face, kneeing him in the gut twice, and I threw him to the ground. Leaning over the back of his head I punched him until he didn't move. To me it felt faster than Gavin's Kung Fu, but unlike that old, fat coward, I fired a Colt round to the back of his head. '*Threat neutralised.*'

Energised, I arrogantly walked over to the wall.

Bang!

I swung around to the floor and aimed the shotgun through my legs.

Pump... **bang**... pump... **bang**!

Both fell back in their red mist. '*Threats neutralised.*' Another head popped up, but immediately he ducked back. Scurrying backwards on my back, I thrust two new cartridges into the loading gate. Planet ran by and fired his Bren from the hip. Reaching the corner he leaned around it, solid, ready for anyone else that tried it on. These lads were now stealing my kills, I thought.

Shrek and Churchill put one hand under my arm and tried to heave me up.

'I'm fine. Leave me alone,' I said.

Churchill looked at the blood on the palm of his hand and then back at my arm.

'Ignore that,' I ordered. 'Watch the other corridor, now, Churchill.'

'What are you going to do now?' Shrek asked. 'You have turned fucking crazy.'

'A faint heart never fucked a pig,' Planet yelled, and opened up the Bren.

I hated that saying, I thought. 'Shrek, go back and find Fish.'

'But...'

'That's an order, Private Harding,' I barked.

I let his irritating cursing under his breath go as I poked the shotgun over the wall. Suddenly, an object came over, landing next to Shrek. In what appeared to be a casual walk and a slow bend to pick the object up, he then tossed it back.

'That is Corporal Harding, you fucking twat,' he raged at me.

BOOOM!

What's eating him, I thought; perhaps he wants some recognition. 'Great idea, young man.'

I threw my last grenade over the wall and, as soon as it had exploded, possessed with speed and agility, I was aiming down the shotgun sight.

'Bastards,' I muttered.

This time I kept the trigger pulled whilst pumping six shots in super-quick time. As the last cartridge flew out, I chucked the weapon over. Un-holstering my Colt, I aimed through the cordite smoke. '*Threats neutralised.*'

With Planet streaming the Bren's hell again and Churchill with his sub-machinegun, I knew there was only one way down to finish the job. I landed awkwardly on some sort of large radio and fell backwards, but the floor was soft—no pain. A pair of eyes stared up at me, his limbs completely shredded. Tucking into the table, I looked around, suspicious there were loads of them. Planet and Churchill had gone silent. Small electrical fires had broken out, the operators slumped in awkward positions. A dying groan sifted in between the arcing and crackles. Were they pretending to be dead? A tiny squeal of a German voice played out in a pair of headphones on the floor next to me. I picked them up and listened: the voice heightened with anticipation; I shot the radio.

A coughing from the room behind alerted me. One of the bastard Germans had survived. Colt out in front, I went to unclip a grenade, but had none. I nosed the barrel around the open large oak doors, like those of a castle, and I was the King. In the corner was a crying German soldier next to a decoding machine, like the one in Simon's intelligence office. The fucker hadn't seen me. I aimed at him, finger slightly pressing the trigger. He looked up, the fear emanating from him. I stared wide-eyed at his young eyes. Tears rolled down his cheeks, sweat poured down mine. Trigger's face flashed in my mind; this lad looked younger.

Desperately, he glanced at his rifle that was propped up next to one of the radios, and then he stared back at me. Arguing with my mind not to shoot him, I raised my pistol, slightly shaking my head at him not to go for it. But why give him the chance? His hand slid back along the floor, and then he raised both.

'*Bitte tötet mich nicht,*' he said sobbing.

'Shrek, get in here now,' I shouted, my voice had almost returned to normal, confusing me.

First to raise his weapon was Churchill, but I knocked it aside; the round hit the decoder; the young lad started to hyperventilate.

'What the fuck are you doing? Kill him,' Churchill ranted.

I faced Churchill, backing up to the cowering boy. I wasn't sure what was going on, but it felt right. Shrek and Planet eyeballed me as they entered. Shrek also had his *Volkssturmgewehr* rifle raised, the kid now in full crying mode.

'Lower your weapons,' I ordered.

'He is a bastard Heinie,' Planet said.

'*Bitte ersparen Sie mein Leben,*' the boy said.

Shrek laughed. 'He wants us to spare him,' he said patronisingly. 'Like you fucking spared my comrades.'

I had started to tremble and feel light-headed. To the side I quickly vomited, noticing it mix with something red on the floor.

'Rice pudding; nice,' Shrek said.

'I said, lower your fucking weapons.'

'Are ye OK, Vinnie. Ye have gone white as a sheet,' Planet said.

'Shrek, ask him his age?' I said.

'Bugger. You are bleeding heavy,' Churchill said.

I wiped the dripping sick from my chin and then looked at the blood that had pooled on the floor. Weirdly, a severe pain hit me in the arm and leg. I turned to the boy who was moving his feet away. Facing the lads, Planet had lowered his weapon.

'Shrek, just fucking ask him his age,' I said.

Shrek sighed. '*Wie alt sind Sie?*'

'*Dreizehn,*' the boy answered, hardly audible. '*Mein Vater macht mich in den Krieg zu kämpfen.*'

'He is barely a teenager, Vinnie,' Shrek translated. 'His father has made him fight.'

'We cannot trust him. Our orders are to kill them all,' Churchill said.

'Like the orders we were not to return to our injured, dying, or dead mates. That's why you cleared off at the farm, isn't it, Andy.'

'These fucking bastards killed my parents, wife, and brother.' He spat at the lad. 'My best friend was burnt alive. Yes, fucking burnt alive.'

'Sarge. Sarge, look at me,' I yelled.

Andy turned; face contorted with emotion.

'He is about your son's age,' I said. 'Lower your weapon. Very soon, this place will be overrun by an invasion on a scale I doubt you could even get your head around. Many soldiers and innocent people are going to die, on both sides. I think saving one thirteen-year-old German kid might help the stability of peace many years down the road.'

'*Du hast meinen Vater getötet,*' the boy said, nodding towards the other room. '*Ihre Flugzeuge bombardierten unserer Stadt, tötete meine Mutter und meine Schulfreunde.*' He started to cry.

'What did he say? Tell him to speak fucking English,' Churchill said.

'I doubt he can speak English as he has just said we bombed his school, and with the loss of his mother and friends, his father also lies dead in the control room,' Shrek translated.

Churchill sat back on the table and put his head in his hands; reality had hit him.

Shrek finished tying off a bandage around my arm and then began on my leg. I noticed the blast dust had stuck to my sweat soaked clothes, and I had become very cold. Fish came in, skidding to a halt, out of breath.

'Fuck,' he rasped. 'Three truckloads of Germans have turned up.'

'How many?' I slurred.

'Jesus Christ,' he said. 'How many Benzedrine did you give him?'

'Just a handful,' Planet said.

'But your hands are like fucking shovels.'

German voices and boots thundered in.

'*Schließen Sie die Türen,*' the boy said.

'Who the fuck is that?' Fish said.

'Ignore that he is a German, and just do as the lad says,' Shrek said.

All three of them pushed the tall, heavy, oak doors shut. I sat dizzily on the floor next to the boy, feeling like I had the worst hangover, ever. I patted the boy on the knee as the three metal slide bolts were nosily pulled across. I was extraordinarily thirsty and needed to sleep.

'What's your name?' I croaked.

'*Heinz Otto Fausten.*'

'I'm Johnny Vince.' I put my bloodied hand out and he shook it.

'*Danke.*'

'Fish, tell Heinz he is going to be all right,' I said, and yawned.

'He may be, but we have hardly any ammo between us, Vinnie.'

'Tell him, Fish,' I said lamely.

'*Heinz, du wirst in Ordnung sein,*' Fish said.

The doors rattled with the first shots. I opened my drooping eyelids to see the oak timbers had held fast. The radio in the corner yelled out instructions in German. Heinz looked petrified. Churchill slapped in his last mag.

'Bollocks. We are cooped up like chickens ready for the abattoir,' Churchill said.

'They are going to blow the doors,' Fish said, and shot the radio.

'Ye fool,' Planet growled. 'That was our way of knowing what they were planning.'

'I know what is coming,' he replied. 'Trust me, you have not enough bullets to kill them all.'

No one said a word.

A larger calibre machinegun pounded the doors; splinters exploded out. Planet returned fire until I yelled at him to stop. The silence that enveloped the place was killing us. Were they laying explosives? I then visualised a German infantryman with his Panzerfaust-60. Heinz tapped my leg and then pointed at the large cupboard.

'*Wir können durch einen Tunnel entkommen,*' he said.

'Planet, help me move this,' Shrek said.

Shrek was straining to move the huge cupboard, his bandage loose and bloodied. Planet shoved Shrek aside and, like a man mountain, he heaved it across the floor. He then pushed it over against the main doors. Churchill looked at the hole in the floor and quickly ordered everyone to get out. However, getting to my feet wasn't easy. Churchill slapped them all on the back as they went below ground. Where was all my spirit and strength? My legs and arms became jellified, my head pounded. Churchill grabbed the boy by his shirt and told him not to cross him, then he patted him on the back to follow the others.

BOOOM!

Lying awkwardly facedown, coughing up and breathing in more dust, I couldn't move the rubble from my body. Churchill's voice mumbled amongst the high-pitched ringing in my ears. I wiped the shit from my eyes to see the blurry wall and equipment spark in a barrage of incoming rounds. Blinking hard, I made eye contact with the eyes of Churchill at floor level, then he disappeared. The large piece of timber pinning me down was lifted and I managed to suck in some air. Looking up, in the last second I saw the rifle butt.

CHAPTER THIRTY-TWO

A cool breeze chilled me. My head was thumping. Not only did I feel nauseous, I tasted sick. Nose blocked and pumping with pain, my jaw ached as I spat out the particles of teeth and blood. Above the aching was the severe pain to my calf, thigh, and shoulder. My hands were swollen, being bound behind my back. Clenching my teeth to lessen the shivering, I listened in—silent. I tried to think of what had just happened, but the memory was sketchy, like waking up from a heavy night on the town. With no light coming through my sore eyes, thinking it was night-time, my heart fluttered as I thought I could still be dangling from the rope. Had this all been a dream? Would I open my eyes and find the tiger above and the river below? Was I at the bottom of the ravine, or better still, in the cave with the weirdo tribe?

'Boss,' someone whispered.

I knew the voice. The dreadful events of the Chinook crash flicked through my mind. I opened my eyes, suddenly to be greeted with the soil and sporadic blades of grass. Could I really be on the forest floor in Afghanistan? Had my squad found me? I arched up my stiff neck.

'Planet?' I croaked.

'No, it is Churchill.'

My gut knotted, disappointment and sorrow flushed through me. I put my face down and sighed. Churchill squeezed my arm.

'I came back, boss.'

'What happened?' I asked.

'Thanks, Churchill,' he said flippantly. 'You are in a bad way, old chap. That was not a good idea to stay in that room.'

I grinned through the pain. 'I'm in the killing house at the airfield, aren't I.' Maybe I had been blown up, I thought.

'I am afraid not. The bastard Hun have beat you up, but I suppose that is little compared to how many you have killed. You owe that to

275

the amount of amphetamine in your blood.'

Sadly, against what I wanted, I had to accept where I was.

'Did we finish the job?' I mumbled.

'Totally fucked their communications.'

'Andy, got any of Planet's Scotch Whisky? Or Shrek's wine? I need to numb the agony.'

'No, boss. You are going into unconsciousness. Stay awake.'

'But I need to rest,' I said, enjoying it.

'Johnny,' he said sharply. 'Oh bugger. We have company. I will be back.'

★

My thoughts turned to Newquay. I was now lying in the sun on the comfortable, grass-topped cliffs looking out at the surfers on the shimmering sea. The gentle rhythmic beeping was hypnotic. I so longed to be back home.

★

Suddenly, pain rippled through me. I opened my eyes and tried to suck in air. A shiny knee-length boot drew back and kicked me again. Curled up in a ball, coughing and spluttering, I was dragged away with my tied hands pulled up behind my back. Still trying to get my knees to work on the ground whilst being hauled along the floor, I wailed in pain. Eventually, I was dumped to the earth like a bag of rubbish. Still groaning, I dreaded what was coming next and curled back into a ball, waiting for another beating.

A new sound made me jump. Were they playing mind games? The metal on metal clanged behind me, again, and again. Then it stopped. Slowly, I squinted to see where the shiny boots had gone, but flinched back when a pair of eyes were a couple of inches away from mine. A hand wearing a black leather glove grabbed me around the throat and pulled me back towards his face. The officer's eyes studied my features, his nicotine stench breathing over me. I tried not to show he was cutting off my air supply as he squeezed harder. He grinned at me. When he let go, I choked for air. Grabbing my throat again, he quickly snatched out his Luger, poking the end in my mouth. He smirked, as if to ask, strangulation or a bullet to the brain? I pulled my face to the side. He let go. Now was the time to be passive, I decided.

'How's Adolf doing?' I said.

I spat blood in his face, and then I blacked out after he had pistol-whipped me.

★

I was now pain-free, back in Newquay. Tying off the rope, I gently lowered myself over the edge of the cliff. The sun was beating down on my back; nobody was around. The mesmerising sea below crested the rocks, seagulls fluttered on the vortex of hot air currents. Shingle landed on my gloves, so I looked up. Weirdly, a pair of legs dangled over the edge. I stopped abseiling. Even though I could only see the hiking boots, I knew who it was.

'What are you doing here, Roy?' I asked.

'Going to kill myself.'

'What? Why?'

I moved the quick-up ascender to get back to the top, but it wouldn't work...

'The pressure of living has got to me. The littlest thing, day or night, I can't take it anymore, mate.'

Roy shoved his arse to the edge...

'No. Stay there,' I said.

A chilly wind blew off the sea as I reached out to touch him...

'Wait. Hold on,' I yelled.

The distant thunder rolling in with the black clouds had drowned my plea...

'I'm so sorry, Johnny, but I've been trying to get your help for months.'

He was now on the final balance...

'You're always too busy. My family hate me. It's time to end the suffering.'

I couldn't see his face, but his tears fell onto my hands as I frantically tried to get the equipment to work...

'No, Roy. I'll save you.'

'It's me, or your family,' he bluntly said.

Further stones fell from his position as I'd made touch...

'What do you mean?' I asked.

His hand pointed out to sea.

I sharply turned; my hand released his leg. The violence of the storm smashed a boat, tossing it around like a matchbox. Holding on for dear life were my family, except my dad. I wanted to save them. I looked back at Roy, but he was gone. I knew he had jumped.

'*Wach auf du Schwein Englisch.*'

The acute pain shot up from my bollocks, almost making me throw up. Hunched over, legs tight, I dribbled the blood that was in my mouth. The beeping in my mind was fast. My arms were tied to something behind me.

'*Wie ist der Phantom-Major?*'

The officer slapped me with something around my bowed head. At least it wasn't his pistol, I thought. His hand squeezed my cheeks, forcing them up so that my broken teeth cut the inside of my cheek; I dribbled the goo.

'I don't speak German,' I mumbled.

He took a few steps back. Standing there in his long, shiny black trench coat and imposing peaked cap, he exaggerated his laugh, belittling me. I nearly brought my foot up to his bollocks, but instead I crossed my feet.

He took off his cap and said, 'You see this.'

I flinched slightly as he came in quick, thrusting the symbol on the front in my face.

'Nazi. Heil Hitler.' He did the infamous salute.

'Not for long, motherfucker,' I blurted.

The motherfucker squeezed the bandage on my arm. I yelled, but it didn't stop him digging his thumb into the bullet wound. Smiling, he stood up and began pacing around, hitting the leather glove in his hand.

'So. Where are the rest of your men?'

'The party's over, motherfucker. 'You can go back and get changed out of your S and M gear.' I chuckled—it's all I had left.

'Your comrade. Dead. English black meat. Burnt and crispy like English sausage,' he said, and laughed. 'Let us see what *white* English meat fries like.'

He walked off out of my sight.

Rage and fear bubbled through me as I thought of Benny. I tussled with the wrist restraints, but they were tied securely to a metal pole. I thought about standing up, but it would be impossible to lift my wrists above the height. Searching ahead in desperation, I then noticed the German machinegun outpost I had seen earlier. I so wished one of my lads could be sat behind it. Stretching my neck to the side was the petrol bowser, but the German officer's car was missing.

The officer came back into view. Disturbingly, I recognised the flame-thrower soldier behind him; I've never been so frightened. The smug officer stood with his feet apart, hands on his hips. Three metres to his left was the infantryman, the end of the flamethrower facing down, lit, ready.

'*Irgendwelche letzten Worte?*' the officer said. 'Oh, I forget, you do not speak German. And I was asking if you want any last words.'

The flame-thrower laughed, also letting out a tiny burst of flame.

I gulped hard.

'Where are your men?' the officer said menacingly.

Once the orchestra had started playing in my mind, I relaxed my tensed muscles, and even found a smile. My actions had annoyed them.

Zip… **bang**!

The deathly spurt of flame spiralled around as the flame-thrower fell to the ground, a large chunk of his head missing. The shiny black coat went up in flames and the officer screamed, trying to pat it out.

> *And now the end is near*
> *So I face the final curtain*
> *My friend, I'll say it clear*
> *I'll state my case of which I'm certain*

I kicked out, trying to stop the burning mass reaching me. Between the orange and yellow blaze I spotted a figure running over at full sprint.

> *And more, much more than this*
> *I did it my way*

Churchill jumped the intense fire, and then he cut free my rope, heaving me up. A mass of shouting came from behind us whilst Churchill hauled me along at speed.

> *Regrets, I've had a few*
> *But then again, too few to mention*

Both of us dived for cover as the rounds whizzed over our heads; sandbags sucked up the malevolent that tried to kill us.

> *I did what I had to do*
> *And saw it through without exception*

Churchill was up first and, cocking the German heavy-machinegun, he let rip. A warm spray splattered my face. In the barrage of intensity that ripped into us, I checked his prone bloodied body. His neck and cheek were oozing blood. I shook him. Churchill coughed and, rising like a phoenix, he got back behind the heavy-machinegun, squeezing the trigger, his wounds pouring. The explosion at the far end of the field lit us up. The obliterated bowser's wave of heat rolled across the field. The battle stopped.

A vehicle's brakes squealed behind me. Turning quickly, I was shocked, then overjoyed, to see the German officer's car full of the lads. Just as I looked down to tell Churchill, more incoming zipped over our heads. Worse still, Churchill was foaming blood at the mouth. The lads indiscriminately returned fire into the blaze, but I knew they were low on ammo.

> *Yes, there were times, I'm sure you knew*
> *When I bit off more than I could chew*

Through the chaos that erupted, a lone figure walked calmly towards me from the vehicle's direction. Rounds from both sides passed through him with no effect. Tim? What the hell was he doing here?

> *But through it all when there was doubt*
> *I ate it up and spit it out*
> *I faced it all and I stood tall*
> *And did it my way*

'Who's that?' Churchill gargled.

Tim stood there with his hands on his hips, looking more different than ever. I noticed the Rolex watch, the same as the one I had given my dad. Then the realisation hit me.

'It's my dad,' I said. 'Tim was my dad.'

> *I've loved, I've laughed and cried*
> *I've had my fails, my share of losing*

'Dad, I knew there was something weird about you, but why are you here?' I said, tears welling.

> *And now, as tears subside*
> *I find it all so amusing*
> *To think I did all that*
> *And may I say, not in a shy way*

'Do you see him, Churchill?' I said proudly, above the firefight. 'We're going home.'

'I do, Johnny Vince. I am with him. Please look after my lad when you get home,' Churchill said clearly.

I quickly looked down at him, but he was dead; eyes wide open.

> *For what is a man, what has he got*
> *If not himself, then he has not*
> *To say the things he truly feels*

'You know what to do, son,' Dad said.

My dad and Churchill faded away. I yelled at Heinz in the driver's seat to go. Watching them head off into the distance, I lifted my bloodied hands onto the machinegun and then started spraying the swarm of Germans that ran across the field towards me.

And not the words he would reveal
The record shows I took the blows
And did it my way

I knew what it was as soon as it landed in front of me. I shielded my mate Andrew Graham from the stick grenade, even though, I knew he was gone…

The white flash had disappeared; I searched my eyelids. The beeping wasn't in my mind, but to my left. I rubbed the soft surface by my side, feeling the warmth under a blanket. Opening my eyes to the sobbing, it was all blurred. The crying stopped. Someone squeezed my hand; cries of joy resounded. I went to speak, but my throat was too sore. The first person that came into view was a female nurse leaning over me. For a second I thought I was back in the Cambridge Military Hospital, that was until she moved out of the way. Mum, holding my hand, was crying, sniffing. I stared at Oliver who was also in a state. Panning around the room, Ella, with her striking blue eyes and radiant blond hair, was stood next to the beautiful Lena. What the hell were they doing here? Where was here?

Ella rubbed my leg, but she couldn't find the words. Lena put her arm around Ella, both sobbed. A clunking noise at the end of the room made me take my eyes off them. Ocker was holding a Frank Sinatra CD case; the stereo tray was open. More music was stacked on the table. Were they mine? Opposite to him stood Trevor and Simon, the anguish overwhelming for them. Next to the life support machine and crash equipment was an over-the-bed table. On this was a family photo, and the Omega watch with the inscription on the back facing me.

'Where's Dad?' I croaked.

EPILOGUE

With the shock of everyone in the room, all pandering to me and asking questions, it was too much. I decided to shut my eyes and switch off, pretending I had fallen asleep. The only question I'd asked had upset them. They had either looked uncomfortable at the ground or burst into tears. I now knew why Ocker had told me to abort the mission and get home; if only he had explained at the time.

The nurses made me comfortable and then asked everyone to leave. With the heart monitor beeping to my side, I thought of the possible reasons for my dad having visited me in the form of Tim. Was that why I had been the only one who could see him, except when Churchill had died? Was he trying to protect me, making sure I finished saving the squad? I caught myself up short: What the fuck was I thinking? It had been a dream whilst in a coma, nothing more. I didn't want to look at the watch or think of the argument with my dad before I had left Newquay. In fact, I now wished I'd died in the jungle.

I miss Dad. Wish I hadn't argued. Would I ever get over never having got to say sorry, or goodbye?